SAMUEL R. DELANY

four-time Nebula Award-winning author of *Dhalgren*, *Nova* and
Triton, was called "the most interesting author of science fiction
writing in English today" by *The New York Times Book Review*.
His latest novel, *Stars in My Pocket Like Grains of Sand*, was
termed "unmistakably the work of a genius ... an adventure and
a voyage of discovery" by Nebula winner Michael Bishop.

NEVÈRŸON

is Delany's remarkable imagined realm of fantasy, previously
chronicled in *Tales of Nevèrÿon* and *Neveryóna*. At once shockingly
real and a provocative commentary on our own time, Nevèrÿon
blends the fantastic spirit of such writers as C.L. Moore, Fritz
Leiber and Michael Moorcock with the philosophical speculations
found in John Barth, Italo Calvino, John Gardner or Umberto
Eco.

FLIGHT FROM NEVÈRŸON

weaves the last threads of Delany's fabulous tapestry together in
a tantalizing design of story and symbol, saga and sign. From a
young smuggler's chance meeting with a legendary liberator, to
an old actor's memories of the city's colorful street life, to a
macabre night of plagues and carnivals that merges magically
with a deadly epidemic on the streets of present-day New York
City, Delany shatters the border between fact and fantasy to show
us the world we know as if for the first time.

Bantam Books by Samuel R. Delany
Ask your bookseller for the books you have missed

Flight From Nevèrÿon

Samuel R. Delany

BANTAM BOOKS
TORONTO · NEW YORK · LONDON · SYDNEY · AUCKLAND

FLIGHT FROM NEVÈRŸON

A Bantam Book / May 1985

ISBN 0-553-24856-1

Published simultaneously in the United States and Canada

PRINTED IN THE UNITED STATES OF AMERICA

O   0 9 8 7 6 5 4 3 2

Publisher's Note

Ten years ago a young black American mathematician and cryptographer, K. Leslie Steiner, published a comparative translation from several ancient languages of a brief narrative text (c. 900 words) known both as the Culhar' Fragment and the Missolonghi Codex. That work has prompted several archeological expeditions to find the historical location from which that ancient text most likely originated, most recently one headed by Wellman, Kargowsky, and Kermit. It sets out just as this volume goes to press. In the same ten years Steiner's ingenious translation methods (highly speculative and mathematically based) have inspired three volumes of stories and novels by Samuel R. Delany about Nevèrÿon, of which this volume—now that the site grows less and less imaginary, more and more real—is the last.

For
Frank Romeo,
and
Robert Bravard, Camilla Decarnin,
Mike Elkins, Gregory Frux, Robert
Morales, & Michael Peplow, and,
of course,
Iva,
who printed up file "i"

Contents

There is no such thing as an absolutely proper meaning of a word, which is not made possible by the very impropriety of metaphorical displacement it seeks to exclude. The impropriety of displaceability of meaning and of infinite openness of syntactic reference beyond that circumscribed by proper meaning is a material force. The imposition of a conclusive, self-identical meaning that transcends the seriality of displacement is therefore metaphysical or idealist. Its political equivalent is the absolute state (be it dictatorial or liberal) that imposes order on the displaceability of power through sedition. The political equivalent of displacement—that force deconstruction foregrounds against absolutist philosophies of identity—is continuous and plural revolutions, the openness of material forces which exceeds the imposition of power.

—Michael Ryan
Marxism and Deconstruction

I

THE TALE OF
FOG AND GRANITE

It can hardly be an accident that the debate
proliferates around a *crime* story—a robbery and
its undoing. Somewhere in each of these texts the
economy of justice cannot be avoided. For in
spite of the absence of mastery, there is no lack of
effects of power.

—Barbara Johnson
The Critical Difference

1

Later, the big man slept—peacefully for a dozen breaths. Then, under the moon, a drop, three drops, twenty drops broke on his face. Inside the nostrils loud air snagged. Lashes shook. The head rocked on stone. Dragging a heel back, he raised a hand, first to rub at his cheek, then to drop at his chest. "Get away! One-eyed beast! Get away, you little . . ." His hand rose again—to beat at something. But the fingers caught in chain.

Curled with his back against the big man's side, the little man—either because of the big one's rocking or the neck chain's rattle or the barkings out of sleep like shouts from a full-flooded cistern—rolled over and was on his knees.

Green eyes beat open.

The little man grabbed the great wrist, while heavy fingers, untangling from brass, caught the small shoulders.

"Calm yourself, master!" the little one whispered. "You are my breath, my light, my—"

"I was dreaming, Noyeed—"

"—my love, my lord, and my life!"

"No, Noyeed! I was only dreaming—"

"Of what, master? What dream?"

"I was dreaming of . . ."

The little man's skull blocked the moon, leaving only the lunar halo by which farmers predict rain in three days—though one out of five such predictions brings only overcast.

"I was dreaming of you, Noyeed!"

"Me, master?"

3

"But I was where you are, now, leaning above me. And you—a much younger you, a boy, Noyeed, with your blind eye and your dirty hair—you lay on the ground where I am, like this, terrified. And, with the others, I . . ."

"Master?"

"Noyeed—" Holding the man, no taller than a boy, up against the night, Gorgik's arms relaxed; the small face fell—"either you know something I can never understand and you will not tell me. Or I know something that, for all my struggles toward freedom, I'm still terrified to say."

"Master . . ." Noyeed turned his forehead against Gorgik's chest.

Gorgik's fingers slid to the little man's neck, touching iron. "Just a moment." He slipped his forefingers under the collar, centimeters too big for the one-eyed man against him. "You needn't wear this any longer." He pulled open the hinge. "It's time to give it back to me."

Noyeed grappled the heavy wrists. "No!" Through thin skin and thick, bone felt bone.

"What is it?" Gorgik moved his chin in Noyeed's hair. It smelled of dogs and wet leaves.

"Don't take it from me!"

"Why?"

"You told me you or I must wear it . . . ?"

"Yes. *Here,* yes." The night was cool, dry. "But by day only I need to, as a sign of the oppression throughout Nevèrÿon—"

"Don't!"

Gorgik looked down, moving Noyeed to the side.

The single eye blinked.

A breeze crossed the moonlit roof, while a crisp leaf beat at the balustrade as if, after an immense delay, it would topple the stone onto someone below, who even now might be gazing up. "Don't what?"

The little man thought: He looks at me as if he were hearing all the others who have begged him for his collar.

The big man thought: I could leap up, seize that leaf from the wind, and wrest it from its endless, minuscule damages.

Noyeed said: "Don't encumber yourself with such ornaments, master." (The leaf turned, blew back, then up and over the wall.) "Let *me* wear your collar! Let me be your lieutenant and the bearer of your standard! And this . . . ?" Noyeed reached across Gorgik's chest to rattle the chain on which hung a verdigris astrolabe. "You go to meet with Lord Krodar

tomorrow at the High Court. Why wear something like this?''
He reached down to touch the knife at the Gorgik's side. "Or
this. Go naked, master. Your bare body will serve much better
than armor or ornament to speak of who you are.''

"Why do you say—?''

"Look, master!'' The little man rolled to his belly. "Look!''
Turning to his side, Gorgik pushed up on an elbow.

Part of the crenelation near their heads had fallen. Between
broken stones, by craning, they could see down into the yard.
Near an outbuilding armed and unarmed figures stood at a
small, flapping fire.

"Here we are on the roof of your headquarters. There are
your supporters. You are only a shadow away from being
the most powerful man in all Nevèrÿon.''

"No, Noyeed.'' Gorgik chuckled. "No. My power is
nothing in Kolhari, in Nevèrÿon. I would be the most unfortunate of rebels if I let such delusion take hold.''

"But you may *become* the most powerful man in all
Nevèrÿon. And if you would, to further your cause, someone—
perhaps me—must think it possible. Go naked, master. Let
your fearlessness be your protection. In the meantime, let me
carry your—no, let me *be* your sign!''

"Noyeed, I don't understand.''

"Look, master.'' The little man elbowed forward, staring
through the break. "Just look!'' He pointed, not at the
milling people below but at the horizon's hills black under
moon-dusted dark. "Already you can see fog gathering in the
mountain peaks outside the city. By dawn it will roll down
over all Kolhari, where it will lie till sunlight burns it off.
Naked, you will ascend into that fog, meet it, become one
with it. Abandon the signs by which men and women know
you, and you will become invisible—or at least as insubstantial to them as that mist. Your power—now small, but
growing—will, at whatever degree, be marked at no limit.
Without clear site, it will seem everywhere at once. That's
what such invisibility can gain you. That's what you can win
if you shrug off all signs. You will be able to move into, out
of, and through the cities of empire like fog, without hindrance,
while I—''

"What nonsense, Noyeed!'' Gorgik laughed. "Has your
harried childhood and hunted youth wounded you to where
you can only babble—''

"Not babble, master! Listen! Unencumbered, you can be

as the all-pervasive fog. And if you need now or again to be at a specific place and time, use *me*! Wearing your collar as the mark of your anger and authority, *I* can stand on the city's stones wherever you would place me, leaving you free for greater movement, while I serve you, visible to all, your incorporated will. Oh, among slaves the collar will make me invisible to their masters as it has already made you. Among nobles, it will make me at least as much a reminder of injustice as you were. And among the good men and women who do their daily work it will transform me into that oddity and outrage intruding on them the reality of evils they would rather forget. Though, master—" and Noyeed laughed— "with my missing eye and skulking ways have I ever been anything else? You wear the collar because you were once a slave. Well, so was I. You require the collar to motivate the engines of desire. Well, as you have seen, for me it's the same. We are much alike, master. Why not let me stand in your place? Why not move me as you would move a piece in the game of power and time, sending me here and there, your servant and marked spy? Let me be your manifestation in the granite streets of the cities, leaving you free for all unencumbered missions. I will be your mark. You will be my meaning. I will be your sign. You will be my signification. You will be the freer, relieved of the mark I carry, to move more fully, further, faster."

"Noyeed, I'm afraid to—because I know what I know, and you are in ignorance of it. Or because you know what you know—and I am the deceived."

"Oh, master, I will always be your finger and your foot, your belt and your blade, your word and your wisdom, made real in the open avenue and the closed courtyard. Only I beg you, let me do it wearing your sign—"

"I say no, Noyeed! I say nonsense!"

"As you have seen how I love your body, master, your hand, your mouth, your ear, your eye, your knee, your foot, what I speak is a bandit's, a wanderer's, a one-eyed murderer's long-thought wisdom—"

"You babble! And yet . . . as I visit the court tomorrow, perhaps there's something in what you say about the way I should go. Perhaps for just a little I might . . ."

And still later, when the big man and the one-eyed man came from the dark mansion into the yard among the men and women at the fire, Noyeed still wore the collar, while Gorgik no longer wore either the chain with the astrolabe, nor any sword, nor clout, nor dagger—as if all had been discarded or given away during the descent through the empty building.

2
_____

Some years later, at the ear of his ox, ahead of his half-empty provisions cart, a young smuggler walked through the outer streets of Kolhari.

A gibbous moon still showne.

Call him stocky rather than thin. At some angles he looked even loutish: there'd been little enough in his life to refine him since he'd first run away from the farm for the city. At others, however, he was passably handsome, if you ignored the healed-over pockmarks from an acne that, though now long finished with, had been more severe than most and whose traces still roughened his forehead and marred his cheeks above the thinner hairs edging his beard. Peasant or prince could have had that face as easily, but the hard hands, the cracked feet, and the cloth bound low on a belly already showing its beer were trustable signs, in those days, he was not the latter.

The cart wheels rumbled onto the road generally considered the division between Sallese, a neighborhood of wealthy merchants and successful importers, lucky businessmen and skillful entrepreneurs, and Neveryóna, a neighborhood of titled estates and hereditary nobles with settled connections— though lately the boundary had become blurred. Today there were any number of business families who'd dwelt in the same mansion for three generations, some of whom had even acquired a title or two by deft marriage of this youngest daughter to that eldest son; and more than one noble family had been forced by the times to involve itself in entrepreneurial speculation.

The young smuggler squinted.

Moonlight leached all green from the leaves, all brown from the trunks.

Was it two hours till dawn?

Something moved by an estate wall's turning, way along the crossroad. Something pale, something slow, something huge as a dragon coiled the suburban avenue.

Overspilling the hills above the city, fog had crawled down through wide streets and narrow alleys, till, across the whole town, it kissed the sea with an autumn kiss.

The cart rolled; the smuggler looked left.

Certainly the last time he'd come to Neveryóna by moonlight, he'd been able to see three times as many mansion roofs, even to the High Court of Eagles. Ordinarily such a moon would light the black peaks, which till an hour ago had held back the mist. But now both mansions and mountains were over-pearled, moon-dusted, veiled.

The cart rolled; the smuggler looked right.

More fog had moved in, as if, rippling up from the waterfront to the road's end there, a phantom ocean collapsed toward him.

He looked over his shoulder. The young smuggler had traveled many roads, you understand, and had often looked back at the way winding to the horizon, while he'd thought: *Is it possible I've come so far?* both fearful at, and proud with, his ignorance of the distance a moment before. Behind him, however, the pavement looked less like a road than like a yard—say one from the inner city with a neighborhood cistern sunk in it and closed round by haze. As fog cut away the distance ahead and behind, so it cut away pride and fear, or any other feeling of accomplishment in his journey. What was left him was dull, small, and isolate.

His bare foot squashed damp leaves.

He looked forward.

Visible above the wall, its crenelations irregular in moonmist, the mansion he neared now slowed his gait. Not his destination, it was, he knew, deserted—as were several walled estates near here. But there was a story to this one, and he angled away to see better where tiles had fallen from the facade, and terra-cotta castings had dropped from the cornice to crash—how many years before?—onto the lawns, behind silent stone.

The mansion had once been a lesser town house of a southern baron, Lord Aldamir, who, as his power had eroded in the south, had leased this home in the north to a series of minor nobles. They had not treated it well, had finally abandoned it. And the political upstart, Gorgik the Liberator, had rented the building as headquarters for his campaign to abolish slavery throughout Nevèrÿon. The Liberator's armed men had patrolled its roof and stood guard at its deep-set gate. Horses had cantered to the studded entrance, their riders bawling messages for the leader within.

The Liberator was a giant of a man, so people said, and had once been a slave himself in the empress's obsidian mines at the foot of the Faltha Mountains. Gaining his freedom, he'd continued to wear his slave collar, declaring it would stay round his neck till, whether by armed force or political mandate, slavery itself was obliterated from the land.

Later, people noted that it was not the radicalness of his program that had so upset the country, for, in truth, slavery as an economic reality had been falling away from Nevèrÿon ever since the Dragon had been expelled from the High Court twenty-five years before, when the Eagle—or her manifestation in the Child Empress Ynelgo—had commenced her just and generous reign. Rather it was the radicalness of his appearance that had bothered the nobles, merchants, and their conservative employees—not the Liberator's practice so much as his potential; for appearances are signs of possibilities, at least when one remembers that what appears may be a sign by masking as easily as by manifesting.

Several armed and surprise attacks on the Liberator had been financed from various sources. Gorgik had repelled them. But once a rabble of unemployed and impoverished workers, supplemented by soldiers from the private guard of nobles close to the court (despite their aid, the contributors had managed to remain as nameless as the gods), gathered on a misty night in the month of the Weasel, when the fog lapped late over the mountains and rolled down through the moonlight to obscure the city's corners and crevices.

They'd stormed the Liberator's house.

Here, however, the story crumbled into conflicting versions. Some said that, on hearing the approaching horde, the Liberator had fled with his supporters to the hills around Kolhari and up into the Falthas. Others said, no, that was impossible. The gang had been too stealthy, too quick. It was far more likely that, in the fog, they had simply raided the wrong mansion and the Liberator, hearing of it a mansion or two away, had

had time to escape. Still others claimed they'd got the proper house all right—the very building that rose behind the wall before the smuggler now—but the information that *this* was the Liberator's headquarters hàd been, itself, misdirection. The home here had never belonged to the Liberator at all; the true headquarters were a close and careful secret.

But one thing all agreed on: the building they'd broken into that night was empty. No guards stood at the gate. No soldiers strolled the roof. No furniture stood in the rooms. No garbage moldered in the great pots, three broken, behind the kitchen midden. Oh, perhaps a vagrant now and again had climbed the wall to build a brief fire by one or another outbuilding— but the charred sticks in the makeshift rings of stone were as likely to be years as months or weeks old. How could a powerful political leader, and his secretaries, and his courtiers, and his armed garrisons, and his plans, and his records, and his recruiting forces, and his provisions, aides and officers vanish from a walled estate with, at most, an hour's warning (more likely minutes'), leaving no certain sign?

Not that the story ended here. But now the various versions multiplied more. The Liberator was still at work thoughout Nevèrÿon, now in the south, claimed some, now in the north. The Liberator was no more, claimed others—indeed had never been. Or at least had never been other than an eccentric freeman, wearing a slave collar for his own eccentric purposes, wandering the Old Market of the Spur and talking too much in the taverns about fanciful political schemes. Now some said not only was this the false headquarters of the Liberator, but, though all had thought him that fabled man, the collared giant himself was only a ruse or, indeed, a lieutenant, or one of many lieutenants to the true Liberator, who was actually a wiry, one-eyed man, once a cunning bandit (who may or may not have been a former slave) and who was, for perverse and powerful reasons (that is, sexual), the true wearer of the collar. No, said others, it was the giant who was the Liberator, and the one-eyed man was *his* lieutenant. Each wore the collar, declared others who said they'd seen them. Both wore the collar at different times for different reasons, reasoned others who claimed such reason was only common sense, given the confusion among those who ought to know. There *was* no one-eyed man, the smuggler heard from a drunken soldier who'd declared he'd fought under Gorgik when, collarless, the Liberator had spent time as an officer in the empress's Imperial Army: "That was just a dream he some-times had. I remember it as clearly as I remember my mother's hearth. We'd be standing night guard outside his tent and hear him within, mumbling in his sleep over such a one-eyed apparition. It was only bad dreams." There *was* no scarred giant, he heard from a crippled cutpurse who swore he'd run with the one-eyed man when his gang had holed up in the Makalata Caves. "One time at night as we all squatted by the fire, he talked of a great foreman with a scar down his face who'd been kind to him when, for a few months as a boy, he told us, he'd been taken by slavers. But that was only campfire talk." Still, whatever the version, or whatever the various versions' relation to the ineluctable truth they mirrored, masked, manifested, or distorted, all agreed, as they agreed the mansion ravaged that foggy night had been empty, that it was on such nights as this, when all boundary lines and limits were thrown into question, that the Liberator could be counted on to do his most pointed work—if, indeed, there was, or had ever been, such a man.

The oxcart halted beside the smuggler, who turned now to slap the beast's red haunch.

Ox and man walked again through the fog, the cart trundling.

The smuggler knew, yes, more of these conflicting stories than might be expected of someone with either his past history or present position. Had he been able to write and read of what he knew, we might even call him a student of such tales—though he was an illiterate in a largely illiterate age.

A youth quick to smile, easy of gesture, and slow in speech, his usual talk stayed with genial anecdotes dramatiz-ing (exaggerations, to be sure) his comic incompetence at all callings. Passing acquaintances found him easy to enjoy and easier to forget, and few remembered the way his questions could grow quiet, intelligent, continuous, and committed. Fewer still would have marked him, thick-wristed, beer-bellied, and haft-fingered as he was, as a young man obsessed.

But many times, in the taverns and markets of Kolhari and other towns, in back-country inns and desert oases, he'd listened for mention of the Liberator; and when a story touching on Gorgik began at the counter of some winter's mountain inn or around some summer's seaside beach-fire, he was ready with measured, attentive questions, based on his own assessments, collations, and orderings of the tales he'd heard so far. On three occasions now, he'd found himself having to argue hotly that he was *not* a spy for the High Court, seeking to traduce an Imperial usurper. One night he'd actually had to run from a much louder and less rational argument that started at a forest resting place in the eastern Avila with a dough-bellied man, who, it turned out, had once sold slaves himself and had lost a brother and a friend to the swords of a huge, city-voiced bandit and his barbarian accomplice. ("A yellow-haired dog of a boy with—I tell you, by all the gods of craft—*both* his eyes! They certainly called themselves Liberators—though they were nothing but the scum of all slave stealers!") Another than our smuggler might have let such violences dissuade him from his research. His dubious profession led him, however, to expect trouble anyway, though time had proved him not prone to it: these inconveniences were not too great a price for information.

The situations that resulted in troubles had only impressed on him, finally, that the object of his obsession was not some innocent and indifferent fable, but rather a system of hugely conflicting possibilities and immensely turbulent values. And whether the Liberator was actually that great a concern to the High Court itself, as some maintained, the smuggler had, by now, as much evidence to refute as to confirm.

The origin of his interest had been, as least as far as he could reconstruct it, the most innocent of happenstance. Perhaps that innocence was what justified the intensity of his pursuit.

There had been a girl.

A lively little partridge, she'd come on one of his early trips to the south, with him and a friend—a walleyed city boy, born in the gutters of the Spur, a raucous Kolhari twang in his crude and constant chatter the young smuggler had, at times, found comic in its licentiousness and, at others, comforting on those vastly still, ponderously deserted back forest trails, just for the noise. The two youths had been paid by a Kolhari market vendor to run a shipment of magical implements to a merchant in the Garth who knew of certain southerners who would pay handsomely for the marvelously empowered trinkets— but not as handsomely as the price you'd have to charge if you absorbed the exorbitant tax the Child Empress's customs inspectors would impose.

By now he'd forgotten the girl's name among the names of several such girls he'd taken on several such trips. (At what friend's house had he met her? She'd been in some kind of trouble and had wanted to leave the city. But the details were gone from memory.) Once they'd begun, there'd been bad feelings between her and his foulmouthed friend. Eventually one morning, somewhere south of Enoch, while he lay dozing in the blankets beside their burnt-out fire, she'd bent over him to tell him she was off for water. (Though he'd been half asleep, he remembered that.) His friend had found the empty water pot, a dozen steps from the campsite, set carefully on a stump. They'd looked for her a bit, waited a bit more, had speculated on accident, on passing slavers. But then, she'd run off from them once already, his friend had pointed out.

They'd do better with her gone.

They'd gone on.

He never saw her again.

Indeed, today, had he run into her on the streets of Able-ani or Ka'hesh, he might not have recognized her. What he remembered, however, was something she had said.

On the first day of their journey they'd halted the cart just beyond the Kolhari gates. Sitting on a fallen log, the girl had toyed with a chain around her neck from which hung some odd piece of jewelry, chased round its rim with barbaric markings. (Though he could not recall her face, he could bring back her brown fingers on the bronze pendant fixed to its neck chain. That was jaw-clenchingly clear.) And she had said:

"I met a man, while I was in the city—a wonderful man! His friends called him the Liberator. He walked with me for an afternoon in the Old Market—he knew all about the market, all about Kolhari, all about the world! I mustn't tell you too much of him. That would be dangerous. But I went to visit him again, in his headquarters—a big old mansion he'd rented out in Neveryóna. Oh, *you'd* think he was wonderful, too. I know you would. He was brave, gentle, and handsome—like you! Though he had a scar down one side of his face. He gave me . . ."

But here recollection blurred. Thinking about it since, he'd completed her statement many ways. Did she say he'd given her the knife she always wore in her sash, hidden under her bloused out shift? Or the shift itself? Or the necklace? Or the tiny cache of iron coins, which, like the parsimonious mountain girl she was, she'd always been so chary of spending? But she'd talked a lot, and he'd seldom listened, as she'd soon grown used to not getting back much in the line of answers. (His friend and the girl, both had loved to chatter. Silly to have expected them to get along. It took a quiet person, like himself, to go so easily with such. He hadn't seen his friend in a year.) Months later, when the girl was gone and the storming of the Liberator's mansion was discussed from Ellamon to Adami, the smuggler's numberless encounters with the name Gorgik the Liberator had brought back the girl's memory and made her words from that morning the core of an obsession. (". . . wonderful! . . . He was brave, gentle, and handsome—like you! . . . He gave me . . ." But how could he have listened more when he'd been so surprised she'd felt that way about him at all?) And whenever, later, the Liberator was discussed, her chance mention seemed to have given him a tad more knowledge than the others had. (". . . He walked with me for an afternoon in the Old Market . . . his headquarters, a big old mansion he rented out in Neveryóna . . .") Though he seldom spilled much of it into words, that extra knowledge was supremely pleasurable; and he cherished that pleasure, nourishing it with continued inquiry. Sometimes while considering less likely versions, he had to relegate the girl's remarks temporarily to the same dubious order as other conflicting accounts. (". . . a scar down one side of his face . . ." Well, some said he was scarred; some said he was one-eyed; some mentioned both. And some mentioned neither.) But because hers had come first, most of the time it was easy enough to let her statements stand as the fixed truth around which he organized the other narrative bits into their several narrative systems, thence to organize the systems themselves as to most probable likelihood—while another part of his mind, the acquisitive part, the part that went poking and prodding in other people's memories for any and all fragments, no matter how preposterous (memories failing with time and boredom or inflated with imagination and self-aggrandizement), that part could claim, just as truthfully as the part that privileged a forgotten girl's chance remark, to be equally interested, or as passionately disinterested, in them all.

There'd been other women in his life more recently, three of them actually (and not *that* recent—), one younger and two older than he. Only the youngest had been able to pretend any tolerance at all to his speculations on the Liberator; and even her pretense had lasted only awhile. Could that be, finally, why it had been so easy to leave them?

Would that long-vanished mountain girl have been able to sustain her interest in the Liberator, he wondered, in the face of what his had become?

He turned by another wall.

Behind him the house that may or may not have once been the Liberator's moved into mist.

3
_____

Minutes later, off through fog, the smuggler made out a gate. Odd, he thought, as his cart rolled by mortared stones, for all these moonlight visits he was still not sure *which* lord's estate he went to—but then, he was not working for the lord.

He squinted to see if he could make out guards, only decorative in any case here in the city. Ahead he saw what might be a spear leaning from a far niche—

"Pssst!" from the door beside him.

He halted his ox.

Through a view hole in the planks, a lamp glimmered with butter-colored light.

"Well!" came through muffling boards. "You're here, then. Good!"

Wick flickering in its snout, the clay tub slid onto the small shelf, its base scraping sandy wood. The small moon, instead of holding a halo to the door, cleared the near air.

Metal scraped plank. Plank scraped stone. A board beside the one with the hole moved back in the rock.

He grunted at his stopped ox, as if to stop her again.

The old woman said: "Uhhh! This fog, I don't like it one bit!" She pulled away another board and set it back by the first. Tied up, the daytime leather hangings were bunched above. "Bad things happen in such weather. I've seen enough of this mist, and I know. Though it's all the better for the likes of you, isn't it? Well, I hope it follows you south and leaves some clear suns and moons with us here in the city. Boy!" she called back by her hip. "You could at least lend a hand with these. No, never mind. I've done them already. Bring that bag here. Be quiet! Do you want to wake the new kitchen girl we hired yesterday? She doesn't need to know of our doings. Oh, no. Not her, yet." Someone behind her scrambled over something ("Quiet!" the woman hissed), picked it up, moved with it. She reached behind, then swung forward a cloth sack. "Here, take it, now. And go on. Go on, I say! You have your instructions. They're the same as last time. You've done it before. Do the same again. Deliver it to the same place. You'll get the same reward when you arrive. And the same when you return. Now be off—"

"I go out now, grandma?" a boy shrilled behind her in a heavy barbarian accent. "I go out?"

The servant woman swayed into the glow, her hood putting a shadow on her deeply seamed cheek, which, in the haze, was the darkest thing about. The accent meant there was no possibility of blood between them. The smuggler looked at her brown, creviced, northern face.

"No one see me," the little barbarian went on behind her. "I hide in the fog and be back before—"

"*Not* on your life!" the woman shot back. "You think I'd let you go off in this miasma? Bad men are out in the city on nights like this, believe me: thieves, smugglers, murderers, and worse—like this one here!" She gestured at the smuggler, and her face wrinkled more—yes, smiling, he realized now. "Here, I say. Take it."

He took the bag from fingers almost as large-knuckled as his own. "Yes, ma'am." What she'd lugged in one hand was heavy enough for him to hold in two. "I've got it." He hefted the sack against his chest, turned to the cart, and dropped it, clanking and changing shape, as it slid over what was already there. He pushed it under a cluster of old-fashioned three-legged pots, bound together by their handles and only a month back declared, by official edict from the High Court, incapable of holding magic as long as they were unsealed, and therefore—when unsealed—untaxable. Behind him he heard one board and another scrape into place; then the bar.

"Come away, now, boy." The voice was muffled again. "Give me your hand I say . . ."

He looked back to see the luminous hemisphere this side of the opening shrink, then vanish. The buttery flame wavered behind the hole, grew small, was gone.

Where the haloed moon had hung was a pearly smear. Holding the canvas cover in blunt fists, the young smuggler yanked its edge down more firmly. Stepping to the ox's cheek, he grasped the harness, clicked his tongue against his mouth's roof with an indrawn breath, and tugged the heavy-shouldered beast around on the return road.

Walking ahead of his loud cart, he smiled. Now, he thought, I'm a smuggler again. A bad man about in the streets. (Whatever was in the bag had been metal and in many flat pieces. He'd felt their round edges. Which was odd, though not remarkable.) Once again he was taking a contra-band load to the south, carrying from people he didn't know to other people he didn't know. Nor, save for the metal makeup and disk-like shapes that had come to him over a few moments through the canvas, was he sure what he carried.

Years back when the smuggler had begun smuggling, at one point or another he'd look to find out what was in his sack: salt, silver, jewelry, magic fetishes, or sometimes even the sealed bullae in which clinked the mysterious contract tokens that signed, in those primitive times, a certain level of commerce. But it was common lore among smuggling men and women that the less one knew of what one carried, the better things were both for the client and, finally, for oneself. He'd accommodated such lore by putting off his look each trip till nearer and nearer its end. Finally, somehow, three, then seven, then numberless trips had passed when he'd forgotten to look at all. Now the thought only returned to him as the memory of a juvenile risk he'd used to take. (And am I really that young anymore? the smuggler wondered. Now and again it seemed to him he'd been smuggling an awfully long time.) Perhaps his meticulous inquisitiveness over anything and everything concerning the Liberator came from having to deflect natural curiosity from where, naturally, it was wanted. He'd thought that often. But this was the third time now he'd gone south at the behest of the old woman at the estate wall's secondary door. He'd first gotten the commission from an-other thief (". . . Follow these turnings. Be there with your cart at this time . . .") and could honestly say he did not know her name, nor the name of the family she was servant to, nor whether she worked for her own gain, her master's, or someone else's. I know nothing of you; but then (he spoke along to himself, on the road back into the city) you know nothing of me, old woman. You have no notion you're talking to a man with a passion and a purpose. Only a small stone's heave from here is the Liberator's house, but you've no idea that I may know more tales of that fabled home and hero than any else save probably his one-eyed lieutenant—more, possibly, than anyone in Nevèrÿon, if some of my conjectures are true.

And why should that be anything to me? laughed the seamed servant of the mind he carried with him. (Her words were as clear as if she sat atop his cart.) Will that help you finish your job the faster? Will it make you braver, quicker, more cautious, more clever in carrying out your task?

To which the smuggler laughed back, answering: Ah, grandma, how much you and your kind miss, who judge the rest of us only by how well we can do your work. But you're one of those who thinks there's no more to life than that, aren't you?

His lips moved in the mist.

As the old woman began to defend her position and denigrate his, he ambled along the damp avenue, now posing one argument, now posing another, now revising his own polemic, now revising hers, this time toward anger, that time toward submission, now with the barbarian boy adding his comment, now with the long-vanished mountain girl giving hers.

. . . a man with a passion and a purpose as great, in its way, I'd guess, as the Liberator's, or perhaps even greater, for it covers all the Liberator does and has done, yet has none of the emotions that drive him now to error, that trip him now in defeat, a passion and purpose that, for all its committed disinterest, has nothing to do with this scheming and scuffling, this cheating and wheedling that make up the daily lives of you and me.

But here he was, already turning onto the Sallese road.

Neveryóna was behind.

He looked back for the Liberator's mansion. But while he'd been wrangling with his imaginary companions about the worth of his commitment to this bit of myth and history, he'd managed to wander, without noticing, past the myth's major historical manifestation. Perhaps the fog had grown so thick it had swallowed the empty house?

No. He'd been too busy talking to himself.

Momentarily he considered going back to scale the wall and, tonight, exploring it, adding some firsthand knowledge to all his hearsay, seeing for himself the floors and windows and empty chambers that may (or may not) have been the Liberator's.

. . . make you braver, quicker, more cautious, more clever in carrying out your task? (Believe it, she was *still* going on!) No, certainly this was not the night to trespass on fabled grounds, leaving a cart of contraband outside. What might he expect to find of the Liberator in such a place anyway, years after it had been ransacked by angry marauders? (He walked through vapor.) He'd be back in Kolhari in a few weeks.

There'd be more foggy mornings.

4

He walked; and the city drew in to him.

Either side the street, sandstone walls and planked-over doorways closed out mist. Moon-glimmer on wet flags spoke of recent rain, though no drops had tickled his shoulders.

A large basket on his back, strapped with raffia rope to his forehead, an old man came from an alley, crossed before the ox, and trudged behind a cistern into more mist.

Later, down another street, he saw a door open and three people rush out, followed in a moment by two more. One held up a lamp filled with the cheap oil that burned red. Some moments' mumbling, and they went back in—except one woman who ran away along the alley, while, from inside, with one hand high on the jamb, a man leaned out to call: "Yes! Yes! Tell him they sent me up here to get . . ." He missed the object—probably medicinal and certainly magical. "I'll be down with it in a minute! Now run!" Fog and darkness obscured the hems and collars that might have placed them for socially. The man's voice sounded foreign, however, and better bred than might be expected in this neighborhood.

He passed the incident he would, no doubt, never know more of than this. Certainly it hinted at stories as complex as any he could tell of the Liberator. But he knew them only as inarticulate surmises; and would forget them, he knew too, in moments amidst the voices playing in his mind, would absorb them among the myriad forgettables that were the encounter, over any hour, dark or light, with the city.

Cart wheels wobbled on cobbles.

He turned his ox off Black Avenue onto the Pavē, which sloped down to the Spur. Fog and moonlight grayed the building walls. Planning to leave Kolhari by one of the little southern roads, rather than the northern connection with the great north-south highway, he'd wanted to move out with the earliest market delivery carts so as to have, at least for the opening of the journey, the safety and anonymity of the more traveled backroads below the city.

An hour or so before sunup, the market porters set torches here at the bridge mouth for predawn traffic. This morning the flare at the far wall had already snuffed to a black brand touched with coals. Sickly and silver, the near flame licked and wagged under smoke.

As he crossed the quayside, firelight feeble on the pitted bridge wall showed only how much denser the mist had become—and a few incomprehensible graffiti. Something to be thankful to the fog for: it was harder to see the scrawls and scratches that, day by day, appeared—more and more of them—on the bridge's walls and stanchions or on the houses nearby. The first writings he'd seen, more than a year ago, had been long and intricate. They had been put up (for writing was what they were) by the students who now and again came into town from their suburban schools out near Sallese. But as the old messages washed out or were rubbed off and new ones were written, soon a few signs among them seemed to take predominance, till today they were about the only ones you saw. And he'd caught both barbarians and baronets, as well as students, marking them with a lump of red clay or a bit of burnt wood, believing, as they did so at dawn or sunset, that they were unobserved. The smuggler had it on the authority of his foulmouthed friend (who of course had mastered them immediately and had once spent an afternoon actually trying to teach them to the smuggler, who simply had not been able to remember a one, till both had become angry and frustrated; they'd seen each other a few times since, but that had really been the end of their friendship) that these particular signs transcribed the varied and eccentric curses of the city's itinerant camel drivers, which combined in eccentric ways various terms for women's genitalia, men's excreta, and cooking implements.

Unable to read even as much of them as the scamps who wrote them and could read nothing more, the smuggler had finally trained himself to ignore them; they were marrings to be overlooked while the eye was out for other, more meaningful detail.

Usually when the moon lingered toward the day the torches were not set out, and he'd be able to see all the way across the bridge, into the market square, to the glimmer on the water that plashed in the fountain at the square's center—as long as the stalls and vending stands were not yet up.

But tonight, to fight the fog that now and again closed out the moon completely, the torches had, indeed, been lit. As the cart rolled onto the bridge, waist-high walls at either side and clotted shallows beneath, the weak fire showed the crockery shapes under the lashed canvas; then firelight slid away, leaving them black. And the bridge thrust three meters into dim pearl—and vanished.

He cuffed the ox's shoulder to hurry her, confident that the old structure was the same stone, bank to bank, as it had been by day or by other nights. Still, images of breaks and unexplained fallings drifted about him.

The cart rolled loudly forward.

The haze kept quiet distance.

Somewhere just beyond the flares, the Child Empress's couriers came at noon to cry out news to the people crossing. Was it marked by a raised paving stone? He hadn't caught a courier in months.

He walked.

Mist retreated.

Bridge flags floated out of it.

Ahead he saw a boy by the wall, head down, pulling and pulling at a lank lock. One sandal was missing; the broken straps were still bound around his muddy calf. The other was held by only one of its thongs, so that the sole dragged behind.

The boy pulled.

The fog rolled.

As his cart passed, the smuggler looked away from the mad youth—and into more mist.

During the afternoon and evening, the bridge served not only as entranceway into the Old Market of the Spur, but also as workplace for most of Kolhari's prostitutes. Once the market that made it profitable to pursue such sexual enterprise shut down, however, the women and men and boys and girls listlessly or vigorously hawking their bodies lingered on the bridge only an hour or so past sunset, when the market's mummers and bear-tamers and acrobats and street musicians also left for the night. (Were they not all, so said a mummer with whom the young smuggler had once been friends, merely purveyors of entertainments at different orders of intimacy?) When the last rowdy youngster ceased calling across the walkway after his or her friends, when the last middle-aged man, unsteady with too many mixed mugs of cider and beer, gave up his search for known, if not knowledgeable, flesh, when the last and oldest prostitutes fell in with one another, shoulder to shoulder, to walk tiredly back to the Spur, for a while the bridge might seem empty. But soon you noticed the sparse population remaining—there during the day, certainly, but absorbed, then, by the traffic coming and going. Now, made prominent by isolation and darkness, they became distressingly visible: the mad, the displaced, the sleepless, the disturbed.

At the bridge's market terminus, people leaving the city could gather with their bundles before sunrise and pay a few iron coins to the wagon drivers in from the provinces for a return trip out to this or that near county. Certain wagoners carried more people than produce; the custom had become so established that, off the market end, the Child Empress had recently rebuilt the shelter, with awning, more flares, and split-log benches, where, wet mornings, passengers could wait for rides.

He glanced up for the moon. A quarter of the sky was blurrily bright, but that was its only sign.

The triple facts of sex, madness, and travel lent their certain intrigues here. Though each had its hours of the night or day when it was most in evidence, the young smuggler had crossed the bridge enough times, and at enough variety of times, to know that none was ever really absent if you looked. With his smuggling cart, he himself was now heir to the travel; in earlier years he'd first come as part of the sexual provender—and at least once he'd spent three whole weeks here, during which, if he had not been properly mad, he'd been near enough. As he walked, memories flickered: an argument he'd once had with the mummer before they'd gone to a fine supper on the waterfront; the taste of grit on a parsnip he'd picked up from the pavement here and eaten; a conversation he'd overheard near the wall years back about the kind of boys some lord or other used to proposition on these same flags; the memory of a girl he'd watched pull water from a cistern not far away, her red hair, her freckled arms.

Walking beside his cart, the smuggler thought clearly and firmly, as if his own inner voice could drown the others out:

I probably know details and incidents about the Liberator's history that even he has forgotten. Yet who around me knows I have such knowledge? Not the madmen swaying in the night, nor the schemers behind their planked-up doors, nor the lazy whores and hustlers working here in daylight.

Nearing the market, he first heard, then made out, the naked barbarian boys by the steps that led down under. (Beyond, making minuscule moons in the fog, torches burned by the passenger shelter.) One was running up, then down the steps, leaning heavily on the rail.

The young smuggler slowed his cart to watch with suspended amusement. A young woman and an older man, who till now must have been walking somewhat behind him, moved ahead. The woman carried a bundle against her side. They were going toward the shelter.

A barbarian about fourteen ran across the bridge to squat beside them and, fists and buttocks bouncing above wet stone, cooed: "Where you going? Now come on, tell me! Where you fine folks going?" He cocked his head, blond hair gone silver in dim deceiving light. "You won't tell me where you heading? I won't follow you! I won't rob you! I won't hurt you! You city folks don't need to be afraid of me now!" He laughed.

The dark couple trudged on.

The smuggler pulled his cart up to the stair and walked around his ox to pat the hard ridge between her stubby horns.

Blinking black eyes in blurred-over moonlight, the beast stepped back.

Traces creaked.

Leaving his cart among milling boys, the young smuggler started down the bowed steps. (Strange, thought the smuggler. No one but cutpurses steal in a crowd. And his cart was not a purse.) At their foot a rock shelf extended from the stanchion. Troughs had been cut in it, sloped to the running water. Here men came to relieve themselves. (Women used the stair at the other side, which led to a similar arrangement, visible along the shelf.) The smuggler reached the bottom with a memory of other moonlit nights, when the bridge above had laid sharp shadow on the grooved stone. Most nights when he'd stayed on the bridge, he'd slept down here, his back against the graffiti-marred wall.

Tonight there was no shadow, and the gray light misted halfway under. Several women were busily doing something on the far side. More barbarians lounged here, most notably younger or older than those above. One of the oldest folded his arms and, as the smuggler stepped by, actually said to the shortest: "All right. Tell me: what's a kid like you doing out at this hour?"

"I told you already," the blond boy said, "I'm not a kid."

"Yeah," said another, probably younger. "He knows his way around!"

The smuggler stepped to one of the troughs, and, with the growing heat behind his groin at coming urine, moved his clout aside with one hand and with the other guided his heavy splatter over the rock.

Another barbarian stood a-straddle the trough three away, this one in a loincloth, pulled back now. He held himself, as though he'd either finished or not yet begun to make water. The smuggler noted that he wore his pale hair in a clublike braid over one ear. You saw such braids frequently enough in Kolhari, though usually not on barbarians, since it was a style left from the old Imperial Army, who, years ago, had devastated the lands from which, today, the blond southerners came, in greater and greater numbers.

Beyond the barbarian, just out of the diminished light, a shape moved slowly against the stanchion wall—likely two people in sexual embrace, though whether they were two women, two men, or one of each, was anybody's guess. The smuggler hoped it was one combination, assumed it was another (from what he knew of the bridge) and, had anyone asked, would have stated the third—if only to appease the times' prejudices; though quickly he'd add, with a self-deprecating laugh, that, given his luck, all three probably made out better than he.

Finishing, he shook himself, pinched and pulled his foreskin free of water, shook again with wet fingers, then tugged the cloth back between his legs. (Since he'd been a child, all bodily secretions had given him an odd comfort. Puberty had simply added another. Privately, he admitted, his heavy hands enjoyed them all.) Skirting naked loiterers, he started up.

At the top he heard: "Where you think *you* going, fine Kolhari man? Come on, tell me. Tell me, now! Afraid I'll follow you? Afraid I'll rob you? Afraid I'll beat you? You don't have to be afraid of me, city man!"

In a white tunic with dark ribbon woven round its sleeves, a tall man walked along the bridge toward the shelter, ignoring the boy cavorting by him. He was dressed like someone who should have had a private wagon. That he was here, sack on hip, to engage a public cart suggested to the smuggler he belonged to his toga no more than the boy below belonged to his braid.

"Hey, barbarian," an older boy called from the wall, "why do you talk like such a fool? Hey—" now the second barbarian strode into the central walkway—"barbarian! Why—"

The first danced back, grinning. "I'm just asking these fine Kolhari men and women why they—"

"—do you talk like such a fool?" Suddenly the second grappled the first in a headlock.

"Hey! Let go of me!" His mouth muffled by a forearm, the first giggled. "Let me go . . . you crazy barbarian!" He was dragged past the young smuggler and down the stairs.

The smuggler clicked his tongue. His cart began to roll.

From the far stairs at the women's side, four girls, followed by a fifth, ran up, talking intently. Also barbarians, they struck the smuggler as youngsters who had been in the city a goodly time. Chattering in the sibilant southern tongue, they hurried off the bridge. "Hey, look at all the big boys, out so late!" the one trailing called. She laughed and caught up to the group, while a boy shouted something in their own language after them. At which point—probably unrelated to the baiting—one of the girls remembered something forgotten below and turned back to the stairs, the others turning, running up, chattering after her.

Back against the bridge's newel, another girl squatted beside a bundle corded with vine rope. She was fifteen or sixteen. Her shift's shoulder was torn. In moon-blur the smuggler could see a smudge—or a bruise—on her jaw. She was just clean enough so he could not tell if she were a passenger or a derelict. If derelict, he thought, she'd probably struggled with her attire to bring it up to this ambiguous state.

Wandering by, a mumbling crone dragged her sack, which would contain (for several times on Kolhari streets the smuggler had seen such women's bags tear open) bits of cloth, broken pots, a wooden hairpin, a cheap leather necklace from a province the woman herself had never visited.

The man in the toga passed, paying no more attention to her than he had to the barbarian taunts.

Spitting, whispering, the crone moved to the bridge's rail, searching for something not there.

The seated girl looked away—the sight too painful, too predictive, or both.

The togaed man turned toward the flares at the passenger shelter.

The young smuggler guided his cart off the bridge and into the market.

Under an orange torch, people sat on split-log benches. Nearby, carts had already pulled up. Some of the drivers talked together. Others had wandered off to the warehouses in the adjoining alleys.

By the shelter's wall, a man slept on the brick, head against the wood. One drawn up on the other's soiled ankle, his feet were wrapped in the thong-bound skins a worker would wear laboring on the splintered rock at some city demolition site. By torch-glow and moon-mist, the smuggler could see, however, that the soles were hardly scuffed, as though they'd not yet been worn to work, while the cloth around his loins was threadbare, torn, and dirt-stiff. The thong that held it tight on a belly that creased above it was broken and retied many places.

Was *he* a derelict, the smuggler wondered, or a laborer passed out with drink?

The smuggler headed his cart toward a group of other wagons, as a morning porter tossed water from a ceramic bucket. Water sluiced near the sleeper's head. The porter set down his pail, took up his wide broom, and, with shove after shove, sent rills across the brick.

If one rill wet the sleeper, the smuggler did not see. But suddenly the man pushed up, got his feet under him, and, one arm straight out, staggered to a bench to collapse on it. His head fell back, firelight showing a dirty neck below a neatly trimmed beard.

What, the smuggler wondered, were the stories that would hold the anomalous details of the togaed gentleman taking a public cart, the squatting girl, or the sleeping man to some lucid and coherent truth, rather than making everyone appear simply another counterfeit, barbarian, citizen, or bum?

Stalls and kiosks had not yet been dragged out.

Near the side alley below a flare, wheels crushing dung, cart followed ox in among parked wagons. Did his appear an ordinary delivery vehicle? So much the better. He would leave it with the others for an hour or so, then be off among the first carts returning to the provinces. (He should be neither the first nor the last to go.) There were enough wagons and drivers about so that, even with its contraband, his could stay unattended awhile.

He tied the reins to the peg on the side of the driver's bench, pulled out the feed bag, put in more hay from the sack under the seat, then notched it to the bridle. The ox licked his fingers. Wiping his hand on the hip of his clout, while his beast munched and munched and munched, the young smuggler turned back to the square. He'd thought vaguely to sit in the shelter awhile among the passengers. But it might be better not to stay so long in one place, where he could be seen, observed, remembered.

Better to stroll back and forth a time or two over the water. From this end also, the bridge was still truncated by gray. He wandered onto it. Again he heard, then saw, the barbarians. Thirty steps on, and their argument and laughter ("Barbarian, why you go *on* acting such a fool...?") dissolved in fog behind.

Ahead, someone sat on the wall.

5
___

For the next few steps the young smuggler was not sure if it were woman or man, adult or child.

The shoulders were narrow. The knees angled wide. The feet were back against the stone.

His next step, the young smuggler saw several things at once:

The gaunt face was looking at him. An eye in it blinked. Across the other was a rag. The cloth strip was tied at the side of the small head. Some hair had caught in the knot. Around the man's neck—now the smuggler saw it was a man—was an iron collar.

"Morning." The man nodded. "What are you doing out on the bridge at this hour?"

The smuggler slowed, shrugged, smiled. "Walking." He'd known men to wear such collars before. Slaves were, of course, almost unknown in Kolhari. If you saw a real one it was likely to be in the retinue of some visiting provincial family. But the sexual tastes of such men were assumed, on the bridge, to be odd and unpredictable. "What's it to you?" He stopped; he still smiled.

"The market vendors aren't out yet." The good eye glimmered as though full of tears. "You should be home in bed, cuddling your girl out of her dreams and into morning."

"My girl just got a job as a kitchen maid—in a big old mansion, out in Neveryóna." The lie came complete and natural; he'd often marveled at the way elements from life so easily joined to make falsehoods—the same way, he'd noticed, they sometimes fused to form dreams. "So I don't see as much of her as I used to."

On the stone either side of him, the man's hands were wrapped with leather strips, recalling a custom in some province that, though the smuggler had passed through it once, he could no longer name. "Then what are you doing for sex?" the man asked, bluntly.

The three female faces drifted before the smuggler, one younger than he by half and almost black, the other two a decade or more older and pleasingly brown. After a sexually bleak year, they had suddenly filled six weeks of his life (almost three months in the case of the eldest) with sensual riches and emotional complexity that had been, frankly, too much. (Oh, yes. For certain, rather a kitchen girl out in the suburbs.) But he hadn't seen any of them for a month. He pushed them out of his mind.

"Just about anyone—" The young smuggler measured his admission— "and everyone I can."

The single eye questioned. "You want to come with me, then?" The man's insteps, back against the wall, were leather-bound too, which, yes, was the way they wore them in that province. He pushed from the rail to the ground.

Obvious thoughts often take longer to form in response to life than to letters. And the young smuggler had no letters. Also he was just now considering precisely that which would prevent the connection that has no doubt occurred to you and me. He'd encountered men before with the perversion of the collar; it was, after all, fairly common in Nevèrÿon—as all who'd ever worked the bridge soon learned. Indeed, he'd learned also in those early encounters, the collar was a sign for any number of sexual stances. It's only consistent meaning was that the most common two or three sexual exchanges were not likely to be among the *most* important for those who wore it. And even that was no more certain than a farmer's prediction of rain at a haloed moon. Also, the young smuggler knew from his time on the bridge, the maimed, deformed, and blind had needs as strong as anyone's, and a paraplegic's or a deaf-mute's desires could be as complex as a judge's or a general's. Those among them who could afford it—including the blind or half-blind—were as likely to buy here as anyone. There was nothing to keep a one-eyed bandit—for the little man surely looked a bandit—from the bridge.

Then he remembered:

The Liberator sometimes wore such a collar and was, some said, a one-eyed man, or at any rate was sometimes represented by one.

"All right," the young smuggler said. "I'll go with you, if you've got a place not too far from here. Even if you don't, below the bridge we could—"

"For coin or for free?" The man cocked his head. "There's a barbarian with a braid over his ear, standing at the pee-troughs. He's been down there more than an hour. If I wanted to give away iron tonight, I'd take him with me." He snorted. "But I don't."

The smuggler felt his humor balance on a more distressed feeling, having to do with his own, recently much self-questioned age. But he grinned it down in the three-quarter dark. "You won't give me anything? You know, last week I was hauling barrels over at the docks. The week before I was trying to make some money along here. And the week before that I was up in the mountains, cleaning out the cellar for some tavern keeper. I didn't make much at any of them. Sometimes, you know, I wonder which job I'm the worst at.'' He chuckled; the three weeks' work were as much invention as his Neveryóna kitchen girl. ''Still there're some who'll give me a few coins, here on the bridge. But I haven't spoken to many people lately.'' That happened to be true. ''Kolhari is a lonely city. I'll go with you for the company, and you can give me what you want. How's that?''

The little man considered a moment. ''If 'what you want' means nothing—'' The unsymmetrical face looked grave, turning away— ''then come.''

''Hey, now . . . !'' The young smuggler fell in beside the man, who'd started toward the market end. ''Don't be like that. You make up your mind later what I'm worth. I know it won't be much. That's not what I'm asking. But something. Say, where've you come from anyway, to be walking these wet stones?''

Striding his quicker stride on his shorter legs, the little man glanced up. ''You ask questions like that on a night like this on such a bridge as we cross now?'' His single eye held amusement, also disbelief.

It was the kind of look, the smuggler thought, you might give a fifteen-year-old barbarian whore declaring drunkenly she was a noble virgin.

The smuggler rubbed his earlobe between thumb and thick forefinger, looking down at his naked feet hitting fog-wet rock. His grin mimed a shyness he did not feel. ''Well, now, I suppose if you *had* a few extra pieces of gold—''

''Gold? Ha!'' the man barked. ''No, I'm afraid you're just not that young!''

''. . . a few iron coins,'' the smuggler said, as if repeating himself, ''that you could help me out with, afterwards; well, I'd appreciate it. I'm not working now,'' he went on, ''and my girl can't see me so often anymore. There're days, I guess, she doesn't think I'm the best lover in the world. Maybe I do better with the men. At least I give it a try, hey?'' He raised his face a little, glancing at the one-eyed man, and thought: I may not be that young, little man, but then, neither are you that you can afford to haggle. ''My girl, she doesn't know I come down here and fool around on the bridge. But she doesn't need to know of our doings. Oh, no. Not her.'' Yet he remembered that almost every woman he'd been to bed with since his sixteenth year he'd told about his homosexual adventuring; all had been fascinated. If anything, it seemed to smooth the sexual preliminaries. Only if some other male might overhear it would he hesitate to tell a woman he wanted to pleasure of these masculine explorations. The three so recent (yet so quickly receding) faces returned. He had told them: and hadn't they all praised him for his gentleness and lovemaking virtuosity? Hadn't all three wanted him to stay? As inducement, the youngest had offered him her body in what she took to be all sorts of wild and wonderful positions. The eldest (who did all that the youngest did sexually and with much less to-do about it) had also offered him money. At first he'd taken great offense. Then he'd taken the money. (Had that, he wondered now, put the bridge back into mind?) Then he'd taken his leave, anyway—when it had all become too complicated. The third, also older than he, he'd liked the most. But she'd had children and a great deal to do and, really, had considered him in every way—save sexually—a nuisance. No, though she'd been polite enough about it, she *hadn't* really wanted him around. Well, the truth was, *none* of the three had freckles. And that, for him (as he'd found himself telling himself with the growing belligerence of the mightily deprived), left sex with women not much better than what he might do with animals or men.

Though the intensity of the women's desires had allowed him to make his precipitate exit feeling (animally) well pleased with himself, still they were gone.

One had found out about the others, of course.

The shoutings! The tears! The accusations of crimes enough to make a provincial bailiff start to oil his whip! The youngest had been engagingly stupid. The one with the children had been distressingly sharp. And all three had been, well . . . He missed them. But here he was, running on with this old story about his sexual secrecy as though it displayed or hid some terribly important truth. "I'll go with you," the smuggler repeated. "Now I don't do this a lot. And I don't claim to be much good at it. But as long as my girl don't find out, it can't hurt her. And she's in Neveryóna, not here. You'll see what you can do for me." He dropped both hands to his legs. "Afterwards."

The little man, who wore leather about his loins, strode ahead, past the squabbling barbarians, as though abandoning the smuggler. (A woman passenger, herself a barbarian, was asking: "Well, where do *I* go . . . ?" A blond boy pointed to the stairs at the other side of the bridge.) The smuggler watched the little man move three steps, six steps, nine steps ahead.

Then he took a breath and hurried after him, off the bridge and onto brick. Fog had retreated enough to see the fountain, a rock in the square's center, with a basin carved in it to catch what gushed from its top—before the spill ran over into the ring of drains. From a cart near it, several women in desert robes were taking down folded screens and awnings for their stalls. One held up a torch for the others to see. As they helped each other open, unload, and unfold, firelight lit wet brick, flashed on the jewelry one wore at her neck.

"You know—" The smuggler caught up— "a few years back, I met someone here. He wore a collar. Like yours. He was a southerner. A barbarian—no older than me. He liked me, you see. So I went with him. Like I'm going with you. He told me he'd been a prince in his own land, off to the south. We got to talking: and he told me he'd been taken a slave—a real slave, once. Before he came here. He said he'd been captured from his home in the south, taken north, and sold up in Ellamon. He told me that he'd been set free by the Liberator—you know, the one everyone talks about? Gorgik the Liberator? The one trying to end slavery? He said he and the Liberator had fought together against slavers in the west." Purposefully he did not look for the little man's reaction. "So I told him, I said: 'You must think the Liberator is a really fine man.' And you know what he said? He said: 'I hate him!' He said: 'The Liberator freed me from slavery, but he didn't free me from this!' He meant the collar, you see? 'And for doing only half the job, I'd kill him if I could!'" Now the smuggler looked over. "That's something, hey? What do you think of that?"

The man paid no more attention than a brown citizen to blond barbarian jibes.

They crossed the square.

Over the years, the smuggler had indeed talked to a number of barbarians, also a number of men in collars, a handful of slaves, and several slavers. From these conversations, from hearsay, from observations, and from any number of story fragments about such men, such collars, such slaves, and the Liberator, the Liberator's one-time barbarian friend-turned-enemy had come together for him along with the conviction that, given one tale and another, he was very close to some historical truth that he wanted to try out on someone who might confirm it—though, as they passed between the fountain and the women, it occurred to him that, after all, the construction of this barbarian adversary was not much different from that of any other lie or dream. "I haven't seen him here for a while," he added. "The barbarian in the collar, I mean." (Certainly, he reflected, he'd never *met* him.) "Maybe something happened to him. You know, they say: 'Not to cross the Bridge of Lost Desire again is to die as soon as you leave it.' Well, maybe something happened to him. Maybe he got killed. I heard once that the Liberator killed a barbarian prince who led an attack against him, somewhere in the Spur. Though with all the tales and stories you hear, who could know which to believe."

The little man remained silent.

So, still walking, the smuggler said once more: "I haven't seen him in a long time. Years. The barbarian." Then, on an impulse, he asked: "What do *you* think of the Liberator?"

With that same amusement, that same disbelief, the single eye glanced up. "What do *you* think of him?"

Dwelling on the ease of lies, the young smuggler found himself—surprisingly—a word from truth. Why not say it, he thought: and felt tightness take his throat. As he tried to swallow it away, his heart pounded, and, swinging dry against his sides, his arms felt his flanks grow slippery with a sweat as chill as if he'd splashed into a wet grave—what, he noted with amusement, he might feel the moment he made up his mind to speak to some dark and freckled summer girl, leaning with her bucket on a cistern wall, whose contempt, whose harsh word, whose rejection, he was sure, would strike him dead upon the yard's paving as surely as the fiat of any nameless god. Yet in his trips to the bridge, in his trips from it, he'd learned that to turn from such a feeling was to declare oneself subservient to terror, to name terror itself one's master. To shirk such inner challenge was to admit passion impossible in this world as the nameless gods had crafted it and purpose nonexistent. "I think the Liberator is—" He drew a breath— "is the greatest man in all Nevèrÿon. For me—and I know I am only one and certainly no representative—the Liberator, Gorgik, may be greater, even, than the Child Empress Ynelgo, whose reign is . . ." He searched for something singular, but came up with only the most sedimented saw— "is just and generous."

"You think, then, that if this Liberator were ruler of all Nevèrÿon, he would be more generous and more just than the empress?" The little man snorted, then looked up sharply with his single eye beside the slant rag. "And do you think there's a chance that I am he—that I *am* this Liberator of yours? Or his one-eyed accomplice?"

"No—!" the smuggler protested. But the man's correctness gave him an odd relief.

"You think, perhaps, if you say the Liberator is great and I happen to be your man's lieutenant, then you're more likely to get yourself a coin or two for the night? Well, you wouldn't be the first to think such rot. But it won't do you any good—not tonight, believe me." The man stopped walking.

The smuggler stopped too.

They'd reached some littered yard in the Spur, by a cistern's low wall.

The smuggler thought: Which way did we come? How did we get here?

"Other folk than you have mistaken me for your Liberator. We might pretend that I was him, and that you were only some miserable slave, waiting for his freedom." The one-eyed man chuckled hoarsely. "But that's not my pleasure. Not tonight. Not with you. Me, a Liberator? No, tonight let us think of *me* as the slave—the lowest of the slaves in, say, the Empress's obsidian mines, north at the foot of the Falthas, where once, so they tell it, your Liberator himself toiled in the iron collar. Suppose I was the dirtiest, most miserable half-blind pit slave. What do you say to that?" Sitting on the cistern wall, the little man leaned forward as mist tore apart under the moon.

The eye and one shoulder, above and below black iron, silvered. "What would you do with me, then? If I were the weakest, foulest, sickest of slaves, too frightened to resist any attack, any brutalization, any abuse visited on me by my guards, by my foreman, or by the other slaves about me? Think of me loaded with chains and irons, so that I couldn't resist your assaults, even if I *were* strong enough." He reached up and put his hand on the smuggler's arm. "I know—they don't use such chains in the mines now, except when they transport the workers from location to location. Such horrors still occur only with the slavers in the west. But you can imagine it, can't you?"

No, it was not a response either to the man's touch or his

tale. What the young smuggler felt now he'd felt enough times before to know that, having a moment ago triumphed over a personal terror, having expressed one tiny inexpressible truth, the bodily sign of terror vanquished was a prickling like rain on the small of his back, his belly, his thighs. And because that terror's object, the man before him, had, on its vanquishment, moved toward him rather than away, the focus somehow became sexual: his cock, rolling forward in its foreskin, dragged on cloth.

"Follow me down!" the one-eyed man whispered, dropping his hand to the smuggler's chest. He turned and swung one leg over the wall. "Down into the cistern!" He paused, then frowned. "Don't worry. There're staples along the wall, so you can make your way to the bottom."

A year and a half back, the last legitimate work the smuggler'd done was three months with a filthy crew who'd drained cisterns and cleaned them of the potsherds and children's balls and bits of waterlogged furniture and general muck that collected on their floors. He'd labored hard, done the job at first with energy and soon with skill; he'd liked the men he worked with, had often been praised by the crew boss: "Sure, you joke about what a clumsy lout you are all the time. But I say you're a good and honest laborer, if not the best of them." In his last week, he'd even been promised more money—and a day later had not shown up. He'd never gone back. Now he never mentioned it. But he knew there were staples on the inner walls of all the city's cisterns.

"Come with me!" The little man swung his other leg over, reached in, stood on the inside rung, and stepped down. "This one's been empty for years."

"Sure. Go on." Leaning on the wet ledge, looking at the man's head, with its knot of rag and hair lowering below him, the smuggler felt the pride any laborer in the sexual services knows when he or she realizes: I can show *this* one a good time! "I'm right behind you!" He started over.

Climbing down the staples, the smuggler looked up at the moon. (Below him, a rung had broken; missing the step, he felt one end scrape his calf, but so lightly he didn't look.) Would the banked fog collapse over the stained shield of bone the loud and unnamed god of war arts had hung on the sky? He did not fancy being at the bottom of an empty cistern in pitch dark with anyone—even a miserable pit slave.

His lower foot dropped into water—but as he swung out

from the staple he was holding by one hand above his head, the other out and waving, he felt rock a quarter of an inch below it. He turned, both feet now on the water-filmed floor.

Yes, *most* of the water was out. But three-quarters of the cistern's bottom was still under half an inch. Over it, the reflected wall cut across night, while rills rushed out and back, raddling mirrored fog.

By an irregular section of stone that had come away from the wall, the one-eyed man crouched on dry rock. His leather skirt was gone—there, it lay a meter from his hand, with which, squatting, he supported himself. "Look—" and the single eye looked down from the young smuggler— "you're free now to do anything you want to your slave. Kick him, beat him, molest his body in any way . . ." With the echo, the voice seemed not to come from the little man but rather from the drenched air, as if the city around them, and not the man before him, gave the permission, the instruction, the exhortation.

The smuggler splashed onto drier flooring. The sexual impulse that had begun moments before, instead of being lowered by the cold water and the cistern's fetid smell, was, if anything, heightened. He tugged his cloth aside, felt it fall, so pulled it fully away and tossed it down. It's the voice, he thought with the endless run of thinking that never ceased regardless. What had always damped his performance in his rare encounters with the collared before had been the chidings, the directions, the continuous corrections from the self-elected slave, till, after the delays and displays and hesitations that finally, more than anything, seemed to comprise the act, he'd usually packed his half-flaccid cock back in his clout and, unsatisfied, gone off to face the world, convinced once more that this perversion was just not his to pursue. But now, with this vocal displacement, the words carried no hectoring critique from a new and demanding lover, male or female, accusing him with ignorance of, and inadequacy at, his sexual task. Rather it was a pronouncement of license from the otherwise mute deity of lust's intriguing and intricate craft, as enticing in its deitic dislocation as, in its too-human immediacy, it could be off-putting.

"This is for you!" He kicked the crouching man in the thigh (but not hard enough to hurt his own bare foot), raised his leg again and brought his heel down on the man's buttocks so that he had to catch himself with his hand against the cistern wall. Then he dropped to a squat. "And this is for me . . . !'' Momentarily awkward, he positioned himself, one hand on the knobby back, to push forward. His knee hit the cold rock as warmth bloomed about him. The pushings, proddings, and pokings, the bodily resistance only a step away from emotional rejection, had often sapped buggery of all pleasure. But, lubricated with whatever oils for the night or from whatever previous encounters, the body before the young smuggler received him easily within its astounding fire, and the discrepancy between the cold under foot and knee and the warmth inner flesh raised in friction with outer was, rather than an impediment to erotic amazement, amazement's confirmation. The heat and vulnerability within the body of another, whether he felt it with finger or penis or tongue or toe was always new, always astonishing, always more intense than memory. And wasn't the memory of that intensity when the sensation itself had been forgotten (the smuggler thought without a break in stroke), the desire all frequenters of the bridge, buyers or vendors or seekers after free fare, searched for—the desire, always lost when not alight, that named those stones? His implant in this humid flesh ran to depths in his own body that, as they were surprised into excitation, he knew were equally unrememberable. And wasn't that, when desire was lost, why it troubled so profoundly, why it lay so deep?

The little man pushed back, not in a single thrust, but with a pressure timed to the smuggler's thrusting, a rhythm that, when the smuggler slowed, slowed and, when the smuggler hurried, hurried, till the smuggler thought, with as much surprise as the always renewed surprise of pleasure itself: He wants me to *enjoy* it! While one enjoyed it nevertheless, it was a feeling rare in such encounters. And, yes, it excited him, so that when the man hissed, ''What are you? The fifth? The ninth? The seventeenth to cover me since moonrise?'' the echoing question seemed so far outside their juncture that, like a god's, the voice was devoid of all threat and comparison, all solace and praise.

''. . . if not the best of them!'' The smuggler pushed back, with no idea whether his words or the man's reported a fact or continued a fantasy. And for the moment he did not care. Among the five, or nine, or seventeen ghosts their echoing breaths filled the cistern with, the young smuggler was,

despite his assertion, outside the hierarchy of recrimination
and easy in a community of lust. He lay his beard on the little
man's cold shoulder. As he thrust, spit trickled his jaw.

The little man twisted aroùnd, becoming a face and,
moments later, a voice—"You're hot! Yes, you're hot in me!
It's good! Yes, it's . . . !"—as near and intimate as before it
had been distant and disembodied. One hand on the ground
beside the man's, the smuggler swung, hips and shoulders
hunching and hunching at each end of his bent back to make a
cave for the creature beneath him, as protected and safe and
steady in its contractions as a heart.

Then the little man moved forward, disengaging. "Wait . . . !"
He spun on the rock.

For a moment the two crouched, facing, the man, one-eyed
and breathless, the smuggler, on knees and hands, surprised
with the cold at belly, groin, and thigh as if, with the motion,
rather than simply removing himself the little man had substi-
tuted a corpse in which, under his half-masked stare, the
smuggler was now impaled.

"Come . . ." the man hissed, pushing to his feet. "This
way. It'll be better, you'll see." He moved to the break in the
stone, hand, back, and elbow momentarily in moonlight; they
disappeared within.

Wheeling to his feet, the young smuggler followed. He'd
assumed the dark blot was simply a place where the stones
had fallen or, at most, some shadowed niche. But, as he
stumbled inside, a hand on either wall, he realized it was a
tunnel—through which no doubt the water had run off.

"Follow me . . ." the smuggler heard, breathy in the distance.

As he moved awkwardly and uneasily in the dark, the
narrow space grew crowded with breath. Breath echoed around
him, echoed before him. He was a minute along the corridor
before he realized the exhalations, with their loud halts and
hastenings, were not from the little man meters ahead. They
were his own. Missing a step down, he staggered, almost
falling. Yet through it, his body was locked in its lust. He
groped forward, persistently hard.

Wetting his hand with crumblings from the wall, stinging
his heel on some sandy edge, and breathing, breathing about
him, the tunnel thrust him through dark turns.

A sense of distance, yes; but little sense of time. For
despite the five or seven kinesthetic memories he took from
the passage, the truth was he ran through it very fast.

The light was dim and surprising. Something was piled before it.

Sacks?

Feeling his way by gritty cloth, he heard metal clink metal: links rattled. He stepped around knotted corners.

From two rock niches, torches spilled their glimmerings. The little man crouched by the wall, fastening chained iron at his ankle. He glanced up at the young smuggler. The rag across his eye suggested one color and another under bronze flicker: green, maroon, blue. The smuggler knew from moonlight it was grit gray.

Dragging links over the rock floor, the man stood, turned his back to the smuggler, spread his legs, and leaned his hands on the stone. Jangling against the wall, chain swung. A length lay across the buttocks. Another was wrapped around one leg. The man was breathing hard. His back rose and fell: shadows at nobby vertebrae shrank and lengthened.

The smuggler came forward, was on him, was in him. Fire caught between their cold bodies. But flesh, chill as it was, was still warmer than the metal pressed between thigh and thigh, buttock and belly.

Links swung against the smuggler's leg as he pushed and recovered.

His chin was against his chest. A drop started on his cheek; another rolled down his shoulder. The one on his face, to his hunchings, moved along his cheekbone, through his moustache, stalled at his upper lip, quivered, then rolled over. Tasting it, he was almost surprised at its salt.

The heat between them built.

Then, once more, the little man twisted away, disengaging.

The young smuggler said, "Wait! No, I was just about to—"

The little man glanced back. "Follow me . . . !" His hoarse entreaty stopped the smuggler. With the chains he'd just donned clattering about him, he made for the arch across from the stacked sacks and through its hangings. Hides swung. Beyond them, the clinking muffled and, after moments, quieted over greater distance.

Drying perspiration cooled the smuggler's thighs and chest. Hairs tickled, lifting. Scratching at leg and shoulder, he walked forward. At the hides he hesitated, wondering at these pastimes, then pushed through.

The room beyond was bigger. One brand in its niche lit

several benches and, as the young smuggler walked in, little else. Some of the benches, up on end, leaned against the wall. The smuggler stepped around them. The little man was not behind them. The hangings at the room's far arch swayed.

He walked forward, thinking that this stroll across the ill-lit room was the opposite of his dash in the black tunnel: there darkness had held both his lust and any speculation on it in suspension, while the flickering in this tenantless space, where he'd expected, if not desire's object, at least a quick relief from horniness, kept pushing him to think, remember, speculate on the fact that, after all, neither men nor this miming of submission and domination was his own pleasure. This was borrowed passion.

That was, indeed, his thinking.

But the feeling was that *he'd* loaned out something that had gone ahead with the little man; and he wanted it back—though he couldn't have said what it was; or why.

With this uneasiness, lust ebbed, so that he lingered in the chamber perhaps a minute, breathing loudly, thinking clearly: Should I go on? What might I get from him? What does he want of me? What might I learn about the Liberator, and is it worth all this? He pushed the next hanging aside.

First he thought it was a slate slab inches ahead. Then, blinking away the moment's disorientation, he saw wide steps down into vast darkness.

A dozen brands burned along a distant wall. And in such space, at such distance, a dozen brands gave little light. Somewhere, water gushed. Here and there he could make out balconies around the hall—and a flickering near one torch: water fell between squat columns, rushed along the wide conduit crossing the partially tiled floor, and swept under two bridges that twice blocked the torrent's glimmer.

A giant brazier stood beyond the water. Across its coals, flames scuttled.

At the hall's far end, between leaning torches, a stone seat rose from a stepped pedestal, its ornate back carved into some beast—eagle? dragon?—which, in the play of shadow, he could not identify.

Approaching the throne in his chains, the little man stumbled to one knee, pushed back on his feet, and continued toward the vacant chair. He held most of the chains over one arm. Chain dragged behind him on the tiles. Steps restrained by the links between his shins, he moved awkwardly across mosaic, turned a moment to look over his shoulder, and went on.

Can he see me up here in this darkness? the young smuggler wondered. He let the hide fall behind him and started down the steps, glancing up at the roof, where ropes and grapples looped below beams. The stones under foot were bowed, worn at their centers. Fifty years' footsteps? Five hundred? The odor recalled night on a winter beach down from the city; at the same time, the echoing water suggested high, summer valleys between widely separated peaks. Yet, overwhelmingly, he felt hugely underground. The conflicting senses of place, with dimnesses and distances, further dissolved the sexual surety that, moments back, had been so absolute.

Cool air moved in the high hall, though the fog had not come within.

What, he wondered, am I doing with this collared creature? But as his blood withdrew into its secret sinks and cisterns, its retreat left belly, back, and buttocks, shoulders, thighs, and arms a-tingle—with desire, yes; though, again, not for the man or his chains, but for the state the smuggler had, moments ago, slipped from. The feeling was both less localized and more intense than normal lust.

Reaching the steps' bottom, he started over the dirt floor. It was darker here than at the stairs' top. Like steam, the light seemed to have collected higher in the hall, leaving the floor pitchy. Twenty steps on, his bare foot went from earth to wood as he stepped onto the little bridge.

Froth whispered below.

Beyond the brazier's black wall, he could see the little man in chains at the bottom step before the throne. There were heaps of something—hides? pelts?—one side of the chair.

And if he *is* the Liberator, or connected with him, the smuggler thought in a moment's passing lucidity, what questions *should* I ask?

Which is the exact month of your birth? Some say the month of the Badger; some say the month of the Dog. Though a birth month you only knew by report anyway, and reports could always be wrong. (He remembered his mother and his aunt, arguing once under a plum tree, whether his own birth had come with the Badger or the Bat.) Well, then, which of the three versions of your departure from the obsidian mines for the army is right? And was that before or after you lost the eye? (He stepped from damp wood to dusty tile, trying to imagine the man in chains as an Imperial officer.) And if you're *only* the Liberator's lieutenant, which is it: You and the Liberator have been together half a dozen years? Or you've been together intimately since your time together in the mines?

Above him, the brazier's rim was burnished with the small flames behind it. As he neared black metal, he felt heat through the darkness. The curved wall itself was, doubtless, hot enough to char flesh should you stumble against it. Ahead, chains dropped, then dragged, on stone.

He looked down.

Before the seat, the little man knelt at the steps' foot. Hides hung over the chair's arm.

After a moment, the young smuggler walked from the brazier's wash of warmth. Cool retouched his shoulders.

Ahead, the man lay down before the bottom step, one fist near his cheek. In firelight, his calloused heel was dirt black, with some cleaner skin before the leather under the instep; then more clean skin, before the cracked ball took up walking's dirt. The foot dragged on the mosaic; the tiles' colors were indistinguishable. A chain fell from one stair to the stair below.

The young smuggler walked up and stepped over the man's leg with its ankle iron. (The leg moved; a loose confusion of links dragged out to become more chain.) The smuggler put one foot on the step and looked back down at the little man, who was . . . writhing!

Fingers opened and closed on the step's lip. The spine arched; vertebrae were sharp, shifting knobs. An arm moved so that a shoulder blade rose, then fell, among small muscles. Cheek sliding on gritty stone, the man whispered, "Free me . . ."

The smuggler climbed the next step, a laugh in his throat struggling with his tongue. Then chills started behind his shoulders to cascade his back, pour over his buttocks, and trickle his thighs. "No . . ." he whispered, trying to ignore both the laugh and the tingle: flat and emotionless, the word sounded like something mumbled by a new mummer on a market-wagon platform, its blandness and softness conveying only the new performer's fear, alone before a hundred eyes. "No . . . !" There, at least he could recognize his own voice in the echo. The tingling came on. He stepped up another step. "Me, free a foul, filthy, and wretched slave like you?

Ha!'' All in a syllable, the laugh burst out with mummerly conviction. "No!''

"Free me, master.... You can do anything to me, lord. Abuse me, ravish me, keep me a slave forever or cast me loose. You have the power! For you it's all the same..."

Was it the great brazier, the smuggler wondered as he stepped to the next step, that kept the fog from seeping within this crypt? "I know what you want, you low and lustful slave!" (Declaring it with all the intensity he could muster, he still could not have said precisely what that was.) "You've done nothing to deserve anything from me! You're low as the garbage tossed in the gutters of the Spur! You're low as the refuse the muck crew picks up from the floors of polluted cisterns! You're low as the deepest and darkest hole in the Empress's obsidian pits!" Speaking, he took a huge step onto the seat itself, to stand on it, naked, moving one hand impersonally to his genitals at the return of impersonal lust, as if his body, even to his cock's reengorgement, now began to mime desire as a last resort before the loss of what he'd felt before.

He turned on the stone seat and looked down at the man prone at the steps' bottom.

The small shoulders flexed. The buttocks tightened and relaxed. A muscle defined itself, now in an arm, now in a leg. "Free me, master. You have the power. You've always had it. For all eternity. You stand above me. I lie below you. You only have to use it on my miserable, suffering, enchained body..."

Chains racketing, the little man rolled to his back.

The stomach muscles grew rigid in the firelight as he lifted his knees to his chest. Wrinkled, vegetative, half-embedded in black moss, the man's penis was soft, which surprised the smuggler. Did the traditional mark of passion's absence mean (centered in a body whose twitches and jerks spoke of all sane limits' passionate transgression) age? Did it mean debauchery run beyond function? Perhaps it meant the transgression itself was somehow a mime, and those quiverings and shakings were actually centered about some invisible control. Did it mean that he had not gone beyond a limit but, rather, knew everything he was doing? He's placed me here, the young smuggler thought. Then it struck: And he would do anything for *me* now! As if in some displacement of the inner dialogue, the little man raised his chin above his corded neck and whispered: ". . . anything, anything, master . . . you can do anything . . ." Dragging chains around his raised thighs, the man reached through his legs to probe between his buttocks, with leather-bound hands. The single eye held both the smuggler's, while the face twisted with the breathing, the reaching. The forehead creased above the slant rag hiding the wounded socket. Knees rocked. In his hand, the young smuggler became aware of the hardness, which, as his two forefingers lifted under his glans, thrust from its half-obliterated sleeve, became even harder, the skin along the side to which it curved hurting a little, which it sometimes did when he was very excited. Tearing and straining, the eye below would not blink. In the mouth the wet tongue twitched. The lips moved about a moist exhortation: "Master . . . ?"

The smuggler came.

It was as surprising as that. During the fifteen or twenty seconds of it, a heat started below his knees as if some fire he stood near abruptly flared. The sensation mounted his thighs, his body's trunk, till, within the flame he'd somehow become, a fist of muscle, contracting, propelled his mucus forward. Unsteady between painful gasps, his heart blocking his ears with its thuds, his right leg quivered, near to buckling. A muscle in one flank strained to true pain. His first articulate thought was that, in the course of it, there had been none of the sub-vocal awareness (It's beginning. Yes, it's . . . Now, it's beyond halting. This one's not so good . . . ? No, this one is *really* fine!) which usually made orgasm bearable.

The pleasure—if something so intense, so unconnected with words, could be pointed to with a word—rolled away like water off beveled sand, leaving the beach still saturated. (He took another breath. Pain caught again in his side. He looked about, to see how to climb down.) What lay beneath was fear. Was it simply the surprise of ejaculation coupled with his pounding heart, together miming terror? One hand unsteady on a gritty hide over the throne's arm, he jumped.

His leg would *not* stop shaking!

As he came on down the steps, the little man grasped the smuggler's ankle, which twisted in hard fingers, wet from one or the other of them. "Free me . . . !"

The young smuggler pulled loose, nearly fell, and rushed across the tile, the floor going from mosaic to dirt.

As he neared the brazier, he realized the hall was not empty.

Off by the wall a flame moved sideways, raised, and went on to ignite another. The twin fires lit what one had been too dim for: the head, arm, and shoulder of a yellow-haired barbarian, carrying his brand from niche to niche.

As the smuggler neared the brazier, he heard falling gravel. Someone had wheeled up a stilted ladder. At the top, her chin aflicker, a woman tossed in a pailful of coal.

She glanced down. The smuggler *almost* ran.

Still panting, he hurried over the bridge toward the wide stairs. By a fitful torch, two youngsters, boy and girl, shook out a hide with thudding snaps. Dust rose between the smuggler and the flame. The boy, who was black, coughed.

Had any of them *seen* him? Heard him? He looked back. Had they realized what he was *doing* as he stood a-top the throne? (His back tingled.) At least the little man had been on the floor. But he, standing high in firelight . . . Why did that happen to *me*? he wondered. What is that supposed to *mean* about me? He pushed those thoughts out of his head with the immediate practicality: Return? Might the man need help to carry away his chains? Certainly he was some morning cleaner or porter, who, among these others, had thought to get here before the rest and avail himself of the empty space until his coworkers arrived.

He *must* have known what he was doing. . . .

The young smuggler started up, leaving behind the subterranean matutinal preparations. (He could not imagine the hall's use.) Possibly they had not been observed or, if observed, his action had not been recognized for what it was. (*Do* you see something like that unless you're looking for it?) He pushed through the hangings, thinking that though such sexual sensation was among the most intense he'd ever felt, easily he—

"Excuse me," the woman in the middle of the room said. She lowered the bench from those stacked up. "Aren't you supposed to be down helping them clean out the—"

"No!" He looked about sharply, stepping back. Swinging hide brushed his buttocks and shoulders. "Yes. No . . . ! They sent me up here to get . . ." He pointed beyond her to the hangings in the far arch. "In there! I'll be down with it in just a minute." Then, without waiting for her to speak, he dashed by her through the far hangings into the next room.

And into blackness.

The torches that had burned in the niches before were out. As his hand found stone, his foot clinked some chain still on the floor. Feeling along the wall, he looked back, but the woman had not pushed aside the hangings to follow or spy. He stepped, reached out again, stepped, reached out: as his hand felt sackcloth, he thought:

I'm glad I'm *not* as young as all that! Such sensations as he'd just had, encountered early enough, could become the object of all sexual searching. No, for all its intensity, wonder, pleasure, he could easily live his life without experiencing *that* again.

Sacks were gone. Stone was under hand. A stubbed toe on a step up confirmed that he was, indeed, somewhere within the tunnel.

That's the kind of feeling, he thought, stumbling in the dark, one could kill to regain. But he had known a truth. (He staggered on, surrounded by the echo of his breath.) The truth of the throne of power, the truth of the secret center, the truth of the hidden crypt, the lie of the limit to pleasure. Or had he? He stumbled again. He had told a truth before, to the one-eyed man: about his feelings for the Liberator. The Liberator was the greatest man is all Nevèrÿon. The Liberator—

He halted, as if he'd become aware of someone with him in the tunnel. But it was not the Liberator he imagined breathing beside him in blackness; nor the one-eyed man. It was the Liberator's barbarian adversary of rumor, conjecture, and surmise.

For he knew, with the same certainty by which he knew his own name, that the barbarian who had died fighting the Liberator in some sexual crusade was a lie. The kind of pleasure one might kill to regain? Yes. But for just that reason—because, whatever pain accompanied it, it *was* pleasure, not pain—no one would kill to release himself from it. If there had been such a barbarian as rumor and fable told of, his situation had certainly been more complicated than that which the smuggler, with his care, study, and collation, had assembled from these rumors and fables to speak of so easily in the market. Again, as had happened so many times over the duration of his obsession, he realized he *knew* something about the Liberator, about the collar, if not his one-eyed lieutenant who also sometimes wore it. Indeed, the smuggler thought, the wonder is *that* I know.

Though how the known differed from the lies, distortions,

and displacements that wove together language's dream of meaning he could not, as he felt his way again through the dark, make clear.

And why, now, did his judgment of the Liberator's greatness seem so trivial? (No, his thought did not halt just because it had crossed a certainty.) Could it be that, in the heat of lust's extremity, the very concept of truth had come unstuck from his initial utterance to the one-eyed man and, in its molten state, fused now to this new notion, so that his new "truth" was finally just as much an assemblage, a dream, a lie as all his other stories?

He staggered on, around one corner, around another, and was just wondering if perhaps he had missed a turnoff or, even more likely, had wandered into some side tunnel that would lead him on aimlessly and endlessly through the dark with only his own breath for company, when, ahead, he saw light glimmer on the wet wall.

Seconds later, he stepped onto the cistern's sheeted floor. He looked up.

Gray morning had wiped away night. Five long logs lay across the cistern top, some ropes still lashed to them—none of which he'd seen earlier.

He looked down.

The little man's leather kilt lay on dry stone. Across it was the smuggler's clout-cloth. He stepped over to it, squatted, and lifted it. "Ahh!" He'd tried to toss it toward the dryer rock; one end, of course, had fallen in the water. Leave it? (Above him, he heard female shouts, one over here, then, moments later, one over there.) No. Though he was not above going about the streets like a barbarian, cloth was not so common you abandoned a length of it, until it was soiled beyond washing and worn beyond patching. ("Ayeee!" and "Ya-ha!" Then, "Ha!" and, moments later, "Aye!" above.) He picked it up: wet, it turned out, not only at the end but in half a dozen other spots along it. He rung it, stood, doubled it over his shoulder, and walked to the staples. He fingered the edge of the broken one. Another sagged till it looked as if it might pull free with the next hand or foot set to it.

He climbed.

It didn't under either.

As his head rose above the cistern wall, he looked about the yard.

His first thought was that both were about the age at which

he'd first run away for Kolhari: two young women were throwing a child's black ball back and forth from one corner of the yard to the other. Both wore the same sort of clout whose end clung so coldly now to the smuggler's back.

With her yellow hair cropped for vanishing summer, the barbarian whipped the ball into the air with a snap of her arm— "Aaiii!" —that shook her tanned breasts.

A dark Kolhari girl, her hair bound back in a puffy bush with a leather thong, the other ran across the yard, leapt with both hands high, caught it, and swung her arms down and around her till her fists almost brushed the pavement, then snapped it— "Ya-hey!" —into the air, while the barbarian, staring up, ran a step in one direction, two in another, then raced off in a third to catch it, to cry out, to fling it high again.

Wondering if they saw him, the young smuggler climbed from the cistern. He watched for three breaths, walked a little way off, then turned back to look through four more shouts and tosses. The fog had left only a ghost of dampness in the air. Though the morning was clear and the yellow sun lit the wall across from an eastern alley, down a northern street mist still put the sheerest veil over the houses.

"Ay-ya*haaa*!" The barbarian stumbled on her throw: the ball shot almost straight up.

"Oh! Hey...!" Her companion ran across the yard, stopped a few steps from her friend, who sat now on the stone with her hands behind her, one of her shoulders and one of her breasts and one of her knees in sunlight. With delight, the smuggler saw the copper freckles speckling all three.

The dark girl put her fingers over her mouth, laughing, stepping about, shaking her head, moving from sunlight to shadow to sunlight. In an unexpected and astonishing gift, the smuggler saw her back, so much the darker, was freckled too—with those even rarer points of patinaed bronze that made him want to put his eye an inch away from one, then, suddenly, thrust out his tongue as if it might hold some marvelous taste other than the skin's faint salt.

The barbarian rocked forward, swaying in a torrent of giggles.

Between her fingers the Kolhari one asked: "Are you hurt? I mean..."

The other managed: "Yes, yes, it's all right. I mean, no.

I'm all right!'' Finally she said: ''The ball—did you see where it went?''

Catching her breath, the dark one pointed across the yard: ''In there, I think.''

''Oh, *no* . . . !'' The barbarian began to laugh again.

Both looked toward the cistern.

''I heard it go in,'' the smuggler called. ''It bounced on the back wall and splashed down on the bottom.''

He could not have said, later, if the feeling had come before he'd spoken and therefore had impelled him to speech, or if it were the detritus of speech, composed of the leftover heart pounding from his bravery in speaking at all. But he waited to see if their look, if their laugh, if some word from them would include him.

They looked.

They smiled.

One of them (''You said you . . . heard it go in?'') spoke.

But through the intensity of his gaze, though he nodded, tried to smile, and realized he was only staring, he lost the specificity of the exchange in the dazzle of the sun-swath that tipped the standing one's brown and spotted shoulder, that bronzed the dotted shin, breast, and cheek of the one sitting. The answer? The truth? For a moment everything reeled in a fiery gust (from the far sun? from the distant sea?), while the sky cracked.

Pieces of the day balanced, gray and yellow.

''Well, there's no water in it.'' The barbarian pulled her feet under her, reached about to push herself erect. ''I can climb down and get—''

''Don't you dare!'' declared the other. ''You're going to go down into some old empty cistern? You don't know *what* you'll find in there—!'' They laughed again.

Across the yard, he tried, tried again, tried a third time to make some joke, to comment, to volunteer climbing down for them—but all three left no visible trace on the two youngsters, one a yellow-haired barbarian whore (really, he doubted it; but he hoped she was, like himself, a whore), one a brown and respectable Kolhari girl. His throat muscles had moved, but not his lips or tongue. Certainly, he thought, in the pursuit of such eccentric pleasure it could be no *easier* to whisper, ''Master. . . !'' for the first time than to speak to a woman whose body and bearing moved you in desire's more familiar paths. He started across the yard for the sunny alley from

which, as best he could remember, he'd entered the yard in
darkness.

Walking naked over dust, he glanced at them again: They
are beautiful, he thought simply, bluntly, truthfully. Why use
men's bodies when there are such as these in the city? But as,
from the alley's end, their laughter swirled his nakedness, he
knew what he'd learned of the Liberator as he'd stood on the
throne, whether fog-blurred dream or granite truth, had only
secondarily to do with bodies.

6
___

Certainly these were more primitive times than ours, when
public nudity was a sign neither of madness, rebellion, nor
art. Along with the ceramic-hard soul and the wood-rough
palm, it meant rather, in both men and women, a certain level
of income, a certain order of labor. Since the smuggler's
gains, when smuggling went well, were modestly above that
level and the physical work needed to survive at it had been,
of late, somewhat below it, he could take a certain joy in the
deception as he wandered—naked—toward the market in the
dawn's near empty streets. The few he shared them with,
women and men, were most of them naked too.

Several times he had to stop and go back a turning when
some alley deposited him on a corso where, if the sun were
really over there, meant the market was not in the direction
he was walking.

Clout still over his shoulder, he finally came out in the old
square; three quarters of the stalls were already up on the
worn brick. More were being set out. Vendors called to one
another, and the earliest shoppers already wandered between
counters and under awnings, carrying baskets and bags.

Certainly at this time crime was among those callings
conducted more primitively than today: it did not seem overly
imprudent to a smuggler of his age and experience to leave
his cart unattended for an hour (the encounter in the crypt had

taken somewhat less) among the others parked by the market's side. At any time, the empress's inspectors might be wandering here and there, observing, reporting, fining. But, because of the several new markets that had, in recent years, opened up closer to the waterfront, inspectors were becoming less and less efficient at their never very well defined tasks.

Across the square he could see other wagons rolling up. Having finished deliveries, a few were pulling out. An hour, yes, the smuggler thought. But much more than that was pushing even primitive prudence.

He walked by stalls of cheap jewelry, exotic vegetables, farm tools, and cooking implements, till he reached the donkeys and oxen and ponies standing before their various carts. His own red-flanked beast swung her head and blinked her eyes' black marbles over her feed bag. Unhooking it, he glanced toward the shelter. Most of the passengers from before sunup had already gotten their rides. More recent arrivals sat, waiting. The drunken workman (if he were not a bum) still sprawled over half his bench.

A youngster, naked as the smuggler, walked toward him as he tugged the feed bag away. (The beast swung her head to follow it.) "Excuse me. You've finished your deliveries . . . ?" the boy asked. "If you're going south, maybe I can get a ride with you for a few iron coins?"

"Sure." The smuggler put the bag up under the driver's bench. "For a few stades, that should be all right." He's a student, the smuggler thought, and felt, behind his smile, oddly uncomfortable with his own nakedness before this younger, slimmer nudity. So, just as though it had nothing to do with the boy before him, he pulled his clout from his shoulder, bound it about his hips, ran it between his legs, and tucked it in at his waist: still damp. As he bound it, he thought: And how do I know he's a student? For his morning's adventures had left him feeling analytical.

Well, for one thing, he goes about naked like the poorest barbarian laborer when he clearly isn't one. His black hair is in the side-braid that goes with the military, while equally clearly he is no more a soldier than the barbarian who'd stood below the bridge. At the same time, for all his nakedness, on his feet he wears the leather coverings of some working man who toils on broken stone. But it's all for the potential rocks he might, as a student, tread, rather than for any daily encountered hardship. (The boy's beard was much less neatly trimmed than that of the man sleeping it off over in the shelter.) And this one, the smuggler noted, wears the same bindings around his palms as the one-eyed man had earlier—though on this youth they're probably not from his place of origin, but rather from some custom observed in passing and imitated for its quaintness. Probably the student would be able to tell more of their use and history than the one-eyed man, who, whatever his sexual eccentricity, most likely had been born to them. Making up his mind not to ask more about them, the smuggler put his thick hand between the ox's horns to rub. "You study with one of the masters out near Sallese?"

No doubt having thought his nudity had stripped him of all identifying signs, the student grinned down at the brick. "I'm just an apprentice. Right now I run and fetch, wax boards, and make tablets for the older ones. I won't take up my own field of study till spring, when my reading has gotten stronger."

The smuggler looked past the student at the shelter; the student glanced too.

Still sleeping, the drunken man seemed moments from toppling off the bench.

"You notice," the smuggler said with a considered sigh, "how there're more people out around the bridge, drunk, mad, or just exhausted, who look like they might have been working three weeks ago?"

The student nodded. "That's what my master says. Out at the school, everyone argues that these are hard times in Kolhari."

And the young smuggler, who hadn't heard any more people than usual say such a thing, laughed and clapped the student's shoulder. "Up on the cart with you, and we'll see if we can't at least get you started on your trip!" for basically he was a friendly fellow, and he did not want the student to think his remark somehow chided the student's calling, for youths who took up formal studies were often the butt of jokes from the city's laboring classes, if not of direct hostility. With no gods of their own, the saying ran about Kolhari, were the students not out to give names to everyone else's? "I'm not the best driver. But if we break down—" he gave the boy a grin— "I'll get you to help me push."

Grinning back, the boy grasped the cart's side and pulled himself up while the smuggler walked once around to see if everything was in place. (The booty sack was still wedged firmly under canvas behind the lashed pots.) Coming round to the other side of the bench, he climbed up and took the reins in his hands. "Hi*eee*!" he called, then clicked a bit, looking out over the moving heads and stationary awnings that filled the market. Half standing beside the student, the smuggler, as they started, sat down, hard, on the bench.

Three carts rolled ahead of them. Moving through the women and men with their baskets and barrows, the boys and girls with their sacks and sledges, he heard others—an elderly woman driver hallooed shrilly for another cart to move—start behind.

His departure was exactly as he'd wished it.

But as he rolled through the morning traffic he glanced at the youngster with his forearms on his knees beside him. Regarding this commercial bustle with an enthusiasm silent as the smuggler's, the youth, whose nakedness did not sign barbarism, whose braid did not sign the military, whose bagged feet did not sign labor on dangerous stones, and whose bound hands did not sign distant origin, sat there, observing all with a student interest (freckles on his forearms, too, the smuggler now noticed: and freckles on a male were as physically repulsive to him as they were attractive on women), a collection of appropriated signs, as if he himself were a living lie, an embodied dream—

Reining the beast right, the smuggler saw the little man ambling between a stall of bladed tools and another of painted bowls. He still wore his collar, the bindings on his hands and feet, and the rag over his eye. He's a tired man, the smuggler thought. Whatever had made him bolt the crypt had stilled in him now; and the little man seemed only a diminutive stranger, up the night and making (again, most probably) for the bridge to complete the debauch that had, no doubt, been nowhere near as surprising or satisfying or educational for him as for the smuggler.

Suddenly the smuggler grinned. "Hey there, one-eye!" he called above the market's noise, for he had never been one to pretend next day that the night before had not happened, with either women or men. "You *still* don't have a coin for me?"

The one-eyed man turned.

Then he did something quite as astonishing as anything the smuggler had seen since he'd first come to Kolhari: he reached up, pulled the rag from his head, yanked it from his hair, and stood blinking two perfectly fine eyes in the autumnal morning, while porters and shoppers and vendors stepped around him. There was recognition on his face but no particular humor.

"You mean you're not . . . !" The smuggler sat back on the bench and laughed. "Well!" he called, suddenly glad he was on a moving cart and the little man was not. "Maybe I'll see you next time I cross the bridge! And maybe you'll see me!" Laughing, he shook the reins over his ox, who moved heavily on. The little man turned to walk away. "Now would you think—" the smuggler elbowed the student beside him—"I mean, I'd thought he might be—" But what did this student know of the smuggler's researches? "For someone who manages to get by, I can think some dumber things than anyone I know!"

"You know him?" the student asked.

Recovering from his laugh, the smuggler shrugged. "He . . . owes me a little money. Yeah, he's someone I know."

"He's a slave." The student nodded knowingly.

The smuggler chuckled. "Well—" He shrugged again. "You know . . ."

"Oh," the student said. "He's one of those."

The student didn't say any more for a while, and the young smuggler soon found himself explaining silently to the student of the mind beside him: Ah, you study with your wise master out in Sallese, but you've no idea of some of the things I've learned right on the stones of the bridge back there. Those stones could probably teach even you a few things.

To which the student (of the mind) replied: You think you're the only one who knows of such? Certainly, then, you know that more than one student, down on his luck, has come to the bridge to earn the odd coin or two and learn something of life in the process—though usually we disguise ourselves, for the buyers of Kolhari don't like us when we come in our ordinary attire, as I wear now.

The smuggler glanced at the boy. *Would* he be that kind? (Tell me, are you that kind?) No, thought the smuggler. (No, said the student. No, I'd never do something like that. Look at me. I don't look like that sort, do I? Of course I wouldn't!) Though what the signs were that told him so were anybody's guess.

The silent dialogue ran on as the cart moved between the stalls and out of the market. Without speaking they rode through the wakening city, toward the southern gate.

7

Though he'd taken a passenger to make his wagon seem more like an honest delivery cart, the smuggler had only planned to keep the student till that night, when he would find some excuse to put him down and let him catch some other southbound wagoner. (The boy's name was Kentog. But how long will I remember that? the smuggler wondered.) Out on a three-day journey south, however, the youth proved companionable and, that evening, laughed loudly at the smuggler's story of how he'd been fired from a lumber crew when he'd been found sleeping beyond the lunch break, and how he'd been chased out of an abandoned barn he'd once decided to rest in by an irate farmer, even as he protested his willingness to work for his stay, and how he'd been cursed down a Kolhari alley by a potter for whom he'd been unpacking loads of imported clay because he'd dropped three of them in a row and they'd broken open on the street—all of which had occurred three to five years back, but which the smuggler related as if they'd happened only weeks ago.

Perhaps, he thought, I might take him on for two of his three days' journey.

The next afternoon, when the smuggler's tales of his own fallible labors began to run down, he found the student, so silent before, now full of his own talk. (Once the smuggler had asked him if he had any thoughts on the Liberator, Gorgik, to which the student frowned and said, "Gorgi? I've heard the word. It's a foreign term, from the Ulvayn Islands, no?" which, by now, was an answer the smuggler had gotten enough times so that, for him, it was the sign that more questions would be pointless about his chosen topic. Today, he never pursued his inquiries beyond such an answer.) And it became easy just to listen to the young man run on about this and that; now and again the smuggler grunted to sign that he *was* listening—precisely when his attention was the furthest away.

But the noise was a comfort.

The boy had not questioned any of the back trails they'd taken, and he'd happily gotten down several times, to pull loose a root that had stuck in the wheel, to guide the cart over the round stones of a stream. Could it be, the smuggler wondered on the second evening when they made camp over a fire where the student had volunteered to cook a respectable pot of stew from some dried cod and roots the smuggler had brought along under the canvas (he did such things, he explained, for the others out at the school), that he's so careful with his questions because he knows I carry contraband, and he thinks all this is a kind of adventure? Well, then, his reticence is to be valued as much as his chatter; he's not such a bad sort after all.

So the student stayed with the smuggler's wagon six hours into the third day's ride, till he said: "This is where I was telling you about. Right here," and got down before a house which, he explained for the third time, was an inn run by an aunt of his. After a few moments, standing in the road, the student said: "You're not like a lot of the others, you know?" The boy looked up at the smuggler on the driver's bench. "I've heard them—" and he drew his shoulders up " 'I wouldn't be one of them students for anything. I'm glad I'm a good and honest laborer.' "

From the cart seat, the smuggler grinned down at the youngster, naked in the road and looking up in leaf-dappled light. He, of course, had heard it too. But this was the second time the student had said it. The first had been two days ago at the beginning of their trip, though no doubt the boy had thought the smuggler had misunderstood him or had been thinking of something else right then, for the smuggler had not said anything back. "Well," the smuggler said, "I'm *not* a good and honest laborer," He'd thought about saying that before, too. But as he'd remained silent, the student was repeating it now. The smuggler toyed with the words, *I'm a good and honest smuggler.* Should he add that? No, it would only be a stupid and witless thing to blurt now. So he just kept grinning at the youngster grinning up at him from the road.

"Why don't you come inside?" the student asked, suddenly. "You can stay over for the night. My aunt'll feed you, if I say you're my friend. It won't cost you anything—and we'll call it an even exchange for the ride." The pale brown eyes blinked above the adolescent beard.

Remembering the "one-eyed" man, so stingy with his coins, the smuggler said: "I didn't carry your aunt down here. I carried you. So you pay me the three iron coins we agreed on; it's less than half what anyone else would've charged you. But I'm that kind of a fool, and I know it. Pay me. Then, if you want to invite me in to a free meal just for friendship, that's up to you."

"Oh, well. Yes," the student said. "Sure. I see." He dropped to one knee on the grassy ridge between the road ruts and untied one of his baggy shoes with his bound hands. "That's fair enough. I mean, it's what we agreed."

The smuggler had already decided the loose boots were where the youth kept his meager moneys.

Handing up the three coins, the leather still a-flap about his foot, the student, standing, said: "Actually, you know, I have to walk on another stade to the west before I reach my mother's house. It's just my father's sister who lives here. So, maybe it'd be better if you *didn't* stop here at my aunt's. . . . I mean, I'm just going in to say hello, anyway, really, before I go on—"

"Good journey to you, then, Kentog." The smuggler bent to put the coins in the shadow under the bench, sat up, and flicked the reins. The cart rolled forward.

Stepping awkwardly back, one shoe tied and one loose, the student called, "Thanks. And good journey!"

The smuggler's cart rolled on among huts, by a pile of baskets, past a broken loom in an overgrown yard. (I'm a good and honest smuggler. Yes, I'm a very good and a very honest smuggler. Rehearsing it to himself, he smiled and shook his head. Someday, sometime, believe me, my young student, I'll say it to *some*one. But, oh, he thought, what a decent, law-abiding boy like you won't do to get away with a few coins from a good and honest criminal like me!) The road was empty; a chicken pecked lazily at his left, and, as his cart rounded a curve, to the right and curled under a bush, a sleeping dog swished its tail once, shivered below the leaves, and stilled. But the smuggler was beyond the enclave before he had any picture of its products or processes, the work of its quiet days or evenings.

Leaves pulled their shadow over the road to break up sunlight on the beast's back, to shatter it on the smuggler's knees and shoulders. An hour later, he paused in his dialogue, still rambling on with the imagined student: between the leaves the sky had confounded to one gray. The air was cooler, thicker, heavier. Glancing at a break left by a fallen tree, he saw that the sun-saturated blue had given over to tarnished cloud, like silver lapped about with hammer marks.

Out of sight, lightning flared. As his cart rolled under branches he heard drops batter leaves. Leaves shook, shivered, and—seconds later—splattered down on him. The ox moved her head left, right, looked up, then plodded on as the road became pocked mud about her hooves. The smuggler leaned forward to take the rain on his back. Water ran from his hair, dripped off his eyebrows.

All right, he admitted to the phantom Kentog (who, because of his incorporeality, could still sit tall on the bench despite the peppering), do you want me to say it, then, young student? There're some things you *do* know better than I! (He jumped down from the cart to walk beside it along this sloppy stretch, laughing aloud in the rain.) Yes, and I'll say this too: I'd give you your three coins back for your aunt's roof, a bowl of hot soup, and a pallet to stretch out on for the night. Good and honest smuggler that I am, I must still be the kind of fool I'm always saying, for not taking up your offer. Well, then; I've said it.

Are you satisfied?

Apparently he was; for after that, pulling his bare feet from the mud beside the creaking wheel, the young smuggler walked his cart through the torrent more or less alone.

Once the rain stopped for twenty minutes.

Once it stopped for ten.

Once the smuggler (back on the driver's bench, for here the road was irregularly paved, its slight slope keeping it moderately free of water) looked up to see the trees to the left had given way to rock. Here and there to the right he glimpsed a storm-lashed valley. But rain obscured distances, distorted boulders and pines—it was hard to look up long with the drops beating eyes and cheeks and lips. By now the smuggler was unsure if he were still on the right back road. Perhaps the last town had put him on a side path. He should be going due south, but there was no finding the sun for confirmation.

When the rain stopped again, the trees had closed him round. The smallest breeze splattered his arms and knees so that, by now, it was debatable whether rain really fell or the leaves only shed their leftovers (and an old woman, a young girl, and some elderly farmers whose names he had forgotten years ago debated it). You are lost on a side road that has detoured you into the unrectored chaos where anything may happen and any lie, falsehood, illusion, or reality is game, he said to himself. And a god, who, though she has no name as you have, is still as concerned with smuggling as you are, will find any play of yes and no prey to attach herself to all entire. He countered himself: You are on the right road, headed south, only wet, cold, and uncomfortable. How many times *have* you prayed, 'All the dear gods, *please* make something happen'? As he answered back, 'Not many,' lightning flashed again behind leaves.

It *was* raining.

The cart rolled.

Foot propped on a slant trunk, and sword drawn; that's what he saw first, when the voice barked, harsher and louder than the falling water: "Hey, pretty man! Give a tired traveler a ride . . . ?"

Looking up, he thought to ask for iron. But rain splattered his face. Looking down again, he called: "Come on! Climb up! You going far?" Calling, it occurred to him the figure vaulting the log to slog up the sloppy shoulder might be a bandit. There'd been something odd about the blade—which slid back into its soaked scabbard. But water blurred all, made him blink. The figure came on with swinging arms, behind wet veils, which, as the smuggler turned away, thickened.

A rough hand grasped the seat beside him. The cart rocked. The other hand grasped his shoulder (which was how he knew the first was rough). The traveler (or bandit) rose with a snort and a chuckle. "Get your ox going! Curse this weather!"

Still hunching, he flicked the reins. A warm interruption in the streaming cold as he rocked forward, the hard hand stayed high on his arm; his new companion's side hit his, swayed away, hit him again. "Where're you traveling?" The smuggler glanced over.

There was something tied across his seat companion's face: a rag through whose two holes, even in this shadowed splatter, he saw blue eyes. A *bandit*? Behind the rag mask, affably enough she . . . well, grinned.

He'd been trying to see those breasts as the muscles developed over the chest of some swaggering country man, distorted by blown water; but here, with her sitting up close and leering against the torrent (still holding his shoulder), behind her mask she was, he realized once and for all as he blinked in falling water, a woman.

He started to speak, but an indrawn breath as a gust blew drops into his mouth made him cough—which only saved him embarrassment, he decided. He had nothing to say. Wiping his face with his wrist, he turned to his beast.

They rocked through the rain.

Perhaps the seventh rock jarred her hand loose. He glanced up. With both, now, she grasped the bench by skirted hips, leaning forward to gaze through masking cloth, pelting drops, raging leaves. Half an hour later, when the rain stopped again, she was still silent.

Decisively (though the reasons for the decision he could not have spoken), he looked at the brush and rubble on both sides of the road before he said: "You from around here?"

"Do I look like a native of this wet and woebegone land?" She snorted with an expression below her mask that, on a man, he would have known was a laugh. "And where do *you* come from? You look like you might be bringing your cart down from Kolhari. What are you hauling? No—" She leaned away from him. Within the frayed holes, her lids dropped halfway down ceramic blue eyes. "You don't really want to tell me about what you carry, do you? I don't blame you—though I could give you some advice on how to ease your load along its way. You're probably in a profession I know more than a little about." She laughed again. "My name's Raven." She put out her hand.

He dropped one rein and reached across to shake.

"What are you called? But no . . ." She held his in a hard grip, her small fingers more callused than his own, fleshy and thick-knuckled. "You pretty men of this country, the ones with enough meat on you to make it look as if you might be comfortable to cuddle after sunset, you're too modest to tell every wandering woman your name. Well, that's as it should be, even in a land like this, where the men act as odd as you do—and the women are too beaten down to be believable." She pulled her hand from his and looked around at streaming pines, at leaves all droplet struck.

A black-haired, blue-eyed, be-masked woman, as far as he could tell she didn't have a freckle on her. Tell *her* my name . . . ? And having committed himself to withholding it, he felt a sudden surge of camaraderie. "You're a foreigner, yes? I couldn't say for sure, and foreigners—I admit it—are nothing I know much about, but you look as if you find the most ordinary thing we do here in Nevèrÿon odd." He grinned. "Is that it?"

"My home is in the Western Crevasse. Now, what *I* find odd," the little woman said, all grave behind her mask, "is that the terribly odd things you do here all the time, most of *you* find so hard to laugh at."

"What do you find laughable here?" He was prepared to chuckle at whatever serene normality she might cite under the salting drops.

"Well," she said, serious as the rain, "now *you* surely look like a young man on his way to fight beside the Liberator, whose cause is noble and necessary. He's assembled his forces just east of here. Well, myself, I've fought at the Liberator's side three months now. And I've grown tired of his campaign—noble as it is—and have decided to rejoin the sane and sensible women of my homeland and to pursue our sane and sensible ends." She paused, drawing back. (He thought she was about to narrow her eyes again, but under and through her mask she gave him a great, sampaku grin.) Above, the trees roared. Rain redoubled. "Now you see, I would have expected a man of my own country to find a speculation such as that worthy of a chuckle at least. But you sit on your bench, staring at me with your eyes wide between wet lashes and your mouth hung half open, and not a giggle anywhere in your pretty beard. Of course—" and here she assumed a lighter tone— "in my country, sometimes it seems that the men can do nothing *but* giggle. They laugh at everything and anything, morning and night, as if they believed nothing in the world worth a true thought. Well, perhaps they're right. Our philosophers are always saying so. People say men don't have to think for the same reason they don't have to have babies. But though one doesn't want to insult you with the point, you have to admit it's reasonable, yes? Still, lost in this strange and terrible land, sometimes a woman wants to see a man with a little flesh on him act just a *bit* silly, once in a while . . . ? Say, I bet you've been driving that ox in this downpour all afternoon. You look tired to death. Here, give me the reins and rest." She leaned forward, reaching out as if he'd directly ordered her to take the ox's leads.

The smuggler snatched them aside, so that she looked at

him with the puzzlement she no doubt turned on all this gray-green country. "The Liberator . . ." he said. "You mean the Liberator—Gorgik the Liberator—is fighting near here? To the east?"

"I've been with his forces three months." She pursed her lips and nodded. "His troops are assembled on the Princess Elyne's ancestral lands. She allows him to use her ancient halls for his headquarters. From it, sometimes with his one-eyed lieutenant, Noyeed, sometimes with his most trusted followers, and sometimes totally alone he scouts the land about here, making maps, marking out trails to forage against the earls and barons who still maintain their slave pens. He's a very clever man, this Liberator. When the evil lords expect an attack from his massed troops, he sends in only a single spy to provoke internal upset. And when the lords have doubled and quadrupled their vigil on their own households and have sent their own spies among their own laborers and infiltrated their own enterprises with invisible ears and silent eyes, paid to report by whisper and writing any and all sedition, driving themselves and all who work for them mad under the anxiety that circles like a kite over the house where betrayal is hunted, then the Liberator's troops descend on the demoralized estate. Oh, he is a *very* clever man. But—" (Her frown, the smuggler saw, was actually a strained smile, showing small teeth behind dark lips.) "—I grow uneasy with your Liberator. Certainly he's a moral and meritorious man. And his cause is reasonable and right. But I do not like fighting for a man among men.

"You must understand—" She laid a hand on the smuggler's forearm, where his muscles moved as he moved the reins— "this is not the misandry of some fledgling warrior whose breasts are no bigger than two handfuls of sand one teasing boy might spill on the chest of another asleep on his back at the beach. 'No man can wield a blade; no man can be as strong, as agile, as honest, or as brave as a woman.'" She laughed. "Well, when the little hawks have never flown further than the horizon of some fussy father's eye, what more can you expect of them? I say, if a man can fight like a woman, respect him as a woman. And I admit: I've met more than one in this tortured and terrible country whose single blade I'd think twice about crossing my own honed twins with—though that admission would get me only laughter in the warrior barracks of my home." (Her accent, he began to hear, was not the slurred elisions and apocopations that, as he moved further and further south, became the barbarian tongue. Apparently, he had been imposing barbaric expectations on an accent that, as he listened to it, began to distinguish itself on his ear.) "No, that's not what bothers me." She let her knees fall wide and ran her hands out on her wet thighs. "Once all that's accepted—that a man can be the equal of a woman in war—you still find yourself uncomfortable fighting amidst a bunch of them, relying on them, knowing *your* life depends on *their* bravery, commitment, honor, and skill. And always in the off-hours around the cook-fire or in whatever quarters we can commandeer for ourselves on the march, there are the jealousies and minuscule hostilities, over which they laugh and try to mask under the warriors' bluster they all wear so uneasily. But one can sense in them the same male sulks and uncertainties you find in the men of my own land—where, at least, those uncertainties and sulks can come out honestly and openly and speak their own names, and the men do not have to disguise them as displays of reason and rational right. Now you must know, I've fought alongside men in this country who were true fighters and soldiers, yes. But a woman among them always has the feeling that, for all the well-fitted skills they may have been practicing for months or even years, still they haven't been *real* warriors for more than a week, so that one begins to realize their laughter and horseplay is to hide the fact that, under all, they remain true sons of Eih'f, still carrying Eih'f's shame. Oh, the Liberator's cause is joyous and just. I respect it (*and* I respect him!) as much as anyone's (or anyone) I've found in this odd and eccentric country.

"I first met him many years ago. It was on a clear spring night, with not a trace of halo about the moon. And his plans and ambition were clear and sharp as the moon-shot dark. I was sympathetic, certainly. Still, I only trust such clarity about such basically muddled matters just so far. But as the years went, and in my own travels I heard more and more of him, nothing contradicted what I thought was most valid in what he'd said that night. So, finally, some months back, I came to him to offer my fighting services." She grunted. "I don't think he even remembered me. But that's no matter. Still, it's been rain and fog and mist for the whole time, I tell you!

"Well, he's *still* as fine a fighter as a woman. What's

more, he has something more than dragon droppings between his ears. And I fought my best for him when I was with him.

"But rumor came by, three days ago, that women of my own country have been sighted traveling through this part of Nevèrÿon. And I grow tired of foreign foibles and failings, and long for familiar ones. I've decided to seek the rumor's source and join them. They say that they were seen in Vinelet. That's where I'm headed."

The young smuggler heard this with a controlled and guarded bemusement not much different from yours and mine. It was much the feeling that a point was being put too bluntly, at too great a length—not at all in a ladylike way. But because, for all his disparagement of students, he was not really so far from a student himself, he said: "If you want to find your friends, better not go to Vinelet. Not if the rumor's been about for three days. I'm no certain judge of these parts, and I'd think twice about anything the likes of me said; and I do. But would they likely be traveling north or south? Three days south of Vinelet is the Argini. Three days north is the port of Sarness," for in the past two years he'd delivered sacks in all those places.

The masked woman, who was not tall, leaned away from him with an appraising eye. (Just then the rain really stopped.) "For such a pretty man, you have a pretty mind. That's as rare in your country as it is in mine." Below her mask, her lips' set told him he should feel complimented. And because he was a friendly sort, the young smuggler smiled. Me? he thought. Pretty? Well, I wouldn't go to bed with one like her if she paid me. Unless of course (and found himself wondering what in her unsettling presence he might be responding to) she really *would* pay. But it was hard enough to pry coin from the men on the bridge. How did one even ask it from such a manly woman, and a foreigner at that, on the road? Still, he pondered, it would be interesting, probably, and different, certainly.

Would that she had a speckle or five.

Raven said: "This time of year, they'd be coming north of course. And by now, you're right, they'd be at the port of Sarness. That's no more than three hours' ride from here."

"Is it?" He would have thought it a town for the next day's stopover. But one always mistook distances in this geography whose organization, if not its very existence, invariably came from the hearsay of strangers. And this masked woman was certainly among the strangest.

"But you know this part of Nevèrÿon," she said with certainty. "When we reach the high crossroad, we'll point out the sights and wonders of Sarness to each other. With the boats set along its waterfront and its houses spread on both sides of the Dragon's Way, the town is beautiful from the hillcrest at sunset. It's a sight to tell your granddaughters about." The woman grinned wickedly. "And I'll find my landswomen there."

Laughing, the smuggler shook his reins—though the red beast's gait stayed the same.

They rolled on.

Thrice in the past five summers he'd looked down on Sarness's collection of seaside huts and warehouses. Twice, he'd actually taken his cart into the sleepy port and driven along its somnolent waterfront, looking to buy beer. Under a shoreside canopy at a long wooden table with several landbound fishermen, he'd drunk up four or six or ten mugs of it, while the waters flickered brighter than lightning between the knocking dories. Then, with a light head and a bloated belly, he'd let his ox pull him and the cart back up across the main highway to the side-path, which then, as now, he'd been traveling.

No, it probably wasn't far.

"Well!" the masked woman said, three hours later when the cart had halted on the ridge, and the two of them stood beside the wheel sunk in the soggy earth. "It really *is* a pretty town.... But now, I'm afraid, between the fog and the twilight, you wouldn't know a town was there, much less that the sea lay beyond it."

8

Having drunk in the rain, the rocks and scrub had, over the intervening ride, breathed out a palpable mist, and the crossway they'd halted at seemed some tiny, fallow garden, furrowed by cart wheels.

They stood by the wagon in the fog.

"But I guess," Raven said, her hand up on the bench by her shoulder, "after you've looked down on Kolhari, Sarness isn't much. Still, it's a city with a history. Some of it might interest you."

"Oh?" The smuggler moved one foot and the other in the earth, which, once you stepped on it, was rather comfortable, if cold.

"You'd been asking me about the Liberator...?"

The young smuggler looked up.

"It's too bad the weather has made it impossible to see the Dragon's Way from here; it's the easiest thing to orient yourself by. But then, you must remember it if you've been there before."

What answered was the faintest memory of a wide, dusty road—the royal north-south highway that ran, here, near the coast and on which, so seldom, he'd traveled, with the city on one side, and, on the other, an astonishing drop below which you could see a few waterside warehouse roofs, fishermen's homes, taverns; and the sea.

He stared into fog.

"There was a time, you know, when dragons roamed wild over all Nevèrÿon," Raven went on. "Before Sarness was built, the ledge along which the main highway runs served the beasts as a perch from which to soar out over the ocean, where they would turn above the waves and glide back to land—or so at least the fables run. Myself, I think that's just a story, for I've never found a dragon smart enough, once aloft, to find her way back to the ledge she left from. They're stupid beasts. Nowadays, you only see wild dragons high in the Falthas."

Fragments of half-attended tales about eagles, about dragons, and their supposed habitats returned to the smuggler. He'd only seen pottery stencils of either beast. Both, he thought, were probably imaginary.

"When we last came through Sarness to requisition supplies, the Liberator pointed out a warehouse toward the lower end of the Way, where, he told us, years ago when he'd made his living for a while by smuggling, the back window had been left loose, and he'd climbed in by moonlight to spend ten minutes in the shadowy storage room, hesitating between a load of metal-headed mallets destined for some shipyard in the Ulvayn Islands and a collection of magic figurines, supposed to go to the quarrymen of Enoch, to protect them from falls on the rock face.'' She snorted. "He told us that, today, he doesn't remember which he actually chose to make off with. All he remembers is that he stood there, caught in indecision—and, of course, the warehouse's location: between the bakery's outdoor ovens and the hostelry's side gate. Both were still there last month. Though he says that the hostelry used to be twice as big as now. They've torn down some of its outbuildings."

"If he was just an ordinary smuggler," the smuggler said, "once he made his choice, he probably tried to put the whole thing from his mind. With his load in his wagon, he probably never looked at it again."

"If what I know of smuggling is true—" Raven considered— "you may be right. Just along the Way, where it rises high above the water, to reenter the rocky stretch, Mad Queen Olin, so local fables tell, once warned General Babàra, then leading a fleet of sailors from the Ulvayns, who'd come in their boats from the islands to hear her proclamation, to be on the lookout for some mysterious sign or other involving a tree and a bird." She dropped her hand from the cart and reached round to scratch an elbow. "Odd how fables are. I had a friend once: knew all the stories from the islands, she did." Raven recited loudly into fog:

> *"And the eagle sighed and the serpent cried*
> *For all Mad Olin's warning!"*

When nothing emerged from it in answer, she laughed. "Because of the rhyme that the children of Kolhari bounce their balls to, every child in that city's streets knows something of that particular tale—whether they *know* they know it or not. But my friend assured me that this one never became part of the islands' lore, though it involved so many of their sailors and boats. But what history remembers here, it forgets there."

"And what it forgets there," said the smuggler, who liked the roll of the phrase, "it remembers here."

"Only sometimes," said the masked woman, upsetting what had seemed as pleasant a symmetry of thought as of sound. "That's if we're lucky. Even further along the Way, at the far end of the town, where the road turns among the crags, so Gorgik's one-eyed lieutenant told us, when he was a boy and the slavers who'd stolen him from his home only a hundred stades inland from here first brought him north, it was just over those rocks that they pushed his wounded brother to his death—or at any rate, he said, it was just after they'd passed through a town where the sea sounded the same on its shingle, as did the crying and laughing of its children, and the bickerings and braggings of its skilled artisans and lazy loafers. He'd been completely blind at the time, he explained, sight having not yet returned to his good eye. But though he'd asked the city's name when they passed through, one day a few years back he woke up to realize he could no longer bring it to mind. But if Sarness were not it, he said, it was a town very like it, and somewhere on the Royal Road.'' She looked into the mist before them, as if it had just revealed some immense secret. ''Fables . . .''

The young smuggler said: ''You're among those who say the Liberator is the one who carries the scar, while his lieutenant, Noyeed, bears the single eye . . . ?''

Raven frowned. ''The Liberator, Gorgik, is a giant of a man, scarred down his left cheek; and his lieutenant, the singular and subtle Noyeed, has only half his earthly sight—though I'd wager that what he sees by unearthly means more than makes up for the loss of that eye.'' She let the mist question him.

He answered it with his laughter. ''I've known some before who've said it was the other way around.''

''I've been with the Liberator for the three months now.'' She frowned through her mask: that clearly was *her* answer. ''I was among his most trusted scouts.''

''And now you've left him.'' The smuggler shrugged. ''Not that either means much. My own memory is often weak about details of things I just did yesterday. And you can't expect someone to recall every word spoken or each bit of clothing worn by someone else, when they didn't know anyone else would ever ask about it . . .''

She looked at him oddly. No, he thought. She's not the kind to take such excuses. But he'd had conflicting tales from more ordinary people than she who'd made far stranger claims.

They stood, silent.

Then she laughed, harshly, shrilly. ''So serious, all you pretty men! So serious!'' though he would have sworn he'd been speaking with a fair suggestion of levity. Her laugh went on, long and barking. She clapped him on the arm. "It's the plump and pretty ones who always want to contradict an honest woman at any and every turn. Well, they say in my country, the wiles of wise men are an asset to their beauty.

"So, Wise and Pretty, here's some advice:

"A hundred stades along, this back road joins the Dragons' Way, which, as we both know, swarms with Imperial customs inspectors. Now I have no reason to think someone like yourself should have any wish to avoid those diverse and devious fellows, for you show not the smallest sign by which one might judge you other than an ordinary wagoner traveling from town market to town market—save that you travel on a road smugglers frequently travel, looking so *much* like an ordinary wagoner..." (For a moment, the smuggler thought, her eyes in their frayed holes glittered.) "Yet if, and whyever, you'd as soon bypass those inconvenient men in the pay of the Child Empress, whose reign, all say, is both sane and sensible, you might cut across the lands of the princess Elyne and, on the other side, pick up the little road that runs along the border of the Garth. A gaggle of those inspectors set out every evening in five directions from Sarness to catch those who chance the roads round here, hoping that night's cover will protect them. If you were what you clearly are not, my warning might save you some bother—if not your pretty neck. Heed me, and you *may* have a better chance of ending up where you want to. No—!" She pushed out her hand as if to halt him. "Don't protest your innocence. Nothing I have said has put it in question. I speak with no more direction and intention than the fog blowing here and there about us. A mere stade from here, down from the left side of this road, is a good spot where a woman—or a man—might take a wagon over easy rocks and among wide-spaced trees, till she came to a naturally protected clearing, where you could make camp. At least half a dozen times in the last three months, since I've been scouting the area, I have seen Her Majesty's inspectors ride right by it. The Liberator himself first showed it to me: he used it as a stopping place back in his own smuggling days. You only have to turn your cart from the road after the grove of tall cypresses on the right and just before the rocky outcrop. But that's assuming a wise and pretty man like yourself might need such protection—" again her laugh barked in the mist—"when of course that's absurd!"

She started away from the wagon, taking wide steps in the soft dirt. Skirting a bush bobbing in the breeze, she grew vaguer, less distinct and, finally, vanished on the slope toward the hidden seaside town.

Frowning at her memory, the young smuggler turned back to his ox, clicked his tongue; again the beast lugged forward. He walked beside the racketing cart in the fog.

As man and cart made their way through twilight, the road seemed no longer than it was wide; they might as easily have been wandering some fogbound plain as traveling a striated path. Now and again, the mist smothered all sense of motion, and the smuggler felt he remained in one spot while the earth shifted under him, compensating his steps.

An inner voice chanted some children's rhyme he'd used to hear in Kolhari. Why ponder that now? But, then, Raven had declaimed its closing couplet. Remembering that, he felt a moment's temporal disorientation to match the spatial. Had he been running over those rhyming lines five minutes now? Or fifty minutes—

The tall shadows to the right had to be cypresses. He paused. The cart kept moving; as the tailgate passed him, he started walking again. Yes, that was an outcrop of ribbed rock ahead.

"*Hiii . . . !*" He halted his ox and walked to the road's edge.

Yes, the cart could turn off here. He looked about, wondering how the place might appear to someone who knew the area—not that Imperial customs inspectors were usually native to the lands they patrolled. Perhaps in such a fog an inspector would not be too thorough. He went back to his wagon, led the beast over and off. Some meters along, he halted his ox again, returned to the road—on the way he pulled loose a branch—and swept out cart and hoof tracks for ten meters. Then, backing up, he obliterated his footprints as they emerged under him, till they turned over the road's edge. Tossing the branch away, he walked down to his wagon. Since beginning his sweep, the sky had gone from gray to purple.

The beast lowed.

They started walking.

The way went round rock and under more trees.

The smuggler saw the glow off between bushes, like ground-level moonlight. As he stepped through underbrush, it became pale orange. Leaves hung between it and him, sharply black as ashes. A boundaryless fire, the fog itself seemed to burn.

The young smuggler halted his cart with a hand heavy on the beast's shoulder and a few clicks, took seven deep breaths, and walked on. Ten steps, and of course it was a campfire with stones around it. A man squatted by it, he and the fire misty.

The smuggler moved behind a damp trunk. A twig scraped his calf. Leaves tickled his shoulder.

The man was big, with a thick belly and a beard growing high on his cheeks. Rough hair thinned over his forehead. Shoulders, back, and buttocks were hairy. Behind him stood a cart, much like the smuggler's. A siding of covered poles leaned against it, making a shelter.

Tethered to a tree, a donkey swished its tail—which is why the smuggler saw it; it munched in its bag.

A four-legged pot sat over the fire. Steam whipped from it, joining smoke and fog: unlike the ones in his own cart, the smuggler reflected, those could still hold magic.

The man held out a stick.

On both arms he wore bronze bands; around one ankle leaned carved and cast rings, wood and metal. About his neck hung chains and thongs. A carved peg pierced one ear.

Skewered on his stick's fork, meat broiled.

Juice dripped, to bubble on the rock.

The young smuggler watched, trying to breathe softly, speculating, remembering.

Two men had shared possible paternity for the young smuggler. One had been generally loud, usually angry, and, during the smuggler's childhood, had intermittently descended on his mother's cottage, often drunk, demanding food, money, or a place to sleep—had disrupted his and his mother's life till, by the time the smuggler was seven, he'd wholly hated the man. The other had lived a farm away but frequently rode his mule by the fields where his aunt and mother were employed. Now and again he'd stopped to play with the youngster who may or may not have been his son, to joke with him, to give him a ride or, when the boy was older, take him, with his mother's permission, on short trips to a neighboring village—a genial and woods-wise fellow, whose only fault was that he always left unexpectedly, staying away for months. The smuggler had soon learned it was the existence of both that kept either from living permanently at his mother's shack. But some of his strongest childhood memories (and childhood was a vague and misty time the smuggler did not usually ponder) were of standing at a distance and watching now one of them, working halfway across a field, now the other, sitting and eating beneath a tree, now one, standing in the sun by the farm wall, or the other, sleeping on a scatter of chaff by another farm's barn. Watching, the young smuggler could feel both delight in the one and displeasure at the other leaving him, while the thought replacing the feeling (no matter which possible father he observed), the thought filling his head, the thought pouring from his eyes and nostrils and ears to flood the sun-drenched day was: He's so *big*! And the bigness would grow bigger, and bigger, till it filled not just the day but all nights and days before and after it, till he was light-headed before such bigness and was sure he was smaller himself than a pissant struggling in the grass at his toes.

Half hidden by the tree and the cool fog, the smuggler felt moments of the same light-headedness as he watched the man at the fire. Ignoring the memories that came with it, he thought: Perhaps I'm hungry . . . his roast and his pot look good.

Just then, without glancing up, the man said: "Why are you standing off there in the dark? Come, into the firelight where I can see you."

Chills started behind his shoulders to cascade down his back, pour over his buttocks. . . . It's only the surprise, he told himself. (His foot caught under some ground-creeper, so that, stepping out, he staggered.) Chills trickled his thighs. The earth was spongy under small plants. "That's a good fire you've got there." He recovered his balance, recalling that when he'd thought of fire before, he'd decided not even to try one in this damp.

The man turned his stick one way, then back. "If you bring your cart on down, you can squat here a bit and share it with me." Reaching out, he gestured in a way the smuggler, moving forward, assumed meant 'come here'—though it could as easily have meant 'go on.' The hand was missing most of its third finger, and the man's lower lip looked as if it had been cut through and awkwardly healed. A scar slanted over one eyebrow; the ends of others gouged above his beard. Firelight gleamed on a milky blot over half his right iris. Firelight on his hairy side lit three ropy welts around from his back—which meant, as slave or criminal, one time or another he'd been flogged. The hand dropped. "Now bring that loud ox of yours along."

The smuggler turned to hurry back into what, by now, had become true darkness. With damp leaves beating his cheek, with twigs hitting his hip, he thought:

Now *could* that possibly be . . . ?

But, no.

Though she'd said he sometimes scouted alone . . .

The smuggler pushed back a branch—which scraped the cart's side. By his wagon, he felt along for his animal, who, at his hand, stepped forward. He caught the bridle and pulled back.

The ox lowed again.

The cart rolled.

Leaves about him blotted flame-lit mist. Leading his beast back into the light, the smuggler grinned. "Now, I bet I'm wrong about you." The ox glanced at the fire, at the donkey. "But you look like you know the land about here well." Tugging the bridle, he felt his feet slip on wet ground.

"Just because I know this clearing every smuggler between Enoch and the Avila has been telling every other about for twenty years now?" The squatting man humphed—and pushed down a piece of meat on a second forked stick he'd prepared while the smuggler had been off in the trees.

The young smuggler laughed. "Now you see, *I* didn't know it. At least not before a very odd traveling lady told me of it just a while back."

Beside the squatting man sat a dish in which red meat, some pelt still on it, glistened at the rim. Across it leaned a broad knife as long as the man's thigh.

The smuggler tied his ox's reins to a thin tree growing from the same bole out of which grew the one the donkey's sweat-blackened thongs were knotted to. "You look like a man who carries a bit of authority with him." He turned to walk back between the animals to the fire.

"Because I have a few more years than you?" The man held out the second stick. "Or do you think I'm some customs inspector, waiting here to feed any young thief and bandit who comes along in the night?"

The smuggler took the stick from the three knotted fingers and thick thumb grasping it. "No, you don't look like a customs inspector." He squatted at the far side of the fire.

Smoke rolled from between them to join the fog. He extended the loaded stick into the flame beside the other hanging roast. After a while he asked: "Do you see with that eye?"

The man grinned across the fire. Two teeth to the side of his mouth were gone and the one forward of the gap was badly rotted. He leaned his head to the side, as if he were not used to the question. "I see well enough. You want to stay on my good side, don't try any sudden movements to the right. This eye can tell night from day, a shadow from a light, and—if you're close enough—a smile from a frown. And the other, believe me, misses nothing." He gave another quick, gappy grin. "Why do you need to know?"

The smuggler rotated the stick. "I'd just guess a lot of folks who meet you think that eye is blind. Do some call you 'One-eye'?"

"Yes. Sometimes." The man grunted. "I don't mind it. I knew a dwarf once, in the K'haki: everyone called him Runt. Another fellow who rode the Venarra Canyon was half again my height, with arms and thighs thick as slop pails and a chest and belly like beer kegs sitting sideways on one another. We all called him the Hog. No one meant anything by it. They don't mean any more by what they call me."

"What I meant was—" the smuggler turned the stick back— "you say you have some sight in that eye. So those who only knew you from afar might call you 'One-eye.' But those who know you better might not." Then he said: "And there's other kinds of authority besides the empress's," and added: "whose reign is fulsome and fecund."

"And whose customs inspectors are a nuisance, at least to the likes of us, eh?" The man took his stick from the fire, examined the meat, and sniffed at it with nostrils that sounded clogged. He looked up again. "Why these questions . . . ? You *must* think I'm a customs inspector. Well, it's wise to keep some doubt with offers of friendship from strangers on the road. But believe me, only smugglers come here. Anyone could tell you that. What do you say?"

"That perhaps you were . . . *once* a smuggler?" The young smuggler narrowed his eyes as a shift in the air made the smoke plume rise, then fall away, between them. "Did you wear the collar?"

The man frowned. "What collar?"

"The one that went with those whip welts." The smuggler

nodded toward the man's flank. "The iron collar slaves wear by law."

The man sunk his teeth, good and bad, into his meat, tore off a hunk, and chewed, loudly, with glistening chin, his mouth open a good deal of the time. Finally he said: "You know Kolhari?"

The smuggler nodded.

"I bet you do. You sound like you've spent some time there. You know that bridge that goes over into the old part of the city, the part they call the Spur?" He spoke with his mouth half full. "With the market in it?"

The smuggler nodded again.

"When I was as young as you—" the man gestured with greasy knuckles—"or even younger, and I'd just got to the city for the first time, I was already carrying these scars from an Imperial whip." He thumbed toward his side. "I was a wild boy in my hometown, even before I started to wander. And the whip is all they had to calm you down, whether you were slave or laboring peasant. But one day when I was crossing the bridge—now you know what goes on, back and forth, across that bridge, don't you . . . ?"

The smuggler nodded a third time.

"I met a man there. He was probably as old as I am now. A fine looking man, too. To meet him and talk to him, you'd have thought he wasn't any different from you and me, you know what I mean? But he wanted me to come home with him. Lived in a fine house, too, out near the Sallese. Had his own cart and a couple of horses and a paid servant to drive him—though he didn't use his driver to take him down to the bridge, you can be sure. Oh, no. He didn't want anyone to know what it was he was up to there. He kept a collar, you see: a forged collar of iron, like they lock round the necks of slaves. And he would have me wear it—or sometimes he would put it on. And we . . ." The man cocked his head the other way, as if considering whether to say more. "But you know what I mean. Otherwise, you wouldn't have asked, right? I made good money off him, too. No less than a handful of iron coins—every time I saw him. Oh, and often a gold one! He said my welts for honest punishment made me look like a real slave." He grunted. "But that's a long while back. It never meant anything to me. And I wouldn't do it today. You ever meet anyone like that?"

"A few," the young smuggler said.

"Everyone does on that overground sewer." The man took another bite. "Oh, I bet you met them, too. Now, they say, since the Liberator's been about, they walk back and forth across the bridge and all around the city, wearing their collars right out for the world to see, as if they had nothing to be ashamed of..." The man bit again, chewed a long time, watching the smuggler. "The Liberator himself is one of them, they say. That's something, 'ey?"

So the smuggler said: "But you yourself were never a *real* slave...?"

The man wiped his chin with his forefingers. "And if I was, what of it?" He pointed to the smuggler's stick. "Go on, eat it. Cook it too much, and the flavor goes."

The smuggler raised his stick to examine the seared meat. Juice rolled down against the skin between his thumb and forefinger, making him angle it sharply away—not from heat so much as surprise.

The man chuckled. "If a man's a slave, then he's not a man. If he was once a slave, well then, the better man he is for rising above it. Wouldn't you say?"

"A man that I believe is one of the greatest in Nevèrÿon was once a slave." Saying it this time did not have the same effect on him as it had when he'd last announced it. For a moment he wondered if it were no longer quite as true. "His soldiers are somewhere not too far from here. Over east, I heard."

"The Liberator...? Is he now?" The man nodded. "Yes, well, some folks say he's one-eyed. And some folks say he's scarred. Like me. Is that right? Well, what's it to you, if what they say is true?" The man looked down at his meat, examining the wreckage from his uneven teeth. "You ever seen him? Would you know what he looked like if you ran into him?"

"I've been told he's brave, gentle, handsome—like you, eh?" The smuggler chuckled. "Or like me—for all our scars and pockmarks and your single eye. At least that's what some have said."

"And what do *you* say? Just that he's a great hero, right?" The man chuckled too; then, after a few more moments, he said: "I was once a slave. In the Imperial mines below the Faltha Mountains. That's where I caught these lashes. Now I'm free." He glanced up at the smuggler. "And I fight to bring that freedom to all other slaves. That's what I'm doing here.'' He hesitated a moment. "So now that you know who I am, what will you do for me?''

The pleasure the smuggler felt was like a heat rising through his body, as if he'd taken the flame from between them within himself. He felt a great smile battling out on his face, while a memory returned of a subterranean hall, where the little man stood naked on a throne in flickering torchlight above an indistinct figure groveling on the steps. The young smuggler made some inner gesture to push away the image, for he knew that the one thing he had no desire to do was to serve or service anyone again on either side of such a sexual split. To his surprise, the image vanished, as the pleasure of recognition, strong as relief, rose, filling him, obscuring all doubt and discomfort. "They say you wear the collar—I mean, that you've worn it on the bridge in Kolhari. But you said you only—''

"Well—'' the man pursed his lips— "it's not a thing you're going to admit right off to any stranger, is it?'' (The young smuggler shook his head quickly.) "Not that what I told you wasn't true. Sometimes what you play with as a youngster returns to plague you as a man? How does that sound?''

The smuggler nodded. "And your forces. They're housed in the princess Elyne's castle, not far off . . . ?''

"Oh, well, now.'' The man leaned back a moment. "Some of them are there. Some of them are here. I mean, all around us. A man like me doesn't wander out in the countryside alone—it would be too risky, you see what I mean? I have some of my men up there—'' he pointed over the smuggler's shoulder toward the rocks— "and over there, and back there. Right now. They're watching us. I want you to know that. Telling you is only fair. We're watched, and watched carefully, you and me. That's how I knew you were there. My men saw you and signaled. I only employ the best men, too. They'd lay down their lives for me at any moment. So don't think there's some trick you can try against me and get away with. If you were some spy, say, from one of the slave-holding barons, there wouldn't be anything you could do to me now.''

"Or if I was a customs inspector?'' The smuggler glanced about the foggy trees, grinning.

The man frowned. "You're too young to be a customs inspector. You think I believe the empress would send someone like you after . . . after a full-grown man?'' He shook his head. "No, you're a smart-aleck hustler from up in Kolhari, running a wagon-load of contraband down to the south." He still looked dubious. "That's all."

The smuggler glanced at the trees. He was thinking that those watching them could not be more than twenty meters off in any direction, or the fire would be invisible in this dense mist. "I'd like to join your soldiers and fight for you—of course, I could only do it for a while," the smuggler said. "I'm not much of a fighter, I don't guess. And I have to be somewhere south of here pretty soon. Though, in this fog, for all I know, I could as easily be rolling north, west, or east. That'd be like me too. But I'd still like to fight for you awhile—just to see what it was like. Though I'd be pretty surprised if you needed or wanted me. You want people as committed to the ending of slavery as you are, people who know its evils from the way its scarred their own lives, who'll stand to the death against it. Myself, I've seen old barracks where slaves were once housed. I've seen rows of stone benches with the iron rings sunk along their tops, out in the sun at the edge of an overgrown field, where five hundred were once chained while they ate their gruel in the rain. But there were no slaves left when I went past, and even the manacles on the whipping post were rusted through. I've talked to some old men and women, come to the city with scars like yours, who remember slavery. And I've talked to a few young ones, too, more recently escaped from the west— and mad they were! If you told me slavery makes you mad, I'd believe it. And when I was a boy, on the farm where my aunt and mother worked, we'd see a line of fifteen or twenty scrawny wretches passing on the road, chained to a plank they carried on their shoulders by day, that they dropped between them to eat off at the evening meal, the bunch of them led along by some leather-aproned men, one with red eyes, one with a harelip, and one with a cough worse than any of his charges—and we'd tell tales of slavers for days, and the grown-ups would threaten us with stories of how, were any of us ever to leave the farm or the fields, we'd be taken by such men, prowling around the country, and put in chains within the hour. And the tales would go on for weeks, for months. And maybe a year later, we'd see another such gang pass." The smuggler began to eat his roast, which was hot and tastier than he'd expected. "But you see, I don't know slavery the way *you* do. I'm committed to the idea of *you*—and, believe me, to eat with you, here, tonight, to be able to say I've seen you and sat with you, talked with you while you rested from your journey and I rested from mine— well, I'll be able to boast of nothing better, sitting and nodding in the sun in front of some thatched shack, when and if I reach my dotage. But in the same way I'm committed to you, I'm not really committed to your ideas. I mean: I don't know what you know of slavery to make it real. I only know . . . well, this little part of you.''

''So for you—'' the man snorted— ''the slave pits of the Thane of Varhesh are not real—because twelve of them have been filled in, and three of them are empty? True, he doesn't have the nine hundred slaves his father owned. But I'll tell you: the one pit now open, in which he nightly locks eighty or ninety men and women, still smells so foul you'd puke if you got within thirty feet of it.'' He nodded. ''I puked. And I didn't think I would. You say slavers only came by your farm once a year? Then you've never ridden through some south- ern clutch of huts and yam fields, off in the forest where they only babble in the barbarian tongue and in that so badly even the fifty words you know of the language hardly make you understood; but the slavers have been by only a night before. And you watch the fathers wandering about, crying for their stolen sons and daughters, stopping now and again to beat their faces bloody against sharp-barked palms or on the slant rocks, while the women throw handfuls of sand into the evening's cooking pot, tearful and silent, for the grieving meals they'll eat for a week after such a raid. And I tell you, now: the last time I rode by such wasn't a year, or five years, or fifteen years back. It was only four months by, not a hundred stades west of here. And it made me as sick to my heart as the stench of the Varhesh pit made me to my stomach when I worked on . . . when I rode by it, six years ago.'' The man ripped off another piece in teeth the smuggler was sure would soon come loose at such violence.

With the next bite of his own roast, juice tickled the smuggler's chin; he turned to wipe it on his shoulder. ''Oh, I know slavery's real.'' He chewed, swallowed, bit again; wiped again. ''It's real when you tell me. Anything that was real to you, I would fight to know its reality! I don't think slavery is good. I don't support it. If anyone asked my opinion, I'd tell them what you said seven years ago, in your audience with Lord Krodar that so outraged him: 'Slavery is

the evil that makes a mockery of any man or woman who
stands in the sun, breathes in the air, and dares to think that
freedom, love, or their right to will is untainted by it—or
hopes, even for a moment, that bodily tortures, cuts, and
brandings wait more than an hour or a week or a year ahead
in some government dungeon because of the horror that
would make any man or woman turn from its evil as soon as
fight it.' They spoke of it through all the markets of Nevèrÿon;
they repeated what you said, and many said it wrong. But I
asked and inquired of many more, till I'd finally put the right
version together—that's what you *must* have said! And I
haven't forgotten it. How could anyone forget who's seen real
slaves, or even those in their real collars on the Bridge of Lost
Desire—much less gone with them? I know *about* it. I only
say I do not *know* it. Not as you once knew it. A few times
I've helped ex-slaves that I didn't have to, doddering women
and doltish boys, hugely brave and hopelessly naive, all
confused by the city, come to Kolhari, lonely and lost. For
that confusion and the city that creates it I *do* know. A few
times I've avoided helping those men in rural parts who were
seeking to profit from what remains of slavery. To say I know
what I know—and, indeed, what I don't know—is only to say
that I've listened to all of them, and I know what I've done is
not the same as bearing arms among your troops, as marching
by your side, one of your most trusted scouts, as knocking
the links loose from the hasp that held them. Well, the truth
is, someone like you couldn't trust the likes of me. And you'd
be right not to.''

"But you've helped some slaves and hindered some slavers?
No doubt you have. It's more than I've done . . .'' The man
frowned again. "I mean it's more than, at times in my life,
I've felt I was . . . *able* to do.'' Suddenly he grinned again.
"Perhaps when the customs inspectors become as hard on
smugglers as the lords of Nevèrÿon have been on their slaves,
then you'll start to fight, 'ey?''

The smuggler laughed, bit, and nodded all at once. "And
what I know you've done for the cause of slaves will brace
me in every battle.'' Once more he looked up and about at the
trees. "Your men are watching us? Here we are, at the center,
then—of five, fifty, a hundred-fifty eyes?'' He shrugged, still
smiling, thinking that there could be no more than . . . seventeen
men at most in the woods about them. "I've always wondered what I would say if I met you. I'd always figured my

tongue would stall in my mouth like a cart whose axle tangles in some underwater root halfway over the stream, or the way it does when I want to tell some specially freckled girl who makes me want her more than I want the words to tell her so, and the fear of those words, as she says she doesn't want me, becomes as large as the stone that, when the cart jounces across it, breaks the old axle. But here I am, talking to you. And believe me, what I say, now, it's ... well, it's what I think. It's what I feel. The truth? No, I wouldn't call it that. But it's as close as a thief, a liar, and a bad man out in the night is likely to get—now that was said of me by an old woman who knew me, really, no better than I know you. Yet she was right in her way. And if she can be on so little personal knowledge, then so can I!''

"I bet you're a real bad man too.'' The man laughed.

But the smuggler was going on. "You know that sign with the two lines that cut each other? It's the only one I can recognize—a friend told me it was also the sign for illiterates like us. The students call it an 'X' and use it to mark the maps on which they plot the stories they call history: I've seen them together, examining one, in the taverns they frequent down in the Spur—because they can't afford the prices out in Sallese where they study. Sometimes I've seen it among the marks on the wall of the bridge stanchion down at the piss-trough, where the barbarians have gone and marked over it with their own meaningless scribble, like the ones you see carved all over the ruined walls and monuments in the south. Well, that's the mark we make, you and I: my journey, your journey, here where they cross. And from our meeting you'll go on in your fight for what you believe, and I will go on with my smuggling, hustling, and scheming. Neither one of us will have changed, really. Yet I can't imagine a greater changing force in my own life than you, than such a meeting with you!''

"You sound like some babbling student yourself!'' The man laughed again.

"But it's nothing to you,'' the smuggler went on. "And it shouldn't be. Look, here: you've given me food, offered me a moment of safety, protection, and company in this fog-riddled night. I've never expected that from anyone, much less from you. That you're the one who gave it to me is the only thing anyone could ever remember *me* for. There're thirty, forty— or maybe fifteen, if I'm honest—men and women I remember because they've gotten even less from you than I have. Someone who fought for you told me you sometimes stopped here—and that's why I came here; and that's why I'll remember her, above all her foreign ways! Her name was Raven—''

"Sure, I remember her!" the man declared.

"It's silly and foolish, but you can't imagine the pleasure of it!" Once more he looked about the flame-hollowed dark, wondering what the listeners might be thinking of his outpouring, which only made him laugh out loud. "The pleasure of it! That's the most important thing. Meeting you, like this, knowing that at last I've encountered the person who's meant more to me than anyone else, what greater pleasure could I possibly have? What more could I ever—"

"Hold up there, now." Carefully, the man pushed his stick's end into the ground, letting the wand bend over a near rock; the remaining meat hung above the lowered flame. Reaching toward the dish beside him, he grasped the knife handle. "What are you carrying in your cart? Come on. Tell me."

The young smuggler frowned. "Carrying? What do you mean . . . ?"

"I mean you're a smuggler running contraband from Kolhari down into the Garth. What have you got in your cursed oxcart? I want to know, now!"

"But what's that to—?"

"Look!" The man lowered one knee to the ground and drew in a long breath. The knife handle lifted above the leaves. Firelight slid the blade. "You think running around and freeing slaves is cheap? I need all I can get for my campaign. All right, then. What have you got?"

The young smuggler pushed back on the wet ground with his fists and heels. Twigs and pebbles scraped his buttocks.

"Come on. The way you feel, you should be proud to contribute to my cause. Tell me what you're hauling!"

"I don't know!" As much from the truth as from fear, the smuggler pushed back once more.

In the young smuggler's wagon, under the canvas, along with the pots and the sack, there were blades both shorter and longer than the one the man across the fire held; there were two clubs, one with metal points inset on the end, one without, and a short bow and a quiver holding nine arrows, each fixed with chipped, sharpened, and weighted flints, then five more wrapped at their tips with wadding, which, soaked in expensive oil, would burn strong enough to speed through air without extinguishing; there were five slate knives, and three of various metals, only one of which, despite its regular oilings, had begun to rust; but he had long since taken to leaving them in his cart until some emergency grew, not over minutes, but over hours—at about the time he'd ceased looking in his sack.

The man went from one knee to both feet, solidly as an ox rising from its haunches.

The smuggler tried to push back again; his heels gouged ground.

Then the man sprang across the fire, his blade high. Anklets clattered. Smoke spun under his heels.

The smuggler went down on his back in wet leaves, as the man landed, one foot either side of him.

"Come on! Get yourself up! Let's see what you got!" The man reached down and grabbed the smuggler's arm, yanked it; and it hurt. "Go on! Get to your cart!" The flat of the knife blade slapped the smuggler's chin, hard. It pressed his head back against the ground.

The smuggler dug his fingers into the earth.

"Obey me, or I'll cut your stupid throat!"

Above him, the man's face was dark. Behind, mist glowed. In it, here and there, a pine branch bobbed. Light over the hairy shoulder under-lit the bearded jaw, so that one half of that lip gleamed—precisely to the cut.

The peg shook in the distended lobe.

"Now—sure!" the smuggler declared. "Whatever you want! You take it! You can have it!" He tried to separate two images. But they muddled each other, neither clear enough for him to be certain what it was. "Why would I want to keep anything I had from you? I tell you, you've . . . been my hero for years! Here, let me up. Yes, I'm taking a sack from Kolhari down into the Garth!" The blade jarred his chin: ". . . don't do that!" He forced a laugh. "You think I care if you get it? The kind of witless fool I am, I'm surprised I got this far!" One image was some vague idea of what towns, neither his Garth destination nor Kolhari, he might go to for a year or so if he got out of this with his skin: betrayed clients could turn vicious in these pointed and primitive times. "I'm honored to give anything I can to your cause. Anything I have. Believe me!" The other had to do with the Liberator, his men planted about the clearing, waiting for some smuggler

to come by. The masked woman! She had suggested he come
here! (No doubt, he thought on hopelessly, frantically, all
she'd told him of the scar, the eye, the history had been lies!)
Of course, she *still* worked for this 'Liberator'—

"Get up, now! Show me your booty sack! My men'll be in
here to skewer you six ways to seven if you try anything!"

"Yes—" But the blade joggled his jaw.

"Up slow."

It retreated an inch.

As the smuggler got his feet under him, the point stayed
just out of sight below his chin, now and again touching his
throat.

The man leaned forward and, grabbing the smuggler's arm
again— "There!—" spun him, pulling it up behind his back;
at the same time the smuggler felt metal jab low beside his
spine, hard enough to hurt if not cut. "Let's get to your cart
and see what you have." The man pushed him forward.

One of the smaller knives, the smuggler thought. Perhaps
he could reach in and grab it; then, with a lunge . . . "See,"
he said. "Right in there. I'll get—" He reached over the
cart's edge with his free hand, then snatched it back. The
blade that had been behind him swung down before him to
hack the wagon's sideboard. His arm was jerked up painfully.

"If you want to keep either of your hands, let them be still!
You think you'll pull out some sword or club? I'm already
missing one finger from such a mistake. Don't you think I
know what you've got in there?" He snorted. "I've been
doing what you're doing, boy, more years than you've been
alive. Let's reach in slowly. No quick moves; no tricks;
and . . . yes, go on now."

One arm still pulled tight behind, the smuggler reached
forward for the canvas cover, tugged it aside, and dragged the
sack up from behind the pots. "Here it is! I told you I'd give
it—Ow!" His arm was yanked again. The man shoved him
roughly away from the cart, and, as the smuggler staggered
off, grasped the sack himself in his free hand, strode around
the donkey's hind end (from inside the feed bag, the beast
gave three braying honks), stepped toward the fire, and
hacked at the cloth with his sword. "Let's see what we've
got!"

They fell from the slash, clashing and clattering. The disks
were as big as a man's palm. As they clanked to the ground
by the fire, the smuggler saw that the rims were deeply

embossed with barbaric markings, holding strange curls and curves within. Bolts fixed the centers as if, with each one, there might be several layers together.

Other images contending in the smuggler's mind pulled clear of each other. The same way he could hold separate the conflicting tales of the Liberator, he now began to separate two tales of his own fate within the next moments.

The first ran quite simply: the man before him was, in fact, the Liberator, with or without his surrounding men, and what the smuggler had been told over the years by the most cynical of the Liberator's detractors—that he was, indeed, little more than a bandit, an outlaw, and self-serving villain, whatever his personal lusts or personal politics might be—was true. In which case most likely, the smuggler realized, he would be dead within minutes; because bandits did not rob you on the road, then let you live to seek recompense or revenge.

The second was almost as simple: the man before him was, in fact, no Liberator at all but only a smuggler too, who had gone along with the young smuggler's own ravings—ravings whose preposterousness, no doubt, had decided him to try this bit of banditry in the first place, and which preposterousness, equally doubtless, was the only reason the smuggler was still alive. There were no accomplices off in the trees. But, for the same reasons as before, if not in moments then in minutes, the man would realize he must dispense with him.

What both tales had in common was the smuggler's own imminent slaughter. Where they differed was that in one, there probably were men about them to help with it; in the other, there probably were not. The young smuggler was as unsure of which tale was correct as he was of any other conflicting facts he'd ever collected about his Liberator.

But it was neither bravery nor fear, therefore, that made him turn to flee; merely, rather, the realization that to stay meant certain, while to flee meant only probable, death. And even to be alive this long meant that he was very lucky or had found a very inexperienced bandit, whether the man was the true Liberator or not.

He turned and crouched in a motion, leg muscles bunched to hurl himself into gray that would be black ten steps on.

As he did so, a man stepped out of fire-lit fog with drawn sword: so now, halfway through his first step, with perfect knowledge of which tale was the ineluctable truth, the smuggler veered aside, seeing, here and there, still others coming from

the trees—and slipped, and went down; and rolled, falling, to
his back, because he wanted to see what came, even if it was
only the blade that ended his life.

Behind him, the Liberator/bandit shouted: "No, you—"

And the stranger, who stepped over him now, became a
woman and said, in a familiar voice: "That's no way to treat
a wise and pretty man!" She merely lifted the point of her
sword across the bandit's/Liberator's face.

There was something about her blade . . .

The man didn't scream. He made some great and horrid
gasp, dropping the sack from one hand, the knife from the
other, and grabbed for his eyes. As he staggered back, blood
rolled between his fingers, thickest where the one was missing.

Raven said to him, as he crouched, blind with blood and
shaking, before her: "You see this blade I have? It's doubled,
not like yours at all. It's as sharp on the inner sides as it is on
the outer, all the way down to its fork. Oh, you wouldn't
believe the things I could catch in it and cut. Let me see. First
I'm going to slip your balls between the tines and whack them
off—snick, snick!—first one then the other. Then I'll cut your
nose off with an upward swipe; perhaps after that an ear. And
while you're listening for it to fall, I'll take your penis in my
hand, slip my blade around it, and hack it loose below the
hair. Then I'll pinch your tiny nipples, tug them forward, and
bring my forked blade up around them and cut them free—
Oh, believe me, I'll open up all the scars of Eih'f and make
them run red again!

"Or," she went on, "do you think you'd rather flee . . . ?
There're six good women here." The others that had stepped
out of the encircling mist were also women. "Six double
blades, out and waiting, all around you. And believe me, my
friends are much rougher and meaner than I. True beasts,
each with her own twinned sword, and far more skilled with it
than I am. That one there? Anything I cut off you, *she'll* probably
eat it—and none too neatly, either! And that one—ah . . . !"
Raven made a disgusted grimace. "I can't bear to tell you the
horrors I've seen her perpetrate on a man's body, not even
with her blade but with her dirty fingernails. And she's got
ten of those!" Leaning forward, she hissed: "And she likes
her men fat, weak, and conniving—like you!" On his back,
the smuggler looked around, blinking at the women who
stood, in a ring, about the fire. Only five had swords, he saw.
Hanging back a little, a sixth, with lighter hair, had no

weapon out at all. Flames and blades flickered. "*Do* you want to run?" the masked woman asked.

Raven was the only one in a mask—though they were all bare-breasted, hearty creatures; Raven, the smuggler also saw, was the shortest.

"If I were you," she continued, "*I'd* run. You may get cut a little, as we follow you. But if you stay, the pain, not to mention the humiliation to your male honor, as we move you on your way to death (and death is surely yours if you stay, for we are not likely to let you go to seek recompense or revenge), is such that the notion of civilization as woman conceives it will be defiled beyond redemption. Believe me: a fate worse than death awaits you if you linger." Then she snarled: "Though you defile civilization yourself, with every breath you take! A finger first? Or a toe? Or a testicle? Or a nostril? Each is worth as little, on you!" Here she reached out the blade, and only laid it against his hip, no more heavily than the bandit, moments ago, had laid his under the smuggler's chin.

The smuggler was sure the man, hands over his face and reeling, had not even heard Raven's excoriation. But at the touch of metal, he turned, still blind, and barreled toward the trees, passing between two of the women, who, here, uttered throat-ripping roars, leaped into the air with swords high, to swing them viciously down—clearly and intentionally missing him by a foot!

The fleeing man's shoulder struck a tree. He stumbled to one knee, bloody hands coming away from his face to grab at the ground; he tried to get, and slipped, and tried again, and finally got, his feet under him.

First the two who'd swung at him, then—as he fell again, and was up again, lumbering off in fog and brush—the other women, began to laugh, covering his crashings away with their shrill barkings.

Raven walked back to the young smuggler, stepped across him with one foot and looked down. Her sword, which he finally saw was split into two parallel blades, its twin points only an inch or so apart, was aimed more or less at his ear. She extended her other hand. "Let me help you up, pretty man!"

Again he pushed at the ground with his heels. Again, they gained no purchase in the soil. He shook his head a little. "That was the Liberator . . . ?" He spoke with a despair that,

as he heard it, he knew she could not understand. He lifted a
hand, thinking to push hers or her blade away.

Raven seized his big fingers in her small, hard ones and,
looking to her side, raised her sword to thrust its twin points
into its hairy scabbard. "Him?" She frowned again at the
smuggler, giving his arm a small tug. "That evil, ugly
bandit? Him? The Liberator? That cut bit of earthworm,
wiggling here in the mud?" She snorted. "Though I'll wager
that when and if his wound heals, he'll look a bit more like
the Liberator than he did before!" and the smuggler, whose
thoughts were leaping from moments of muddle to moments
of lunar-bright precision, found himself wondering, still on
his back: Is that because of the scar that will remain, or
because her sword points had crushed his half-blind eye
completely, like an egg? "Oh, my foreign friend," Raven
declared, "it is truly said in my land, 'Men must not trust
other men!' They wait for one another, smiling face to face,
supporting every lie and self-deceit one can offer the other,
yet always ready to distract with flattery or falsehood—and
the moment the innocent turns away, the other is ready to
claw his back as soon as a back is offered. . . . Him? The
Liberator?" She gave a disgusted grunt. "He was no more
than any yellow-headed boy you'd find prostituting himself
about the Old Market of Kolhari. A thief! Less than a thief!
The vilest of highwaymen!" Now she shrugged. "Perhaps
even a smuggler . . . ? No! No smuggler or prostitute could *be*
that low!" She smiled down with small teeth. "A smuggler,
perhaps? We shall look in his cart and see! You might find
something to take along with you! Come. Can you stand?"

His arm shook in her grip—not with fear, he realized, but
with the detritus of a terror worse than any he'd ever known
before.

"Come, pretty man. Up with you, now. Don't you want to
see what you've won from that old and ugly reprobate?" She
tugged again.

Again he tried to stand. Again he slipped—the heel of his
hand, as he reached behind to push erect, no more successful
in the muddy earth than the heel of his foot had been. "You
should have killed him . . . !" he got out, looking around at
the others.

Half with blades sheathed, half with doubled tines still
against their thighs, they grinned at him in firelight.

"If he comes back—?"

"Oh, don't worry about him." Raven tugged once more, harder this time, and the young smuggler in her grip was so weak he nearly fell. For some reason, he felt he was about to cry. The thought of tears before these odd and alien women put him in a panic that, on experiencing it in full, he realized had been with him in miniature since his ride with her on the road, but which, till now, had been hidden, as if under the fog which had obliterated the day. With an expression that, even in this quarter-light, he recognized as patient, desiring, and containing all he could know of tenderness and goodwill, Raven looked down at him. "Don't worry. I have saved you. You are safe. Get up."

Had she announced with rage and snarls that he would be tortured and humiliated as thoroughly as, minutes before, she had threatened his attacker, he could not have been more surprised by the moment's terror that pulsed and, a second later, vanished—because he could not bear it? By an act of will not much different from the one that, in the Kolhari crypt, had allowed what had happened there, he forbade what might happen now if he accepted the extremity of emotion toward which, and beyond which, he seemed to be rushing. Sitting on the ground, he shivered—and kept shivering, as moments became minutes—while, with the same solicitude, Raven tugged, really, so gently and urged, really, so fondly and, finally, lifted him to his feet with the patience of someone who must have done this (once? many times?) before with men who had acted, he was sure, just as he was acting now.

Well, whatever he'd suppressed, the effort, as he stood, unsteadily, against her, left him all but paralyzed.

"You're all right!" she insisted, supporting him, while he realized, clearly, that he wasn't. "You're safe. Don't worry."

The young smuggler looked about the circle of her friends. Raven seemed so small! Surely she hadn't been that small when she'd first ridden in his cart.

"Oh, yes," she went on, beaming at him. "You've been through quite an experience." Now and again she would say something to those around her in her own language. Sometimes they'd laugh. (At him? he wondered, and didn't care.) Sometimes they just answered in their shrill, flat voices.

"You should have killed him!" he said again, when he felt steadier; because that was the long-thought wisdom of such situations in such primitive times, concerning men like his attacker, like himself. "You threatened to. Why didn't you do it?"

One of the older women said something harsh. (About the natural viciousness of men, he was sure.) For a moment, he thought, she must have understood him.

Raven answered with something equally harsh, then said to him in her gentlest tone, "Do you think we are barbarians that we go around killing any man on the road we see? That's not how civilized women act."

Standing a little way from the fire, having picked up one of the sticks to examine the remainder of the roast meat, the lighter-haired one with no weapon said: "He won't come back. Don't worry. He's too frightened. He's too hurt. Besides, there're more of us than there are of him."

Her accent was not theirs. Certainly she was a woman from the Ulvayn Islands. Recognizing a more familiar foreigner, he took a deep breath and made himself stand straighter, fighting what in the last minutes had become a lassitude that, among these strange women, unsettling as it was, still had its blurrily sensuous comfort.

"Why didn't we kill him!" Raven declared. "Kill him? What a strange man you are. Do you think women can go around killing just any and all men, like that? What monsters would do such a thing?" she went on in a voice so preposterously secure in its right to be heard. "Though, truly, in this strange and terrible land where men aspire to woman's place, sometimes you must make a pretense of knowing how it's done by those spiders, mantises, and other vermin who, from time to time, do."

"But then . . ." He stepped away from her, while she stood back herself and regarded him from her mask. "But . . . why did you come here? For me . . . ?"

Again her grin. "Why? You want to know? Well! You are just a very pretty man! When I met my friends—" she gestured toward the others—"in Sarness, I said to them: 'Ah, you would not believe the one who, just moments ago, gave me a ride on the rain-lashed road. Come, come! Come, if you want to see beauty beyond that of all the sons of Eih'f!' "

The one whom, before, he'd thought might understand his language gave a loud humph and turned away, to survey the foggy dark, as if she expected something unpleasant to creep, tentatively and momentarily, out of it.

"They're all true women, the lot of them. What woman *wouldn't* come with such an enticement?"

Another, who'd gone off in the dark, reappeared now and said something that carried anger.

Raven's response was ribald. At least the others all grinned. "Of course when we found your cart tracks gave out just a few meters before the turn off I'd mentioned to you," she went on, "immediately I knew where you must have gone. Here! To this lousy den where every thief and cutthroat highwayman, fearful of the Sarness inspectors, seeks respite from the road between Enoch and Varhesh. Well, I said to them: Let's go in and take a look at where he's made his camp." She glanced down, now, almost shyly. "Only, you were here with another man—pretty enough I suppose, in his way; though not so pretty as you. And we hung back in the darkness, like the lustful girls that linger, I suppose, within all women. We wanted to hear what you might say to one another when there was none of us about to intimidate you into silence. Who knows? Perhaps I even hoped to hear you mention *me* to your treacherous companion.... But like all the men in this land, you had only words for the Liberator. Well, I suppose you're not that much different from the rest—"

"Raven," said the island woman, "perhaps we should go on. There's no reason to stay here."

But the masked woman made a dismissing gesture. "Soon, as we listened, we realized your new friend was not a good man. Not at all. Not like you, who would give a wet and tired woman a ride and a smile, out of no more than the sweet and natural goodness of a wise and pretty heart." Here, smiling herself, she reached out her small, hard fingers to touch his cheek. He looked at her eyes, in the frayed mask holes. In this light they might have been black.

One of the women dropped another log on the fire.

Sparks spun up into the dark.

In Raven's hair, for a moment he saw a glint of blue.

Flames settled again.

Another, in her own language, most likely told the one who had dropped the log that it was a waste of time and that they *should* be on their way. That, at least, was what her gesture suggested.

The idea of moving off in the fog alone appalled him; but the prospect of staying here with these women drained him.

Hating both feelings, he turned from her to walk aimlessly about the campsite, unable to do anything to free himself of either.

9
———

The actual leaving, of course, took quite awhile—as if, he decided, darkness with a circle of trees about it confined more effectively than any wall or barred door.

They lingered there a good hour.

He wanted to be on his way, but he had no clear idea of the severity of the bandit's wound and he did not want to run into the man again, alone on the foggy road, with whatever reinforcements, weapons, or friends he might have picked up in the nearby town.

So he waited with them.

The delay seemed to be some low-key altercation between a barrel-chested woman whose breasts hung flat, low, and far apart, and one, younger, gaunter, the staves of whose ribs bore high only the shallowest nippled cones.

Whatever the argument, from time to time Raven or one of the others would toss in a joke, which would be answered with a snap from one or the other agonists.

The island woman stood off from the others, near the tethered donkey, which now and again glanced over the feed bag's rim; but it had made no sound since the bandit had approached the smuggler's cart. Her lighter hair, he realized, was probably red. Redheads often had freckles. He walked over toward her, just to see.

He'd assumed she was his own age, but as he came closer he saw a certain roughness to the skin about her eyes, and a looseness in that at her shoulders. The firelight had confused two colors in her hair; one was red, yes, but the other was probably gray. She was at least a decade his senior. And if she had freckles, they were pale enough so that mist and flickerings lost them in the shadows playing on her breasts, her clavicles, her cheekbones. To say something, he asked, quietly and suddenly: "Who are they . . . ?"

She looked at him, frowning.

"Who *are* these women?" He nodded toward the others.

"They're my friends," she said, shortly. "At least that one is." She inclined her head toward Raven, who stood at the other side of the fire, her back to them. She had taken out her double sword again and, with one foot on a stone, polished and polished it with a bit of chamois.

She'd been doing it now ten minutes.

"She's your friend . . . ?" His repetition sounded inane. But somehow he could not focus on anything he should be saying, should be doing.

"Well, right through here—" The redhead smiled—"she's only interested in you. Will be, no doubt, for a while. But we go back a long ways, Raven and I. I've been looking for her almost five years now. When I met her fellow landswomen a few weeks back, I thought that traveling with them for a while would be the best way to find her—or for her to find me. And it worked. Only since we met this evening, she's been full of nothing but the wise and pretty man who gave her a ride on the back road." The wryness left her smile. "It's good for you we came along with her!"

The young smuggler looked across the fire at the small, muscular back, at the head bent over the blade—yes, those were blue stone beads in her hair—at the twin tines turning and running on kidskin. He'd had no sense at all of any particular relationship between Raven and the redhead—no more than there seemed at this point (even though she had saved his life!) any relation between Raven and himself.

Is that, he wondered, a woman obsessed?

But with the notion that he himself might be the center of that obsession, the whole idea crumbled and became impossible to hold in his mind. For he had been rendered by the whole evening a nothing, a vacancy, an absence in the foggy night. How could she be obsessed with nothing?

"And the others . . . ?" he asked, turning back to the redhead.

"Actually," she said, "they're rather horrible. At least I find them so. I keep trying not to, telling myself they're simply from another land, wher things are done differently. But then, just when I've convinced myself they're really good sorts underneath, one of them will turn around and do something that . . . well, I suppose they find me strange and terrible too.'' She gave a little shudder.

"Then why don't you leave them?"

She looked around at the damp night. "Certainly I've done enough traveling on my own in Nevèrÿon. Yet, somehow, when you have a bit of protection, you're not so quick to give it up. With all this fog—'' She glanced around again— "I think I'm afraid to. Besides, I've only just found my friend. *She* won't stay with them too long." Again the redhead indicated Raven. "That I know. She never does. Oh, she gets lonely for them when they're not here. But soon she'll grow restless. And we'll be off on our own once more, the two of us. At least we will if five years ago is any sign of today.''

The argument on the other side of the fire reerupted. Then the thick-set one he'd suspected might understand his own tongue said something loudly and angrily in hers and threw down a piece of branch from which she'd been restlessly stripping the bark. She stalked around the fireplace and came over to where the redhead and the smuggler stood.

The ox stepped back, hooves squishing and sucking in mud in moist leaves. The donkey turned his long face away and went on chewing.

Planting herself before the young smuggler, the big woman said, brokenly, her impatience edged with anger: "Please! You come now? Please? To the bandit's cart. Take your share! Now! Quick! So we can take ours. You let us go? Now? Please?" She took his arm and led him firmly forward, as the smuggler realized that, somehow, they'd been waiting for *him*. His own inaction had been the center of the women's alien bickerings all along.

As she steered him across the clearing, twice he started to speak, to protest. Everything in him yearned to blurt some appeasing anecdote about how, the last time somebody had been talking about him, it had taken him even longer to realize they'd meant him—about how much trouble it had gotten him into. And that, even, had been in his own language. "You know, I remember once . . .'' But only Raven and the redhead seemed to understand his tongue enough for such a tale as he sought to invent now from bits and pieces of the real, the feigned. Also, the fact was, right now he could remember almost nothing. The story he wanted to tell would not coalesce. His companionable strategies had all shattered before these strangers from the mist.

The woman pulled the poles with their sagging cover away from the side of the bandit's cart. For a moment they seemed to balance. Then they crashed over, revealing a fur blanket, another pot, a large knife stuck in the ground, and bits of cord—all with the sour smell the smuggler remembered from his own bedding after some particularly exhausting trip where the detours had extended things by weeks.

One sandal on the fur, she reached over the edge, grabbed the cart cover (of impressively tooled leather, full of shadowed, arcane designs), and yanked.

Two of the thongs holding it popped.

Three didn't.

So she yanked again.

And broke two more.

She made a movement of tossing it away, but it only dropped, mostly rough-out, to hang, by the remaining tie, down over the back wheel.

The young smuggler had expected to see beneath the leather something much like what was under his own canvas. As he gazed into the shadowed wagon, however, a sudden memory struck:

The crone dragging her bag about the bridge.

The pots and furs and rope and—yes—the weapons he made out in the dark below him seemed the mad spillage from such sacks.

"This!" the woman demanded, reaching down and bringing it up—it was a pot. And badly chipped. "For you?"

The smuggler shook his head. "No . . ." The word was flat and emotionless.

Disgustedly, she grunted—"For nobody!"—and flung it over her shoulder. "Or this?" (Behind her, the pot shattered on stone.) What she drew out now was an ornately worked blade, perhaps a foot and a half long, the bone handle intricately carved and, here and there, banded with metal that might have been precious, with complex chasing. The woman grunted again. "Stupid," she declared. "A blade like this? Stupid. The swords of this country. All outside. No inside. No . . ." She paused for a word. "No *two* blades. No good. Just stupid man sword. Unity. Like a silly penis. Nothing. Not even balls." She thrust it toward him. "You?"

"No!" He said that loud enough to hear his own voice somewhere in the denial.

She leaned over and began to rummage. "This junk. What you want? We see."

"No," he said again, turning from the cart. "No, I have to get..." What, he wondered, was he trying to convince them of? He felt like some new mummer on a wagon platform in the town market, who, in the midst of the skit, had suddenly lost all sense of the part he was supposed to be playing.

Behind him, she said: "Or this, yes?" He did not even look at what she held up now.

His sack lay just off from the fireplace. Squatting to pick it up, he reached for one of the fallen metal disks.

He wanted to put it in the bag without looking at it. He wanted to see what it was.

The eyes of the woman at the cart—which, he realized as she went on taking out one thing after the other, would *not* look at him—generated in him all the anxiety of a disapproving parent.

He stuffed the metal through the tear and picked up two more.

As his clumsy hand carried them through the firelight, he saw each was actually several disks of metal, layered and bolted together, the top one just a rim with a crossbar, the one below that a strange cutout of curlicues with little prick-holes in the points; the disk below was scored with maplike markings that the other two turned over. The rim markings were the sort he'd seen in the barbarian lands. Yes, he remembered, as, with the memory of some young habit, he looked at it: sailors used these. It had something to do with the stars...the word *astrolabe* came back to him. That's what they were called. Someone—perhaps his mummer friend—had pointed one out to him, hanging around the neck of some waterfront seaman. (It was one of these, he remembered, suddenly and with astonishing clarity, that the long-gone mountain girl had toyed with on her chain that day!) But their specific use was still mysterious to him, so that the meaning or magic they contained was unknown.

A shadow darkened the disk in his hand.

He looked up as Raven dropped to a squat before him, her face in shadow, firelit fog behind. "Here! I'll help you!" She reached about for the fallen astrolabes and handed them to him. He took them from her, thrusting them through the tear.

Between his knees the sack grew heavier with each clank. Picking them up here and there, Raven said: "So this is what you're carrying to the south. It's pretty work—barbarian craft. One wonders what it was doing in the north, yes? Well, that's not our concern, is it. What will you be carrying with you when you return to Kolhari?''

He took more disks from her, put them in—clink!—and frowned. ''Nothing.''

''You mean you make the trip back empty-handed?''

''They pay me well. For the trip I make south..''

''But there're things you could take north. Before you leave, ask around. It won't be hard for you to find something profitable to return with. Your northern masters won't punish you if you make a little extra.''

Another time, he would have explained: If I get stopped by an inspector on my way north and my cart is wholly innocent, I have a much better chance, on my next trip south, of being waved on if I meet the same inspector. But for now he only nodded. ''I'll remember.'' He took the next handful.

''And remember, too, what I told you about the lands of the Princess Elyne.''

He took another handful.

From the bandit's cart, waving half a dozen implements in her grip, the woman barked something down.

Raven barked something back. Then she looked again at the young smuggler. ''You don't *really* want anything out of there, do you?''

What he wanted was the tooled cart-cover. But even to say it seemed exhausting. ''No.'' Oh, why do you go *on* acting such a fool! More clinks. ''This is all . . .''

Raven looked up, speaking in her own language.

The woman at the cart said something gruff and, obviously, uncomplimentary. But it brought the other women over to the bandit's wagon, laughing. They fell to pulling out this and that.

Looking about to see if any more of the astrolabes had rolled away beside or behind, he stood up with his torn bag.

''Here. Let me help you,'' and, somehow, it was away from him and up in Raven's arms. He followed her to his cart, protests weak under his tongue, while she dropped it, clattering, over the edge, and shoved it down, pulling up the cover, pushing it out of sight, stuffing back inside those that had fallen again through the tear. She turned to him, a great smile on her face that asked for nothing but complete gratitude and total approval.

Then why, he thought, can't I give it? Why does she make me feel empty—as though I no longer had anything to give?

"Thank you." He managed a smile. "Thank you. But I have to go. Really, we should be on our way."

"Come with us," Raven said, suddenly, brightly, "on our journey. We can offer you protection, companionship, even, perhaps, amusement . . . ?"

"Where are you going?" he asked.

"Oh, now," said the masked woman. "That shouldn't concern the likes of you. Such things are not the business of a wise and pretty man."

"What is your business?"

"Now, there," said Raven, "you're at it again; asking after things that are not your concern."

"But I can't come!" he blurted. "I mean . . . I can't come with you!" He blinked at her, while she questioned with masked eyes. "Thank you—for wanting me. Certainly, for saving me. I mean, I'm pretty much of a loser; I can stumble into more trouble than any three men you'll meet. I know it. It's true, I've always been like that. I could be flogged for it, and it wouldn't change, believe me. I could use your protection, I know. And I'm grateful to you for offering it—"

The masked women beamed.

"But I've got . . . my *own* task to do—"

At which Raven (and one of the others passing by) let a knowing chuckle.

"I've got to go," he said. "I just don't . . . well, I don't feel *safe* here! Not with that bandit about in the bushes." But what was there to be frightened of, he thought with hopeless illogic (realizing the lack of coherence as he thought it), in another man? "Really, it's dumb of me." It's them, he thought; it's *them* I'm terrified of! I know it. (Ask her for the cover . . . !) But why, when they're the ones who saved me? "But I . . . well, I want to go! Please, you have to let me go. Now. I'm sorry. Please!"

"Please?" No longer smiling, the little woman dropped her eyes and bowed her head in a manner that spoke of total acquiescence. "Come with us . . . ?"

The smuggler was suddenly frightened all over; and angry; and hurt. Because he would have to say, again, no. And because, with all three women he had been sleeping with back in Kolhari, he'd often felt the same, suddenly and naturally he did what he'd done with them when he felt this way, though he experienced less desire now for this hard little woman than he'd felt for any man who, from time to time, he'd indulged on the bridge:

He took her small face in his big hands (her eyes beat, in their mask, lifting, surprised) and pulled her to him. Only (as had the others, toward the angry, unhappy ends) she stiffened and would not come. So he came to her, with his heavy body, and let his hands go down her neck to her shoulders, then behind them, and across them; and he hugged her. Like them, it was like hugging some stone or tree that would not give. He remembered the last woman he'd put his arms around— the little, stupid one. And yes, just as rigid, just as stiff. (Are all the women in all the world, he wondered, really alike, no matter the seeming difference . . . ?) Holding her, he tried again to remember her getting onto his cart bench in the rain. When he'd offered her the ride, the signs she'd displayed of aspiring to some masculine power had surely masked, at least for him, something unquestionably and quintessentially feminine, so that the signs of aspiration themselves had been eccentric, amusing, playful; and she'd seemed merely a playful and amusing, if eccentric, creature. But now, with the advent of her friends, it was clear that she no longer aspired to that power; it was—and had been all along—hers. Whatever had been quintessentially feminine was an illusion (in her? in all women?). Certainly he'd had enough experience with the women and men of his country to recognize that the signs she displayed toward him now all spoke of a certain masculine weakness. (He looked down, brushing her forehead, almost inadvertently, with his lips.) Yet they were all saturated with that same astonishing, displaced, and dispossessing power, so that, as he had not with the others, he released her more hurriedly than he had them and stepped back, his heart beating a bit more rapidly than he'd expected, his breath coming a bit faster than it had before. (That, he knew, was simple fear!) How many women of his own land, he wondered, had stepped too quickly back from their saviors, granting them only a half measure of what they needed above all things to go on? Where, he wondered, had she, had they—he looked about the clearing at her friends—seized such power? But because there was nothing in the whole of his primitive life from which to construct the lie, *from me* (as there would have been with any who'd ever before questioned the sources of his own strength), he felt as uncomfortable, as unsettled, as discommoded as a girl.

As had all the others, she smiled.

"I'm going..." he whispered. "I have to—"

"Hooop-ah!" one woman cried as, having finished with the spoils, two others lifted the bandit's cart, racketing loudly, to overturn it. Its remaining contents crashed out on leaves.

Startled, the smuggler looked back at the wrecked campsite. It wasn't just the cart: stones about the fireplace had been kicked away. The cooking pot had overturned. And the dish from which the bandit had prepared the smuggler's roast had been broken and the meat stepped on in the wanderings back and forth.

The others walked over. The barrel-chested women who'd taken him before to the cart said, not to him: "We go now? Yes?"

The smuggler stepped to his ox's shoulder; looking at the tree with the donkey's and the ox's reins, for a moment he was unsure which set went to which beast. "The donkey," he said, at last deciphering the twisted lines; he began to untie his ox. "What are we going to do with him?"

The barrel-chested woman said: "We leave it here, yes? For him. If he come back, he want it? He need it! It be good for him. Right?" Then, in a movement, she turned, pulled out her twin blades, raised them high over her head, and hacked, breath-jarringly hard, at the donkey's flat neck. It took her down into a crouch, as she tugged on through the broad neck muscles. The head didn't sever at the blow, though the smuggler expected to see it fall free. The animal gave a breathless gargle, staggered to the side, went down on its forelegs, got up again—staggered into the ox, into the woman (who stood now, breathing hard), stumbled out to the end of his reins, spurting and splattering, its mouth working wildly inside the bag, lost its hind footing, lost its fore-footing again—and fell over. The ribs heaved for three loud, clotted roars, then stilled.

"There." The woman put her sword away. "We leave it for him. He find it."

In the canvas feed bag, the donkey suddenly snorted; it kicked, quivered, gasped again—then, over a few more seconds, died.

The ox stepped about.

Where he'd been splashed, blood dribbled the smuggler's calf. He didn't even reach down to wipe it.

His heart hammered; this surround of terror was as pervasive as the fog.

Raven had gone off again.

Looking about, he saw that the redhead was watching him. He blinked, questioning, confused—in the middle of it, he realized he wasn't breathing, sucked in a great gasp (harsh enough to make Raven glance back over at him) and, with it, the sweetish smell of slaughter. His ox was lowing, steadily, loudly, and not looking at the carcass. Catching her bridle up short, the smuggler freed her reins and led her away. Her lowing and the creaking cart behind covered the mutterings with which he tried to quiet her.

The women, including Raven, were talking rapidly in their language.

The gaunt one took a long stick and plunged it in a pot they'd pulled from the bandit's wagon, raised the dripping end, and thrust it in the fire. It splutterted, as flame contended between the damp wood and the easy oil she'd soaked it with.

Then it flared red.

With the bright brand high, she kicked apart the fireplace, damping coals with sandalfuls of earth.

As the woman stamped about in the ashes, the smuggler looked back at his ox. Its shoulder and flank were matted with donkey blood.

Still talking, the others moved off into the trees, the mist. The smuggler took his cart along behind. Leaves got between him and the flare the gaunt woman carried aloft. Then, at the spot he'd first left his cart, red flame caught in an equine eye, on a dappled shoulder; there was neighing and the sound of hooves in brush.

They'd left horses tethered in the darkness!

One and another of them mounted, while he stopped his cart again, wondering would they just ride off and leave him in the pitchy woods. Hooves smashed about in the undergrowth toward him; blackness blocked the brand; and Raven's voice came down at him from what—since he could not see her at all, really—might have been some tree's upper branches. "Don't worry. We'll go slowly. So you can follow."

They did, for a while—long enough, anyway, for him to get the cart on the road. Two more flares had been lit from the first; there were three brands now. Among the half-dozen riders cantering before him in the black, red flames smoked from cheap oil.

Once alone and twice with a companion, once holding up one of the torches, then twice in the dark, Raven rode back to him.

"Where will you go?" he asked her the last time, walking along by his animal.

"To the Cravasse!" Some jollity had begun among the women ahead, and, stamping and cantering, Raven had carried it back with her. "The Western Cravasse! We are leaving Nevèrÿon at last!"

Ahead, one of her landwomen shouted something into the night, waving her brand—the one who'd slain the donkey.

"There," Raven explained to him in her most reasonable tone, "all will be well. The lips of the Cravasse are shaped as the inner blades of a sword. Once we ride within them—" and here she clapped her hands over her horse's head—"we will again be in a land where sanity and civilization reign. And the madness of this nation, with its slaves and liberators, this land that boasts an empress but is really governed by scheming men whom you can never find when you look for them, will be behind us for good! Will you come with me, wise and pretty man?"

"I *can't* . . . !"

Raven rode round his cart once, then, without acknowledging she'd heard him, galloped ahead, leaving him plodding in black.

He wondered if the judgment of the redhead (who rode her horse up with the others) about her friend, would turn out to be true.

A stade or two along, he stopped his cart to climb up on the bench, now feeling behind him for this, now checking under the seat for that. Should he take out one of his weapons, just to have it beside him? But the resolve ran from him even as he considered it. He let himself slouch forward, sucking in long, moist breaths from the cricketless night. The cart rattled on beneath him. When he looked up, the brands were only a pink, wobbling blur, through mist. Now and again he could hear the women's shouts, their laughter.

As the distance between them increased he thought to call out. What wouldn't I do, he wondered, to have them continue this frightening protection?

He felt truly abandoned.

Just to see what happened, the smuggler tried to imagine himself in the Kolhari crypt, standing on the throne in torchlight, with Raven in chains at the foot. Or perhaps the *other* way around . . . ? Varying the pictures in his mind, he waited for desire's stirring that might reveal to him where all the night's anxiety had lain.

But the wells of his body remained silent, offering up not the faintest quiver of confirmation, so that, in the dark, he could believe for a moment that the wells themselves were not there.

No; that, he thought, considering the absurd and fading fancy, is just what we could never do. It's too close to something real (and, like all unexamined reality, therefore truly unknown) for me to trust myself *or* her in such chains before the other.

Let them go ahead, he thought. Let her go . . .

With the wagon's shaking in the darkness, did he drift off . . . ? Because now, though the cart still jogged and the beast still followed whatever ruts, there was *no* light ahead. The women had finally ridden off, as if they'd never stepped from the fog.

He was surrounded by black.

The smuggler held the reins, which now and again shook over his knuckles—though, in truth, if they led to an actual ox or if she'd been replaced during some moment of inattention by a winged beast who now crawled with him across the sky or over the sea or through towering clouds, he could not have said for certain.

Should he stop?

Perhaps he should curl up in the cart itself, waiting for sunlight (or a scabbed and bleeding face . . . !) to peer over its edge?

Should he try to sit where he was, wakeful, while they wandered on the road or off the road, to what dark destination he could not possibly imagine, in wait for light?

For the moment, even to form the question in the rattling dark was exhausting, so that all he could do was return to the dialogue that had been running on beside him. Yes, he repeated to the grizzled smuggler of the mind, you wouldn't believe how much of my time, of my life I've spent following the Liberator, like some fool looking for a hero to give his life meaning. I went around as if he were my passion and my purpose! Then, one night, just like this, riding through the south in my cart, I finally ran into him. It was at a campsite, just down from the road. Him, a hero? He was only a bandit! As soon as he'd thrown me off my guard with a pretense of friendship, by offering me food, he turned around and tried to kill me! Even wanted to steal my wagon load—said it was for his cause! Oh, it was definitely him. I'd met one of his women—no, one of his men. She told me the place where I might find him. I mean, *he* told me. The man had his scars, all right. But it turns out the single eye they talk of is only a half-milky iris. I escaped with my life. Usually, you know, he has his men with him—if not right there, then stationed in the woods around him, waiting to come to his rescue at a call. I was just lucky that this time he'd chosen to go on a scouting mission alone. Not that he didn't try to lie about it. But I fugured he was bluffing. With one of the blades I keep in my cart, I gave him a cut across the face—perhaps I lost him his other eye! He didn't stay to let me see, but ran off. I overturned his cart and killed his donkey. I should have gone through the cart for spoils, but I wouldn't touch a thing in it—it had a handsome tooled-leather cart cover. I should have taken that, at least. But I wouldn't touch it. Well, that's the sort of fool I am! He must have been too scared or too hurt to follow me.

You just hope he doesn't run into you again some day, opined his phantom companion. I know these highway murderers . . . And the young smuggler looked about in the blackness.

Oh, I managed to get my cart away, and struck out on the dark road in fog thick enough to blot all moon and stars, if not the sun itself! You'd think, wouldn't you, a man like that with all the trust and faith people have in him throughout Nevèrÿon—and I know they do, for I've talked to many of them and, indeed, once had it myself—would feel some obligation to honesty and right behavior. Imagine such a man, sneaking up behind you in the dark, leaping on you from the back, trying to stab you like some thief in an old Kolhari alley—

Is that what he did to you . . . ?

No. No, the young smuggler explained, taking a great breath and looking about again. But he would have if he'd had the chance. For now, since I met him, I know the kind of man he is. He only exploits for his own ends the faith that fools like me have in him. Believe me, I know that now, from firsthand experience. I mean: Can you imagine it, Gorgik the Liberator, the man everyone talks of, only a common cutthroat? Fool that I was, I thought he was a great man, committed to the relief of human suffering, when all he does is lurk about at every campsite and crossroad, at every—

With a shudder, the smuggler blinked, staring into black as if it were a slate wall inches or feet ahead. The truth! he thought, desperate in the dark. The truth! Is that the kind of fool you are? The wise men and teachers of Nevèrÿon who talked of truth as if it were some glowing and generous light? The truth was a blackness into which anyone might be reasonably terrified to enter alone; any and every horror, he knew, could wait there.

And what is the truth? (He moved a little on the bench.) You are a frightened, ignorant man on a foggy, moonless night.

The young smuggler began to cry.

He did not make much sound doing it.

The companionable voice running on beside him certainly didn't notice. I've heard many people, it confided, gruff and fatherly, who don't approve of the Liberator at all. They say he's out for himself like everyone else. And you must admit that in these harsh and hazardous times that's a reasonable assumption for anyone to make.

Crying quietly, the young smuggler answered: Well, believe me, I can say from what I know: he's a liar and a murderer and a self-serving thief, no better than you, no better than me. Believe it: if only because I know me, I now know him...

No, I'll never tell that story, the smuggler thought. Tears still rolled his cheeks. I'll never tell it to anyone!

First of all (he snuffled, then spat to the side in the black; a wheel jarred over a root or rock), it's a stupid tale. Anyone who knows anything about the Liberator at all could catch me out in a minute. A fool I am, yes; but not *that* big a fool...

Taking another breath, he shivered. But, as his cart rolled through black fog, he went on telling it to himself.

10

Barefoot, two carried the trunk across uneven stone, the tall
one grunting more than the heavy one. A look, a word, a
jerked chin to coordinate their toss: the wood crashed into the
fireplace wider side to side than the length of both, laid head
to foot.

Gorgik looked up from the goatskin map on the plank table
as sparks rose before small flames.

In billowing smoke, the soldiers danced back, grinning and
beating bark bits from their hands, one against hairy thighs,
one against bald ones.

The heavy barbarian was a woman.

Gorgik nodded to them.

Saluting, backing away, then turning, they ambled off.

A year or a hundred years ago a roof beam had broken, one
of its ends crashing down to the floor's center, the other still
lodged at the ceiling's corner. The soldiers stepped around it
to join the others.

Between the six beams remaining, the sooty inlay had not
even sagged. But since the fall, torch holders had been bolted
to the slant beam's side, weapon hooks and woven hangings
had been fixed to its bottom, so that, however awkwardly, as
if awaiting some never begun repair, it was, today, part of the
hall's architecture.

Beyond it, a soldier stood up from among the others, to
turn his sword, examining it in torchlight. Were there two
blades rising from its hilt—

But that, Gorgik thought, would be a trick of the fire; or a
trick of the beer he'd decided he would not drink and had
anyway.

Squatting on the table's end in his iron collar, arms locked
round his knees, Noyeed stared, not at the flame, but at the
joined stones beside it.

106

"I dream..." The little princess swayed on the split-log bench. "If you only knew my dreams, my one-eyed monkey, my great Liberator..."

In firelight, her face was lightly lined; her hair was thin enough so that, in full sun, you could see much of her scalp through it. Strands shone with dressing. The princess sat close to the fire, a position of her own choosing. Her face was bright with sweat, though the soldiers, seated before them, now mumbling, now laughing sharply, now falling into altercation hot enough to notice, yet too distant to detail, would soon be complaining of the chill on this damp night.

It's having women among them, Gorgik thought. They give their all to the cause, certainly, as much as the men or more. They come and go, sometimes. But that was true of them all. Yet often it seemed to him just the fact of their being there led to problems—or at least to misunderstandings among the men who were still nine out of ten of his soldiers.

Leaning back in her stiff gown and blinking, the princess moved her hand—blemished, freckled, and liver-spotted—toward the heavy goblet of an estate cider hard as applejack; her fingers missed the stem. "I dream," crooned the princess Elyne, "of the time when you and I, Gorgik, were children, lost together in the halls of the High Court of Eagles, trying to find our way about—like children following some trail of crumbs to the treasure, starving peasant children in some summer, country fable."

"We were never children together, my princess." Gorgik chuckled, feeling little humor. "Our childhoods were very different. Nor did *you* ever starve when you were at the High Court."

The princess Elyne reached her goblet, got its edge to her lips, and drank. "But how do you know, my Liberator? Certainly—" Cider dripped to the table as she leaned forward— "certainly *you* did not starve, there or before. Real slaves don't have the kind of muscle you carried so handsomely about the palace—which made it rather easy to question the whole slavery story. Noyeed is a bit more what I'd expect an ex-slave to look like."

One end of the new log was wet, and the flames, already low at that side of the fireplace, began to hiss and sputter at it, as if castigating the wood for the sappy tears rolling its gleaming grain where the bark had come away.

Gorgik looked back at the map. His blunt forefinger had

traced the route with only half his concentration; now it was following an irrelevant path, as if, during his inattention, it had wandered onto an improper turnoff like a traveler lost in the autumnal night. "Noyeed," he said, "what are you staring at?"

Noyeed jerked about, long hair dragging his shoulder. "The stones, master. You see the stones, beside the fireplace? I was thinking, master, I was wondering—"

"He was thinking—" cider splashed the rim to wet the princess's spotty knuckles—"he was planning, he was speculating, while I, you understand, I was dreaming . . ."

"Between the stones." Noyeed released his knees to point. On his arm, muscle and bone made knots of equal seeming hardness. "See—where the wall's rocks are set together? A mist drifts from them, into the hall here. I was curious if that was moisture caught between them, heated to steam by the fire beside them; or if it was fog from the outside, leaking in from the night."

"Ask her. It's her castle. Ah—!" Some wrangling among the soldiers made him look up. "What are they arguing about now? These barbarians I have for soldiers. Is it the women among them or the men, I can't tell. Well, they must learn to support one another, not turn on each other at every little failing."

"Support, you say?" The princess chuckled. "Consider, my Liberator. It is only my being free not to support you that allows me to support you as I do. Yes, while you've been here, I've financed your cause, fed and paid your troops for you, welcomed them into my home. Proudly. Oh, so proudly! A man may learn a lot by losing the support of a woman. Ask any of your barbarians, and they will explain. But often I'm afraid that's just what you, above all, will never learn. It *is* my castle, you know. This is the new wing, too. Look up! It has a roof! I lodge you—and me and your lieutenant—and your soldiers and scouts in the little chambers dug in the walls of the old, roofless great hall—"

"But why not inside?" Noyeed spun on thin buttocks. "If it rains, we need a roof. Don't you think so, mistress?"

"Rain?" asked the little princess. "But it doesn't rain. Not at this time of year, my monkey. Not in Nevèrÿon. Now there's only fog." She waved the goblet, spilling more cider, her speech more unsteady. "Be still, or I shall order you roasted. On a spit! And I shall eat you up, as Mad Olin once

ordered her own sons so served, when, indeed, it *did* rain
with such torrential fury that—''

"Master!" Noyeed was up on his knees on the table.
"Master, when we quit this castle to move on to some
other—''

But the princess was chuckling to herself, over her drink.
"I dream . . ." she repeated. "I dream, here on the border of
Nevèrÿon. In my old, cold castle, I dream of nobility and
grandeur and truth. I dream of using my meager hoard to
finance a great man in his humane and wondrous cause,
which I know is benevolent and brave. His truth and commitment will reintroduce purpose, passion, excitement, and wonder among these ancient stones. I will love and revere him in
his commitment to his truth. He will respect and cherish me
in my commitment to him. Oh, I dream . . ." As she smiled,
firelight burnished her drab collar, her goblet. "If I escape
this dream with my life—" she sipped again—"I will be
satisfied. With less, and I won't complain. If I escape with
my life in any way enriched, well then, I shall count myself
the luckiest of women. Oh, I'm old enough to know that
dreams have their own beginnings, their own climaxes, their
own ends—that, when a wandering tale-teller imposes such
orderings on her stories, it makes those chaotic compilations so
much less like life, yet so much more exciting. No, when I
began this dream, one of the things I was determined to do
was dream it to its end, if only to see what such a dream
might leave me with. Life, I sometimes think—like dreams,
like stories, like plans, even like lies if you will—is to be
pondered on, interpreted, interrogated: but you had best not
try to change it too radically in the middle, or you risk never
finding its secret. If you must leave my dream, my great
Liberator, my one-eyed lieutenant, to follow yours, you must
leave. I can stand being left again with mine.''

Beyond the beam, the soldiers' noise rose, with clattering
arms and laughter. An officer with a sheaf of parchments
ducked in through the far hanging, now pausing to call
something to one soldier, now making his way through
several others in comradely converse.

Gorgik raised a bushy eyebrow.

On the table edge, Noyeed grasped his knees once more.
"And how did you learn to dream such wise dreams, my
mistress?''

But the little princess was gazing into her cider.

Reaching the table, the officer dropped his bunched parchments on the map. "You might look at these, my Liberator, if you're still making plans to depart . . . ?"

"Leaving me," mumbled the princess. "Yes, here on the border of Nevèrÿon, you're already making plans to leave, to go on. But where are you going?"

Noyeed turned toward her on the table. "My princess, the further we get from the center, the better the fighting. Haven't you said so yourself? And so, we plan, we dream of going on, going further, going beyond . . ."

Gorgik picked up one and another parchment, putting this one aside, handing that one back, gazing at the next and nodding. "It's going well." Most stayed on the table; Gorgik looked at Noyeed, at the princess. "Reinforcements for us have come from friends both to the east and the west. But the empress's troops are still new here and unacquainted with the territory. When we started, I didn't think it could be done. But we're holding off the small forces that the local brewers and less powerful nobles have been able to muster. They have no trained fighters among them, other than those the Child Empress has been able to send them. How many of them can *read* a map, much less make one?"

The officer lingered. "My Liberator . . . ?"

Gorgik looked up.

"The guard told me to tell you he's caught another smuggler. Outside the castle, he was trying to sneak his cart across the princess's grounds."

"A smuggler?" The princess put down her goblet. "A smuggler, you say? No! What would a smuggler be doing on my lands? I allow no smuggler on my grounds—"

"He may be a spy, master . . ." Noyeed remarked, softly and intensely. "Soon, they will be sending even more spies than they do already."

Gorgik looked up. "We've had enough experience with spies by now to know how best to take precautions. Bring him up," Gorgik said to the officer and, turning, to the others, "so that we can ponder on, can interpret, can interrogate this smuggler, this spy . . . But first—" Gorgik stood up behind the table— "clear the hall!" This was a bellowed order.

Soldiers began to stand, as if they were used to such directives.

"Clear the hall, now!" Gorgik looked down. "You too, little princess. Retire now, and leave the hall to me."

"But why, my Liberator...?" She was clearly annoyed at having to move.

"If he is a spy," said Gorgik, "I would rather he not know who I am."

She rose from the bench, taking her goblet. "I don't understand all this secrecy. This is not the way my father or my uncle would have conducted such a campaign from these halls."

"I'm a public man, my princess. That means my only meaning is the web of signs I publicly inhabit. Thus, I would appear to our visitor as close to naked, unarmed, and without ornament as I can."

"But—"

"We do not have many soldiers. Those we have are so few they can vanish easily among the corridors and chambers of your great castle here, or into the lands around them if they have to. I have few—and our smuggler will leave here thinking I have none. Or, at any rate, he will think I have no more than the guard who captured him. Later, if he meets someone who has fought against our brave handful, that one will say I have many—while he will declare I do not. And what will .happen in the course of their altercation? Believe me, the number of fighters I have will double, treble, quadruple by the end of their argument on one side—while, on the other, even the guard who took this smuggler will, no doubt, vanish completely as this smuggler insists I carry on my campaign entirely alone. Princess, I have made a point never to be fully present within the central crypts of power where I'm reputed to reside—at least never in the full force, true complexity, and complete organization by which most hope to know me. It is a strategy I learned many years ago when I worked for Lord Aldamir in the south. Such subterfuge has laid about me a fog of confusion and misinformation that has often aided me—"

"But then, master," stated Noyeed, "you are seldom fully absent either."

The Liberator chuckled. "And that I learned simply from the exigencies of the times." The chuckle—"Now go, my princess—" as he looked about, again became a bellow: "And clear the hall! Quickly! Clear it!" He glanced at the one-eyed man. "You stay, Noyeed."

"Yes, master!"

*   *   *

The dripping roof brushed his hair and made him crouch again, as he clutched the sack to his chest.

"Get in, now!" The guard shoved the small of his back, hard, so that, staggering, he reached out with one hand to steady himself against the wall that crumbled under his fingers like dried mud. Behind him: "Get in!"

He rushed toward the hanging, thinking to find blackness, pushed through, ducking under a sagging lintel, to hear the echo of his breath change timbre. He stopped and stood, slowly, in the flickering room. A beam slanted through it, ceiling to floor. Beyond, a plank table stood by a wide fire.

A man sat behind it.

Another squatted on the table itself among mugs, goblets, and parchments.

When the young smuggler had realized the guard who'd accosted him was taking him to the Liberator, he'd thought pretty much everything he'd thought before, felt pretty much everything he'd felt before, when he'd met the man on the bridge or, again, when he'd found the man in the clearing. There was curiosity and pleasure and wonder. There was fear and disbelief and—as the guard had shoved him through the corridor—outrage at betrayal.

Because of his two earlier encounters, for all he'd felt, for all he'd thought, he said none of the things he'd said before.

But as he stood in the flicker, however, he began to think and feel something new:

I have just become one of those people who, from now on, must say: There are two of them, not one. There's a big one, with a scar down his cheek. And there's a little one, with one blind eye, who goes about in a slave collar. And, for all my researches, that is *not* who I was only moments ago ...

Or *have* I become that...? (The smuggler narrowed his eyes, for the feeling of disorientation was different from the other times: it was smaller, clearer, more precise.) In this ill light, *have* I really seen them? Or am I only putting that upon the shadowed faces before me, like a student come down to write his unreadable profanities on some wall in the Spur? Be clear. Be certain. Be careful with this truth. Because I am better equipped to see it than most, I above all must not let my equipment itself fool me.

The big man stood up at his bench, walked to the table's end, and came around it.

The young smuggler edged forward, hugging his sack.

The big man was naked, with only some leather web pouching his genitals. At one ear, his hair was braided with a bit of thong.

On the table, the little man rested a sharp chin on his knees.

The smuggler squinted, trying to clear both faces in the flames' light. But, looking back and forth between them, trying to hold on to the full and heavy features or the small and acute ones, the fire and his attention itself seemed to distort vision.

On the cheek of the big one standing—a veritable giant— that *could* have been a scar...

The little one squatting blinked one eye. His other was sunken; or sealed; or perhaps was only in shadow...

"Are you..." the young smuggler hazarded.

"—the Liberator?" The big man laughed. "What do you think? What do you see around me?"

The young smuggler shook his head, bewildered, and hugged his sack higher.

"Do you see here all the Liberator's hundreds of troops?" He gestured about the empty hall. "His dozens of secretaries, aides, and orderlies? his spies and provocateurs? the whole elaboration of the fighting forces with which, carrying on his campaign, he has freed thousands of slaves throughout the nation and has made even the Child Empress herself and all her ministers quake in the High Court? Or do you see, perhaps, a single man with a guard or two in an all but abandoned castle?"

The smuggler frowned at the man on the table, who laughed, sharply and shortly.

"Or, perhaps—" The little man spoke in an accent very different from the big one's clear, Kolhari diction—"you think you see *two* men...?" Pushing parchments with his hip, he moved to the table edge to drop one ankle over. "You don't, you know." Yes, a metal collar, nearly black, hung on his scrawny neck. "You don't even see one. No human forms stand or sit before you. You face only some illusion that mimics the form of men as, without names, the gods do. No real castle of granite and fitted stone stands around you. Think, rather, that as the night fog drifted and formed about you, making one shape after another, as the night sounds rose and fell, twittered and cheeped, at some unfixable point in your journey they came together for a moment in the suggestion of the man and his shadow some have called the Liberator, as well as this castle about him, and the guard who your memory says brought you here. Realize that, there and here, those wisps and chitterings have played on your imagination to suggest even me and the words I speak, now, here. Wandering in the mists, you merely *think* you've come into the presence of the Liberator, when actually it's the fog-filled night's autumnal sorcery—''

The Liberator raised his hand. (The little man silenced.) ''What questions do you have for me? Do you want to know who I am? Or where you are? Or what I intend to do with you now that I've had you brought here? Talk.'' The big man actually smiled. ''You'll find we autumnal night wisps are not that frightening.''

The younger smuggler took a breath and, with one hand, released his sack and pointed to the table. ''Those . . . ?'' Because that was all he could think of now: they were the only thing that seemed solid.

Frowning, Gorgik glanced back; Noyeed looked down beside him.

''Those skins,'' the smuggler said. ''They have writing on them, don't they . . . ?''

Gorgik nodded.

(A scar? A shadow . . . ?)

''Can you read?''

Glancing back again, the big man frowned at the little one. The little man hazarded: ''I can't. But he can. Can you?'' The young smuggler shook his head quickly. ''Oh, no!''

''You can't? Not at all?'' The big man stepped closer, observing. ''Oh, I bet you know the signs for . . .'' The green eyes narrowed in the flickering light— ''women's genitals, men's excreta, and cooking implements, in all their combinations, the curses that are forever scratched and scrawled on walls up in the city—you sound is if you've spent some time in Kolhari. Am I right?''

''Oh, yes. *Those* writings, yes,'' the smuggler lied. ''I can read those.'' Momentarily he was back in that hot afternoon when his Kolhari friend had labored with a stick over a stretch of mud down at the edge of the Khora, ineffectually trying to teach him the written forms of profanation.

''Like everyone in this country,'' the big man commented over his shoulder to the smaller, ''slowly he is learning to read and write. Take a lesson there, Noyeed.''

"But what do . . . *you* use it for?" (Noyeed! Then that *was* the little one's name! Then the big one *must* be . . . No, he must wait.) "The writing, I mean?"

"I use it to remember. To remember, clearly and accurately, what I have, what I need, what I've done, what I must do, where I've been, where I must go, what I've seen, and what I must still look for. Memory often plays tricks on you even minutes after your thoughts have settled somewhere else."

"Oh, I know!" The smuggler nodded.

"With writing, you are free to use your thinking in other ways. I can observe clearly and carefully what I have to—but do not have to worry about recalling it later if it is written down. It's an interesting system, the one that actually puts down words themselves. Myself, though, I use an older, commercial script, from before the current system made its way to Nevèrÿon from the Ulvayns. It's one my father used back in Kolhari, when he worked on the waterfront."

Kolhari, thought the smuggler. And his father (story fragments moved up in his mind. Other fragments receded), on the waterfront . . . ?

"Why do you ask all this?" The big man frowned. "If you can't read and write anything save wall scratchings, what difference does it make to you if *I* do? But tell me, what does someone like you think of this new writing?"

Was it fear? The smuggler blurted: "I hate it! The students, they use it all the time. They started all that scratch and scrawl. When I first saw it, I used to think they were putting up messages to each other—putting them right out there on the walls, too, just because the rest of us wouldn't know what they meant! Because they can pass them out in the open like that, they think they're better than we are. I *hate* students, and I hate their writing!" *What* was the name of the boy he'd given the ride to, down from Kolhari? Many *did* feel that way about the students and their script. But why, he wondered, was he saying, here, when questioned, that *he* did? Still, once started, he could not stop. "*I* wouldn't be a student for anything! I'm glad I'm a good and—"

"—honest laborer?" the Liberator finished for him.

The smuggler swallowed.

"Or, perhaps," said the Liberator, uncannily, "you were about to say, smuggler . . . ?"

The smuggler blinked.

"My guard caught you trying to take your cart across the

princess's land here—to escape the Imperial customs inspectors of Sarness, no doubt. I know them well. They're no friends of mine, either.'' He stepped forward. "Too bad you couldn't admit you were a smuggler. We might have had more to say to each other, then. But we don't. Cutpurse or potter's boy, that's still the kind of honesty I look for in the young of our nation—and so seldom find. But that you are like so many in Nevèrÿon is not anything I can hold against you.''

The smuggler thought: When I came in, this room seemed so big, its roof so high. But his head comes just beneath the ceiling beams he passes under.

"You're a youth of your times, like so many others. Who'd blame you for being the victim of those times? Who could chide you for trying, in whatever misguided way the times provide you with, to master them? What are you carrying there?" He reached out a hand. "Here. Let me see.''

The young smuggler glanced left and right and, holding the sack still tighter, pulled back.

The Liberator snorted—yes, it was a chuckle. "Come. Show me now. Tell me, are you taking your contraband up to the north or are you traveling down to the south with it? Speak; now!'' The Liberator grasped the sack in the young smuggler's arms with his great fingers at the same time as he stepped up, blocking the firelight.

The young smuggler blurted: "South! I'm going south—running contraband from Kolhari down into the Garth. I'm the most foolish, the clumsiest, the most incompetent of smugglers. But you know that! You saw it! I needn't tell you. But I know running around and freeing slaves isn't cheap. I know you need all you can get. All right, then—''

The great hand tugged; the sack fell away from the smuggler's chest. As the Liberator turned to the fire, the light fell on his heavy features clearly enough to show the scar that dropped across one eye and down the broad cheek. The two green eyes looked over at the smuggler. The heavy lips thinned. "You think I want to steal your haul from you?" He yanked at the cord binding it closed. A tear of some sort had been recently sewn with rough vine. The tie pulled loose. Holding the neck with one hand, the Liberator looked in and reached inside.

What he pulled out was a small, round ball. He frowned at

it, frowned at the smuggler, reached in again. Now he drew out a whole handful of balls. "You're taking these . . . south?" One by one he dropped the black spheres back in the bag.

One caught on the neck, fell to the floor, and rolled. Noyeed was off the table to retrieve it. "Here!" He thrust it over the man's arm and in.

The scarred giant pushed the sack with its tie-cord at the smuggler. "Here, take it, now. And go on. Go on, I say!"

The smuggler grabbed up the sack, cradling the neck against his shoulder to keep the toy balls from spilling over the floor; he grasped at the cord, trying too quickly and too clumsily to bind the neck closed. "I'm only the poorest, most careless, most clumsy—" He glanced up again; the little man in his iron collar waited beside the Liberator, like the big man's foreshortened shadow. Yes, one eye was definitely missing. The flesh had sealed within the socket, leaving only the scar lid and lashes made within a depression deep and round as if it had been rolled into the sharp face by one of the balls.

The smuggler whispered:

"Master . . . ?"

"Out of here," the big one said, "before I change my mind!"

The smuggler swallowed, turned, and rushed under the low beam, through the hangings, and into the hallway. He'd expected to find the guard who had led him up here. But the man had gone.

He hurried with the sack along the corridor. Under torch-light here and there, he tried to recall the brief interview with the Liberator and his one-eyed lieutenant—unless the great one speaking to him had been the lieutenant and little Noyeed was, indeed, the Liberator . . . ?

And the scar?

And the single eye?

He'd seen them now, yes? Unless, of course, that *had* been a trick of firelight, or even the detritus of the terrors from out in the mist that, even now, drifted before the torches in their wall niches—the fog that seeped through the walls about him as if the stone itself were stream. *Could* he trust his memory? Or anything else? *Why* had he lied to the Liberator's questions about his direction, about his ability to read? "Master," he'd called him! By all the nameless gods, had he uttered a word of truth? *Could* it be, he wondered, he'd only thought he'd seen what he'd seen because of his own desires, researches, expectations?

The Liberator was certainly no murdering highwayman.

One had certainly worn the collar.

But then, he'd known that since the night how long ago on the Kolhari bridge.

The real and solid meeting in this foggy night had left him the same entanglement of suppositions with which he'd begun his journey—oh, slightly adjusted, slightly shifted, but in ways almost too subtle to name. The illuminating and major change he might have hoped for in an encounter with the real, taking him from night to day, had, equally certainly, not occurred. Just as before, he still carried with him, unknown and untaxable, the intricate, frightening, many-times questioned and faulty certainties called, at the behest of what ill-understood forces, truth.

That was all.

Now pausing, now hurrying again, now making his way hesitantly, his sack mercifully safe in his arms, he rushed through castle corridors, down steps, and out the door where his cart waited for it in the fog.

At the turning of a corridor under a guttering torch in its iron cage, they encountered each other later.

Feeling along the cold wall, the little princess walked unsteadily in her stiff gown, humming to herself.

"Well, master—" Noyeed laughed, for, in truth, both men thought that she would simply wander tipsily by without seeing them—"it seems that my plan—"

"Your dream, little monkey?" The princess chuckled. She stopped. She swayed—but she did not look at them.

"—my plan has worked, master!" (It was well she did not look, for with the torchlight above, both the one-eyed man and the scarred giant looked truly demonic in the dark hall.) "We've been able to move you and your forces out to a part of the nation where slavery is a reality and real force is needed to end it! Here, master, you and I—and you—" The princess might have thought from their conversation they ignored her as she appeared to ignore them, but the little man reached out to seize her wrist, gaunter than his own— "we've been able to turn revolution into reality!"

Gorgik nodded in the dark hallway.

The princess did not appear to realize her arm was in Noyeed's grip.

"Only sometimes," Gorgik said, "I wonder if my own dreamings—"

"Your plans," said the princess, like a mother correcting a child's diction.

"—if my dreams are that real, after all. You and I have observed slavery as slaves and as free men, Noyeed. You have observed it as the daughter of a slaveholder, my princess. All three of us, together and apart, have debated and interrogated and argued about it through a thousand firelit nights and on into the fatiguing glare of dawn. We all know what drives slavery from the land: a new farming technique, a more efficient yam stick, the spread of minted coin, some imperceptible warming of the very earth itself over fifty years, or an equally unpredictable increase in the rainfall, yielding the greater affluence that makes slavery impracticable and paid labor more profitable. Yet somewhere, through all this experience, observation, and speculation the object must remain intact: slavery. But where is it? Unless we can truly locate it, what can the likes of us do, *really,* to affect such a thing?"

She turned to peer at the shadowed faces, one above hers, one below. "Yet what are necessary to move a country from slavery to freedom are insight, energy, and commitment," declared the little woman, clearly and most undrunkenly, as though the conversation had strayed into an area with which she was totally familiar, totally at ease. "Men and women caught in one set of habits do not shift so easily into another merely because the sun shines and the rains fall, my Liberator. You have brought your passion and your purpose here to serve your nation, your times. Could anything be nobler?"

"The idea that a man is a slave to the times may be just as much a dream as the idea that a man can be a master of them—or less than a dream, my princess. A lie, if we know ourselves to be dreaming." Gorgik turned to wander a few steps up the hall. "Perhaps, the times notwithstanding, I am only here because of a dream, just as much as the empress's troops, which, true, would not fight me in Kolhari and its environs, but which her minsters send, with their dreams of victory, to fight me at the borderland."

"We *must* fight here, master!" Noyeed released the princess's wrist, to look after Gorgik, who'd wandered some steps by

the stony wall. "And we must triumph here. Then we must
move on, beyond Nevèrÿon. We are at the border now. And
we must move even further. Do you think that the evils we
fight to eradicate here end with the ill-defined boundary of
this nation? What we fight is the nightmare of oppression and
lies. Where we come, we wake men and women to the light
of freedom and truth!"

"Ah, yes," said the princess. "I still recognize it. That
was, indeed, my dream. Yet just as I recognize it, am about to
reach it, just listen to you, my one-eyed monkey; already *you*
are dreaming of leaving!"

The one-eyed man turned back. "No, my mistress—!"

"—leaving me, leaving Nevèrÿon itself, for whatever chaos
no civilized person can say. No, do not protest. If that must
be part of my dream too, then let it."

"My mistress, I did not want to suggest that—"

But the princess was walking away again—was indeed
beyond them in the dark. Once more they heard her, in the
dark, humming.

11

The two men walked together through corridors, up turning
steps, and under narrow arches, to come out on the castle
roof, just as the moon cleared through a tear in the fog,
which, wider and wider, wavering and billowing, ripped
across the night: for minutes, abutments and balustrades
silvered.

Gorgik stepped to the edge to gaze between the crenellations.
A sea of fog surrounded them, so that the castle seemed to
float in it with, here and there, a treetop bobbing, nor many
of those. "I dream . . ." the Liberator whispered.

Behind him, chuckling, Noyeed dropped to a squat on the
chill stones, forearms balanced on his knees. "What do you
dream, Master?"

"My dreams? Sometimes I wonder how I can know for

sure. When I was at the mines, Noyeed—when we were slaves together at the mines—I abused you like some master might abuse a slave; and, sated from that abuse, I lay my head down on my straw pallet, and I dreamed. I dreamed of freedom. I dreamed of struggling toward it. I dreamed of the ways to secure it. I dreamed of having the power to grant that freedom to the slaves around me, even you—even to you, Noyeed. They were dreams that, today, strike me as not far from the princess's, however more intense mine might have been. And you were part of my dream even then. Only none of the other slaves around me knew of them. I could not tell it to any of you. I could not even speak of it clearly to myself. I could only dream. The language had not yet been given to me. But then, soon, somehow, I *was* free; I was able to struggle for more freedom. I was able to secure it by that struggle. I was able to seize and nourish enough power to grant it to others. Thus I became a liberator. But all through my freedom, through its growth and coming to power, from the very moment that it began, I have been troubled with other dreams, with dark and violent dreams, dreams of that initial abuse that I and six other miners—slaves, guards, and I, a foreman among them—visited on you when you were a sick and helpless child. And that abuse, you tell me, now, you do not remember. It is as if, somehow, once again, I cannot make you know my dreams.''

"And so, you sometimes think, *we* abuse each other only to make me remember whatever truth it is that I've forgotten? A truth, you call it, that I cannot believe is true if only from what I know, what I remember, of my time in the mine with you, master?''

Gorgik turned from the wall and stood with his back to the stone in moonlight. "You are not a forgiving man, Noyeed.''

"I can be a very vengeful man, master.''

"And you took no secret pleasure in the violation we miners—slaves, guards, and a foreman—visited on your body.''

"It was agony and terror beyond humiliation, master. Believe me, master.''

"Then aren't you a fool, Noyeed, to love and support someone who openly admits he was among their number—even more, to mime again and again, night after night, now as master, now as slave, the very abuse you suffered?''

"Master, I cannot fight *all* the evils in the world. Therefore I must fight the ones I have known, the ones I can recall.''

Noyeed shook his head. "What occurred that night in the slave barracks below the Falthas so many years ago was not written down. No spy lurked there in the darkness, taking notes and noting names. What's left today is dreams, memories—yours, mine. Well: that you have such dreams means only that you are human. But you are a fool, master, to be a slave to them." Noyeed cocked his head in the silver light. "I remember the abuse, master." He said it tiredly, as if he'd said this many times before in response to what he had, indeed, heard many times. "How could I forget it? But it was years ago. Many, many years. And I have no specific memory of you among my abusers. In truth, the more we talk, the more I wonder if I would recognize *any* of their faces if I encountered them again—even if time had not scrawled over their features with age the way you mark out some miswritten sign on one of your parchments. It was dark that night. And I was ill. Perhaps it was another boy, at another time, you fell on, master, and misremembered as little Noyeed. Or perhaps you confused the time you received your scar with some other incident concerning me. You say it was not the first time you committed such abuse. My memories of you at the mine, master, are only of your kindnesses to me, time after time after time. Now, perhaps the foreman with the scar, called Gorgik, whom I remember saving my life again and again was not really you but some other. Perhaps *I* misremember . . . ? Oh, master, I let you have your memories! Let me have mine!"

Standing at the wall and squatting on the stone, the two watched one another, till finally Noyeed turned his single eye away.

"I have not forgiven you your cruelty, master. I have forgotten it. And that, for you, has been a cruel forgetting."

"And suppose, Noyeed, someday you remember. Suppose, someday, it comes to you—the way the name of a street you once lived in for a month, which, a decade later, you cannot recall, suddenly returns in the night to wake you sharply from half-sleep. Suppose, some moonlit night like this, as you watch my face, laboring and sweating above yours, suddenly you recall my scar from years ago—"

"Years ago," Noyeed said, "I was on my belly, not my back—"

"But what if—"

"It's the game we play, master." Noyeed blinked his eye.

"If I remember, then I may, indeed, forgive you. Or I may strike you dead. It's an interesting game, master. But till that happens, what can I do? What can you?" He leaned forward. "This forgetfulness of mine, it plagues you, doesn't it?"

"Yes, Noyeed."

"Then my forgetfulness is my revenge." Sitting back, Noyeed looked up in the moonlight. "You see, master, I am not a forgiving man. Even to one I love. If I were a forgiving man, I would lie, say I remember—and forgive you." Noyeed suddenly reached up to grasp the iron collar at his neck, pulled it, creaking, open, and placed it—open—on the stone before him. His hands came back to his knees. "What we do together, you and I, we do very much awake. How you take it apart and put the fragments back together again to make those monstrous dreams, and your memories of those dreams, and your waking talk of those memories—master, that is your affair. I can listen. But I cannot forgive . . . because I cannot judge." At the wall, the Liberator was still, till after a time the one-eyed Noyeed said, "South . . ."

And Gorgik, as if released by the word, stepped forward across the roof, laughing.

"He lied, didn't he, master!" Noyeed laughed too. "That smuggler we took? Oh, but you caught him out! You knew he could read a few signs. He was a smuggler, and yet, master, you forgave him! You let him go! But now, master, as he goes on his way through the land, he goes knowing your power!"

"South?" Grunting, Gorgik dropped to squat before Noyeed. "No one smuggles such trifles *into* the south! Of course, he's on his way back to Kolhari. But that kind has not a true word in him. I wouldn't be surprised if everything he said were a lie. Such as he lies as he breathes. Truth is something he's never even learned to speak."

"But *you* knew the truth about him, master! Didn't you? You knew the truth of his lies. And the truth is the source of your power!"

"Ah!" The Liberator chuckled again. "What power, Noyeed? Believe me, I have no power with his sort. That's why I sent him on his way. A better, more honest man, and I might have asked him to join us. But him . . . ? The kind of fight we engage in here would mean nothing to him."

"But your fight means more and more!" Noyeed declared. "And to more and more people! Master, the last time I was in Kolhari at your behest, I met one not so different. It was on the Bridge of Lost Desire—yes, it was! And as we talked, he spoke your name—*I* didn't mention it. He spoke it first. But he thought with my one eye I might even *be* you, master! Imagine! But you were his hero. He had searched out all he could of you. For him, you were the greatest man in all Nevèrÿon! Greater, even, than the empress! Oh, I suppose he was not really a youth like this one. He was sharp and intelligent and talked like a student. But I would wager there are many such in Kolhari, in Sarness—all over Nevèrÿon! *You* do not hear of so many because, as they go about this fearful, fogbound land, they meet too many counterfeits, too many imposters, too many who only mimic the gestures of those with true purpose, true passion, true power, from whom they learn nothing about truth. But then, master, when they hear another fable of your exploits, when they hear something of the truth of your deeds and doings, their vision is cleared—"

"Now *is* that the truth?" From his squat, Gorgik made a dismissive gesture. "No, Noyeed, you only say this to please me. Nor is it necessary. Certainly when you were last in Kolhari, you met some boy. You probably met many. And one told you this, and one told you that, and one you didn't meet but only heard of may have said something like it to another friend who, to flatter you, repeated some distorted version of it. And from them all, you've put together this little tale. But if I let such delusions take hold, believe it, I'd be the most unfortunate of . . ." But here he stopped. "It's too easy to put together such lies, Noyeed. I've put together too many myself. South . . . ?"

They faced each other across the few feet of stone, on which the collar lay, both of them grinning as the light about them brightened and dimmed.

Fog blew across the moon.

"Yes, you know his sort well, master."

"Sadly, I know him as well as I know myself, for once I was such—perhaps am only an accident or two away from being such now."

"Ah, master, you say that of all you meet. You say it of every thief and whore and smuggler. You say it of every merchant and princess and minister—then you tell me it is the source of all true power!"

Gorgik began to laugh.

"What dreams you have, master! What a dream of power!" The little man grinned. "Where do the pieces of such a dream come from? How do you put them together, master? Where does one learn to dream like that? No, master, we cannot stay here. Soon we must go. We must leave the princess, leave Nevèrÿon, and take your dream, your knowledge, your power beyond this ill-bounded land and truly right the wrongs of the world!''

But as fog closed out the chill moon, for a while the two men squatted together on the roof, with their dreams, laughing in darkness.

—New York
January 1984

II

THE
MUMMER'S
TALE

The limit and transgression depend on each other for whatever density of being they possess: a limit could not exist if it were absolutely uncrossable and, reciprocally, transgression would be pointless if it merely crossed a limit composed of illusions and shadows. But can the limit have a life of its own outside of the act that gloriously passes through it and negates it? . . . For its part, does transgression not exhaust its nature when it crosses the limit, knowing no life beyond this point in time? . . . Transgression, then, is not related to the limit as black to white, the prohibited to the lawful, the outside to the inside, or as the open area of a building to its enclosed spaces. Rather their relation takes the form of a spiral which no simple infraction can exhaust. Perhaps it is like a flash of lightning in the night which, from the beginning of time, gives a dense and black intensity to the night it denies, which lights up the night from the inside, from top to bottom, and yet owes to the dark the stark clarity of its manifestation, its harrowing and poised singularity . . .

—Michel Foucault
Preface to Transgression

1

So, *that's* done! Come in, come in. Myself, I thought I was brilliant. Step over that, my young friend. Oh, not so young anymore, you say? Well. You've still got twenty years on me. Always had. Always will. No, around *this* way! Don't mind the clutter. A bit hot for you? Here, let me open the trap in the wagon's roof. That will give us both air and light.

There!

Sit now, on that shelf with the pretty weave over it, just under the monster's wing—yes, it's the same beast the Hero slew out on the platform. But since that was at the very beginning of the skit, they just toss it in here during the second scene while the Baron and the Peasants are singing that awful song about the Unconquerable Sea, when everybody down in the audience—*and* up on the stage—feels so insufferably noble. If it creaks and crashes while we're back here putting it away, you're supposed to assume out front it's just the wind on the rocks.

Now *look* at that sword, hanging on the wall. Split practically in two! In here it seems like nothing more than the painted wood it is. But I've seen our Leading Lady snatch it from the Hero's scabbard to plunge it into her heart, and I've heard grown men off from the platform cry out, "No! No, don't do it!" till that great lummox dashes it from her hand and plants a kiss on her breast instead, begging her to forgive his unfaithfulness.

From the platform we always hear the market girls, crowded together down front, start to weep.

No, that's true: they didn't today. But Kolhari is a sophisticated city; the audience demands more. Really, I was speaking of the way they receive us in the provincial markets. Here, they're much more likely to appreciate my—

No!

I won't endure either your praise or your carping. You took time off from running your school to come all the way in from Sallese and see our opening afternoon performance. What greater compliment could you pay me? Oh, it's funny. . . .

Now, lean close, because I don't want any of the others loading things outside or scrambling over our roof to hear. But we've been friends for years, you and I. *I* know you were born a prince in Neverýona; and I also know that well before you set up your school, you dropped your title so that people would deal with you as they would with any ordinary citizen. Believe me, it's a gesture that, in the eyes of us who know you, makes you extraordinary indeed!

But about a season back, the oddest gentlemen joined our troop while we were off somewhere to the south. What talent our Director saw in him, *I'll* never know, for he was older than I and had never acted before in his life. Wouldn't you guess, after a few days the rumor went round among us that this odd old man was actually a great southern lord, out of favor with the ministers about our Child Empress, whose reign is proud and prudent. There he was, running about the countryside and cavorting on the platform with a drum and a lot of feathers, just like the rest of us. But that's not the funny part. He left us very soon. Oh, off the platform, he was pleasant enough, and though I sometimes felt his onstage shenanigans rather overlapped my own, nevertheless, just as a fellow artist, I was sorry to see him go.

Well, don't you know a day later, the little flute player, whom you saw open our performance this afternoon and who doubles as a driver when we're on the road, told everyone that she, too, was actually a deposed lady of some status. Then, the young man who plays the comic servant confessed, one night after much cider, that, though he didn't *really* have a title himself, he had been brought up as the companion to a northern earl and could, indeed, ape all the manners of a lord if he chose—perhaps the Director might consider spreading the rumor that another aristocrat was part of the troop . . . ? And that otherwise sane and sensible man consented!

Within the month, I tell you, it all became too preposterous.

Our horseboy became a duke. The three rather bosomy young things who play the witches in the morning skits and the lost peasant girls in the evening had all been, they assured us, ladies in waiting to various titled dames. And the Leading Lady herself was suddenly a distant relation of our empress—a duchess one week, a countess the next. She could never keep it straight. Oh, my friend, I tell you! Out there in the Nevèrÿon countryside, titles broke out among our company like sores among the plague-ridden! And the height of it was that, one night as I lay right on my pallet there—yes, you're sitting on it—with all the false beasts and birds and weapons and armor you see around us now, just a-clattering as we jounced toward some tiny town on the coast, I actually thought of . . . you!

And of your discarded title, my friend!

I wondered: since he has no use for it, would he really *mind* if I took it up . . . for just a while.

Yes, I'm glad you think it's funny!

I'm welcome to it, you say? Oh, you're only humoring an old artist! You might not have felt so if it had gotten back to you I was using it, now. We must retain some sense of propriety about these things.

I came to my senses, you understand, even before the next performance. After all, I told myself, as I put the blue paint on my eyes and the gold about my lips: If my Neveryóna friend has cast it aside, why should I take it on? Let those who have never been within the walls of a lord's estate dream and scheme to be something better than they are! I have the friendship and esteem of a true prince of Nevèrÿon. I have lunched with you in your garden; I have performed my mimes for your family and friends. You have come to sit in my cluttered quarters, the two of us grinning at one another like tickled boys with mutual admiration. You have even lectured on the fine points of my art to the young men and women whose educations have been entrusted to you by the better-off merchants of Kolhari and its environs. Oh, how good you've been to me, from the beginning! It makes me weep. I have need of nothing more from you than your good opinion.

And I shall not keep that, I told myself out there in the boondocks, if I sink to this theatrical madness for appropriated nobility.

Now, tell me I was wonderful, thrilling, amazing this afternoon! No—

Let me stop!

Your good opinion, yes. I enjoy praise as much as anyone. But just as you don't need my advice on how to educate the sons and daughters of your ambitious tradesmen and artisans, I don't need your advice on how to move an audience to laughter, tears, and the recognitions supporting both—though I know you well and also know how anxious you are to give some.

But I saw you, out there among the others, only smile— yes, at the end of the third scene—when those around you roared. You and I both know the joke I'd just told was one of my most vulgar—merely a concession to what our Director thinks will please the most insensitive spectators, and worth no more than a smile, no matter how the other onlookers hooted and clutched their sides. Well, I *also* heard your laughter come, full, rich, and flowing, at that little business with my goblet in the penultimate part, while the Heroine's Father is asking for more wine . . . ? Even though half the audience missed it and the half who noticed gave it no more than a titter, you must still know: I have been working on that gesture for *months*! (Did you recognize the eastern count on whom my original observation was based? But no. My art lies in its universality, not in its specificity.) To appreciate that turn of my hand as I glanced down with that complex expression of befuddlement (which my makeup is, you can still see here if you examine my face, designed entirely to enhance) is to appreciate what I *really* do.

And you appreciated—I heard you.

And applauded loud as anyone, at least at the end.

So you see, I've already had your critique. For us to sit here, then, face to face, while I go on to beg you for more and more empty plaudits only demeans us both.

Yes, they all seemed to have liked it—the whole thing— pretty much.

Oh, you mean the one with the thinning hair and thickening belly who stood a little off from the others, laughing and clapping heatedly at everything I did? He liked it particularly, you say? Ah, then, you noticed him.

His is the kind of critique I prefer most?

Oh, you *are* unkind to an aging actor! But the truth is, he too is a friend. He comes to see all my performances in the city, when he's here. And, yes: unlike you and the general audience, critical for your separate reasons, everything we do delights him. Once or twice, when there were new and inexperiencd mummers recently joined with our cast, and everyone was badly rehearsed, and the audience, sensing it, hardly raised a smile, I've seen him applaud just as thunderously as he did today, even scowling at the others as he stalked off afterward—unnoticed, in most cases, by all but me. But those are the days when I think he is perhaps our most perfect spectator and that we need no other. Indeed, I've known him almost as long as I've known you. And that must be fifteen years now—or is it twenty? Why, I believe it *is* twenty, if not a little longer!

But the way I've been honored by your friendship, I fancy he's been honored by mine. And though it doesn't make me enjoy his applause one whit the less, you will understand: honor is the motivation for his delight far more than any critical capacity. And he honors himself by never having claimed otherwise. He's known one of the actors personally— me—and for that he will clap the calluses off his hard hands. In a sense, he applauds himself for knowing me at all. Or, perhaps, more generously to us both, he applauds our friendship—more truthfully, he applauds what our friendship once was. And I will also say this (for it particularly pleases me to recall it on those days when he is the only one who claps): though I've often found him charmingly naive, for a man of his class and caliber he is not stupid. And you yourself have said it within my hearing many times: Ignorance is never a sin; *only* stupidity. He was really just a year or two too old to be called a boy—as were you—when I met him.

How?

He was born on a farm some stades to the west of the city. At seventeen or eighteen, he ran away, here to the great port. A few months later, I found him where one finds such boys, loitering on the Bridge of Lost Desire, beside the Old Market outside.

Yes, many—boys and girls both—get there much younger.

My supposition as to why he took so long? I don't know if you got a close look at his face, but you can see by the roughness there that, as a child, the pimples, pustules, and angry pocks that so often mar the cheeks of the young must have been, on him, particularly severe. By the time he came to Kolhari, they were more or less healed over; but from observing their traces I've suspected since the day we met that in full flower they could not have been very prepossessing.

I've just assumed they had something to do with why he stayed at home as long as he did.

Traditionally handsome? No. Even as a boy, he was on the stocky side, though there's always been a good bit of muscle in with it. Once in the city, he took to beer like a fly to honey—I use the many-times repeated phrase because nothing is new in his story there. Often during the first year of our friendship, I suspected that, like so many others, he would end a drunkard or a derelict. Not to mention all the petty illegalities that can catch the young and, in these variegated and violent times, kill. More than once, when, in later years, he would be some months away, I'd imagine that the next time I saw him he'd be carrying the welts of some Imperial whip and with them the story of his year or three at hard labor on some prison detail—that's if I didn't just learn that on some chill night he'd died in a doorway or in a back alley, too cold, too wet, too long exposed to the elements.

But, as you've seen, it didn't happen thus.

I may have even had something to do with that—though life is hard for everyone, and we must not take credit ourselves for the little that others can do with theirs. Rather look instead to whom we can give credit, if not thanks, for what little we have been able to do with our own.

Certainly it would be more generous, if not more accurate, to say that he gave me quite a bit of pleasure, at least for a time. Truly, he was then and is now the most genial of men, if somewhat self-deprecating. And the goodwill he maintains to this day allows me to remember that pleasure and continue to call our relation friendship, if only as my memorial to the friendship it was.

What does he do?

Your interest makes me suspect you might like to meet him, in which case I'll tell you only what he, certainly, would wish me to say, leaving him, in due time, to say more, if and when it pleases him.

Frankly, he doesn't do much.

He lives as best he can, sometimes in Kolhari, sometimes away from it, now and again taking up menial work, though seldom steadily or for any length.

Oh, you *don't* want to meet him?

Well, then: He's a smuggler.

Has been for years.

Yes, that's my friend, as you saw him there. Though after

he quit the bridge—trading one dishonorable profession for another—our friendship reduced to smiles, nods, a few words exchanged on the street or in the market. They were warm and sincere enough words. But on the whole it's been little else. Oh yes, by then he was coming regularly to see me perform. And he'd always stand a bit off—and clap and cheer the loudest. In that he did no differently then from what he does now.

That he still does it, I assume, is his own memorial—if not habit.

I'd say once a year or so—though, more recently, it's been more like once every eighteen months (and believe me, sometimes more than two years have elapsed between)—he waits around after the show to meet me. It happens so infrequently, I always invite him in. He sits where you sit now, leaning forward with his heavy hands hung between his knees. We talk. He smiles. I tell him a little of my life. He tells me a little of his.

I say it's been twenty years?

A *thousand* times we've waved and nodded when both of us have shared the city (and in his profession he is away from it as much as I), but within that same period we've actually sat together for serious conversation less than ten.

In the early days, when I still thought of him as a youngster, on a few of his visits he had his arm around some girl's shoulder—on one occasion two at once. Beaming, he introduced them, showing them off to me, me off to them: his old friend, the wonderful, talented, much applauded, madly and marvelously magical mummer. I found it amusing; and, politely, he didn't stay long, so that in the end it was harmless.

Was it five years ago? Ah, more likely seven! Sitting where you sit now, he told me he'd been living with a widow, just outside Kolhari, by whom he'd had two children. It only made me realize how long it had been since I'd seen him.

I remember glimpsing him out in the audience a few times after that, once with some terribly young and frizzy-haired barbarian tucked under his arm, as freckled as a quail's egg and who, I'm certain, was not his widow at all but the grubbiest of prostitutes from the bridge across the market.

They didn't come in to see me.

I confess I was relieved.

Once, when he dropped by and we went down to the waterfront, where, rather uncharacteristically, he bought me a

mug of cider while he had a few beers, I learned, in the
course of our talk, that he'd collected a wealth of information
about the Liberator—you remember, that political upstart
everyone in the country was talking of ten years back or so,
when his headquarters were raided out by your uncle's? Well,
he knew every battle and skirmish and story and rumor, every
fact and surmise about the man. You wouldn't have thought it
to look at him, but he'd been collecting these tales for years,
keeping them all in his head. And only once had he met him,
he said. But it confirmed for me what I'd dreamily suspected
from the beginning: there really had been something unusual
about him—though no doubt it would never come to anything
that brought him reward in the socially managed markets, old
or new, of need and necessity. What makes a boy interesting
does not make a man interesting. Yet the interesting boy had
become an interesting man: it would be the rare student from
your school who could give you so rich and so textured an
account of his field of study as that man you saw today could
give of his perfectly pointless and obsessive pursuit.

Oh? *Fifteen* years back, you say was the raid on the
Liberator's mansion? Well, you should know. It was right
out there in your neighborhood.

The last time he dropped in, when I asked after his family,
he told me that, oh, he hadn't seen the widow in almost a
year—nor his children; nor hers.

I believe that was when it struck me: by no stretch could I
think of him as a youngster anymore. What in his youth I'd
been able to look on as a handsome solidity had, in the man,
run simply and brutally to fat. You saw—and I think you'll
admit, though I'm twenty years his senior, too—I've kept my
figure a bit better than he. Also, he's losing his hair. Mine,
miraculously, has only thinned. Yes, he's very much a man
and is today as close to middle aged as I am to being simply
and brutally old.

No, I don't really think he's been doing as well of late as
he once did. It pains me to admit it of one who, for so long, I
thought of as a child, but his decline is just another of those
little shocks by which the nameless gods remind us of death.

Thank them all, whoever they are, that I can still mime,
however clumsily, can still sing, however reedily, can still
dance, however stiffly, and can skew each to the other in a
parody of age's failings artfully enough to make an audience
laugh.

Why, yes. I suppose you *could* say that. In a sense, my friendship with him *has* gone more or less the way of my friendship with you. But whatever the cares and concerns in your various undertakings—not to mention my own—you are both doing well enough, in twenty-plus years, to come here to the market on the first day of our return from our triumphant provincial tour and catch our opening performance.

Which is only my too self-centered manner of saying, I suppose, that, in my different ways, I really *do* value you both and know you value me.

Yes, I suppose I too am surprised you haven't seen him before. But then, your lives and concerns have really been quite different, don't you think? After all, you are a prince, a teacher, a philosopher—while he's little more than a thief!

Indeed, I'm sure you're right: many people *wouldn't* be surprised in the least.

Tell you more about him? Well, all right.

2

No doubt that stolid man you saw today came to the city as a boy like many—to the bridge, where such boys come—with the dream of selling his sexual services to some fabulously connected countess, who would take him off to her private rooms at the High Court, where he'd be presented to various nobles at various intimate but elegant suppers. His rough, country charms would be made much of as he amused the lords and ladies with his anecdotes of common life, for he was seldom more than three beers away from being a good, comic raconteur: he had that fine sense of self-mockery that is the social point from which we begin all later self-criticism, without which none survives long on the very bumpy road. No doubt in the palace his rough, if scarred, good looks would cause (he dreamed) a few noble ladies to catch their breath; and perhaps even once, at some great party, into which he'd wandered only by accident, he'd exchange a few lines of banter with the Child Empress herself, whose reign is glittering and glorious, causing waves of jealousy and ire among the lords gathered at the affair, so that, after a month or six of such dalliance, his patroness (who, by this time, hopefully, would have taken up another lover, perhaps a young nobleman whose arrogant ways would make her fondly recall her nights and noons with him) would finally secure him an officer's commission in the Imperial Army, at some fascinating outpost in some exotic mountain hold, sending him on to who-know-what great and gainful adventures. . . .

But with what seemed then, even to him as he looked back on it after only a few months, idiot slowness, he soon accepted in practice if not in theory that such dreams were as insubstantial as moon-flicker on the shallows down below the bridge rail.

In his first days on the Bridge of Lost Desire, so he told me later with a laugh, one man took him home to make love to a perfumed, sultry woman he claimed was his new, young wife. As such work went, he liked that a lot. But it didn't happen again for another three months: next time an older man picked him up, describing his handsome, noble-born mistress, who, he said, was forty—my age, incidentally, when I met him.

Well, he'd always been partial to older women. But when they arrived at the gentleman's large and well-appointed mansion, the woman was out. They waited, sipping wine together and talking for several hours. Then the man apologized to him, paid him half the agreed-on fee, and sent him back.

These two incidents exhausted his professional contacts with women during those first months.

What he actually did when he looked up from the garbage-clotted shallows—what he'd done in the few days before the first of these encounters, what he did in the many days between them, and what he did daily after—was to sell his services, often for distressingly little money and more times than not simply for a meal and a place to sleep, to a succession of artisans and clerks and laborers and merchants and army officers and market vendors and wagon drivers and still others who did not want anyone to know what they did, all of them men.

Though very occasionally they passed across it, with their parasols and paramours, their secretaries and serving maids, in search of some rare item rumored by an acquaintance to have been sighted in the market beyond, titled ladies did not, as a rule, stop on the bridge to purchase pleasures—not in *this* part of Nevèrÿon.

I had been with the traveling troop here only a few years, and you probably recall that, in those days before my current comic eminence, mostly I played for the other dancers and actors who worked on our portable platform, coaching them in rehearsals and helping to devise the skits.

Our actual meeting?

No doubt as I passed across the bridge from the Spur to the more commercial neighborhoods of the city, I'd seen him among the loitering hustlers of both sexes, now sharing beer with one of the other boys, now calling to one of the women: "—Hey, little gillyflower, I see how you're looking at me!"

And I'd thought what a man such as I was would likely think (of him and, indeed, many others): One time I would find him rather attractive in a vulgar sort of way. (Should I approach him. . . .) At another, I'd decide: No, he was not my type at all . . . It would be silly even to smile. And at least once I saw an elderly grain-seller stop to talk with him, and heard him call the man "Papa."

Clearly he had gone with that mercantile gentleman before; though if "Papa" were a nickname of his own devising or part of his client's previous personal instruction, I never did have the temerity to ask—though at that moment I convinced myself I had really been about to speak, that given my preferences he was, certainly, the most attractive young man on the bridge. What a fool I'd been, my momentary jealousy told me, to hesitate this long in making my interest known!

Those who never browse in the commercial markets of sex assume that we, who do, shop there in order to escape the wounds, self-recriminations, and hurts to the soul associated with timidity, opportunities missed through hesitation, and the simple pains from rejection that plague those who limit sex purely to the results of social encounter. They feel a moral superiority through the sufferings that they have agreed to bear and which they are sure we avoid by barter, convinced their social courtship agonies chasten them in ways we can never know and—like youngsters' plunges into cold mountain streams—harden them to life. They do not know commercial possibilities in no way abolish such pains and hurts, but rather add to them a certain sting that, if anything, makes them the more excruciating, the more gnawing. The commercial only multiplies the opportunities to risk such hurts again.

Oh, yes! A day after I saw him with his gray-haired old man, I passed him once more, only to realize that it *was* he when I was a step beyond—by now my mind was that deeply on other things!

But one evening when the clouds were high and yellow and the sun was like a copper gong half-hidden among them—for some reason, there were only a third as many people out on the bridge as usual—as I was crossing I saw him, naked, leaning back against the wall, an elbow either side of him on the ledge, a drinking skin on the stone beside him, one foot up on the wall below.

I looked.

He smiled.

I thought to look away and didn't.

As I passed, still looking, suddenly he thrust out his hard farm laborer's hand to me and said, simply:

—Hello! How you doing?

We shook.

I stayed to tell him; to ask him the same, while he took his skin down and offered me warm beer; and I, who markedly prefer cider, accepted.

Oh, first there was a bit of small talk as we leaned together against the wall. I know now he did not think himself handsome and took a boyish delight when *anyone* stopped for him at all. But the sexual worker who can evince sincere pleasure at the coming of a customer seasons his or her fare with a rare spice! Five or ten sentences into our exchange, and I brought out some frank and specific questions as to money and positions. (If I were taken at all, I wanted to be taken as a serious customer.) About both he gave reasonable, frank, and specific answers.

That settled, I offered to refill his skin with drink.

About that he was grateful.

Since then I have known boys years younger, soliciting years longer, who merely wanted to do the deed, take their pay, and go. Today, I would not fault them. But the fact is, a mere five years before that warm afternoon, I would have sworn to anyone who asked that *I* would never pay for sex! In my own way I was as new to buying as he was to selling. Oh, we had both bought and sold before. That is not the level of innocence I am trying to establish. The surprise to me now, however, was that he was not so experienced that he took my offer of a little sociability mixed in with our transaction as a sign of what, eventually, we would both learn it was: in terms of any continuing monetary relation, I would be a rather poor-paying customer.

But perhaps another observer, knowledgeable in the ways of sexual commerce, might say that our friendship, if I can call it that, began with a little more promise than most. I'd recently gotten a small windfall; from what private party, where I'd performed brilliantly, I no longer remember—*was* it yours?

Now, at that point it would have to have been. Ah, you must be right! I'd completely forgotten.

I'm embarrassed to go on and let you know where the moneys your uncle so generously—

Oh, of course! Of course, I understand—after all this time, how could it mean anything to you?

Well, then! From your family's most generous fees I not only brought him his few mugs of beer that evening and fed him, but I gave him some coins for himself and paid a week's rent on a cheap room where I let him stay.

After I'd enjoyed him, I returned to pass the rest of the night in the wagon.

Mornings I would show up at his door and knock. Sleepily he would call me in. There, sitting on the bed, we would talk.

Or I would talk—for the morning hours were not his most communicative, though he was always certain to make me promise to come see him again the next day, as if the simple sound of my nattering on about this and that, if not the physical exchange between us, comforted him. He would listen to me or, at any rate, pretend to listen.

And the truth was, whatever he thought of our sex, he liked me: it was the first time in months he'd slept three nights running under the same roof.

I brought him to visit our wagons. To give you some idea how provincial he was: though he knew the bridge to twenty meters around it at each end, until he came to see us perform he'd never walked farther than the fountain at the middle of the market. He did not even know that on the other side of the square we have traditionally set up our wagons since we began to call at this city!

Once I let him watch our skits from the privacy of the prop cart.

Ah, and after that he talked!

At some point during the performance, he'd glanced aside to see one of our dragons leering at him from the clutter—like the one you're sitting under...?

Oh, it startled him!

Well, with his great grin, if he told me about it once, he told me about it twenty times over the next week.

—What a fool I am, he'd say, to be scared by such a toy. But from his smile as he said it, you knew he'd never known a happier fright.

I often asked him about his sexual history—indeed, I told him tales of mine. Yes, he had his own sexual quirks. I believe it was summer women with—

But then I have quirks too, about which he was always obliging. (—No, come on. You like it. You said so. *Do* it! You see, I want *you* to have a good time! I did not know then just how rarely I might expect to hear that from such a young man, and so, in my way, I took him for granted quite as much as he took me.) Also there were several times when I was sure my particular peculiarities had become common knowledge from one end of the bridge to the other, thanks to his banter with the other hustlers—only to discover it had never even occurred to him to mention them, from nothing more than a natural reticence which would have done honor to someone far more nobly born. Therefore I see no need to detail the particularities of his tastes. Suffice it to say, they were harmless, even charming, and I was touched that he chose to confide them to me.

At the time, you understand, he'd only gone to bed with seven women in his life—the first six of whom were sundry country lasses and ladies, and the last of whom had been the wife of that early customer on the bridge. When we were talking of this in his room one morning, I declared:

—What a coincidence! That's the same number of women I myself have bedded in my forty-odd years! And here I'm more than twice your age.

Like so many youths who drift from country to city, when not thinking of some titled lady (or lord) to keep him in lackadaisical luxury, he would daydream, now and again, of a son and a wife—in that order—and perhaps several adoring daughters with them. That, he would explain, is what he needed to settle down. All of them would live together on some small farm that he would manage to own, a miniature, I finally came to believe, of the one on which he'd lived and labored so thanklessly before he'd come to Kolhari.

At which point I would quip:

—Then all you'll need is a job that will take you away from it at least eight months of the year; and *all* your problems'll be solved.

He would laugh. But I wonder if, later, with his country widow, he remembered my advice; for certainly, those many years on, he seemed to have taken it.

Oh, in those days with me he had his bouts of homesickness. They troubled him greatly; I listened as sympathetically as a man with other concerns could, till finally I suggested:

—Then *why* not simply go home? At least for a visit.

—Oh, no. My home is much too far away. It took me four days of steady walking to come from there to the city.

How would he ever cross such a distance again?

I pointed out that what one can walk in four days, one can ride in an oxcart in a day and a half. Also, though I had never visited his village, I'd heard its name before and knew that it simply was not that far off. If it had taken him four days to walk, that was because he'd probably been lost at least a third of the time. But supporting him for a week, I was beginning to feel responsible for him, a feeling that, first, I did not enjoy and, second (not to slight your uncle's occasional early munificence), I could not afford on my ordinary mummer's earnings from spectators' donations at our day-to-day fare.

On the night before his week's rent was to run out, therefore, I proposed to call for him before sunup next day, take him to the market end of the Bridge of Lost Desire, find a wagoner finished with his morning deliveries who was returning west, and pay an iron coin or so for his day-and-a-half's ride home. Just to show you how naive he was, he hadn't even known you could do that. Today, of course, it's an established institution, but at the time I don't believe the empress had yet set up the passenger shelter that's been rebuilt twice in the last decade. You just had to go and ask around till you found a wagon going where you wanted— though enough folks did it, anyway.

Anyway.

The next dawn I got myself up from my cluttered bed, went to his room, rolled him sleepily out, and we walked to the market. The second driver I asked pointed us to a third, who hailed us heartily as we strolled up. A pleasant and blustery fellow, in my memory, he was then the spit of my erstwhile friend today. Sure, he'd take the young man to his village. His journey passed right by it.

—Good. I said, as my friend climbed up into the cart to grip the back and sides, blinking about at the market square still dim in the summer dawn. You'll be there by tomorrow afternoon, I called as I handed two coins to the driver.

—Tomorrow? the driver demanded. We'll be there by tonight! and returned me a coin. You've overpaid me, and I'm a good and honest laborer! It made me smile and I wondered how this further comfirmation of the physical nearness of his home struck my young friend, who blinked, still red-eyed, in the back of the wagon, as they rolled off by the fountain where the first of the stalls was only then being set out.

His room, of course, was paid for till sundown and supper that day—a custom I miss in these times when innkeepers expect you out and off by noon. If I recall, I was back there an hour later with another . . . friend. This one was a little older, a little more experienced. At the time I thought myself far more attached to him than the young man I'd just sent off to the country. We carried on lubriciously till I realized I was late for my performance—a sin I have committed only three times in my life. And today, though I have tried many times, I cannot recall the name—much less the face—for whom, then, I committed it.

3

He was gone some three or four weeks. However or whenever he came back I'm not sure, for he had the tact and good sense *not* to look me up immediately on his return. He had interpreted my sending him off, however friendly I'd been about it, in the terminal sense I had intended it, a sensitivity, I confess, I admired him for, and which no doubt eventually influenced

me to see him again. Was it a month later that I glimpsed
with some surprise someone I thought was he turning onto the
bridge? A day or two after that, as I was crossing, I nearly
bumped into him—though he was deep in conversation with a
barbarian youngster and an older man who, no doubt, wanted
them both; he didn't see me, or pretended he didn't.

I thought it politic not to interrupt.

A few days later, I was on my way to join my fellow
mummers at a street carnival in another neighborhood where
we were to perform. Some had left with the wagons in the
morning to set up. I was to join them that afternoon. I recall,
I didn't *have* to cross the Bridge of Lost Desire to get there; I
could have gone the few streets north to the perfectly unexcep-
tional overpass that leads to those ethnic enclaves in the city
where, on carnival days, our theatrical talents are so in
demand. It was just habit, sedimented no doubt by past
pleasures, that took me over the bridge.

He was leaning there in what I'd come to think of as His
Spot.

We smiled; and while I was wondering if I should stop to
talk, I found myself slowing.

—Hello! How you doing?

For a moment I wondered if he actually remembered me:

—Fine. How did your trip go?

—Fine. Fine . . . ! It was great! Fine!

He'd seen his aunt. Yes, he knew who I was. No, his
mother hadn't been as pleased to see him as he'd hoped.
There'd been some problems before he'd left that, though
he'd mentioned some of them to me before, he'd all but
forgotten till, really, the cart had pulled up by those familiar
fields. Still, he'd had a couple of good, or at least interesting,
evenings with his village friends. But as he talked, every now
and again he would glance at me curiously. Did we discuss it
that afternoon, or did I only have the strong feeling that it was
now known? Today I couldn't say for sure. But from somewhere I gained the conviction that it was clear to him that the
vast distance to his home over which he had tramped for four
aimless days to reach Kolhari was not that of stade after stade;
rather it was a distance of mind, of temperament, created by
his urban education even in so vulgar a version as he had
received it during his handful of months on the bridge. And
that was far vaster than the one he'd imagined he'd crossed by
foot or by wagon. In comparison, save by some machinations

of the unnamed gods beyond both his powers and mine to conceive, the true distance could not be retraversed.

That was why he was back.

—Where you going, today? he asked as I was about to leave.

I explained about the street fair.

—Take me with you? he asked. After all (and he stepped from the wall to look down at himself, naked on the bridge flags in the warm autumn evening), how long can I hang around here, shaking this old turkey neck, hoping some guy with bad breath and no teeth is hungry enough to buy my turkey milk.

—I have work to do there.

—Oh, come on, he said. Take me. I won't be in the way.

—Well, I suppose you can come. But I made it clear, as he fell in beside me, that there would be nothing monetary in it for him. He made it equally clear: he'd heard of the various Kolhari festivals since before he'd come to the city, but he'd been afraid to go to any of them by himself. If he had a friend, like me, he wouldn't be scared. And he couldn't pass up the chance to go with somebody actually part of the festivities.

When we reached the crowded streets with their colorful revelers, the grills set out on the corners with their spitted lambs, the drunken singers, the arguing parents, the racing children, the colored hangings roped below the windows, he stayed very close to me. The neighborhood (to him) was full of foreigners; and foreigners were what, at home, he'd been taught to fear.

Once we reached our wagons, for the first minutes he simply stood by the back corner, blinking and staring a lot. Of course there was still more setting up to do, and I turned to lend a hand. Minutes later, I looked up to see him suddenly let go of the wheel whose rim he stood clutching and throw himself into our preparations as if he were one of our troop, now asking some groom, now one of the propmen, what he could carry here or there, what he might fetch, what he might hold, and even the Leading Lady if there was anything he might go bring her—with a blown kiss she sent him running off after something or other, which, in only a little longer than one might have assumed, he returned with.

I admit I was somewhat wary of all this, but the others

seemed to take to him, and soon they were sending him there and here, with this load or that.

His labors clearly left him braver. Now, as the day wore on, he would actually go off by himself for a while, and an hour later I would see him, from the platform, as I played my gongs and cymbals, threading through the crowd, munching on this or that bit of carnival fare, given him by whom or pilfered from where, I would not presume to guess.

Eating, watching, grinning, he would wink at me.

And, indeed, I would grin down at him—and go on playing.

That night when the flares burned low and it was time to dismantle the platform and take down the lamps and lanterns, again he threw himself in with our work. Once I saw him nearly slip with a plank of wood balanced on his shoulder. A little later, I saw him unsteady with a load of masks in his arms. Somehow in the course of the evening he had managed to get satisfactorily drunk—but then, in such conviviality where strangers offer you drink practically at every corner, that was not surprising. And it certainly had not dampened his energy.

He stayed with me that night in my wagon, the two little dancers with whom I then shared it having found some sailors after the performance who wanted to take them to see their ship on the waterfront by the moon. (*They* didn't get back till two days later and received quite a dressing down from the Director.) We had rather drunken sex in the littered dark. One or the other of us, I suspect, fell asleep in the midst of it.

Once, in the wagon, he woke up, somewhat disoriented, and made me lead him, unsteadily, outside into the surprising moonlight. He kept on repeating, still drunk, that he'd *heard* something. Then, with his head down, his feet wide, and his hand against the crumbling daub of some dilapidated wall, he began to urinate—in amazing quantities, with astonishing force—wetting his feet, my feet, splattering his knees, soaking his own hands, making almost as much of a mess of himself as if he had never left the bed.

The next morning he was up, however, standing out in the quiet morning, only a little squint-eyed.

We saw the wagons off, on their way back to the market. Then we walked together, the long way, toward the bridge. Halfway across I told him:

—I must cut you loose here. It's been fun. And I don't have *too* much of a headache.

—I do. He grinned at me, his young beard, unbrushed that morning, looking as grizzled below his rough cheeks as one of his elderly client's. I'm going down under the bridge and sleep for a while in the shade, he told me. (I was planning to crawl right into bed as soon as I reached the wagons back in the market square.) Hey, how about letting me hold a couple of coins? Oh, I don't mean for last night. I wouldn't charge you for *that*. That's free. But just for all the work I did? For you, and everybody?

What could I say?

—We get together soon? he called after me, as I left him, standing there with the iron in his hand. The bridge was quiet that morning, and I had the momentary feeling that his voice, with its all too expected proposition, echoed not only from end to end but throughout the entire city.

—Yes, of course!

I believe I also called back some tentative time for meeting him the next day (—I'll see you at about . . .), an appointment that one or the other of us didn't keep.

Of course.

And whose party was it a week later? No, not yours that time—because I recall distinctly I rehearsed with that marvelous, messy woman who composed the wonderful music that made me, finally, decide to give up tootling to become a serious mimic. And *we* never performed together in *your* gardens. Yes, that's right. It was for your friend, the baronine. You were present at that elegant afternoon affair? Well, that's certainly possible.

At any rate, it was probably that same evening, when I was returning from Neveryóna to the market, over the bridge:

—Hello! How you doing?

A few more beers. A few more coins. Another room. In another inn, which another boy had told me was somewhat cheaper. And as I sat at the edge of his bed over the next few days, our conversations ranged back over pretty much the same topics as they had the last time.

The son.

The wife.

The farm.

—I was married, I decided to tell him one evening. Once. For almost eight years, actually. Before I became a mummer.

Or, at least before I permanently joined the troop. I had two sons and a daughter. Ah, what a good father I was! I've never worked harder at any role in my life. Well, that's finished with now, and though it may be my finest performance, I wouldn't give a minute more to it, that I tell you.

He laughed with me; but he was curious:

—What about your fooling around? Did you do it back then? With men, I mean?

—Certainly. Probably a good deal more than I do now. After all, I was young. About your age, actually. At least when I married her.

—Did she know? I mean about you and . . . men?

—Of course!

—You told her?

—Well before we were married. What sane man would ally himself with a woman and not let her know something about himself as serious as that?

—How did she feel about it?

—At first it rather excited her. (From the way he grinned, I knew that even with his seven women he'd already learned that anomalous truth about the complex engine of sexual interaction.) After the children came, I suspect the topic began to bore her.

—Did the kids know?

—Toward the unnecessarily ugly end, the two who were old enough must have suspected. A lot of things were yelled that had nothing to do with anything save how deeply they could wound. You know, my wife was quite talented herself. Still lives out in Yenla'h. At least I think she does; it's not on our summer itinerary. Oh, she could make anything: houses, pots, stage sets. Also, she was rather an adventurous, if moody, woman. But I was fond of her; and most of the time I treated her as such. With me, that involves a certain amount of honesty. I suspect it does with most.

—Then why aren't you together?

The most difficult part to understand for him, I think, was that the reasons for our separation (Oh, final happiness!) were simply those that split any pair who each finds that the company and habits of the other reduces her or him to a sniveling, furious, pitiable, and paralyzed beast no longer capable of acting like anyone's notion of a reasonable man or woman as the gods first formed and molded us.

—*How* many women have you been to bed with? he asked.

And before I could answer, he begun to tell me a clearly preposterous story about a sexual triumph he'd had with a beautiful woman he'd slipped off with for a while that night at the carnival. He hadn't told me before, you see, for fear I might be jealous. But he hadn't drunk that much, yet. So of course once he'd gotten her down in a pile of leaves behind some old shack away from the merrymakers, he'd come too fast and—In the middle of his tale, however, it was as if he suddenly remembered we too had entered into a certain arena of honesty, and he halted. Well, actually, he said, he'd *seen* a woman in passing, older than he, ordinary enough in other respects, but with a certain... Well, she was just leaning against a wall and eating from a netted sack of fruit at one of the crowded corners. Standing across the busy way from her, he'd considered going up and trying to talk with her, hoping possibly to bring her to the wagon, where he'd intended to ask me to let him fuck her while *I* stood guard outside.

That's why he'd come back and worked so hard!

He had left her and returned to look at her several times. She'd apparently stood there quite awhile, as though she were waiting for something. (—Almost as though she were listening for something, I believe is what he said with a moment of poetry to his pensive look that now and again would illuminate his most work-a-day accountings.) But he still had not been able to bring himself to speak. Eventually, on the fifth or sixth time he returned, she was gone—alone or off with someone else, he did not know.

—Like the fool I am, he told me, shaking his head, I couldn't say anything.

For both of us, then, the answer was still seven.

I don't remember which of us asked the next obvious question: Well, how many *men* have you slept with? (Oh, it *must* have been me!) We sat on his bed in the tiny room with the bare walls and sloping thatch, trying to figure. Twenty-five? Fifty? (Did I throw such absurdly low numbers out only to tease?) Well, he'd come to Kolhari with half a dozen from his childhood play on the farm, and he'd seen a hundred go by months ago: he remembered passing the twenty-five mark in his first *week* on the bridge.

Laughing, we agreed that for both of us it was certainly high in the hundreds. I was forty. He was not yet twenty. I wonder why I felt obliged to tease:

—Well, then, you're just like me. Obviously you like

men's bodies better than you like women's. *I* certainly do!
Always have. Always will.

—No! he protested. I like women's bodies *far* more than I
like men's. Men's bodies? That's only a kind of play. I don't
take them seriously. I only go with them when women aren't
around. And I want to get paid for it when I do.

—Well! and I had to laugh. I *thought* such things once
myself, though I never really felt them. When I sleep with a
woman, it's only thinking about a man that allows me to
enjoy myself. Which thinking I did very well, thank you,
twice a week for eight years. Of course, too often when one
does go to bed with a man, one has to think of *another* man.
Really, it *does* go on. What do you think about when you
sleep with a woman? Or a man—me—for that matter?

—Nothing, he said a little wonderingly.

—To be sure, I said. he doesn't think of anything.

—Well, sometimes, he admitted at last, a man and a
woman doing it together . . . but while you were married, you
still did it with men?

—Who do you think I was thinking about that let me enjoy
my wife? My young friend, I say it, and I mean it: I like
men's bodies for the inspiration, stimulation, and relief of lust
far more than I like women's. And going through the proper
nuptial rituals with a woman, as your village prescribes them,
will not change that if that is, indeed, your case. Also (and
here I frowned askance at him with one lowered brow), for
two who *feel* so differently, don't you think it's odd that what
we've *done* is so much the same?

That only made him protest the more. Indeed, as he argued
with me over the next quarter hour he got quite angry. Now
and again he actually threatened me. I only pooh-poohed him
the more. Finally, I declared:

—Well, whatever you do, and like, and feel, and think,
you must learn to accept them all and live with whatever
contradictions between them the nameless gods have overlooked in your making, like cracks in an imperfect bit of
ceramic still pleasing in its overall shape. Certain strains,
certain tasks, certain uses one does not impose upon such
pieces. But everyone has them. Learning what they are is,
no doubt, why we were put here.

Though by now I suppose I had a somewhat worried look,
for he'd already overturned the bed during one outburst and
had several times struck the wall with his fist.

—That's the only thing that matters, I went on. Calm down, now. Our wagons leave the city tomorrow. Let me buy you a farewell meal tonight.

I took him to eat at a waterfront inn where tables were set on finely broken shells and lamps hung from the poles overhead and you could look down the docks at men walking through the evening, some holding up flares, some rolling barrows in from the side streets, some loading bales off the boats:

—Have you ever been here before?

—No . . . His eyes were big with the waterside wonders, and he clutched his mug in both hands.

—Well, then, it's about time.

We ate a meal and drank a lot. It was the first in all his time here he'd even *seen* the docks—in our port city so famous for its waterfront. The ships and the confusion around us scared him a bit, I think; and excited him; and made him grin.

The argument earlier, back at the inn, seemed forgotten. Everything here spoke of travel, with its commercial support not so vividly contaminated by lust and madness as it was in his part of the city. It gave the waterfront an excitement, a purity he'd never known in the infamous quarter that had been till now, for him, almost all of Kolhari. In some ways, however, I'm sure that realization of the greater vastness to this city, which had already educated him well beyond anything he'd even dreamed of knowing on his village farm, deeply unsettled him.

That night in his room I left him, sprawled on his bed, as drunk as I'd ever seen him.

That, and perhaps something unsettling I'd felt myself, put all thoughts of any farewell intimacies from my mind; although, for a moment, I think, as he swayed in his dark room, demonic in the light from the clay lamp I had just set on the rickety corner table, blinking and bleary-eyed, he expected it or even wanted it (do I flatter myself?)—before he closed his eyes, slowly, to collapse, half on the floor and half on the bed, where I gave him a few tugs to straighten him.

I blew out the lamp and left.

The next day, of course, our parti-colored wagons rattled away from the city. He was certainly not up to see us off. With the kind of hangover such a drunk leaves, I'm sure he spent that day sick in his room. The day after that, his rent ran out at the inn. So he must have returned to the bridge.

But somewhere between the time I left him and the time he was back on that walled stone walk above the water, so I learned later, my friend went mad.

Yes, just like that.

It was a quiet, inward sort of madness. Most of the first day he ambled from one end of the bridge to the other and back. The only way his actions differed from before was that, now, when the other hustlers spoke to him, to call hello, or to suggest they go there or here together on this or that mildly questionable pursuit, he walked by them, not speaking, sometimes with an angry, startled look. When men glanced at him, he did not grin and step up to begin talking with a hand on their shoulder, nor stop to lean beside them at the wall, with a comment about a passing whore. He walked to the end of the bridge.

He turned.

He walked back.

Mistaking him for a potential customer, some tired prostitute called:

—Come on, darling. We'll go out tonight! (They always say "tonight," even when they accost you at ten in the morning.) But he did not fall into the usual banter, about how *she* should pay *him* since his services were *clearly* superior.

He walked on.

He walked the bridge most of the night.

Toward morning, he stopped for a minute, then, a few steps on, stopped some minutes more. Finally he sat down with his back against the stone rail, his mouth wide for breath, sometimes closing his eyes tightly, sometimes opening them in the dark.

He woke to the day's traffic raging about him. Getting to his feet, aching and unsteady, he began to walk again. The usual bridge voices—wagoners cursing, pedestrians chattering, pimps and prostitutes shouting to one another—had been joined by tens, hundreds, thousands of others. It seemed he could now hear every voice in Kolhari reverberating along this stone strip. Angry voices, cooing voices, wheedling voices, greedy voices, bewildered voices, cajoling voices all knitted and nattered in argument and antiphon, a tangle of altercation and contention, haggling over commerce, lust, madness, travel, as if there were no other topics in the city, all of them centering on this bridge, all of them on him on it, as he walked from one end to the other.

He saw an apple an ox's or a camel's hoof had squashed a section of, before it had rolled or been kicked against the wall. He picked that up and ate it. Later a parsnip fell from the tailgate of a wagon as a wheel jarred on loose paving. When it was still on the ground at his fifth trip back and forth, he picked it up and, with the gutter dirt and all that had darkened one side, ate that too. He didn't eat too much else because there was little else lying around, and because the sound of his own teeth and jaws and saliva and the food bits sloshing and grinding as he chewed and swallowed nearly obliterated the voices. And he was sure by now that at the core of this contestatory hubbub some secret was being discussed that, if he could only overhear it, would net him untold wealth, power, and fame—enough to make the empress and all her ministers at the High Court of Eagles grovel before him.

He ate little

He slept little.

For much of the time he did not look very different from any other madman you might see ambling over the Bridge of Lost Desire. Sometimes, in his effort to listen, to keep his step in rhythm with the voices, he would clench his jaw so tightly that his face and shoulders would shake. His steps became, then, staggers. When he bumped into someone, he turned and stared, astonished, bewildered, and furious at them for distracting him from his infinitely important task; sometimes he would curse them through gritted teeth—at least in the first days. Later, when he bumped someone (which happened more and more rarely, as people avoided him more and more widely), he did not notice.

What this madness was, or where it came from, or what lay at its center only the nameless gods can know. Certainly not I. Possibly it had no cause save the exhaustions of his life, myself a part of them, my former efforts at friendship and my various moments of selfishness all equal in that they had only helped to wear away whatever in him had till then been able to endure. What I can say, however, just as I can say it began: after fifteen, or twenty, or twenty-five days, the madness stopped.

Naked on the ground by the bridge rail, he woke for the fifth time in fifteen minutes—or five hours.

Three men stood talking beside him. One with a shaved head had dark wings of paint around his eyes and wore jewels at his ears. One could have been some tall, merchant's clerk, with his short, drab tunic, his long, thin hands. The third was a squat workman, a hammer hanging from a noose on his belt the way a soldier might wear a sword. His brown hands and naked feet were gray with rock dust.

—Do you remember, cried the bald one with the makeup, how Vanar used to come to the bridge here, to pick up the boys?

—Sure, declared the workman. I used to see him all the time! People talked about him down here. Why didn't he take me, I always wondered. But he never did.

—Oh, *there's* the kind he liked. Like that. The bald one pointed at the young man sitting against the wall. I tell you, the filthier, the crazier they were, the more he wanted them. Just let one of those wander, dirty and deranged, onto the bridge, and he'd be off with him in a minute—

—No! countered the workman. That wasn't what he was after. *His* eyes were all for the yellow-headed barbarian scamps hustling down at the market end. (The workman's own hair was black as raw oil, bubbling up from some swampy spill.) Oh, he might take a poor beggar like this one here for a meal or a drink, or maybe help him to a doorway out of the rain—I've seen him do that. But he only wanted the little yellow-haired southerners. I saw him with enough of them, going and coming.

—At least once I saw him take a plump little moutain girl off from here, said the clerk; though he didn't look southern, his accent was, somewhat surprisingly, barbaric. (Still slumped against the wall, my friend glanced up—but only with his eyes.) He was a fine man, Vanar. A character, yes. But I've always thought that must be the real taste of such a man. Perhaps he took a boy now and then. But I'm sure he only did it either to make people talk—or because he truly wanted to help. Everyone speaks of him as a good man. It's a sad comment, I know. But he wouldn't have the reputation he does, unless he liked his girls. And there're more than enough of them out here. The boys are always about, but they're a very small part of the business.

—Oh, no, my dears, declared the bald man in the eye makeup. I remember both of you, and you were only visitors to the bridge in those days. I was a daily denizen and a fully paid-up guild member in the sisterhood. I saw more of this overground cesspool than either of you. And I know what he went after, believe me.

The workman chuckled and said:

—The way Vanar would carry on down here used to make me laugh. I knew he was rich, sure. But you could have sat me down and picked me up when I learned he was a count.

—A count, my dear? the made-up one declared. That man was in line to be a suzerain! "Count," you say? You must have heard people call her "The Countess." The way she went on here was a terror, as if there were no Neveryóna waiting for her back home!

—Well, observed the clerk, when you are as rich as Lord Vanar was, there are some things you don't *have* to worry about.

—This bridge has seen it all, declared the bald one, touching ringed fingers to both jeweled ears. And it has seen more than I'll ever tell you. Do you remember...

But, walking again, they were out of earshot.

That was when my friend, sitting against the bridge wall, realized he had heard only the three of them. He had no idea, nor would he ever know, who this "Vanar" was. (Though it's good to see *you* smile at his name. Indeed, it *might* have been Vanar they spoke of back then; but it could have been any number of others who would have made you smile as broadly.) They had made sense; he had heard them. Save a donkey cart, trundling by across the walkway, it was quiet. Whatever great secret he'd been listening for, it had been uttered.

Oh, it had turned out some profoundly trivial, self-evident homily like: *You are only yourself, with your name, and nothing more.* No ... that wasn't it. (When he tried to tell me later, he actually seemed surprised that he still couldn't remember it, as if his whole reason for recounting the occurrence to me had been to prompt its full return.) It was much simpler. It was so simple that, once heard, even with having forgotten it, there was little pull to think about it any longer. But at its utterance, the extraneous babble had ceased.

He raised his hand from where his fingertips touched his shins. His knuckles were black with dirt. He turned his arm over. His palms were only slightly lighter, and their crevices bore black lines as if someone who could write had inked them.

He touched his cheek. Dry skin against dry skin—a foul

dryness, too. It let him know his face was probably as dirty as his hands. In the filth over his calf he saw several small sores—and a larger one on his ankle where, he remembered vaguely, a day or so back someone had pushed him against a cart wheel, and he'd scraped himself to the bone.

He got slowly to his feet, hips aching, shoulders sore, knees stiff. One nostril was raw inside. As he gained his balance, loose mucus trickled into the hairs on his upper lip. Limping a little, he walked to the bridge's end—and kept walking, into the loud market.

4

Most people hurrying around him did not look. But now and again, one or another at a distance would stare till he looked back. By the nameless gods, he thought, what kind of half-beast, half-man have I become? And grinned; and walked on, making for the public fountain.

A man-high stone in the market's center, the fountain spewed water chattering from the natural cleft at the top, down into a carved basin—and how many times have you yourself, and how many others, stopped to drink there, if only on your way to, or on your return from, our performance?

He took his place in a line of five. In front of him a young woman with a green rag bound on her unevenly cropped hair glanced back and pulled forward, shrinking the distance between herself and the tarry-handed sewer-worker before her, while the fig vendor joining the line behind, his basket near empty and strung round his neck to rest on his hip, hung back, not actually staring.

He closed his eyes a moment, took a breath, and grinned again.

The woman in the head-rag drank hurriedly, left quickly.

He stepped up to the basin, plunged his hands into the spring water, and doused his hair and face. His naked flesh drew into bumps, as if feathers there had been plucked from

pullet skin. He sloshed water under his armpits, rubbing the
hair there with his fists. He sluiced freezing water over his
arms, turning them this way and that, working at the black
and wrinkled nut of his elbow, at the thick and scaly knob of
his wrist. He splashed his neck, his chest, his chin. He
rubbed his groin, his hips, his buttocks.

His legs were streaked with mud.

Brick swirled with dirty wash.

Once he glanced behind. The fig vendor, two more women,
and another man still waited for him, nervously. Behind
them, a fat market porter muttered something bitter, turned,
and stalked off with his brooms over his shoulder, to disap-
pear between the stalls of garden implements and spices on
the left, cooking utensils and honeys to the right.

He went on washing.

Finally he leaned his buttocks against the rock and, with his
wet forefinger, first on his left foot, then on his right,
scrubbed between one toe and another, now and again scooping
out another handful of water that ran down his leg as he
cleaned off the ligaments of his feet. (The fig vendor gave up
and went; one of the braver women behind moved in to take
her drink and, when he'd started to reach in the bowl, gave
him a harsh look so that he pulled his hand back and waited
for her to finish.) Wet, shivering, he stood up and splashed
through the muddy puddle he'd left before the fountain where
the brick has worn down to gray-green stone around the
inefficient drains. He walked to the market's edge and loped
twice about the whole square, sometimes flapping his elbows
to let his flanks and underarms dry.

Then he walked onto the bridge.

Two youngsters, one a barbarian with whom he'd once
traded tricks, called to him:

—Hey!

He nodded, waved back to them—struck by a sudden and
ungainly sense of the community in this awkward spot, where
all the city's fragments jammed together without quite filling
the space, so that a certain play in the engine of the port
was apparent here, a shock, a shiver that was doubtless felt
from the real and resounding waterfront to the elegant and
unimaginable High Court.

—Hello, there! That was the grain-seller, who always took
him to the warehouse five streets off, where the late sun fell
through the roof chinks onto the loft's scattered straw.

He swung around, grinning, went up to the old man, who regarded him strangely, and put his hand on the shoulder of the brown tunic:

—You'll be around for a while? he asked. I'll be back in a few minutes, Papa. You stay here, I'll be back, now—

—Well, I don't know...the grain-seller said. What was the matter with you last week, anyway? I came by here and I saw you—at least I *think* it was you...

—You wait for me, Papa! He pressed the grain-seller's arm. You wait for me, now. I know I don't look too good right through here. But I'll be back. Papa, let me hold a couple of coins—no, don't give me anything! (The elderly man had started to move away.) You just wait for me. We'll have a good time. Down where you used to take me. In the warehouse, right? I'll be back! He turned and sprinted toward the bridge's far end.

—Where you hurrying, darling?

He looked around at the listless voice to see a thin woman, her eyes winged with paint and a colored scarf wound high on her ribs just under her darkly aureoled breasts.

—You want some fun tonight? she went on, not even looking.

—Sure, little gillyflower! He stepped up to her. How much do you want to give me for the best piece *you'll* ever have?

—You? The woman frowned nearsightedly at him. Me, give *you* anything? I'm not even *talking* to you! I'm not even *thinking* of you! I was addressing another gentleman entirely.

—Think about me, little flower. Think about me and weep! I may not look like much, but I could give you a time to tell your grandchildren about. No, and he narrowed an eye at her, you couldn't afford my prices.

The woman made a sound between a laugh and snuffle and turned to call to another man passing:

—Hello, darling? How you doing?

Shaking his head and pleased with himself, he hurried to the other end of the bridge.

A few streets down the Pavē was a yard with a cistern, where, with ropes still attached, a few ceramic buckets were always left near the wall. Though he'd taken off the surface grime, the dirt felt as if it had somehow worked into, if not through, his whole body; as determined as he was to be rid of it, he was not sure if water could wash it away.

At the cistern's wall, he chose a chipped pail, lowered it,

felt it hit, then bob on the slack; he waved the rope wide till the lopsided container filled and sank. Then he hauled it, sloshing, up beside the iron staples, caught the bucket's bottom with one hand, hefted it high, and dumped cold water over his head.

It seemed even colder than the fountain's gush—because he was already half dry.

He hauled up another bucket.

And another.

Somewhere around the fifth, with his mouth wide and water running into it from his moustache, drops falling from his lashes to his cheeks, trickles from his beard running down his chest, he paused.

At the other side of the cistern, a heavy girl, with her wet jar dripping onto the cistern wall, was just looking away from him with a serious expression. She wore a rough robe. Her arms were lightly freckled. Shaking water from her fingertips, she pushed a wisp of hair aside, where it stayed, moist, against her temple.

In a house behind, an old woman pulled back a raffia curtain to call shrilly:

—Get in the house! Get in the house, now! You have work! Get in!

The girl turned from the cistern, her jar on her hip, to amble away, her arm out and waving, gently as some gull's wing, for balance.

Women's bodies?

He looked in the bucket, still half full, lifted it again, and dashed it over himself.

Men's bodies?

No, he preferred women's bodies. And however many men he went with, however few women, and whatever contradiction anyone might see in it, he had to accept that too. And if, in two years, or ten years, his preferences changed, that would simply be something more to accept—though if they hadn't changed in *these* few months (he started to shiver in the faintest of breeze), he doubted they would!

He watched her go, her arm with its light speckling still waving, beckoning him on, beyond the cistern, beyond the yard, beyond the bridge, beyond Kolhari, till it seemed suddenly to indicate a border to the entire country that, truly, he had never even thought of before, a border that, simply because, however uncertainly, it must exist, he now realized, as the girl with her jar turned stolidly into another alley, if only because the city had taught him that such borders were not endings so much as transitions, he now knew he might someday flee across, down whatever street, across whatever bridge, along whatever road, through whatever tangled wilderness, into whenever and wherever, the possibilities vaster than the seeable, endless as the sayable.

To flee beyond Nevèrÿon itself was no more impossible than his flight across the unknown to Kolhari, his flight across whatever madness to this new sanity.

He went back to the bridge.

The grain seller was gone—probably with some barbarian. But the warm weather, he could see as he stood there, looking now up, now down the walkway, had brought out other men.

Was it three weeks, or three months later? While he lay on his back in the warehouse loft with a chink of sunlight falling through the roof into his left eye, he glanced down at the gray head on his belly:

—Hey, Papa. You can give me something to do besides this, can't you?

—What do you mean, the elderly man asked sleepily.

—Give me some work. Reaching down to rough the man's sparse hair, he chuckled. I can't spend my whole life on the bridge, Papa, waving this half-peeled goose gullet at hungry men who want to go off tumble about as though we were boys behind a barn! I'm a good worker. I can work hard.

—You're a good drinker. The man laughed.

The young man blinked up at the chink. No, Papa. I don't drink that much anymore. You haven't seen me drunk in a month.

—I can't give you any work here, the sparse-haired grain-seller said. I have some drivers taking some carts for me down to the Vinelet market . . . but I couldn't hire you. It wouldn't look right. I mean if someone in town recognized you. No, I—

—I can handle oxen. The young man gazed up at the beams across the ceiling. You got oxen to pull your carts? Oxen don't give me any trouble. I've been thinking of going south.

—Of course, said the man, who'd been doing his own thinking, there's *one* cart that I have to send along . . . it will carry grain, certainly. I have an ox for it. But there might be something else in it too, you see? Whoever drives it would have to take it mostly down the back roads. Certain customs inspectors—for this cart—I'd just as soon avoid.

—I could take it down any roads you want.

—You've always struck me as pretty trustworthy; and anyone seeing you would just think you were some country farmhand.

—Me? asked the young man. But that's what I *am*, Papa! Not too clever, not too wild, not too talkative, hey? A friendly fool, that's me, isn't it? Just look at me. What could be in a cart someone like me drove *besides* grain? Come on, let's go have a beer. I could take an oxcart of grain down to . . . wherever you wanted me to, deliver it to whoever you wanted.

—Well, perhaps you could. I wouldn't send any of my regular drivers. Some of them are family men, you see. If the gods do only their customary job as they work at the world, all should go well with the trip; nevertheless there might be some danger attached to it.

—I'll take your cart down. Hey, and I'll bring it back too! I need to get out of the city. I won't go back to the farm. Don't worry, Papa. Just tell me when you want me to leave.

And so he made the transition from hustler to smuggler as easily as he had made any of the others that had split his life into its various befores and afters. Possibly the last one had been violent enough so that the others in wait along the roads for him held little terror. I've often wondered who it was, in the intervening days— another hustler with a bit more experience than he, or perhaps a world-wise client—who told him some of the real dangers of his new undertaking. Did he ponder the fact that for the grain-seller to entrust such a mission to him was far more a sign that the elderly gentleman considered him particularly expendable rather than particularly dependable?

No matter. He did the task. And several more like it.

It was some weeks after our return from the provinces that, at the end of an afternoon's skit, I saw him, at the edge of the audience, clapping and shouting so loudly, so enthusiastically, with that look of special knowledge, of intimate privilege, of personal connection with the wonder, the magic, if not the very madness of our performance. As we began to tear down the platform, I motioned him up, and, with a grin, he vaulted onto the stage and walked with me among the other actors and musicians and dancers still in our makeup and bright attire, nodding now to the Leading Lady, waving at the groom he'd helped back on carnival night, here to my wagon, where he told me . . . well, *some* of what I've told you.

No doubt I made much of him, aghast at the depths he'd fallen to, and as delighted at his newfound success as some merchant when his child brings home a particularly fine report from your own bright institution. His attitude both to the madness and to the fortune that had followed it was the sensible gratitude of the spared. Oh, I'm sure that the deeds of that dim period of unexplained derangement, while they seemed behind him, still were able to frighten him at those moments when the chaos of the city around him would momentarily join the inner voices with which, truly, all of us spend so much of our lives in dialogue. If he did not, here with me, seem wracked by the fear of madness's return, I suspect it was because he was, finally, very brave. In no way denying that bravery, I also felt, as he sat on my bed, telling me of all this, he truly saw himself as too insignificant to be visited by such an experience more than that once—as long as he kept his drinking down. His pleasure was to be part of the city, to know an actor in the play, to have an interesting tale of inner and outer adventure to tell, when he was called back-stage as a sign of his privilege.

My own response to all this?

It was of the lowest. I kept wondering, while he sat there, what would happen if I enjoined him to stay with me a little longer, perhaps, than he'd planned—oh, certainly for his usual fee, while we did, oh, only some of the things we'd done before. Yet, I was also honored enough by his confidence to fear that he might be offended if I suggested it. I fancied that part of his reason for attending the performance, for clapping, for coming back to talk with me, was because he somehow felt I had had some part in the whole incomprehensible transition.

Unlike his scare from the prop dragon, however, after he told me once of his mad moment, the tale dropped from among his anecdotes. Yet, over our next few encounters, it lingered for me under the various comic mishaps he would recount, now in the spring, now in the fall, about his new nefarious activities. I even wondered if he didn't see the glimmering and gaudy characters we gave voice to, as they untangled the mystery of each other's plottings and schemings,

out on our sunlit or lantern-lit platform, as some controlled
image of his own many-voiced days of disorder: that, indeed,
he saw me, us, our whole theatrical company as living
constantly with and within the polylogue chaos he had
traversed so surprisingly and unexpectedly, and that his applause acknowledged in *us* a certain bravery, which, he felt,
we now shared. But whatever you say of them, finally I had
to dismiss such notions as the ratiocinations desire can entan-
gle about the most sensible of us.

After he left that afternoon, I went walking across the
market, to wander back and forth over the bridge, curious if
his new success as a full-fledged petty criminal hadn't been
somewhat exaggerated; wondering if, indeed, he mightn't
have stopped to loiter, in his usual place, hoping for a coin or
two, where, if I saw him, I would have no compunction
asking from him what I had been too diffident to request in
the wagon. On my third trip back and forth, after searching
His Spot and many others, when I realized that, no, he was
really no longer there, I told myself I was simply horny and,
certainly, one of the other boys out could satisfy me.

Still, I came back to the genial and boisterous supper at
the communal actors' table behind our wagons, alone. And
thus we both made another transition: to friend and friend.
But, by the hem of your royal cousin, whose reign is enigmat-
ic and eternal, that is really all I can tell you about him that I
didn't tell you before.

5
———

Yes, what a fine idea to quit that stuffed and stuffy wagon for
a stroll out here. Mind you, we must not stray too far from
the market; I have to be back for the evening performance.
Will you be staying?

Of course, I understand.

You have responsibilities waiting at the school. It is already
beyond amazement that you've managed to get away to see

our entertainment, or to talk with me, at all. It would be base ingratitude to demand, to expect, even to *think* of more.

But after all this discussion of my meeting with your erstwhile contemporary, I can't help wonder: do you recall when *we* met, young man? And don't protest that you're now forty. It's still the right of a sixty-year-old to call you young if he likes.

Yes, no doubt I *was* among the more interesting guests at the to-do your uncle threw for you, out in Neveryóna, in honor of your return from your youthful, year-long trip across our magnificent and mysterious land.

That's where you think we met?

But how in the world would I have received my invitation?

I knew no one in your circle, then, to bring me along to the party.

Yes, it *was* from you. You yourself.

You really don't remember inviting me?

Truly, I suspect the gods have crafted a different city for each of us, specified not only by our different points of view in it, but also by the random and irrational discontinuities into which our hopelessly faulty recalls endlessly cast and recast our diverse and separate lives.

It was on a little street, not far from here. For me it's all quite clear and sharp. A harness mender used to have her shop there, oh, perhaps three alleys over from where we walk now. She was a firm-voiced, hard-armed little woman, with a look in her eyes not unlike my abandoned wife's—though their personalities were quite distinct. (I always felt her laugh was larger than she was.) Those who patronized her business were fond of her, for she was an evenhanded worker and a fair-minded dealer with them all; but her life was harder than most women's because she had an idiot son, whom, now that he was almost grown and her husband dead, she would sit outside her shop on a bench in good weather. Pear-shaped, soft-shouldered, bean-headed, and often drooling, he had a spindle, a piece of wood that hung on a cord, which he would hold in one stubby hand, spinning the weight with the other, hour after hour, examining it, cooing over it, batting it now one way, now batting it back.

Ah, you *do* remember the idiot.

Well, I used to go there mornings simply to observe him, her, her customers. For wagoners, harness makers, smugglers, idiots—all of them figured from time to time in our skits, and

you know I have always liked to observe from life what I
interpret up on the platform. One morning when the sky was
limpid and sun-drenched but the clouds down at the seaside
were piled like metal shavings, I came there, as I often did in
those days, just to watch; and while I was watching, I noticed
a young man standing a ways off, clearly doing much the
same as I. His tunic was simple—but far too clean for anyone
to think him native to any near neighborhood. Did that fine,
dark face hold a full two decades behind its youthful beard?

I decided to include him in my observations, which have
always been of the active sort. Approaching him, I asked
what he was doing on that fair morning, and how did he like
the weather of late? Do you recall what he said—for, in truth,
he was you.

Now, you say, you begin to have the faintest recollection? I
can only wonder what my smuggling friend remembers of *our*
first meeting, what words, images, impressions, or even
misremembrances he retains from it, if any. Given his
homeless state, the daily pressures of his life—the amount of
beer he drank in those days!—I might expect such vagueness
from him. But really, my friend! From you?

—What do you do? I asked. How odd. Followed by, "And
how much do you charge to do it?" that was my first frank
and specific question to my friend on the bridge. . . . (I won't
bother you with the particularities of his answer, generally
liberal forward, admittedly limited behind.) You said to me:

—I am struggling to become a wise man, and some say
I've even made a stride or two in that direction. But sometimes I'm afraid my knowledge is wholly dependent on my
ability to watch for minutes at a time the quivering of a single
leaf, deep green on its upper face, olive gray under, with
yellow veins all through—and a bit of brown at one edge,
scalloped by some caterpillar. It's a quality, I'm afraid, I
share with that creature drooling in front of the tackshop. So
it probably doesn't mean very much, whatever others make of
it.

Oh, I see I have tickled you. Look at you laughing there.

Yes, that really *is* what you said.

Well, you were the kind of young man who went around
saying things like that. Believe me, I was no less impressed
with your answer than with his. People made much of you in

those days, I was soon to learn—even as they do now. That you were able to keep any humility about you at all was an accomplishment.

The arrogance and presumption of it, you say?

The measured and honest insight of it, I would say rather. That's certainly what struck me at the time. But I suppose that only means your liberalities and limitations fit comfortably with my own interests and needs. We talked for quite a while, there in the street. You had recently returned from your year-long trip, in which you had traveled all about Nevèrÿon, searching out this or that monument, looking for the site of that or the other fable. Because I, in the ordinary course of things, just happened to have visited many of those same places, and many more you hadn't, and had heard a few of the fables myself, as well as some that were new to you—not very astonishing given that I had spent most of forty years doing what you had done in one—you decided I was clever. Also, I think you found the *idea* of an actor interesting.

That's when you told me your uncle was throwing a party for you, out on his estate. It was to be the next day. Why didn't I come...? And later that evening, much to my surprise, your servant came down to the market to present a formal invitation at my wagon door—which rather impressed my fellow mummers.

You say, now, you have the vaguest memory of something like it, but, really, you only assent to it because I have said it? Oddly that's the way I recall the multi-voiced derangement of my smuggler friend. From his really very bare account, from my own observations of other madmen, and from the little flights and flirtations I've had—yes, I confess it—with madness on my own, I suppose I've decorated my tale.

The result is very like a memory of something that never really happened—at least not to me.

The party itself—that you'd thought was our meeting? For me that's really quite vague. As I wasn't performing, I suspect I found it a bore. A moment after I arrived, however, I recall you came by the gate—looking as though you didn't remember me even then, I might add. But all at once you smiled, and we strolled in among the others, the two of us talking together, though of what I couldn't tell you. Oh, you'd invited quite a collection, somewhat to your relatives' dismay. It was not that I didn't feel at home in such opulence, for a few times in my then forty years I'd been within comparable gates; but it was intriguing to observe the endless ways in which everyone—with the possible exception of you—seemed to feel equally uncomfortable with all those, well, oddballs you'd gathered about.

Ah, I'm glad accounts of your youthful manner can still amuse you. I found you amusing too. Also touching. For all the distance between us, I saw a bit of myself in you.

Several times we ended up in conversation. There was talk of my entertaining at some future gathering—a plan which, over the next few months, on several occasions blossomed. (You were, and still are I know, a generous man.) If it hadn't I might have missed out my friend at the bridge. But the rest you certainly remember, at least in outline. And unlike my bridge-bound infatuation I recounted to you this afternoon, our friendship—yours and mine—without the sexual element, grew and deepened over a much longer period before it eased to its present amiable stasis.

But you must recall, in later days, going with me various places about the city to observe, if not the idiot and the world of wagoners and harness menders that moved about his oblivious head, then other denizens of Kolhari, now in one neighborhood, now in another.

Well, I'm glad you do!

You must also recall that wonderful, frustrating, endless argument we had back then, which I thought would occupy us as obsessively as money occupies the working men and women on the bridge or off it.

You claimed that the habits and mannerisms, which I collected in our travels to decorate the characters I played or coached in our platform skits to make them more real and recognizable to our audience, were ultimately invalid because I would embroil those same carefully and colorfully constructed barrow-pushers and counts and wagoners and cutpurses in perfectly preposterous actions, during the course of which each would declare with great eloquence things that no count or cutpurse would ever possibly say. And if any ever even thought that he or she felt such things, you maintained, it was only from having been taken in by our skits in the first place.

And this much was certainly true: I'd play the most eloquent of idiots, while both of us knew that, whatever leaf he observed, the poor creature slobbering on Netmenders' Row had little to do with the carefully organized carryings-on with which I so delighted the market strollers, however accurately I let the spit spill down my chin or spun my bit of wood.

In the same way, I suppose, you could say that I informed the young man I told you of this afternoon with a voice, or voices, not his—that, indeed, however cleverly I decorated them from whatever experiences of my own, on any sort of reflection one of your perspicacity must see that, finally, they *could* not be his; even if, hearing me tell it, he himself thought he recognized those voices and applauded my performance, as heatedly as is his wont.

—It is as if, you would have said back then, you are presenting on your platform not people, but rather the nameless gods on whom all are modeled; then you sully them with human names.

My argument to you, during our same observational forays, was that what *you* collected, studied, and catalogued—the same habits and mannerisms as did I—were only the various silences of these same poor slaves and masters, workers and wastrels; and until you pried some voice out of them, alone or in concert, whether the voice of their secret fears and desires as you suspected them or even some desire or fear of your own, unless you gave them a meaning that was significant to you, what you observed was *only* silence. It spoke to no one; even its meaning for yourself was muffled, and it could have no other for either gods or the faulty humans they model, regardless of what names either humans or gods were or were not called by.

You remember our endless colloquy?

Well, I'm glad you nod your head to *some*thing.

In the interim between then and your present visit, I must tell you, however, I have thought of a much better answer for you: the voices I give, however decorated with observations and interpretations of the other, are, nevertheless and certainly, very much my own.

But they do not speak *for* the other—and therefore speak falsely.

They speak rather *to* the other: the other in me, the other in you, the other in my other friend—assuming he would not finally and for the first time turn at this particular outrage to the real we call "his story" and laugh with undisguised derision at my preposterous fancy with no relation at all to his life, his madness, his city—instead of giving out with his usual applause. They speak against the other. They speak always in dialogue with, in contest to, in protest of the real. They are always calling out to the other across the bridge on whose wild span madness and desire endlessly trade places, creating a wilderness at their center as palpably dangerous as that observed at any ill-mapped border. The monologue of art must be reinterpreted as the many-voiced argument of the artist with life, with life's images—indeed, as the wrangle between the articulate and everything else, with desire never fully possessed by any party, but endlessly at play between.

Oh, of course. I know, you must be on your way.

I have tried your patience much too long in the name of our eloquent friendship. And there I was, I see it now, daring to encroach on grounds that should be wholly yours. But you know how an old man—or even one not so old—can babble on. You must be off?

So must I. So must I. The evening performance is at hand. What?

You plan soon to send your students again to see us, just as you did last spring? Oh, you *are* too kind to an aging artist! You say it is their most pleasurable assignment? Really, you say too much.

But let me repeat it: I've known you for a while, and you have done this before, so this is not a complete surprise. Thus, I have something of a—though not a complete—surprise for you! We're preparing a new skit, back at the wagons, largely under my direction. Certainly it will be ready by the time your students troop down to join our common audience.

In it, they will see students like themselves, idiots, actors, barmaids, businessmen, teachers, tradesmen, harness menders, housewives, philosophers, philanderers, prostitutes, and princesses—all of them pursuing each other with mayhem and hilarity, song and dance, now through the halls of a school out in Sallese, now through the Old Market of the city. You can be sure that on our platform each of them will have more to say to, and more to do with, each other than any of them ever might be expected to in life. Oh, you have no idea how carefully I have been observing. Their eloquence will be unbelievable! Their significance will be overpowering. You have no notion what wonders I shall give voices to! The plot, I think, will turn on the theft of something magical, smuggled away before dawn—something, anyway, of incomparable worth.

We know, of course, who is hired to carry it off at the bottom of his grain cart. But who was the *original* perpetrator of the crime?

Now *that* is the mystery!

It's the part, of course, I haven't figured out. But all my spectators, even you (deny it, now, I dare you), love to see a mystery solved, the hero applauded, the villain flogged—

To the bridge?

Oh, you can go the short way that turns onto the quay. It's right through there. That will take you to it. But I'm going down here, as I want to get back to the other side of the market as quickly as I can. Oh, forgive me if I laugh a little now.

But was my tale this afternoon so powerful as that? Well, it's good for an old reprobate like me to know that even a young man as high-minded as you can consider looking in that common lane for some loud and hearty wench just up from the country, some rude and boisterous boy just down from the hills—

But you frown more deeply. Oh, forgive me, young master! I certainly did not mean—

It was only a joke!

We are old friends!

But see, I have transgressed some limit of politeness I never dreamed would offend you.

When I was off in that provincial wilderness, beset with all temptation, would I appropriate your noble name? (The nameless gods alone can hear what voice in you I've momentarily called up to contest your usually most decorous behavior!) Could you then suspect—?

Might I even *think* that this afternoon's performance would lead you to appropriate my own low practices and preferences, grown from an evil upbringing and a licentious existence on the periphery of all society, in the wilderness between far provinces, at the sordid center of our city?

Please, do not take offense at an aging actor's jest!

I merely meant to say that it lies there, on the way from the Spur to Sallese—a bit of madness one must cross to get from here to there.

—New York
February 1984

III

Appendix A:

THE TALE OF PLAGUES AND CARNIVALS,

or: Some Informal Remarks toward the Modular Calculus, Part Five

Ours, too, is an age of allegoresis...
> —Allen Mandelbaum
> *Inferno,* Introduction

"If you believe that," the tutor remarked, "you'd believe anything! No, it wasn't like that at all!..."
> —Joanna Russ
> *Extra(Ordinary) People*

Does this amount to saying that the master's place remains empty, it is not so much the result of his own passing as that of a growing obliteration of the meaning of his work? To convince ourselves of this we have only to ascertain what is going on in the place he vacated.
> —Jacques Lacan
> *The Function of Language in Psychoanalysis*

1. On—th Street, just beyond Ninth Avenue, the bridge runs across sunken tracks. Really, it's just an extension of the street. (In a car, you might not notice you'd crossed an overpass.) The stone walls are a little higher than my waist. Slouching comfortably, you can lean back against them, an elbow either side, or you can hoist yourself up to sit.

There're no real walkways.

The paving is-potholed.

The walls are cracked here, broken there. At least three places the concrete has crumbled from iron supports: rust has washed down over the pebbled exterior. Except for this twentieth-century detail, it has the air of a prehistoric structure.

At various times over the last half-dozen years, I've walked across it, now in the day, now at night. Somehow I never remember passing another person on it.

It's the proper width.

You'd have to double its length, though.

Give it the pedestrians you get a few blocks over on Eighth Avenue, just above what a musician friend of mine used to call ''Forty-Douche'' Street: kids selling their black beauties, their Valiums, their loose joints, the prostitutes and hustlers, the working men and women. Then put the market I saw on the Italian trip to L'Aquila at one end, and any East Side business district on the other, and you have a contemporary Bridge of Lost Desire.

It's the bridge Joey told me he was under that sweltering night last July when, beside the towering garbage pile beneath it, he smelled the first of the corpses.

2.1 She pushed her old hands into the dough, which pulled away, still too moist, leaving yeasty bits inside the crock. Outside the high kitchen window, one of the maids was beating a rug. The thwacking echoed over some garden bird's complaint.

Just then the new kitchen girl, whose name was Larla, swept down the steps and through the arch, wiping her hands on a brown cloth, moving toward the open fire on whose slate hearth the morning rolls, hot and gilded, waited on a brazen tray.

"Should I take these up to Lord Vanar?"

"He's not going to eat them," the woman said. Her face was deeply seamed. "Bring some water with them. His stool's too loose for milk, though he'll ask you for it. Give it to him only if he insists. He won't take much of that either."

The rolls were up, out the arch, and gone.

The servant woman fell again to her kneading.

2.2 Diseases should not become social metaphors, Sontag informed us in *Illness as Metaphor*. (I've already seen her analysis of cancer-as-social-model quoted in a discussion of AIDS [Acquired Immune Deficiency Syndrome].) When diseases generate such metaphors, the host of misconceptions and downright superstitions that come from taking them literally (misconceptions that, indeed, often determine the metaphors themselves in a system of reciprocal stabilization) make it impossible, both psychologically and socially—both in terms of how you feel and how others, with their feelings, treat you—to "have the disease" in a "healthy" manner.

"Dis-ease." Non-easiness. Difficulty.

"Health." Via the Old English "hælp," from the Old High German, "heilida": *whole,* or *complete.*

Metaphors fight each other. They also adjust one another.

Can a person who is "whole" also be "dis-eased"?

The answer, "Yes," would seem to be what modern medicine is all about.

But consider a variant of the same question: "Can a whole person be diseased?"

To answer, "Yes," is to give *one* answer to *two* questions with nearly diametric meanings. That the common form of the question can be deconstructed in this manner is the sign of our dis-ease before anything that might bear "disease" as its proper designation.

2.3 Sitting in his ground-floor study at his school in Sallese, just back from seeing Toplin in the rooms set aside for the school infirmary, the Master looked at the dusty bars of light slanting through the shutters to put their evening grill on the pale stone. He fingered the wooden chair arm. There was no hope for it. The boy would have to be returned to his mother.

These things spread.

An interesting boy, he mused.

A troublesome boy upon occasion.

A bright boy and a fine athlete, also: Toplin, bosom friend of students, Quetti and Bozar, of teachers, Kentog and Gisnik. Always talking, Toplin, with those two shy, brilliant girls just up to study from the Avila, Larni and Callee.

Toplin had a spirit, the Master had said, which, when he bridles it and learns to ride, will take him far.

But now he was feverish, with swellings in his neck, groin, and armpits. Infirmities that announced themselves with such symptoms, the Master knew, could kill.

A handsome boy, the Master mused . . .

The previous term there had been that embarrassing incident. Someone had told someone who'd mentioned it to someone else who'd whispered it to the Master: Toplin had been seen *selling* himself to men in the city! The Master was not an unworldly man. He was aware of the sexual play that went with adolescence; he could even see its healthy side as long as it did not go too far. But this was not a rumor the school could tolerate.

He'd called Toplin in.

On presentation of the accusation—delicately enough, the Master felt—the youngster had been embarrassed, seemed confused, and denied such a thing had occurred; yet his distress spoke not only of embarrassment but of guilt. Thus it had gone till the Master said: "If you need money, you must talk to your mother. She's a sensible woman, and I'm sure she will arrange an adequate allowance. But we cannot have our students running about the Bridge of Lost Desire like a bunch of barbarian ragamuffins, doing things even a barbarian would hestiate over!"

At that point, something had seemed to lift itself from the boy's confusion. Standing red-faced before the Master's chair,

Toplin had drawn himself up and declared: "If I were going to sell myself, why would I go *there*? Look, I *don't* sell myself! And don't *you* know that there are other markets for such things in this licentious city?"

It was a brazen answer, and so out of keeping with what he'd expected, so at odds with the way the boy had been acting thus far into the interview, that, indeed, it was easier to ignore. (When he thought of it later, he would mutter: "... spirit.") "This is only a rumor, Top. And rumors must not be confused with truth. That would demean me as well as you. Still, I must *not* hear anything like this again!" he had declared. "Or you will be in serious trouble!"

"Well, you *won't* hear anything like it!" Toplin had declared, surprisingly, back.

Thus it had ended.

The Master sat in the darkening room. There were student voices on the lawn, and little light. Laughter surged by in the hall. Pondering questions of magic, disease, and power, the Master sat alone.

2.4 Without a virus, in a sense AIDS is not a disease. It's a mysterious and so far (February 23rd, 1984) microbically unagented *failure to fight* disease. It is connected with sex—"perverted" sex. It is connected with blood—"blood products," as they say. Suddenly the body gives up, refuses to heal, will not become whole. This is the aspect of the "illness" that is ravenous for metaphors to stifle its unsettled shift, its insistent uneasiness, its conceptual turbulence.

2.5 This past summer, when one of the aging street people was suspected of having AIDS (because he'd lost perhaps forty pounds in a month) and the hustlers and dope dealers rallied to get the man to the hospital, Joey, talking about it with me in the Fiesta, said: "AIDS, that's where your body just stops healing, and even an infection from a little cut, or a cold, can kill you ...?" There was the faintest interrogation at the end of his pronouncement that a question mark distorts. Still, he seemed to be waiting for my confirmation.

How do I explain that this questioning is what we share—not what either of us can relieve for the other.

This is the absence that will be filled, one way or the other, by metaphors, his, mine, or someone else's.

The man, of course, turned out not to have AIDS, but lung cancer.

3. Perhaps the job is to find a *better* metaphor and elaborate it well enough to help stabilize those thoughts, images, or patterns that, *in the long run,* are useful—useful to those with the disease, to those who care for them, or even to those who only know about them. (Needless to say, what is useful in the long run is not, necessarily, in the short.) What is most useful in the long run is what destabilizes short-run strategies, the quick glyphs, the clichés, the easy responses history has sedimented.

3.1 AIDS is like unto a flower in the sunlight, beautiful to all graced creatures, a glory and a wonder. (Most recently, I think it was: "We must consider AIDS an opportunity for consciousness raising, rather than a disease.") "Bull," answers a person with AIDS. "Communication, fellow support, and shared insights may provide a little consciousness *about* AIDS. But AIDS itself provides you with shit. Expensive, painful, mortal shit!"

AIDS is like unto a Scourge of Satan, the Wrath of Khan, and the most awfullest thing that can happen not only to the sniveling faggot (whose unthinking phrase was that . . . ?), who, doubtless, deserves it, but to the whole lax, doomed, and immoral nation, which, evil as it is, doesn't deserve a fatal disease *just* yet! (Over *how* many radio talk shows have I heard that one?) A frustrated voice takes another breath and says in the levelest tone it can muster: "Since it obviously isn't, *why* say it is?"

But that's why metaphors stuck on this good-bad scale won't do. What is needed is a metaphor or metaphor system in which restraint of judgment as well as a certain order of complexity are part of what is metaphorically suggested.

AIDS is the sparkplug in a social machine of which we are all—people with, and people without, AIDS—a part, including the metaphor maker.

A step in the right direction? It only turns out to be so if you're willing to step much further.

The criticism of this one is harder but just as real: engines break down into their parts, basic and superfluous, central and peripheral, whole and diseased, good and bad. And in this kind of engine, the parts are simple metaphors, on that old scale; the "complexity" of the metaphor masks a notion of structuralist simplicity. But I am truly interested to discover— and am as willing to accept no as I am yes for an answer—if there is anything among these fancies that might be useful in thinking about what was first dubbed "the gay plague."

3.2 A new illness, AIDS, began to infiltrate the larger cities. Some saw it as a metaphor for the license, corruption, and decay that is the general urban condition. (Well, after all, "metaphor"—*a transfer,* something that *carries* something else, *after* it—is as much a metaphor as is "disease.") More interesting to the more interested citizens were, however, the strategies people used to avoid thinking of the illness. Certainly the relation between the facts of the infirmity and these strategies—as many noticed and several said—was anything *but* metaphorical.

4. She fled between counters piled with leather, counters piled with cloth, sunlight striking between awnings at her, the news bubbling behind her eyes, bursting her ears from within as the vendors' shouts and halloos battered them from without. Half a sentence squirmed on her tongue, fighting toward completion, as the words bumping one another between her running breaths awaited her voice.

He caught her shoulders before she saw him—"Nari . . . !" —and swung her around in sun, not meaning to hurt her arms with his fingers, while he grinned at her with his bronze, barbaric grin, above his rough brown beard, below his rough yellow hair.

Shoulders drawn up between his hands, Nari blurted: "Oh, Zadyuk, he's so sick! I didn't know . . . We didn't know . . . !" And where was the rest of it? She watched Zadyuk's smile fall apart, leaving bewilderment.

He said:

". . . Pheron?"

"You asked about him this morning . . . ? We hadn't seen him this week, and the last time, he said he was feeling so tired, and looked so . . . awful? After you left today, I went by his workshop. It was all closed up, and the man in the shop next door said no one had seen him in Crescent Alley for days! So then I went to his room—he couldn't even answer the door, Zadyuk!"

Bewilderment crumbled, leaving fragmentary expressions

moving among Zadyuk's features, impossible to say where, among hurt, anger, and fear, they would settle.

One hand dropped from her arm.

The other's grip, in three stages, loosened, before it fell.

"He's so thin—he must weigh only half of what he did when we saw him! His joints and his neck are all swollen. There're terrible sores on his leg and his side! His eyes are red and runny. And he's . . . sick! He can't even put his arms down. Underneath hurts too much!"

"But what's wrong with—?"

Nari looked aside.

Zadyuk blinked, then looked too.

She'd been speaking excitedly, and the two men passing arm in arm watched with the curiosity one gives to any street encounter. The older man's head was shaved. Both had dark wings of paint around their eyes, which emphasized astonishingly the pale lashes and gray irises of the younger. As they turned away, walked away, Nari looked back at Zadyuk, knowing he, too, remembered how Pheron would fasten on the colorful swatches he wove and dyed himself in his workshop and, in the same eye-paint, with a cider jar hooked on his forefinger, and already a bit tipsy, would visit their rooms after work. "Parading about the streets like that!" Zadyuk would declare. "People will think you're some prostitute from the Bridge of Lost Desire!" and Pheron would mime a show of great surprise, and exclaim, "But, my dear, I never go anywhere *near* it! There're too many other places in the city to get what *I'm* after!" Then he would show Nari the hard, bright colors and the metallic threads he'd worked into his fabrics, while at the table Zadyuk would pry the cork from the wine jar with his sandal knife.

Nari shook her head a little, as if already answering a no or an unknown to what Zadyuk was about to say.

"What's . . . the matter with him?" Zadyuk asked anyway.

"The island woman who lives in the room next to his, she's been in to take him water and things and help him clean himself—I met her outside, as I was leaving . . ." Nari tried to compress her voice the way, moments back, Zadyuk had compressed her arms. What happened was that voicing itself dropped from her speech, leaving not even a true whisper, but a gesture at words, which Zadyuk, narrowing his eyes, read from the movement of her lips and tongue rather than heard:

"She says it's plague! She says she's seen it—" Nari

caught her breath, shivered once, and spoke out again: "She's seen it before, she said, in the islands. When she was a girl. It killed—!"

"Nari . . . !"

They looked at each other.

But around them, complex and glittering like some choice weave Pheron might swirl above his head in Zadyuk's and Nari's small, second-floor, stone-walled room, lay the New Market, to its east the waterfront, down the side streets between the recently completed warehouses and storage buildings, to its south the artisans' shops, their dull storefronts and colorful displays at the sides of badly paved alleys with names like Potters' Lane and Netmenders' Row, to its west Her Imperial Majesty's Public Park, where mothers brought their children and students brought their studies and where Nari had often brought her fancies to tell Zadyuk (and sometimes Pheron) as they walked there after work on summer evenings, and to its north the vigorous business district about Black Avenue and the ethnic enclaves beyond it, the trade and traffic constant among them, the movement back and between them endless, from the Spur with its reeks and wailing barbarian babies to the palm-lined avenues of Neveryóna and Sallese, with their dark-skinned, dark-robed nobles and their anxious, amiable merchants, ambling by the falls and fountains in their walled estates.

4.1 Twenty-three years old, Nari was born in the autumnal month of the Badger, off in Adami. Both her parents came to Kolhari when she was two, a few years after the ascension of the Child Empress Ynelgo. Nari was an only child, rather a rarity in that time, that place.

When she was seventeen and beginning to "experiment with sex" (as another epoch would put it), Nari'd wanted a son passionately—in that age with no birth control. But she knew with a definiteness that sometimes astonished her, she did *not* want a daughter. Indeed, her deepest and most secret desire was for a little, yellow-haired, barbarian boy—something of an impossibility, as she was a small, brown girl with thick, black hair, whom many people complimented by telling her she could easily be taken for some aristocratic daughter of the nobility.

"If I got pregnant," she said once to a girlfriend (other young women her age were getting pregnant and having little

girls and boys all around her), "and it turned out a girl, I
think I'd *kill* myself!" Her friend laughed, but Nari was
worried by the strength of her own feelings. "I'd give her to
another mother," she corrected herself, "and *then* I'd . . . kill
myself—" which, as she said it, seemed neither wise nor
probable, if, after all, the unwanted daughter had already
been got rid of.

One could try again.

Her *very* best friend was an older barbarian named Meise,
with three sons of her own, all by different men, who was
now pregnant for the fourth time by some vanished yellow-
haired ne'er-do-well and was anxious for a girl. Meise was
one-third owner of the Kraken (where, as far as Nari could
tell, Meise did all the work), just off the Alley of Gulls. Nari
herself sometimes helped in the kitchen.

One evening, when rain pelted the street and chattered on
the tavern roof, and the younger woman and the older woman
leaned on opposite sides of the counter, each with a half-
finished mug of beer, lazily wiping out one crock after
another and moving them from the dripping ones on the left to
the dry ones on the right, Nari got Meise to promise that if
Meise's new baby was a boy, and if Nari herself should get
pregnant and have a girl within the year, they'd trade.

A day later, Nari was sure that Meise had forgotten the
whole, giggling exchange. Or at least she pretended she had.

That bothered her, too.

Nari had several barbarian boyfriends in those years; and a
good number of chances to get pregnant.

Yet she didn't.

At nineteen, when she met, and again, at twenty, when she
began to live with, Zadyuk, her parents, out of despair, and
Meise, out of real delight at her nice young friend's nice
young man, decided they liked him. He was certainly an
improvement on Tarig, Kudyuk, and Bedog—Nari's last three
barbarians. For one thing, Zadyuk looked a great deal more
like what Nari thought a real barbarian ought to and acted a
good deal less like what even she had begun to think *must* go
with such looks at this age and epoch.

But though she had not talked about it with anyone,
including Meise, she'd also begun to wonder if she were one
of those women who just wasn't going to have a child.

After the first year with Zadyuk, he suspected it too. They

talked. Nari was not all that surprised when Zadyuk didn't think it was so awful.

"You know," she had said, speaking almost into his armpit in the room lit only by moonlight through the back window, "I'd always thought I wanted a nice, yellow-haired son. I mean, with the kind of life I was leading, I always thought, soon, I'd *have* a child, whether I wanted to or not. Since I had to, that's the one I wanted." She snuggled into him; they were lying on the bed. (Pheron had visited earlier in the evening; they were happy.) "But I don't really *like* children, Zadyuk. Boys *or* girls. Oh, they're nice enough when you don't have to take care of them. But Meise's new brat, whom I used to think I'd even trade for, drives me crazy when I'm over there! And he's the cutest looking little barbarian I know—besides *you*!"

Zadyuk chuckled into her dark hair.

"I think the baby is why I stopped working there," she went on. "Just so I didn't have to help."

Nari had occasionally worked as a laundress among barbarian women in the Spur; but for the last year and a half now, she'd been managing her own group of washerwomen, with two young drivers (one girl, one boy) who went out to collect washing even as far as Sallese. (They did all the students' laundry for at least one of the schools on the near edge of the city's merchant neighborhood.) She was becoming rather successful in her business.

4.11 If a mid-twentieth-century orthodox Freudian could return to Kolhari and present Nari with the theory of "penis envy" (to explain her girlish desire for a son) and "sublimation" (to explain her new success in her work), though myself I think the analysis would be false, Nari, a primitive woman in a superstitious time, would probably find the notion intriguing, even plausible.

There were a number of such fables about in that land in those days—especially among the barbarians.

4.2 Twenty-five years old, Zadyuk was the middle of three brothers. (Kudyuk—a different Kudyuk from Nari's former petty-thief boyfriend—two years older than Zadyuk, had been gone from Kolhari six years now and had more than likely come to a bad end; he was seldom mentioned in his family. Namyuk, a year younger, had had a string of not terribly good jobs and a few times actually had got himself in trouble. He lived in the Spur, was going from bad to worse, and didn't seem to care.) All three boys had been born in Kolhari, Zadyuk in the month of the Finch. Their father was a barbarian from the south. Their mother, half barbarian, was herself actually born in the city. Zadyuk's parents' life in Kolhari predated the coming of the Child Empress to the High Court of Eagles, and they clearly had mixed feelings about the most recent influx of southerners.

Zadyuk worked as a sandal maker at one of the leather stalls in the New Market, where, last year, he'd had an interesting bit of luck. The sandals he made were popular with the students out in Sallese. One evening, when he'd taken a wagon load of laundry out to the school for Nari (she was between drivers), in the yard among the school's three buildings he saw a student wearing not the usual sole-with-straps (or, more usual, going barefoot), but rather the full, somewhat baggy leather foot-coverings that workers on rough and stone-filled construction sites used around the city.

Just then another boy recognized him from town as a sandal maker and approached: "Do you make shoes like that?" the boy asked.

Zadyuk said: "Sure. Do you like them?" Then he grinned. "Come on down to our stall. In the New Market. You know where it is." The next morning he went into the leather stall early and made two pair by opening: they took more leather but were simpler to make than the interweave of straps and buckles that were the stylish sandals of that day.

Toplin was in for his the hour the market opened.

Over the next three months Zadyuk sold over a hundred pairs of "work shoes" to students. Zadyuk had begun that month as a worker at the stall of an aging boss who seldom came in. By the end of it, he was foreman of a stall of his own, employing three more leather-crafting artisans. And had been since.

But at Zadyuk's counter, the youngsters did not have to put up with the teasing and, occasionally, outright hostility they met with when they purchased their work shoes from the usual workmen's shoemaker.

4.21 Zadyuk carried a deep, if now settled, resentment toward his parents for giving him and, indeed, his two brothers the three *most* common male barbaric names in Nevèrÿon.

Performing in their wagons in the city markets, the mummers, when they portrayed a barbarian character in their skits, *always* named him Kudyuk or Zadyuk. And at least once, when Zadyuk was sixteen, he'd actually seen a show in which there were three barbarian brothers named, yes, Kudyuk, Zadyuk, and Namyuk—big, brawling, brutal fellows, so stupid they could not even keep their own names straight; and there was a running joke about a nonexistent fourth brother, "Yuk-yuk." While the rest of the audience laughed and applauded, Zadyuk had watched with pursed-lipped fascination, his fists in sweaty knots that cooled when, suddenly, now and again, he would force them open. Indeed, he was never sure when people called him "Kudyuk" if they were honestly mistaking him for his brother, or if they just felt one barbarian monicker was as good as any other.

Back when he'd been sixteen, he'd tried to change his name to something nice, northern, and innocuous. Yes, "Pheron" was what he'd picked. What an impossible three weeks! His friends, yellow-haired barbarians and brown respectable folks alike, kidded him endlessly. Everybody seemed to realize immediately what his motivations were and teased him mercilessly. There was nothing but to give it up. Well, Zadyuk *was* a good barbarian name; and Nari, whenever he grumbled about it, said she wouldn't want him called anything else.

4.22 Six months after he and Nari began living together they met Pheron.

Nari started a conversation with the thin, green-eyed, brown-skinned youth one day in the market when he came in with an armful of his fabrics. She brought him to Zadyuk's leather stall, where the three of them began to talk; then a woman buying a pair of sandals decided she also wanted to purchase one of Pheron's pieces for a scarf. It was a great joke when they told her where, if she ever wanted to, she could have it laundered . . .

The three young people marveled at how little time it took them to become the closest of friends.

But, though he'd started to a couple of times with Nari, Zadyuk never told either Pheron or Nari directly about the attempted name change nine years before. Especially not after he decided that Pheron really was his closest friend in Kolhari.

4.231 If a mid-twentieth-century orthodox Freudian could return to Kolhari and present Zadyuk with the theory of "repressed homosexuality" (as the basic force behind civilization)—though myself I think the analysis would be false—Zadyuk, a primitive man in a superstitious time, would probably find the notion intriguing and even plausible.

There were a number of such fables about in that land in those days, especially among the established classes of Kolhari.

4.3 Pheron? Where does he come from, with his nice, northern, innocuous name . . . ?

His workshop was not far from the New Market. With a shifting string of young assistants, he worked harder than both Nari and Zadyuk over any given week, sold to a clientele slightly higher socially, to make somewhat less money than the laundress and shoemaker together.

Pheron's father had worked on the New Market when it was being built. (It had been completed five years ago, after three years of labor.) Seven years back, Pheron would sometimes bring his father his dinner in the afternoon to the construction site.

Watching men dig and roll barrows about the site, Pheron had sometimes thought: "There is nothing, nothing, *nothing* I could do here—except, perhaps, carry a slop bucket for the workers."

His mother, whom he'd always considered a terribly interesting woman, with her songs and jokes and eccentric opinions and furious energy, had died, after a brief illness, when he was fourteen. He'd missed her desperately. But two things soon grew clear.

His relationship with his father became much better than it had been—for his parents had always argued over him. As Pheron himself took over the cleaning and cooking and general household duties, rather as if he had been (and he and his father both joked about it) a daughter, a kind of friendship took over between father and son. At one point, as he recalled some of his parents' wrangling, it suddenly struck him: it was not *him* they had disapproved of, but only of how each other had treated him.

And with one of them gone, unfair though it still seemed that it had taken his mother's death to bring it about, the conflict had ceased.

4.31 If a mid-twentieth-century orthodox Freudian were to present Pheron with the theory of "penis envy" and "sublimation," he would probably have said:

"The only thing is, *I* envy them too. And I've *got* one. Nor is it small. And heaven knows, I don't sublimate. I go right for it!"

And if the orthodox Freudian went on to present the theory of "repressed homosexuality" as the basic force behind civilization, Pheron's comment would most likely have been:

"But *what* makes you think it's repressed?"

4.32 There is something incomplete about Pheron. (Since there *is* no Pheron, since he exists only as words, their sounds and associated meanings, be certain of it: *I* have left it out.) My job is, then, in the course of this experiment, to find this incompleteness, to fill it in, to make him whole.

But at this point, however, there's a real question where to look for the material: in the past? in the future? on the roaring shore where imagination swells and breaks? in the pale, hot sands of intellection? in the evanescent construct of the here and now—that reality always gone in a blink that is nevertheless forever making history?

4.4 The lintel's shadow pulled away, and he narrowed his eyes in the sun spilling on the grass between the buildings. A younger man, the Master wondered, did I squint as much, stepping out of doors? How odd one can close one's eyes to such light but not one's ears to such noise.

The students shouted and tossed their balls and roamed the lawn.

He stood with his lids near met, smiling. Because, walking out among his students, he smiled.

Toplin would have been in the thick of their ball tossing . . .

Can I hear his absence through their games? Eyes all but shut, the Master caught the shadow of three dashing by his left indoors and, a moment later, one sauntering out on his right. With a tiny joy, he (who claimed to know all his children by their footsteps, even around corners) recognized none of them. Then, as if in reaction to the joy, there was . . .

Nothing, he thought. An absence. But it's an absence in me. What will I fill it with?

Work? Fear of the illness? Mistaken notions? Brilliant

speculation? Care and concern for the ailing Toplin, whose distraught, angry mother had taken him away only an hour ago, back to her somewhat pretentious house in its somewhat unfashionable neighborhood?

That he truly did not know *was* the absence. He opened his eyes to the sun and stalked among the young women and young men laughing and loitering in the light—certainly—of his knowledge.

4.41 If a mid-twentieth-century theorist of any sort could return to Kolhari and present the Master with just about any modern notion, say Freud's concepts of "the unconscious," "transference," "repression," or "infantile sexuality" (I believe these theories to be basically correct), the Master would probably not put much stock by them—even though there were a number of such fables about in the land in those days.

The Master has too many carefully worked up theories of his own, however—and even a few small, but clear, hopes that they are coherent and rich enough to interest people into days well beyond ours, however foggily (powerfully?) he conceives "the future." But he is a primitive man in a superstitious time, and though he has a surprisingly sophisticated intuition of this, it is precisely when his theories turn to grapple this most important problem of his day that they became truly incomprehensible to those coming after him even by a generation, much less millennia.

4.5 The nameless old servant—the crevices broken into her cheeks and forehead are what medicine will eventually call Touraine-Solente-Golé syndrome—stopped beside the leather hanging over the scullery doorway, in the dawn's cool and rustle. She'd not yet gone to wake the new kitchen girl. (That, indeed, Larla needed to be awakened quite so many mornings did not speak well for her first month at the estate. Still, she didn't mind working on at a house with a lord gone suddenly and so distressingly ill. There were some who wouldn't stay for that.) She thought of Lord Vanar and, as an aged woman might at that time, pondered magic, disease, power, and felt...

An absence? She noted somehow it was hers. No. It's not. It has been inflicted on you by...

That's me, of course, protesting ineffectually across the

ages. But my inability to reach her on that morning, millennia ago, only confronts me with my own failings, incompletions, absences.

I content myself with noting, then, that she does not much resemble our housekeeper when I was a child, Mrs. Bembry. (*Her* face was round, brown, and lineless.) Mrs. Bembry, who cooked, cleaned, and baby-sat for us, lived at home with Mr. Bembry and was, indeed, *Mrs.* Bembry from the first time my father introduced my sister and me to her when I was four and my sister just beyond two. But this was because we were a black family hiring a black maid in the forties:

My Father (while my mother looked on): What is your name?

Mrs. Bembry: Cora.

My Father: *What* is your name?

Mrs. Bembry: Cora . . . ?

My Father: What is your *full* name?

Mrs. Bembry: Cora. Mrs. Cora Bembry.

My Father: Sam, Peggy, this is Mrs. Bembry. She'll be helping us in the house and sometimes taking care of you.

Mrs. Bembry: Oh, you all can call me Cora . . .

My Father: We'll call you Mrs. Bembry.

And for a dozen years we did. I think Mrs. Bembry and the nameless servant both believed in magic. But at this remove, I couldn't say which believed in magic *more.*

4.51 I hesitate before any notion about the reception of theory for this prehistoric woman. (In both our urban and rural landscapes, so overwhelmingly based on service rather than production, the nineteenth-century "house servant" or "body servant" is a very weak model for modern maids and housekeepers, cooks and gardeners, mail carriers and delivery men and women, wait-persons and counter people, supers and maintenance folk, civil servants and secretaries, not to mention live-in baby-sitters. Still, what draws us to it and what makes us hesitate before it are both historical—that is, composed as much of nostalgia as of curiosity.) Only the most minor character in what is to follow, her minority masks an incompleteness (a dis-ease in the writer) clear and close to that which makes Pheron so uncomfortable.

4.6 Six-thirty in the morning, and I have been up since five-twenty-three, sitting in the living room, drinking coffee, reading desultorily at the Mandelstams—Osip and Nadezhda—Tsvetaeva, Pasternak, preparing for the big plunge, two weeks hence, into the Russian Yeats, Ana Ahkmatova: generally putting off the rewrite on "The Tale of Fog and Granite" with an eye (and an urgency) to handing it in on Monday.

It's Saturday, January 14th, 1984, my daughter's tenth birthday. (Through childhood she ran around with her sunny crew-cut till, three years ago, she put her foot down and, since, has developed Long Blond Hair.) She will be up in an hour, if not in minutes.

Last night she and I sat, where I sit now (writing this), watching a TV Charlie Brown special. Then, the shutters were open. Now they're closed against predawn black. Morning traffic is cut by a fire siren; I can hear the slush under the tires from the last days' snow. The vacuum cleaner sits, as it does all too usually, by the jamb of the double doorway between the living room and the dining room, half on the red rug, half on the green.

Last night.

My arm around her, I joked: "This is the last time I can watch TV with my nine-year-old," and, a minute later, took another trip to my word processor in the office—checking for corrections, formatting this, that, and the other.

"You know," she told me suddenly, when I came back and we sat again together, "I remember my *seventh* birthday!"

I raised an eyebrow and looked down.

"It was after my party . . . ? All the paper from the presents was lying on the floor, and I remember standing there and thinking: Finally! I'm seven! I didn't think I was *ever* going to be seven!"

I smiled. "Was that here or at your mother's?" I just wanted a better picture of it.

"I think it was here," she said. "But I'm not sure."

And though I could write twenty pages detailing her fifth, I realize that I have no memory of her seventh birthday at *all*!

It gave me an astonishing sense that this marvelous microperson, who has been so much a part of me for a decade, has her own inner life—a life which I've always known was there, wanted to be there, but, as a parent, I so rarely catch the signs of.

Hingley's *Nightingale Fever*, some notebooks, *Zhivago*, Clarence Brown's *Mandelstam* (among the volumes of translated poems) are scattered on the tweedy couch-cover. Soon she'll be up and off to her horseback riding lesson, the day's presents—the actual party will be a sleep-over with a handful of her friends. The great change marked by ten? Well, as *I* remember it:

No more writing down your age with *one* numeral!

Odd, after all these years, to be catching up on the Russians.

Odd, too, that this sort of moment (in its domestic, not its literary, aspect) is something I've decided to deny to Zadyuk and Nari by an offstage quirk of biology. (But then, offstage biological quirks are what this whole tale is about.) Odd also that, ten years ago, just before my daughter's birth, when I began the Nevèrÿon series, I wouldn't have thought it odd in the least.

5. "...*including* Lord Vanar?" The minister lifted a palm, leaving his fingertips on stone. "That is a great many people in the city to have such a singular and serious illness. Already six others have died of it, you say; and *none* has recovered...?" The small window of the council room was high and deeply beveled; a bird beat by outside, its shadow flicking the stone table. "It would not be a lot of people for headache, or stomach distress, or a cold. But certainly any number over fifty is an unconscionable amount for fevers, pains, incapacitations, and fatal swellings. We must observe this carefully and be prepared to act..."

5.1 Joey is a Boston-Irish hustler and heroin addict (when he can get it) who lives mainly on the street. Of his four brothers, one killed himself in a drug-induced depression when Joey was out at the store. At twenty-one or twenty-two, they were trying to kick together. His brother wasn't doing very well. Joey came back from the grocery carrying a paper bag with a quart of milk and a pack of cigarettes in it to find his brother hanging by an old jumper cable from the kitchen light fixture above an overturned chair. A year later he watched another brother get pushed out of a third-story window to impale himself on a spike fence below. (Revenge for money owed on drugs: "Sometimes, afterwards, I'd see the fuckers who did it on the street. They'd say 'Hi.' I'd say, 'Hi.' That was all I could do.") The two other brothers also died violently. So Joey left his mother in the hospital ("What the hell she need with me—though I like to go see her, sometimes. She's still there") to come to New York.

The quality of street dope, he says, is better in New York than in Boston.

Joey says he used to lift weights. ("I was up to a hundred and ninety-eight pounds, and *all* muscle! I was doing tournaments and getting third, second place. Can you imagine me that strong?" Today he seldom weighs in at over a hundred-thirty.) At twelve he got a job washing dishes in a Boston diner, thanks to an affair with the twenty-five-year-old man who'd inherited the place: that lasted till he was eighteen—when his drug involvement and the owner's interest in younger boys ended it. Briefly, when he was nineteen, a woman a few years older than he married him for a couple of years. ("That's when I was lifting weights. She thought I was cute.") They had a daughter. Drugs again. Another male lover, this one another weight lifter. Joey drove an ice cream truck for a while—managed a fleet of trucks, he sometimes says. By the time he was twenty-five, it had all gone bust: marriage, lover, job. And someone had blown up the truck(s?), which he'd used to move drugs and illegal money around between whorehouses, anyway. At twenty-seven he came more or less permanently to New York. (Just before he made the change, someone hit him in the mouth with a baseball bat, knocking away most of his upper teeth; the broken ones have rotted out by now, helped by a couple of trips to the dentist, a year or so apart, to remove a few of the stubs.) Living on the street, he says, is easier in New York than in Boston.

Among the stories Joey has told me, he says he thinks about this one a lot. It's from his first months here in the city.

A drug friend of his had taken over an abandoned apartment in some half-burned building in Hell's Kitchen. No heat or electricity in the place. But as Joey was outside that winter, he considered his friend lucky and—compared to him—prosperous. Joey went to see him one cold morning, hoping he might get some dope. There was never any lock on the door. Joey just pushed in. With his works out beside him, the man sat shirtless on a mattress on the floor of the chilly tenement kitchen.

"Hey!" Joey said. "How you doin'?"

The man looked up and said, matter-of-factly: "Oh, you're here? I was just gonna kill myself."

"Yeah? How?" Joey squatted down before the mattress to watch.

You gotta understand, Joey told me, I thought he was joking. I was livin' in my clothes and sleeping out, which means I wasn't sleeping much. I was pretty sick, so I wasn't too alert, and I was trying to act nice—you know what I mean? And this guy had a place to stay, sometimes drugs, and sometimes food—I never thought anything *could* be wrong with him!

The man jabbed an empty hypodermic in his arm. "Air," he told Joey.

If he'd said "bubble," Joey told me, I would've known what he meant and done something. ("A bubble to the ticker" is the usual drug slang for this.)

"It ain't supposed to hurt much." He pushed the plunger in.

Nothing happened.

Joey thought he'd just interrupted his friend's shooting up.

"Sometimes you need two or three," the man said, sliding the needle loose, pulling out the plunger, and injecting himself again.

"Hey . . . !" Joey said, "That's kind of dangerous—"

"No," the man said. "It's what I wanna do." He pulled the hypodermic free again, again filled it with air, stuck it back in his arm a third time, and thumbed down the plunger.

He didn't even get the needle out, Joey said. Suddenly he sat up straight, like someone hit him with a hammer in the small of his back, and he falls over on the mattress.

I hadn't been in there thirty-five seconds!

I stayed around for another five minutes, to see if I could do anything. I tried to give him mouth-to-mouth artificial respiration. (And doing that with somebody you *know* is a corpse already is weird!) There was no breath, no heartbeat, no nothing. So I left him there with the needle still hangin' off his arm.

But he'd just decided it was time to go.

In the almost three years I've known him, I've seen Joey dragging through the retarded slough of pain that is his biweekly bout of heroine deprivation sickness. I've seen him with his arm in bandages, shoulder to wrist, because the night before he'd rushed into the parking lot to help a woman who was being mugged and got his arm and hand knifed open for the effort. And—most recently, after not running into him for three and a half months—I've seen him in clean clothes, with a fresh haircut and weighing thirty pounds more than I'd ever seen him before, showing off arms that have doubled their diameter from a vigorous exercise program. He's been off the street three months, he says, and swears he's touched no heroin since just after I last saw him.

"I ain't sayin' I don't take a snort of coke if somebody offers it. But you ain't gonna get me near that other shit again. I mean, look at me. I'm the best lookin' guy in here—" and he grins about the Fiesta— "long as I don't smile at nobody."

5.21 At nineteen, *the Master explained,* I took stock of my prospects (did some work to find out which of my titled relatives would get what) and realized, by the end, my title would get *me* little.

Well, not too long ago such things got you killed.

So I abandoned mine.

That simple act of unnaming started something of a fable, which still grows and moves and develops in the city and its suburbs, quite apart from me.

Oh, there've been moments when my reputation seemed a light rippling out into darkness, myself its central flame. More often, however, it's some gnarled, preposterous monster, inhabiting my city with me, whom I've never met, but whom, for incomprehensible reasons, people who should know better still mistake for me. It goes about, parodying me with misquotation, mocking me with stupidities and homilies, giving my actions false motives—oh, doing things somewhat as I would do them, yet always for absurd reasons, and finally doing them differently enough that I don't recognize them when the reports come back.

Of course the misunderstandings brought about by this malignant entity are all laid at my door. I wonder if it isn't the main reason why, when I decided to open my school, it never occurred to me to settle it in any of the available Neveryóna estates (though I had enough connections there) but rather here, at the far edge of Sallesse, where it becomes one with the District of Successful Artisans: here where, nearly ten years ago, in the three adjacent buildings with the yard between, I began to interview, house, and instruct the young people whose parents sent them from all over the city and beyond.

The monster often comes close, but it refuses to confront me personally: I must wait for people to tell me about it. Yet I'm astonished how boldly it trespasses on my personal circle. (Again and again, I meet those who find the monster acceptable—its most disconcerting aspect!) But the doorsteps of Neveryóna, my real home, I now suspect, were what I wanted to protect from the grotesquerie all knowledge becomes when it moves too far from the knower.

5.211 In "The Paris of the Second Empire in Baudelaire," Walter Benjamin quotes the first modern poet of the city: "The time is not distant when it will be understood that a literature which refuses to make its way in brotherly concord with science and philosophy is a murderous, suicidal literature." This notion was expressed, of course, by various other people besides Baudelaire at various times and places throughout the nineteenth century.

5.22 Youths of my titled class traditionally visit the High Court of Eagles between our fifteenth and twentieth year, *the Master said,* sponsored by one or another relative already in residence there. We stay between three months and—those of us destined for government work—three years.

There's a story about me, though it was never told till after I gave up my meaningless honorific:

When my invitation from court arrived (I was seventeen, so runs the tale), I refused to go, declaring that I would seek my education from the land rather than in those gloomy and official chambers. So instead of my Courtly visit, I took off on a trip from one end of Nevèrÿon to the other. That's the story.

No, I never went to court.

Yes, I took a year-plus trip around the country, departing a few months before my eighteenth birthday and returning a few months after my nineteenth.

The distortion, then?

Let me say, rather, when I heard the tale's first inkling.

I don't recall how many months after I'd gotten back from my trip. But while I stood in a fountained garden of Sallese, filled with matrons and merchants congregating in honor of someone not me (a party, somehow, I'd felt obliged to attend), a tall, soft-voiced countess (suffering regally the same obligation) with green stones on a leather braid about her somewhat hairy forearm, to whom I'd been outlining some of my immediate plans and past adventures, bent her head to the side and exlaimed: "I see what you did now! In place of your traditional time at court, you sought out your education in the world! How wonderful! The empress herself, whose reign is luminous and lively, should encourage the same of all the bright and imaginative young people in Nevèrÿon!"

I thought: What an interesting—and complimentary!—way of stating what I'd done. Was it factual? That didn't occur to me. Nor, I doubt, to her. Rather the words seemed much like those some traveling tale-teller sometimes tosses out: an extraordinary phrase for the most ordinary occurrence, which, from then on, makes both occurrence and phrase hold in memory. I smiled. We went on talking. And I had no idea of the story I'd just heard the beginning of.

Perhaps a year later, I first heard the tale complete, in its more or less final form: I'd been asked to speak at another party—a gathering of some of our interested citizens, back when I first had thoughts of running a series of exploratory programs for intelligent young people. (A decade more, and these programs would become the school I now head.) While the smoking brands kept away the insects, a gentleman introduced me to the people sitting on the benches or standing near the tables filled with drink and food about the lawn:

". . . and when he was presented with the traditional invitation to court in his seventeenth year, he declared to his parents that he would not accept it, and demanded that he be sent, instead, on a journey about the land, where he would learn many more things of interest and importance than he might ever glean within court walls. His wise parents consented, no doubt proud to have such an intelligent and resourceful son . . ."

But here, as it hadn't that afternoon in the other garden, the pressure of fact assailed me:

No such interview ever took place between me and either my mother or my father. Mother died suddenly when I was nine, while she was away visiting relatives in the Avila. Father's long and drawn-out illness through my sixteenth year, till at last in murmuring delirium he died, was no doubt one among many reasons that, in the confusions his terminal sickness wreaked on all his affairs, the topic of my official visit to court was indefinitely postponed. I'm sure when he saw me off in my caravan, my mother's brother, who generously housed me in the months after my father's death and who, indeed, sponsored my trip, was glad to see me go.

But when I was making plans to leave, I never thought of court. I don't believe my uncle did either.

There on the lawn, however, as I heard this gentleman refer to that fabulous parental encounter, I remembered the countess; somehow, in my failure to nip the rumor, which had no doubt budded back in that other garden, I saw now that I'd indulged a dishonesty that had returned as this outright false fact. But as the man went on, I also heard his tone of voice: he was speaking not as someone informing strangers of new happenings and new ideas. Rather he was reminding his friends, many of whom were my friends also, of things they already knew.

In thanking him for his generous words, I made only the most modest correction of what still seemed the exaggerations of someone only overanxious to speak well of me. The man considered himself my supporter—*my* friend. There was no need to make him out before his peers as either a liar or a fool. (Among those who knew me and my family, surely some recalled my age at my parents' deaths.) But even the modesty of my corrections soon joined the tale itself: many times over the next years, I would hear that, though as a youth I had, indeed, confronted my parents with such an ultimatum, I was too self-effacing to admit it—another sign of my high character.

It was only the most minor annoyance.

But to repeat: my parents were dead by the time of my trip. And I received no invitation to court, nor was I really expecting one. Why? Well, I lived in Kolhari, in Neverÿóna, not in the country: I have, and have had, many relatives at the court all my life. Even by my fifteenth year, I'd been through the great Eagle Gates many times, now to stay for a weekend with one earl, now for two weeks with another duchess, now to visit this young, provincial cousin in for his own official visit, now to attend a party honoring that one; I had gone riding and picnicking on the royal grounds more times than I and my two younger sisters had fingers and toes among us; and I'd already spent more time with, or at least within sight of, my third cousin twice removed (whose reign is awesome and adamantine) than many folk have who've lived at court for years. I'd already gained most of the experiences and benefits provincial nobles must travel to the city for. To skip my officially sponsored stay deprived me of very little. And by the time I was seventeen, everyone at court and pretty much everyone in my family simply assumed that, for all practical purposes, I had been.

Indeed, I'm sure that is what my uncle assumed.

As a practicing wise man, I'm concerned with mastering truth. To insist on such petty details, however, about what is, after all, only one's own personality seems to discredit the enterprise. Isn't it unseemly to dwell with such intensity on so minor a misprision of my personal history—especially one to my benefit?

Yet, annoy me it did.

A decade later, the school was becoming real; and various of the city's finer men and women who supported me from time to time would come to consult with me about my plans. One day I found myself in conversation with an intelligent young man from a successful merchant family. My noble friends still had their reservations about these alliances of mine within the world of trade, and my friends among merchants and tradesmen were aware of the nobles' misgiving. Yet I felt, finally, both sides respected me for trying to bridge the gap between the classes, whatever their personal reservations.

The young man and I had gotten down from his wagon to stroll a bit along the palm-lined avenue that runs between Neveryóna and Sallese. It was a warm spring evening. Behind the palms the wall of the old Aldamir Estate was topped with coppery light beneath a sky smeared over in the west with gray and violet clouds. A tall brown fellow, who'd done much traveling for his father, the young man wanted to identify his adult travels with my youthful ones; and I was happy to let him. As we ambled along the orange dust of the shoulder beside mud-mortared flags, he said to me with the pleasantest smile: "Years ago I heard a story from a friend of mine that, as a boy, when the time came for you to make the noble's traditional visit to court, you told your parents that you refused, and proposed instead that you go traveling. Were they really as pleased with your decision as people say?" He smiled at me, his green eyes in that earth-dark face suggesting relatives three or four generations back from the Ulvayn Islands, which he himself, no doubt, had never known by name. "There was no prospect of court in a childhood such as mine," he added. "Still, my father is such a stickler for tradition, I'm sure that if there *had* been, he would never have put up with such a suggestion from *me*!"

I looked at this intelligent, merchant's son. I remember I had a very strong sense of what, I thought, he wanted to hear from me: some speculation on the contrasting personalities of the aristocrats and tradesmen of Nevèrÿon. Doubtless, he both romanticized the nobility some—and disdained us. But that particular evening he was ready for some aristocratic speculation about how, perhaps, we nobles were sometimes more liberal with our children than his own hardheaded and practical relatives. And I also thought, while I walked with him: What nonsense! He's far too smart a boy really to want that kind of drivel—even if, this evening, he thinks he does. I also thought: He's not of my class. He's encumbered with none of the fables that weigh down the Nevèrÿon nobility like sinkers on a fishnet. Speak the truth to him directly, simply, firmly. What better ears than his to hear it! "I've even heard the story myself," I told him, chuckling. "Alas, there's nothing to it. There was never any talk of my going to court. With young nobles who actually live here in Kolhari, this is sometimes the case. My parents were dead by the time I was of age for my official court sojourn—and my uncle, who'd taken me in at my father's death, had too many of his own problems to think about such things. When I proposed my trip about the country to him, I saw it as a chance to get out of his way; and, though I'm sure he liked me well enough, I suspect that's how he saw it too and was at least a little grateful to me for wanting to leave just then. I took my trip. And I did not officially visit court—though I'd visited it unofficially many times. But the story of that brave and intelligent youth who conscientiously replaced one with the other by a concerted declaration of intent to his parents—parents who were, after all, in my case, quite dead at the time—is only a fable. I simply do not deserve the praise usually heaped on that so astute, so well deserving, but finally nonexistent lad."

There was no flicker in my young companion's green-eyed smile—no sign he'd misunderstood, or disbelieved. We talked about the new school's location (it was his father who'd just volunteered to sell me two of the Sallese buildings and to speak on my behalf to the owner of the third, as well as to

supervise the necessary renovations); we discussed the benefits of travel to students, the nature of intellectual inquiry, the
necessity of theoretical knowledge in practical matters.

And we returned to his cart, where he drove me back to my
gate.

Some three days later, my secretary rushed in to halt before
my chair. Light fell in slant lines through the shutters over his
agitated face: "Master, people are saying the most appalling
things about you! Now it's been decided that the school
buildings are definitely to be located not in Neveryóna but in
the artisans' district, it's rumored you've been telling the
merchants that you completely deny your noble connections.
They even say you've been spreading falsehoods about your
parentage, saying they were not really of the noble class! The
other nobles who have been sponsoring you have heard of this
and, of course, resent your pandering to the merchants'
prejudices; and the merchants themselves think you are trying
to play them for fools!"

I was, of course, bewildered, and tried to figure what,
indeed, could be the basis of such a tale. It took me three
days of careful inquiry among both merchants and nobles to
learn what had happened.

The tale had gone around that I'd told some merchant
youth that, as a child, I had not been *allowed* to go to court
because my parents were dead! This, I had explained to the
trusting young man (according to the rumor), was some sort
of *tradition* among local nobles! But the next person to whom
this youth—clearly the merchant's son with whom I'd been
talking that evening on the avenue—recounted his version of
my story happened to *be* a noble himself, who knew (quite
rightly) there had never been any such tradition among
noblemen of Nevèrÿon and that I was of no such disempowered
class: in much consternation, he'd explained all this to the
young man, while decrying my falsehoods. And the two of
them had gone on to speculate on what my motives could
possibly be for such outlandish prevarication!

Though among a few people with whom it mattered I was
able to set things more or less aright, the incident still remains
for me a sign of the pressure toward misunderstanding that
haunts all social communion:

For in this city there is still a monster all expect me to
speak of as "I."

"I" was a youth who, at his invitation to court, refused to

go and proposed to his parents (some say his uncle!) a trip across the country instead.

Sometimes, today, "I" am too modest to talk of this essentially admirable act.

At others, however, "I" simply deny it for my own exploitative ends.

And it is "I," they think, who lives in this city, runs this school, teaches these children, and is respected or criticized for it by the populace.

5.221 Placing Benjamin's quotation from Baudelaire in a fantasy context produces a very different effect from placing the same quotation in an SF context. And both effects are distinct from that which would result from placing it within an example of the literary genre Todorov called "the Fantastic" —or, indeed, placing it in a piece of "scientific" literary naturalism, e.g., Zola, or Sinclair Lewis.

In both paraliterary contexts, the Baudelaire dialogizes heatedly with the text. In both literary contexts, the Baudelaire merely approves or condemns the specific narrative tropes that evince what is usually called "the plot." To create true dialogue there, beyond this near-mute judgment, would require real critical violence.

5.23 My detractors in Neveryóna (many, after all, my relatives) say that by situating the school where I have, I've made both the pursuit and dissemination of knowledge a craft or trade, *the Master explained*. They see this as debased and appalling in these so unaristocratic times. But suppose I *had* located the school in one of the available Neveryóna estates? Would it have been any better to have made the pursuit and dissemination of knowledge an aristrocratic accomplishment?

5.3 "Now let me restate what you have said." The minister pulled his hands to the edge of the stone table. "First you tell me that of the hundred-thirty-seven persons who have so far been reported to have the disease, *all* are male . . . ? Then you cast your eyes down, become nervous, and tell me, well, they are not *all* male . . . ? Lord Vanar I am, of course, personally aquainted with. Should I assume, then, that this is a way of saying that those men with the disease are men who, in the eyes of many, might be considered *less* than male . . . ? If that is the case, then it is a truly astonishing illness!" Outside the small, high window, the sky was hot silver. ''Our position does not, however, afford us such coyness. We must observe this carefully and be prepared to act..."

6. with a thumbnail, nudged and nipped the dark, beneath bark's brown the yellow wood   beneath green, copper   under oil the ashy slate

stepped into hip-high troughs with hides floating, nudged them with poles while the gray gunk you waded in took the hairs off the leather   later on the sandy ledge examined his newly hairless thigh

Zadyuk had never worked in the tanning troughs   but he had six months at seventeen

Nari her hem hiked up and dripping among her tubs, the yard she worked her women in awash with lye   shrill shouts

something else to scrape away apparent color loved color because it appeared   wove wires in the warp   stretched thin, beat flat as foil   threw it away if they broke (once) put it up after that and sold it cheaper   this pain poled through and poked by his arm's prod, his knee's pole, under pain only more   would make it different from everything else and he didn't believe that   comfortable positions when you're sick as rare as beauty when you're not working well   his workshop

was it necessary to feel a little superior to friends to love them

that anxiety   he wished the workshop   hide hanging behind the planks in wait for summer   to be at the shop   not opened   wasn't closed

nothing superior now

resting on his bed and not entirely there, he skidded about a circle of words surrounding a fire finger brushing its char on the side of some terra-cotta pot when he was six, skimmed years and alleys and facts that fell in a turbulence that was more its swing and rhythm than its settle)when he was seventeen(and stop

watching the small furious woman who had been his mother die, as a fourteen-year-old he'd thought the happiest death would be one   like hers at the end   where you were too exhausted by the facts of dying, the hour by hour bargain with pain, the moment by moment barter for breath, bargains and barters you always came out on the short end of, to fear

fear of death was something you indulged if you were

healthy, perceptive, alert   dying took up too much of your diminished strength

afraid before, among so many weeks of illness, what once had been fear now only rose to annoyance

sunlight wedged in the window corner lay on jamb and sill like a lock of hair from a certain lively afternoon hour pausing outside to catch her breath, where voices talked of traffic, boiled grain and pepper smell, of what was happening across the street he'd always thought cluttered, convenient, and picturesque

to lie here in his room was to be sick but not that sick

when he was that sick he was usually someplace else

6.01 "Shannon decided that English is about 50 percent redundant when we consider samples of eight letters at a time. If the length of the sample is increased, the redundancy is much greater. For sequences of up to 100 letters it rises to approximately 75 percent. The figure is even higher in the case of whole pages or chapters, where the reader is able to get an idea of the long-range statistics of a text, including its theme and literary style. This means, Shannon said, that much of what we write is dictated by the structure of the language and is more or less forced upon us. Only what little is left is of our own free choosing."—Jeremy Campbell
Grammatical Man

6.1 On the raised paving stone beyond the mouth of the Bridge of Lost Desire, on the speakers' platform at both old and new markets, at corners in the business district along Black Avenue, on the waterfront and in the central squares of the ethnic neighborhoods, Imperial criers, wearing the sign of the Royal Eagle on breast and back, shouted:

"There is danger in Kolhari of plague. To date there have been seventy-nine probable deaths—and of the several hundred who have contracted it, no one has yet recovered. We advise care, caution, and cleanliness, and Her Majesty, whose reign is brave and beneficent, discourages the indiscriminate gathering of crowds. This is not an emergency! No, this is *not* an emergency! But it is a situation Her Majesty feels might develop into one."

And on the bridge and in the market and on the street corners and in the yards, people gathered, heard, glanced at their neighbors, and dispersed quickly.

6.11 "Once the plague is established in the city, the regular
forms collapse. There is no maintenance of roads and sewers,
no army, no police, no municipal administration. Pyres are
lit at random to burn the dead, with whatever means are
available. Each family wants to have its own. Then wood,
space, and flame itself growing rare, there are family feuds
around the pyres, soon followed by a general fight, for the
corpses are too numerous. The dead already clog the streets in
ragged pyramids gnawed at by animals around the edges. The
stench rises in the air like a flame. Entire streets are clogged
by the piles of dead. Then the houses open and the delirious
victims, their minds crowded with hideous visions, spread
howling through the streets. The disease that ferments in their
viscera and circulates throughout their entire organism dis-
charges itself in tremendous cerebral explosions. Other victims,
without buboes, delirium, pain, or rash, examine themselves
proudly in the mirror, in splendid health, as they think, and
then fall dead with their shaving mugs in their hands, full of
scorn for other victims.

"Over the poisonous, thick, bloody streams (color of
agony and opium) which gush out of the corpses, strange
personages pass, dressed in wax, with noses long as sausages
and eyes of glass, mounted on a kind of Japanese sandal
made of double wooden tablets, one horizontal, in the form of
a sole, the other vertical, to keep them from the contaminated
fluids, chanting absurd litanies that cannot prevent them from
sinking into the furnace in their turn. These ignorant doctors
betray only their fear and their childishness.

"The dregs of the population, apparently immunized by
their frenzied greed, enter the open houses and pillage riches
they know will serve no purpose or profit. . . . The last of the
living are in a frenzy: the obedient and virtuous son kills his
father; the chaste man performs sodomy upon his neighbors.
The lecher becomes pure. The miser throws his gold in
handfuls out the window. The warrior-hero sets fire to the city
he once risked his life to save. The dandy decks himself out
in his finest clothes and promenades before the charnel house.
Neither the idea of an absence of sanctions nor that of
imminent death suffices to motivate acts so gratuitously absurd
on the part of men who did not believe death could end
anything. And how explain the surge of erotic fever among
the recovered victims who, instead of fleeing the city, remain

where they are, trying to wrench a criminal pleasure from the
dying or even the dead, half crushed under the pile of corpses
where chance has lodged them. . . .''

6.12 Artaud's bit of *feuilletonage noire* about the plague
(above) is basically the image Ken Russell mounted so vividly
in his film *The Devils*.

This ''plague'' has the same politically reactionary relation
to the reality of present-day urban epidemics that Elias Canetti's
description of the violent, hostile, mindless mob in *Crowds
and Power* has to the two most common manifestations of the
contemporary urban crowd: the Audience and the Protest.

6.2 ''You mean to tell me—'' and the minister placed his
hands on his brocaded lap beneath the stone table—''that
among the more than three-hundred-fifty persons with the
disease so far reported by our inspectors, which till now we
assumed were all males, and homosexual males at that, there
are at *least* seven women? and five children under the age of
four?'' Outside the high small window, the evening had fallen
into a brilliant cobalt. ''So far, there have been seventy-five
deaths and, to date, no recoveries. I am afraid we are past the
time of preparation and observation. We must act.'' The
minister turned to the head of the table. ''Your Highness, let
me propose . . .''

6.3 ''It's interesting about its social patterns,'' Peter mused.
''There I am, working at the Gay Men's Health Crisis three
days a week, interviewing people with AIDS every day, and
yet I don't know anyone in my personal circle who's come
down with it. On the other hand, I know of people who have
eight, nine, ten friends who have it.'' White wine stood in
three cut crystal glasses. A fringed cloth covered the round
oak table. ''The thing you have to remember with AIDS is
that all these statistics about the average number of sexual
contacts a year for the average person with AIDS—sixty a
year, three hundred a year—are very skewed. And the range
those averages are drawn from is immense. There're guys
with it who claim only one or two contacts for a lifetime, the
last of which was a couple of years before they came down
with it. And there're some who claim truly astronomical
numbers of contacts, three or four thousand per year. And
with a subject as touchy as this, *both* could be exaggerating in

either direction for any number of reasons." It's July 1983. Peter has been doing volunteer work for AIDS in New York City for six months now.

"Peter," I said, "you know what three hundred contacts a year can mean." I said: "You go out to the right movie theater with some action in the back balcony for an hour and a half on Tuesday night, and on your way home from work Friday you stop into the right public john for twenty minutes. You can easily have three contacts involving semen in each. With only two hours a week devoted to it, that's six contacts a week; and *that's* three hundred and twelve for the year. You know as well as I do, you can keep up an eight-hour-a-day job, an active social life, have your three hundred contacts, and not even be late for dinner. Thousands of men in this city live that way." (I pondered the dozen-plus years I did it myself, with a wife who was agreeable to it, which is how I managed to combine married life and a child with an active gay life that continues more than half a dozen years after our divorce.) "And that's without ever going to the baths or a bar with a back room—where you can up that by a factor of two, three, or more without really trying. The fact is, the straight people who're dealing with AIDS—say the ones in the media—simply have no notion of the *amount* of sexual activity that's available to a gay male in this city!" I said: "Most straights, Peter, don't realize, when they're putting together these statistics, that a moderately good looking gay man in his twenties or thirties can have two or three contacts while he's in the subway on his way to the doctor's to see if he *has* AIDS. . . ." I was surprised at my outburst. I think the two other people at the table were too.

Peter said: "We also know that there're many, many gay people—probably many more thousands—who can count the number of sexual contacts they have a year on one or two hands, Chip." (That's my nickname that replaced "Sam" when I was ten.) "Still, the people with AIDS I've been working with—" He speared a fried potato from his plate and held it a moment on his fork— "have *really* been living life in the fast lane. But we still don't have any reliable statistical prototype for sexual behavior. In my own experience, I see a leaning toward IV-needles and passive anal. But that's what they're calling anecdotal evidence, these days. And everyone's got some, and it's all different."

Slightly pinkened, reflecting from the stained-glass window, open this July morning, sunlight gouged slivers in the stainless-steel-ware.

6.31 In Nevèrÿon there is, of course, a model for the outbreak of the disease: some years before, an epidemic struck the outlying Ulvayn Islands, during which the empress, whose reign has been, on occasion, both caring and compassionate, sent ships and physicians to help evacuate those who were still healthy and who wished to come to the mainland.

The leaders of Nevèrÿon's capital and port, Kolhari—most modern, most sophisticated, most progressive of primitive cities—, have some sense of the conservative nature of the Artaudian plague, even if, without Artaud's text, they carry that sense on a more primitive level than we do. Thanks to reports from the islands, they know that *that* is what their city must never come to look like.

6.4 Once, that night, Pheron, who was twenty-four (a fact that, several times in the midst of all this, had astonished him), woke in darkness, feeling better. Well, that had happened before; he did not consider miraculous cures.

Lying on soft straw and under a cover he had given its luminous oranges and ceruleans, he turned to his side (his lower back throbbed, distracting him from the queasiness pulsing in his throat), thought about his father, and smiled.

He had been seventeen, working out at the tanning troughs.

His father had been laboring at the construction site of the New Market.

One day in every twelve his father had off, coming home late that night and sleeping far into the next morning.

Pheron had two days off in every ten.

His third off-time coincided with one of his father's, to both their surprise; the evening before, they sat in the dark room with the lamp on the table Pheron had lit from the cook-fire coals.

His father leaned his arm in front of his bowl. Lamplight doubled the number of hairs over blocky forearm strung with high veins, putting a shadow hair beside each real one on the brown skin.

The lamp flame wavered.

Half the hairs moved.

With a wooden paddle in his other hand, his father ate

noisily from the grain, peppers, and fat Pheron had stewed together. "Maybe then, tomorrow," his father said, "we'll go someplace. You and me." He gestured with the paddle. "Together."

"Sure," Pheron said, unsure what he meant.

Then both went to bed, Pheron sleeping with his heel wedged back between the big toe and the toe over of his other foot, fists curled in straw by his face, fingers smelling of garlic and the new barbaric spice, cinnamon (one of his recent enthusiasms his father put up with), and the acid from the bark that soaked in the stone troughs, their tides and ripplings littoral to his day.

Lingering at the mouth of the Bridge of Lost Desire, his father pulled at his earlobe, where gray hairs grew, with heavy workman's fingers and said in flat tones that signed a kind of nervousness (as a boy, Pheron had feared those tones because often they presaged punsishment): "You ever come here before . . . ?"

Certainly Pheron had crossed the bridge to the Old Market. As certainly, he knew that that was not what his father meant. But "No" would be easy and appeasing.

Perhaps because the tanning work meant he was grown, or because being grown meant you stayed tired enough that the appeasements you'd once indulged you didn't have the energy for now, he said, anyway: "No . . ." Then, louder: "I mean, yes. I've been here. Yes. Before."

His father smiled a little. "I thought it was about time I took you to get yourself a woman. After your mother died, I came here enough—more than I should have. I don't too much now. But we may still meet some lady who remembers me." His father rubbed his ear again. "Only now you tell me you've already beat me. That means, I guess, I *do* neglect you—more than a father should. Well, then, you know how it's done."

With the veil of exhaustion that lay, these days, over both working and nonworking time, blatant confession seemed as out of keeping as blatant denial. "Why don't you find yourself a woman," Pheron said, "and I'll meet you back here in a few hours?"

"No," his father said. "Come on. We'll go together, you and me. Besides, if we both use the same room, it'll be cheaper."

They began to walk across.

"Go on," his father said. "Tell me which ones you like the most."

A strangeness in it all—it *was* his father—made him want to smile. And, very deeply, dark discomfort streamed through. The strangest thing, however, was how ordinary it all—humor and discomfort—seemed. Father and son? he thought. Two workmen, an older and a younger, come to the bridge for sex? It was a pattern someone must have fit in the very stones of the bridge itself. "I guess . . ." Pheron shrugged. "Well, that one's cute—"

"Ah, you like them young!" His father chuckled. "Not me! Even when I was your age. I always thought the older ones would give me a better time. And I'm right, too. Your mother was four years older than I was—and if she'd been fourteen years older, it wouldn't have been so bad."

"Father," Pheron said, suddenly, recklessly: "I don't want a woman." Then: "If I was going to buy anyone here, it would be a man. And besides: when I come here, men pay *me*!" And added: "Sometimes." Because he'd only done that three times anyway, and that at the instigation of an outrageous friend he didn't see much of now.

He walked with his father half a dozen more steps. He felt light-headed, silly, brave. (He imagined some tangle of shuttle and warp quickly, agressively, finally unknotted.) Yes, his heart was beating faster. But the tiredness was gone. The soles of his feet tingled in his sandals; so did his palms.

His father stopped.

The sky was clear. Under Pheron's jaw and on the back of his arm, where sun did not touch, were cool. Across the walkway, a redheaded boy herded ahead half a dozen goats. They lifted bearded muzzles to glance about, yellow eyes slit with black, bleating and bleating. One raised a short tail, spilling black pellets from a puckered sphincter, only to get pushed on by three others. Two older women at the far wall laughted—though whether at the goats or the goatherd, Pheron couldn't tell. A donkey cart passed in the opposite direction.

"Then your mother was right," his father said, finally.

Pheron thought, *He must be furious*, and waited for the loud words, for the recriminations, for the distance glimmering between them to be struck away by anger.

"I suppose I knew she was. But I always said it was something you'd grow out of. Now, there! See, maybe you *will* grow out of it."

"I'm seventeen, father. It's just the way I am. I don't . . ." He shrugged. "I don't *want* to grow out of it!"

His father started walking again; so Pheron walked too.

His father said: "You should try a woman. You might be surprised. You can find nice ones, here. I don't mean just pretty. I mean ones who're fun, even kind. Someone like you, you see: you need one who's kind, patient—that's because you're sensitive, young, unsure of yourself. I should have brought you here before. I know that, now."

"I've tried it," Pheron said. "Before. With a few women." Well, one, he thought. And there'd been another boy with them. "I didn't like it that much. Not like with men. That's better. For me, I mean . . ." His father was getting ahead, so Pheron hurried. "You like women. Suppose someone told *you* to grow out of *that*?"

"Ha!" his father said. "No. No, I guess there's not much chance of that!"

Pheron laughed. "Then what do you want to do? You get a woman, I'll get a man?" (For some reason, that morning there were no male hustlers in sight, though there were many girls and women about.) "And we'll *both* share a room? Maybe *you* should try a man!" He laughed again, feeling nervous. Not his father's nervousness, either. It was all his. "Men are cheaper than women, here. Did you know that? It's true. Some people go with either. If you were one of those who could do that, you could save yourself some money—"

"Oh, no!" his father said, still a step ahead. He waved his hand behind. "No—"

Then he stopped again.

The sound he made was not a shout:

"Ahhhii—!"

A grown man might make it at sudden pain: a sigh with much too much voice to it, perhaps a quarter of the sound a full shout might carry.

Pheron stopped too.

His father looked back. "You don't want this? With me? Go on then!"

"Maybe—"

"Go on home," his father said. "You don't need to be here with me, for this. Go on, I say!" He looked back. "What do I want you here with me for? Get out of here—now!"

Ahead, goats bleated.

Their arms around each other's shoulders, two prostitutes walked by with a third chattering after them.

Pheron turned back toward the bridge mouth. By the time he came off, he was trembling and angry. Halfway home, wrestling the anger silently, he felt the tiredness again. He walked half a dozen streets he wouldn't have ordinarily taken—a long route home. When he reached the door to their dark rooms, set back in the shoulder-wide alley between the stable and the brickyard, he was mumbling: "I'm too tired to be angry. I'm too tired . . ." It was something his mother had occasionally said. Usually she hadn't meant it either.

Under his bed frame was a handloom. When he got inside he pulled it out and sat in front of it cross-legged on the earthen floor. The strip he'd been weaving was wide as the length of his forearm laid across it. The finished material was rolled in a bundle on the loom's back bar. Currently he was in the midst of a ten shuttle pattern, at least for this part, for he'd varied his design along the three meters he'd done so far, now using yarns of different thicknesses, now of different colors, now varying the pattern itself, sometimes using a knotted weave, sometimes a plain one, the whole an endless experiment.

He wove furiously till the window dimmed.

Then he got out the jar of expensive oil and filled and lit three lamps from the banked coals under the ashes in the fireplace. He set two lamps on the corners of the table and one down on the floor at his side—waiting for the moon.

A running argument with his father went: "If you're going to work after dark, Pheron, don't waste expensive oil. Take it up on the roof and work by moonlight!" which Pheron always said he would do, only—"I'm just using the lamps till the moon comes out, anyway, father." But often, once started, he would weave by lamplight half the night, while the full moon came, went away again, and he, refilling the lamps half a dozen times, never even looked out the window to see. "Pheron, I *told* you—"

He wove again.

He got up and went to look out the window; for the moon should be full or near so. But it *wasn't* out yet. So he sat back down on the floor.

He wove some more.

The hanging across the door whispered. He heard his father push through and didn't look up.

His father moved around the room and, after a while, said: "Here. You like this stuff."

So he glanced over.

"I got you something."

The yarn bundles dropped on the table. One rolled between the lamps and fell to the floor, spinning in the air on dark string.

By the lamplight, he could only make out the brighter hues.

"Oh." He put the shuttles down. "Hey . . . !" He pushed himself up to his knees.

"In the Old Market," his father said. He stood by the table, beard all under-lit, his arms still bent with the ghost of their gift. "I don't know whether they're colors you want. But I figured, you could use them. For something." He reached up to pull his ear. "Some of that stuff is expensive, you know?" Now he picked up one and another of the skeins, frowning. "I just thought . . ."

Pheron stood, his back stiff, his thighs aching from crouching so long on the floor. "Thanks . . ." He tried to think of something else to say. "You want something to eat? I'll stop and fix some—"

"No," his father said. "No, I ate. You fix for yourself if you want. Not me. I got something while I was out."

His father, Pheron realized, was slightly drunk.

"Is this stuff something you can use? You like it?"

"Yeah," Pheron said. "Yes. Thanks. Thanks a lot."

"You go on," his father said. "You go on working. I just thought you might like, might use . . . some of these."

"No," Pheron said. "I'll stop for a little." Then he asked, because there just didn't seem any way not to: "Did you find a woman?"

His father pretended not to have heard.

The two of them sat at the table together awhile.

Some of the skeins had come undone.

Several times his father buried the fingers of one hand in the yarns to lift a tangle from the table in the lamplight, blinking through the strands as if to determine the color in the inadequate glow.

His father said, finally: "I didn't get a woman. I didn't want one. I got you this. See? Instead."

Pheron thought: This isn't the kind of apology I wanted. I wanted him to have his woman and I wanted him to say, too,

"I thought about it, Pheron, and I was wrong. I'm sorry. You're my son. And I want you to be my son any way you are. Any way. You have your way. I have mine. But whoever you are, it's fine with me. Do you forgive me?'' (How many times while he'd woven had he rehearsed what his father should tell him?) But, as he leaned his elbows on the table, he thought: That's just not who he is. That's just not what he can give. And I'm too tired to ask for it, or even—he realized after a while—to want it that much.

Through raised strands, his father blinked. "What's the matter with you?" He put his tangled hand down.

Sitting back on the bench. Pheron rubbed his wet eyes with two forefingers which were growing rougher with each day at the troughs. "Nothing."

"The moon's out," his father said. "You want to work, I know. Take it up to the roof. So you don't waste good oil."

"No," he said. "I . . . Well—yeah. Maybe. All right." He stood up, looking at the dark yarn piled on the table. "Thanks for all this stuff. Thanks." He picked one of the skeins to take with him, though he wasn't sure what color it was.

His father grunted.

Pheron turned and picked up his handloom. Shuttles swung and clicked. "You all right?" he asked.

His father nodded. "Don't stay up too long, though."

"I won't," Pheron said.

Behind him, his father blew out first one, then the other lamp, so that the only light came from the one still on the floor, below the table.

Pheron lay in the dark (seven years later), not thinking of his father's death three years before, but of this; and of squatting before his handloom on the roof, moonlight bleaching the colors from his design's intricacies, while he wove on into night.

7. A woman writes from the Northwest:

"What really angers me about the AIDS business is that women, *we*, find ourselves again in the position of *helping men*. Out of the goodness of our hearts. . . . Where were they when *we* were fighting the health-care system because of what it routinely did to women? Nowhere, that's where. . . . It pisses me off to find myself in the Helpmeet Business again, especially since the whole situation *is* so bad—the right wing screeching, 'God hates gays!'—so that, in all conscience, really, I can't do anything but be appalled by the disease itself *and* the homophobic capital being made out of it.

"What we must do, politically, is make it clear that the bigotry that sees AIDS as a sinner's punishment (or merely assumes that gay men's lives are expendable or trivial or not important) is the *same* bigotry that hates and fears women and wants to keep us in our place, i.e., squashed. This is the *same* ideology that allows most people, of both sexes and all sexual persuasions, to swallow a government that is spending more and more billions on war toys and lining somebody's pockets thereby. . . . I'm afraid that only the usual radicals are making this connection (but they always made it). . . .

"Of course the epidemic is a terrible thing—and the satisfaction with which so many Americans regard it as God's fulfillment of their own extremely disgusting system of values and fantasies is worse. I HATE the antisexual use of AIDS even more than its use against homosexuality *per se*. To be morally upset about how other people take their sexual pleasures is surely the weirdest human quirk ever. It is utterly silly, especially when one knows nothing but myth anyway. (Here the usual voices come in, "But violence—" *Of course* I don't approve of rape or murder!)

"People are biologically so constituted that they not only *like* being sexually aroused and satisfied, but they tend to get antsy or cranky when none or far too little of this is happening. This seems to me quite simple and totally amoral."

7.1 Conferments in the High Council Chamber; conferments before and after that in several lower ones.

Discussions in the throne room. (In still another room someone declared: "Oh, she will stamp her small foot, but Lord Krodar will have his way." No foot was stamped, however, and the conference with the Child Empress Ynelgo lasted a third the time the most sanguine courtier had predicted. Later, however, the Empress called her aged vizerine to her to meet privately.) Details, pronouncements, instructions made their way through the High Court; messengers were dispatched—finally a messenger returned; so that on a balmy morning in the month of the Ferret, Imperial couriers shouted from every street corner—indeed, the announcement was first made at dawn but was repeated throughout the day and the city, both by proclamation and rumor, till, that evening, few did not know it:

"Her Royal Highness, the Child Empress Ynelgo, in a reign both greathearted and gracious, has sent an Imperial deposition to the very borders of her empire to confer with the man known to the people as Gorgik the Liberator, with an invitation to come to the capital, Kolhari, and assume the post of minister at the High Court of Eagles, where he shall work with the empress and her other ministers and employ his talents for the betterment of the nation and the alleviation of the suffering of all classes, high and low, slave and freeman.

"He has consented.

"In honor of this joyous occasion, a week of Carnival will shortly be declared throughout Kolhari, at which time all employers must cut their work to half-time for five days, so that no one labors more than six hours consecutively, followed by an entire day of leisure and license. The city and the nation will officially celebrate with carnival the coming of the Liberator to the High Court of Eagles!"

7.11 And that, said the minister, should get their minds off this unbearable plague!

7.2 For several years she had traveled with her cart about the land, telling stories—now in the great houses scattered over the country, now in the markets of outlying cities, now to strangers who stopped by her evening camp. Her rewards had been as varied as her tales: sometimes food, lodging, and entertainment; sometimes money; sometimes the simple satisfaction of a grin from a young girl or a smile from an old man whom she had brought to some affective understanding of the taking of joy or sorrow or wonder. Sometimes it was introductions, verbal or written, to other great houses, other markets, where there would be more food, more money, more children and oldsters, and more introductions.

It is the rare society that does not abuse its artists, and Nevèrÿon was not rare. Norema had suffered its abuse, but she had come through it with a minimum of bitterness, a maximum of goodwill, and a little money saved—with which, on returning to Kolhari, she had rented a small room for a while, planning to relax, recuperate, think.

Recently a friend whom she'd found after long searching had gone off again—this time probably for good. But then, after she'd been in the city only three days, while walking in the Old Market of the Spur, she'd run into another friend she'd thought lost to her forever—a wealthy merchant woman who lived in her walled estate in Sallese and for whom Norema had once worked as secretary years before. The woman had welcomed her warmly and had been materially helpful to her several times since, so that, once more, for both better and worse, life had again gone against expectations.

But the man who lived in the room beside her—talking to him a few times when she'd first moved in, she'd decided she liked him—was very ill. When she went out for her own water to the cistern in the back, she had taken to filling one of the chipped jars to bring back for him. Now and again she went in to help him clean himself or to bring him food from the market.

As the evening put bright copper along the edge of her window, and the air outside fell into dark blue, in her room Norema sat on the bench by the clay wall and thought—

7.3 CMV, ASFV, HTLV, Hepatitis-B model, retroviruses, LAV, the multiple agent theory, the "poppers" theory, the double-virus theory, the genetic disposition theory (the eternal Government Plot theory!), the two-population theory; and I just learned today that the average person with AIDS is in his upper thirties, rather than in his mid-twenties, as I'd thought— that is, he's much closer to my age than, say, to some of the more sexually active people I know. To date (March 1984) there are 19 cases under 20; 831 between 20 and 30; 1,762 between 30 and 40; 813 between 40 and 50; and 330 over 49, with another 19 cases where the age is unknown.

A hundred-fifty-eight of these are women; and because the women with AIDS are, so insistently, both socially (most are IV drug users and/or the sexual partners of men who are) and statistically marginal, you can bet dollars to doughnuts that *they* are getting the truly shitty end of an already inhumanly shitty stick. Should I change Toplin, Pheron, or Lord Vanar, then, to make them more characteristic . . . ?

Should I modify them as to age, sex, or class to make them even *less* so . . . ?

To tell any tale in such a situation is to have press in on you the hundreds, the thousands (the most recent headline: GUESS WHAT HITS FOUR THOUSAND?) you aren't telling.

I could write a small pamphlet on every one of the above acronyms—as could, I guess, just about every nontechnophobe gay male in New York City at this time.

The CMV theory still makes good sense, but I put a lot of hope in the two-population theory (a comparatively small, vulnerable population, a comparatively large immune one) if only to preserve sanity—though I am highly interested in the LAV work (as is everyone this month—along with the "too good to be true" Dapsone treatment for KS, with its entailed "variably acid-fast" mycobacterium theory), as we wait for the release of a report by the Atlanta CDC that's expected later this month from the French Institute Pasteur—officially confirming LAV as the agent—in hopes that it will begin to consign this period to the past of historical nightmare, from which we can start to shake ourselves awake. It's much the same sort of excitement, however, as we had about ASFV six months ago.

What was the old Chinese curse?

"May you live in interesting times!"

This kind of entry, incidentally, is just what makes a great book like John Reed's *Ten Days That Shook the World* all but unreadable to a later generation.

Still, no one will understand this period who does not gain some insight into these acronyms and retrieve some understanding of how they *must* obsess us today, as possible keys to life, the possibility of living humanely, and death.

7.4 It is not that easy to flee, *Norema thought. When I was younger, the world was a series of loud and foaming oceans. One after the other, I launched out into each, with as much excitement as fear. Today it is a sequence of badly tended fields, each to be struggled across, the waves and the cities as difficult as the woods. Someone ran by outside, banging a ceramic drum, shouting. The mention of Carnival, and they act as if, finally and at last, they've trapped their Liberator, hauled him back from what moment of flight, and fixed him in one of their empty halls, like a beast or a prisoner chained in some void cistern. Will he be strong enough to act from within court walls, to make himself heard through the granite that, from now on, surrounds him? Will he be able to thrust his arm through the fog of protocol, tradition, habit, the very constitution of power with which he now becomes one? Will he be powerful? What is possible from within the paralyzing citadel? She looked about the darkening room, at wooden statues by the fire, at ornamental jars on the table, the parchments beside them on which she kept notes for her tales.*

Some were piled at the corner, some—the most recent—were spread on the table itself. What an array of aids to memory! There's the small, glazed jar of rinds and spices given me by that old dear in Ka'hesh. Open it in a room where all real filth has been cleared away, and it will cleanse the remaining mustiness from the air inside an hour. Opening it here three months ago, pungently I recalled the giver. (Polished bone rings on her earth-stained fingers . . .) Sitting on high rocks by the sea, I inked my skins with notions for "The Tale of Time and Pain": *Lean-masted ships sailed into the sun-shot harbor . . . among dark bushes children muttered magical rhymes . . . that morning the Queen ordered the captured slave-girl to dress herself as a count.* That parchment's on the table now. Looking at it this morning, *what* did I recall? (What do I recall I recalled . . .) Perhaps the question is: Who is the giver in such situations? Myself? The sea? The rocks I sat on? Time? Or the nameless god of language skills, who is at once so niggardly and so profligate with the blessings she holds back from living song to bestow on silent record?

Twice as I roamed this country, I've been set on by bandits. Both times I was lucky and escaped. (Both times they thought me a smuggler.) Both times, when they found my cart contained nothing of salable value, but rather the old marked-on skins where I work out my tales, they let me go with only the most perfunctory threats.

It happened once, and I moved on through the forest after it in a transport of self-congratulation and gratitude. Six months later, it happened again; this time when the scarred criminal who set upon me recognized what I carried was writing, he became furious as he pulled the vella out and threw them in the leaves, now ripping this, now crumpling that. Indeed, he ruined many of them, while I stanched all urge to plead with him that he cease, lest he think his ravages did me more harm than they did, leading him on to destroy systematically what he now ruined at random. When I finally got to go on my way through the dappled wood, I was nowhere near as joyful as before—and chose my routes more carefully.

Another parchment there on the table bears the sentence I wrote about the second of those two outrages, hoping at some point to use it in a tale: "The peg shook in the distended lobe." How long have I spent looking at it, rereading it, rewriting it now this way, now that. Should "distended" be there, or not? ". . . in the lobe" hangs from the sentence's end as the lobe of that rough man's ear hung from the curvital cartilage, as he stood above me after he'd pushed me to the ground. "Distended," then, distends the phrase that gives the experience, miming it: two dancers make two identical gestures in one dance. That doubling bespeaks the art that belies the improvisatory quality of their practice. But we have all seen those carved pegs such men thrust through their ears; we know their forefinger thickness, their intricate scrimshaw. Perhaps, then, I want the words to move *against* the experience, to tug in tension with the reality, like a dancer moving away from himself in a mirror. (Drop "distended" then ...?) Certainly that's no *less* artful. But which verbal gesture do I want? Support or opposition? And does Pheron ever weave and unweave at a single row as much?

What to think about, instead of that man's pain?

Once, some weeks after his illness began, I sat in his room and watched him weave three hours. I drank a tea, chatting with him while he worked. Work, he says. Work is what makes him feel human, those days at a time he can do it. Now, I've watched women weave before. Did his slow, bright pattern bring it to mind, then? As his shuttles went in and out and under, carrying color over, dropping one hue beneath another, I thought: *That* is what *I* do when I make a tale! Whatever god oversees the making of webs and nets and fabrics must also oversee the construction of stories. Oh, putting them together is so very different from the assemblage of the words and phrases, the joining of hearsay to hoped-for by which common workers and wastrels make up the speeches they tell some laboring girl to aggrandize themselves in her blinking and distracted eyes, speeches in which truths and lies trip over each other the night long. *More singing outside in the street broke up into laughter. One woman began to sing again.* When I was younger, there was a plague in the islands. I will not rehearse what I lost there. They dare this merriment here only because the illness is so limited—to men, though I've heard otherwise, and, at least in the general mind, to men like Pheron.

But what must such laughter say when it rings beyond the windows of those, women or men, who are sick to their death?

When I was a child on my marginal island that I thought, then, was the world, inland tribes sometimes held festive navens, where everyone dressed up in everyone else's clothes, the chief hunters and the head wives pretending they were beggars and outcasts, while the social pariahs were obeyed like queens and kings for the day. Women pretended to be men; men dressed as women. Parents made obeisance to their children, and children strutted like adults. It was a wonderfully healing practice. In the midst of it life itself became a wonder-studded tale with endless lessons for later use woven through with delight. I am truly pleased at this carnival time in Kolhari. Some go, rather, to a monstrous calling—not I. I will walk out in the streets, singing among the festival's celebrants.

For the Liberator has come to Kolhari...

Still, when I think of what those songs, that laughter must mean to those who are excluded from it, I want to flee this city, this country, this land ready to think of anything but the pain within it. Only considering what lies on the other side of such flight stops me. And when I consider, I imagine in place of my personal exile, some text, a tale I might weave together, here, now, in this room at the end of this Kolhari alley, a luminous fabric that leaps from the loom of language for a monstrous, phthartic flight, soaring, habromanic, glorious as song and happy as summer, till finally it sinks into the savage and incicurable complexities of its own telling, to be torn apart by what impelled it: angry criminals fall to ravage a cartful of parchments.

This will be a fine celebration.

This will be a dark carnival.

7.5 Historically the official reaction to plague in Europe was the one described by Defoe in *A Journal of the Plague Year* (1722): "The government... appointed public prayers and days of fasting and humiliation, [and encouraged the more serious inhabitants] to make public confession of sin and implore the mercy of God to avert the dreadful judgment which hung over their heads.... All the plays and interludes which, after the manner of the French Court, had been set up, and began to increase among us, were forbid to act; the gaming-tables, public dancing-rooms, and music-houses, which multiplied and began to debauch the manners of the people, were shut up and suppressed; and the jack-puddings, merry-andrews, puppet-shows, rope-dancers, and such like-doings, which had bewitched the people, shut up their shops, finding indeed no trade; for the minds of the people were agitated with other things, and a kind of sadness and horror at these things sat upon the countenance even of the common people. Death was before their eyes, and everybody began to think of their Grave, not of mirth and diversion.''

Defoe's last few lines may betray that this is the official interpretation of the response as well as the official proscription: if there was, indeed, ''no trade,'' why would these merry-makings need to be ''forbid,'' ''shut-up,'' and ''suppressed''? At any rate, even in Artaud's conservative schema, once ''official theater'' is banished during the plague, the reemergence, here and there, of spontaneous theatrical gestures in the demoralized populace at large throughout the city represents, for him, the birth of true and valid art/theater/spectacle.

Though not burdened with a modern theory of germs—not obsessed with acronyms—Nevèrÿon certainly has some intuitive knowledge of contagion. And despite (or because of) the inhabitants' suspicions of its officially sanctioned carnival and its official invitation to the Liberator to take part in its cabinet, this unusual response has opened a marginal space for a certain radical gesture.

Do I, however, know what it is?

7.6 That morning Pheron sat at the table, sore at groin, back, and flank, not thinking as much as possible between moments of yearning after his workshop. But his walk to the end of the block and back, which he'd been forcing himself to take (almost) every morning, had again confirmed that he was not strong enough to go the three quarters of a mile through the busy city and return.

Where *was* the scamp who'd helped him out at the work-shop the week before the illness had forced him home? Not that he expected to see him again. Oh, definitely a girl next time. No more boys. Not in the shop at any rate. The girls appreciated his wit, were impressed with the stream of (impressive) clients in and out, fell in love with him a little, and worked dreadfully hard because of it. With the boys, however, even the ugly awkward ones he'd offered jobs only out of compassion, sure he could never feel anything but pity for them, it was always he who began to fall a little in love (or into too great a pity). He grew lax. They grew lazy. No, definitely a girl—

A chill moment caught him up as if a wind had come through the window: because he was not getting better, he knew. He was only teaching himself to live with the decayings, failings, breakdowns in the body that marked an inexorable deterioration.

Hung in a fringe across his window, yarns were black with the sunlit blaze beyond.

Somewhere outside a wagon stopped.

Two of the three planks still leaned in the door frame, but the leather curtain hung in front of them. When leather moved, he thought it was Norema come with more water.

Backed by sunlight, the figure swayed.

Pheron sat up—not as quickly as he might—and blinked.

The boy—it was a boy's voice and a boy's body outlined by the sun—put his hand on the side of the door and leaned.

Further out in the sunlight stood an older man. His brocaded robe suggested that he was a lord. There were others as well—

The boy said: "Excuse me. You're Pheron, the dyer and weaver?"

Pheron nodded.

'You are very sick . . . ?"

Pheron squinted.

"So am I," the boy said. "I . . . so are we. My name is Toplin. I'm a student from one of the acadamies near Sallese. At least I used to be before they sent me back to my mother's. And this is Lord Vanar, with me. May we come in and talk with you?"

"I'm not very . . ." Pheron began. Then he said: "Yes. Please. *Please,* come inside! Sit on something—yes, there. Please . . ."

8. There was another hustler, twenty-four or twenty-five and maybe six-foot-three, very thin, very blond (very curly), who'd also had his top teeth knocked out at one time or another, so that when he smiled, his canine fangs hung either side of his grin. Like Joey, he lived on the street and used to sit on the stoop next to the drycleaners or hang out with his hands in his pockets in front of the comic-book store, sometimes asking you to go into some grocery and purchase something for him if he gave you the money—beer, a sandwich—as he was (like Joey) usually too dirty and too disheveled to get served.

Sometimes I used to tease Joey: "You have to work hard

when you're out here, man. You think you're the *only*
toothless junky hustling? Your competition's right over there.''

Toward the end of last July, about ten o'clock one hot
morning, as I was coming up Eighth Avenue I saw Joey
wandering down the street. Fingertips under the waist of his
shorts and wearing a grubby maroon tank-top, he came over
to me: ''Hey, Chip, is there any way you can get me a room
somewhere? I *really* don't wanna be sleepin' on the street for
a while!''

Occasionally I'd given Joey a few dollars. On his more
presentable days, I'd take him into the Fiesta for a beer. In the
first few months I'd known him, when a cold snap got me
worried about him, I'd rented him a cheap room for a week.
But such needs as his are endless, and to remain friends with
him, I'd known from the first I would have to disentangle
myself from his survival—which, for a couple of years now I
had. ''I can't spend that kind of money,'' I told him.

''Please,'' he said. ''It's really weird out here.''

''What's weird?'' I asked.

''You remember that kid you always used to say was my
'competition'? The other one with no teeth?''

''Yeah, what about him?''

''He got killed.''

I looked surprised.

''Last night. And he's the fifth!''

''What in the world happened?''

''Oh, man,'' Joey said, ''It's been crazy out here for the
past few weeks. You ain't been down here. But some guy's
running around the streets at night *killin'* people. And it's
gruesome, too. When they're asleep, in doorways and places.
About three weeks back one night—'' we walked past the
comic-book store and the boarded-up windows of the old
Haymarket, along that stretch called by only a *very* few
people, for reasons I've never learned, the Minnesota Strip; in
this neighborhood, most of the stores and shops that are
going to open up, are open by now. The others are permanently
shut— ''I went over by the waterfront to shoot up, by the
tracks under the bridge, where there's this big garbage pile;
and while I was going under there, I smelled something, man.
You ever smell a dead body? I mean, after it's been there a
few days. In heat like we've been having too.''

''Yes,'' I said. ''As a matter of fact, I have.''

''Well, that's what it was. I didn't even take my works out.

I mean over there. Then. I just got out. I didn't want to even see it, you know?''

"You didn't report it?''

"Naw. But two days later, I heard they found it. Some girl got cut up and dumped over the bridge, right on top of the garbage pile. But the same night I went under there, a guy got sliced open down on Thirty-eighth Street, sleepin' in a doorway. We all heard about that one the next day. Then, a few nights later, two kids got killed, a boy and a girl together. They were sleepin' with their knapsacks under some steps. He left a note on them: 'Death to the Street People!' But he doesn't just *kill* 'em, man! He really cuts 'em up! That why they think it's all the same person doing it. The guy I told you about—my 'competition'—that got killed last night? It was right around on Forty-sixth Street, over there. Right near to that restaurant where all them young actors go.'' He thumbed toward Restaurant Row. "Him and his partner went over there to sleep under the steps. About four o'clock in the morning, his partner woke up and said he was goin' for some breakfast. The toothless kid said he was gonna stay there and sleep, you know? And an hour later, his partner come back—and the kid's stabbed to death. And hacked up, too. His nuts were cut off. And his stomach was split open and his *heart* was pulled out! But that's the kind of stuff this weirdo's been doing. People all up and down here are scared to go to sleep!''

"Jesus!'' I said.

"The others were like that too,'' Joey said. "Can you imagine, doing something like that to someone?''

"That's a pretty messy thing to do,'' I said. "How do you get home through the streets after you've done something like that?''

Joey shrugged. "Well, he's done it five times now—*if* the first girl was done by the same person. She was cut up pretty bad, but not quite as bad as the others.''

A few minutes later, after Joey had wandered off somewhere else, I walked across Forty-sixth Street. A section had been roped off along the south side. A few policemen still stood around. The remains had been removed, but apparently the forensic crew hadn't yet (or had just) finished.

8.1 The conversations were muted in the high council room:

"...not what we were prepared for, with this Carnival...''

"...I am afraid so, yes, that every sedition...''

". . . certainly in the streets, but I have heard that beneath them . . ."

People left the room, with sweeping robes. Others entered and swept by still others bending to clean and straighten up after the meeting.

Near the door to the antechamber, a minister approached a woman in a white dress, her dark hair cornrowed severely over her head. He moved his hand toward her arm, not quite touching her; it was only because she chose to glance at him that he actually spoke.

"The Liberator is coming; yes, this we've all agreed to, Your Highness," the minister said softly in unaccustomed agitation. "But are you aware that certain elements come, not with him, but no doubt because of him. Certain subversive and dangerous elements have arrived to exploit the days of merry-making entirely in terms of this accursed plague that the carnival you have declared and the man it honors was called precisely to distract them from. How does one say this to such a noble presence as yourself? But our customs inspectors have found a wealth of magic fetishes being smuggled into the city of late—and rumors of a terrible Wizard descend upon us; oh, and in one cart of contraband, when the tooled-leather cover was pulled back, what was there but a miniature model in exquisite detail of Kolhari herself, with all her avenues and alleys, her secret sinks and cisterns, from the Spur unto the High Court—like some hugely outsized garden maintenance maquette! This is not right. There is rumor that a woman cooked a two-headed goat and sold it for barbecue from a cart in the Old Market, that bloodred ships have drawn up to the old docks along the port where the fog refuses to leave the streets, and that certain children with green eyes and coppery hair have added strangely improvised nonsense names to their gaming chants as they play ball by the cisterns of the inner city: names that make even the wisest of our sages, who pass them in the sunlight, suddenly chill from their unspeakable implications. We do not talk of this in the council, Your Highness. But are you aware that these unmentionable things are all anyone mentions—and with grave trepidation—going to and from it?"

To which the Child Empress, who was soon to be forty-seven and had her own annual carnival in the month of the Rat, when her birthday was combined with the anniversary of her ascension for a similar week of celebration during the winter days of short-light, answered crisply: "Yes. I am aware of all things in my land," and started ahead to join her maids and servants, who turned to her now in a flurry of forehead knocking, with lowered faces and raised fists, ready to depart for the royal suite.

Before she joined them, however, she turned back. "Have you heard, as I have, that there are plans and plots afoot in the city to call up the old named gods and ancient powers: Hellwart, Gauine, The Thrine Sejcenning; Oning har'Jotheet, the Amnewor, and Ropig Crigsbeny; possibly even Dliaballoha, and Doonic Yenednis . . . ?"

The minister's silence went out to all corners of the room like cords from some tangled knot at the center; here and there a servant or another minister glanced over. Yet it did not rope in the entire space, for the conversations and motions that halted here and there began again at other places. The minister drew up his arms within the long sleeves of his robe, and said at last: "Your Highness is well aware that these names have not been spoken within the walls of court since—"

"—since eternity's dawn, when the nameless god of count and accounting sorted the night into her left hand and day into her right and began to juggle the two." The empress did not smile. "They have not been mentioned within these walls since I came to live among them, Lord Krodar. And as they were not gods local to this part of the country, they have never been mentioned much outside." She paused a moment, lifting her hand to touch her low collar. "Or were Dliaballoha, Gauine, or the Amnewor, some of the 'nonsense names' that the children have been gaming with? You know, when I was a very little girl, before I came here, those names would terrify me. Then, when I arrived in the north, to be given a whole new gallery of nameless gods and the promise that they would protect us from those awful, ancient demons, I was terrified all over again. Do the old or the new gods terrify you now?" Suddenly she smiled and took the minister's arm. "Look about you, Lord Krodar. Suppose I had mentioned these same evil entities ten, fifteen, twenty years ago, toward the beginning of my reign. The whole room would have dropped into a stunned paralysis as palpable as the stone walls themselves. But look. Listen. Many of these around us now were born here. They live in precisely the world we once hoped to create: a world where such gods as once terrorized a third the nation now sound, indeed, as silly as the nonsense children babble in the streets in time to their ball bouncing. The nameless gods have created a barrier of silence that has imprisoned these malignant and alien deities and demons till their callings have been stripped of terror." She looked at the floor, considering. "We feel, Lord Krodar, that we can indulge a certain flexibility—indeed, *must* indulge it, if our reign is not to be fragile and friable. I have been conferring with my good vizerine. She reminded me that my grandfather's mother—her own great-great-grandaunt, you no doubt recall—whose reputation is glorious in the south and somewhat . . . awkward in the north, nevertheless put the northern dragons under her Imperial protection, to the glory of Ellamon. I think that we in Kolhari can afford to have a similar attitude to these ancient and endangered monsters. Who knows. It may even win for us a similar glory. At least in carnival time."

8.2 A friend since my high-school days, Queenie works the night shift as a registrar in the emergency room at a better New York hospital. She called me up for a breakfast date, and in a Columbus Avenue coffee shop with tile-top tables and aspiring actors for waiters, we ate overpriced fruit cup, toasted bagels, and drank cinnamon shot coffee: "Chip, I see one, two, sometimes three AIDS cases come in to the emergency room a *night*! I read somewhere that for the whole city they're coming in at the rate of five or six a week, but we get more than that during the night shifts where I am. Maybe that means it's going up—Right now, I'm about at the point where I can look at somebody across the desk and tell if he's got it—I mean, you're *very* sick, and you're not pretty. Like I said, this is the night shift in the emergency room in a hospital that doesn't *have* that big an emergency service. And someone who suspected that that's what they had would probably go down to St. Vincent's anyway, where they have that special AIDS clinic. It's very scary. And I'm worried. About you."

I reassured her I'd put some sharp curtailments on sex outside my main relationship. (When sex is as available as it is in New York, monogamous gay relationships tend to be the exception.) "The problem," I told her, as we went on looking for a waiter, which we'd both been doing almost ten minutes, "is that since they still haven't discovered what virus it is yet, there's no way to be sure of the incubation period. People are theorizing up to thirty-six months. I've been being very careful since February of eighty-two." (This was spring of eighty-three.) "But how am I supposed to know what I *was* doing three years ago, if I should come down with it?"

8.21 Personal knowledge of deaths from AIDS? Well, I note that six months after Peter came to talk with us at my house, when he said he personally knew no one with AIDS, other than the men he worked with on a volunteer basis, he now reports than an ex-therapist of his has since gotten AIDS and died. (I saw the obituary myself a week later in the *Native*.) This is tax month—which is how he found out last week that his accountant had died from AIDS only a week before.

He, a solid African black, she, an East Indian brown, the couple who run the print shop where I get most of my manuscript copying done told me a few months ago of a recent death from AIDS in the neighborhood—the owner of a local boutique I often passed, also a regular customer of theirs. Then, in letters, a San Francisco friend tells me of her landlord with KS (Kaposi's Sarcoma), and AIDS opportunistic disease.

The closest I get, I suppose, is George Harrison, Jr., who, for some years, I knew only as "Hibiscus."

In 1967, when WBAI's "Mind's Eye Theater" produced my radio play, "The Star Pit," George's then fifteen-year-old younger brother was in the cast, with the double role of Ratlit/An—though I didn't make the connection till some years later.

Around the beginning of 1970, as I entered my second year in San Francisco, Link brought news that the new commune he was living in had a number of fascinating people, including Hibiscus and Scrumbley. Their interest was theatrical: flamboyant, colorful, energetic—eclectic? No, that suggests a careful and measured choosing here and there. They were inclusive and accepting, rather: it was not that they would take *from* anything. They would take *everything*, then transform it into rampant, lively theater.

The group was called the Cockettes.

Some of their shows I saw, between San Francisco and New York: "Dorothy and the Wizard of Oz," "Pearls over Shanghai," "Babes on Broadway." On the stage of the sprawling San Francisco movie house where they did their early shows, one night when the audience was still mumbling to itself and wandering about in the aisles, a scrawny young man dressed in a white slip, with a maroon stole about his shoulders and collapsing basketball sneakers showing beneath his hem, climbed unsteadily up on a gold drum, lit a Fourth of July sparkler, and held it aloft like the lady at the heads-out end of how many Columbia Pictures.

The audience went wild—and, from that moment on, so did the show, which flamed and flaunted itself over the next few hours, ribald and energetic as a gaggle of baby tigers.

"Whose idea was that wonderful Columbia colophon?" I asked Link, later.

"Hibiscus's."

The only thing I know of that still remains of the Cockettes is a rather sickly, sixteen-millimeter color film, *Trisha's Wedding,* a spoof on the nuptials of the daughter of our then president, with some heavy-handed commentary on the Vietnam War. (In it, Link makes a brief appearance as the reactionary Madame Nhu of South Vietnam, who, through a barrage of pointed political questions, has "Nothing to say.") The Cockettes were a mad and marvelously integrated improvisatory ensemble, full of beards and bangles. Their aftertaste was, oddly, somewhat similar to that of the far more austere and low-key, khaki and denim dancers of the Grand Union Construction Company, that sublime collection of serious artists who did so much to make New York livable, if not lovable, a few years later. *Trisha's Wedding* is a series of talking heads in drag—and is, as such, in its basic effect, almost the opposite of the company's hot, noisy—now and again stalling on long, hysterically awkward silences and stases—panache. Hacker's poem, "Imaginary Translation III" (*Presentation Piece,* Viking, 1974, p. 73) gives a somewhat stylized account of a Cockettes' performance. Rex Reed, who came to one San Francisco show with—at least it was rumored that night through the audience—Truman Capote, published an article on the evening that did a surprisingly good job of capturing the flavor, if not the intensity, of their carnivalesque shenanigans.

I met Hibiscus once (on some North Beach street?), with Link and Scrumbley, who introduced me: a hefty, blond, bearded St. Sebastian in his mid-twenties, he wore a blue robe, a gold collar, and half a dozen daisies in his hair. His voice, when he spoke, was just a little higher than I expected it to be.

But by the time I'd decided that Hibiscus, one of the

originary masterminds behind the group, was a true theatrical genius, he had abandoned the Cockettes as too commercial and, frankly, no longer fun.

I came back to New York and moved into the Albert Hotel on West Tenth Street. A year or so later, so did the Cockettes—taking over most of the eighth floor, so that now the whole hotel, always colorful, for years a haven for rock groups, ragamuffins, and the generally outrageous, stumbled up new crags of chaos, with invasions of Hell's Angels and admiring cross-dressers from several states—Divine's and Holly Woodlawn's visits were the talk of a month—and student leaders of Gay Liberation university groups from Jersey trooping through all day. I came down from my tenth floor room to visit Link (now playing Madame Gin Sling in "Pearls over Shanghai") in their suite a few times, said hello to Scrumbley, took Link and his visiting brother out to dinner at the Cedar Tavern across University Place from the hotel.

Over Rose Marie's Hand Laundry within the high walls of the Albert (where Abraham Lincoln had slept the night before he delivered his Cooper Union Address), again and again I found myself sharing the elevator with one or another six-foot-two, football shouldered, teak-black prostitutes in miniskirts, with mouths red as a Christmas ornament, some of whom, an operation or so ago, had been men; and some of whom had not. During that period I lost what till then I'd often suspected was genetically ineradicable in the human brain (after all, it might have been a species survival factor . . .): I stopped *wondering* what the sex of the person standing next to me had once been. Saturday and Sunday mornings—after Friday and Saturday nights—the same elevator's floor would be awash in urine, on which floated handfuls of glitter. And once, on the elevator wall, someone wrote in lipstick:

> For Good HEAD
> Do NOT call Patti:
> 515–4136
> I Am TIRED!

The feel in the theatrical suite was colorful but, usually (like Patti), tired after the energy output of their performances.

For nightly, over at the old Anderson Theater on Second Avenue, in a series of spectacularly uneven shows, the Cockettes galvanized all in the city who could *be* galvanized. (I must have seen them four times and dragged by how many friends . . . ?) *The Voice* started by panning them and returned, a week later, for a measured rave.

Yes, it was a strenuous, aleatory art that required an education.

But for years, deep among my inner organs, I was certain you couldn't really *know* what art was unless you'd seen frail, tone-deaf Johnny, the eponymous hero of ''Babes,'' with his blond beard, green eye-shadow, and silver lamé gown, belt out ''Lullaby of Broadway,'' one and a quarter tones off-key and an inconstant beat and a half ahead of, or behind, the accompaniment, while the audience cheered and stomped and applauded, till, crying real tears, he would call out, ''Oh, I didn't *know* it was going to be like this! Thank you! Thank you, New York. Thank you *all*!'' blowing kisses and throwing glitter at the front rows, while the rest of the cast pell-melled from the wings for a thunderous finale: ''I'll Build a Stairway to Paradise,'' inspired, no doubt, by the closing of Part One of *Camp Concentration*—certainly through Link (writer of a good bit of the material), always a great Disch enthusiast.

The Jewel Box Review—while it had its own magic—was never like *this*!

It was an aesthetic experience that gave the illusion, at least for a night, of being all form, yet devoid of content—specifically all the forms of seduction, while wholly and refreshingly empty of seduction's matter, i.e., those moments or minutes of aesthetic production that manage to maintain, through practiced skill or artless intensity, the illusion that form and content are, indeed, one.

Content, of course, must have some form. And form, of course, creates its content/commentary. This is why their chimeras have chased each other through moment after moment of history, the intense perception of one or the other producing the overwhelming effect: Art.

But by now, no longer with them, Hibiscus was starting another, equally innovative, group here in New York, The Angels of Light.

If Robert Wilson and Richard Foreman are heirs to Wagner's *Gesamtkunstwerk*, with its high seriousness and darkened auditoria, then Hibiscus and his communal theaters represent all that stood against the Wagnerian—all that was truly Dionysiac in the modern that leads to the postmodern. (There were a couple of early San Francisco performances where the houselights never did go down—presumably because no one was sure how to work them. But Hibiscus's backstage, "Go on, anyway. Now!" transformed that from a technical disaster into a field of light where art could be observed the more carefully.) With Charles Ludlum before him and Ethyl Eichenberger after, certainly he was not alone. But then, community is what that kind of classical self-assurance and dispassion is always about, anyway. We all have our personal pantheons—there are no canons anymore. Well, along with María Irene Fornes and Judith Malina, Hibiscus was a resident director in the Great Delany Utopia Ltd. Theater of the Mind.

Two years ago, the death from AIDS of the man whose hand I shook once on a San Francisco Street—George Harrison, Jr./Hibiscus—was reported in the *Village Voice*. Indeed, till that particular article, all I'd read of was KS, the "gay cancer," and it was only with the report of Harrison's death that I saw for the first time mention of the more general problem of opportunistic infections (Harrison died of pneumocystis carinii pneumonia) and the Acquired Immune Deficiency Syndrome of which they all were revealed to be a part.

8.3 ". . . said that the Liberator had almost reached—"

Nari heard him stop and felt the clay wall's evening chill under her palm. She looked from the black window to her fingers on the wall in dim red. "Zadyuk . . . ?" She glanced back. "Are we going to go?"

He sat on the edge of the bed frame, leaning on his knees, fists hung between. "You don't mean the carnival, do you?"

"You've heard them talking." She turned from the wall. "You *have* heard them, haven't you?"

"Who hasn't." He looked up. "Nari, it sounds . . . I don't think it's right—"

"It's supposed to be for anyone with a loved one or a relative who's sick."

"Pheron's not a relative."

"Oh, Zadyuk . . . !"

He turned on the bed, drawing both feet up to face away, his back curved toward her, flat and detailless before the lamp's red fire from the table corner. She looked for the mole just below his right shoulder blade and the three small freckles scattered high on his left. (They were so familiar to her. But did *he* know they were ever there?) Vertebrae, blades, muscle, and the troughs between were all flattened under a blood-colored glow. Zadyuk said: "I don't even know where it's supposed to be."

"I heard from two of the old women who work in the yard next to mine that," and she stepped around the table, "it's somewhere in the Spur—"

"Well, I'd heard *that*. I meant where in the Spur."

"They said there's a tavern." Standing before the lamp, her shadow darkened Zadyuk's back and the bed he sat on. "Under it, an old cellar's been dug out. Some ancient crypt, I think, that used to be used for . . . well, I didn't really understand that part. But so many people are going—so many people are sick—we'll find out how to get there by the time the carnival starts tomorrow. Someone will tell us. And I want to go, Zadyuk."

A man shrieked outside, followed by laughter—with four or five other laughs joining. Clear light moved below their window. (Zadyuk and Nari both looked back.) Yellow swung under the ceiling's thatch. Someone was passing below, holding high an expensive brand whose butter-white flame bleached the red about them to pink, before the deeper maroon refilled the room.

When Nari looked back, Zadyuk had gotten up to stand beside her. He blinked down at her with eyes a little too close-set for his heavy features (but, she always said, she liked it), then turned to lift the lamp. "We'll go. If we can find out where." He blew it out. "And we will."

She reached for him in the dark, again, to be, as she had been for years now, surprised by his body's sheer size. She felt him set the clay lamp back on the table. His arms went round her.

8.4 A few weeks back, before going off to the laundry, Nari had put out some apricots, pears, plums, and peaches on the stone slab up on the roof, which the sun had already shriveled to a tart, chewy sweetness. With the skin behind his ears still chill from the cold water he'd splashed on his face at the roof trough, and gnawing around a pit, Zadyuk stepped out on a street the color of drab pear and, where the sun between the buildings across from him hit the wall, dusty apricot.

The little girl wandering down the dawnward alley was fat, no more than five, and naked. She carried a stick like a staff. Someone had taken a cat's skull, run the shaft in the neck hole and out one eye, whipping the yellowed bone to the upper end with half a dozen loops of leather.

At first he thought she was wearing a mask over her eyes, but it was only a smear of charcoal or makeup.

She looked odd and infinitely cute. As he grinned at her, the notion seized him. "You're going to the Carnival today?" he called. "Wait a minute. I have something for you. Just a moment—" He ducked back in the door, noticing that she hadn't stopped at his call, though her morning amble had no particular dispatch.

Less than a minute later, he was back out the door, more dried fruit in one hand and holding a piece of cloth in the other.

She was still there. As he came across the street, she planted her cat-skull staff in the dust and stopped, looking up at him with dark and dark-banded eyes.

"Here." Zadyuk squatted before her. "These are for you. You can take them to the carnival." His hand was full of prunes and dried peaches.

From a thong around her neck, an astrolabe hung against her round, brown chest. She was holding three toy balls against her stomach with her other hand. She and Zadyuk looked back and forth between the fruit he held out and the toys she clutched, both realizing that she couldn't possibly take them without abandoning the balls or the staff. She said at last, nodding toward the fruit: "Well, I don't like those anyway. I'm not going to the Carnival."

"Oh," Zadyuk said. "And . . . what about this?" He held out the cloth.

It was a black-and-orange remnant Pheron had decided he was going to throw away, when Nari had rescued it—only to decide herself that she thoroughly disliked it and could think of no use for it.

"I'll tie it around your shoulders, like a cape. Would you like that?" He stuffed the fruit into the leather sack at his own waist. "For Carnival. Really, it's very you," which was what Pheron always said when he brought him or Nari some little bit of this and that.

After sucking her lower lip through half a minute's deliberation (while Zadyuk wondered if he should be squatting here so long), she said: "All right. But I'm not going to the carnival. I'm going to the Calling of the Amnewor."

Half a dozen loose cords hung off the swatch. Zadyuk

flipped it over her head while she ducked, blinking made-up eyes. Reaching beside her staff, he caught up one cord, pulled it loosely around her shoulder, and knotted it to another. "There." He stood—

And a surprising cramp knotted his right calf. Pain pulsed hard enough to make him blink. He grunted but kept his smile. (How, he wondered wildly, do you explain to a strange child you've just given a present to that, inexplicably, you are now in crippling agony . . . ?) With it came a sudden fancy: whatever entity she'd named was actually an ancient demon from before the reign of the nameless gods, and her pronouncement of it had brought this cramp down on him. (How idiotic! Zadyuk thought.) The air flickered before his eyes.

The little girl said: "You're a barbarian, aren't you?"

"Yes . . ." The pain peaked, then slipped away. Zadyuk stepped uneasily from one foot to the other.

"Are you Kudyuk?"

"Kudyuk's my brother," he said. "No, I'm not."

"You're going to like the carnival," the girl said, nodding. "My father says the barbarians like Carnivals more than anything.

"Oh," Zadyuk said, "well I'm not—" at which point the sunlight falling on the back of his neck made him sneeze, obliterating his: *going to the carnival either*. Still sore, his leg throbbed again.

The little girl blinked.

"—you'll like it too," he managed to say.

Then he turned and walked off along the street, feeling extraordinarily silly. Overwhelmingly he wanted to turn back and ask her, *where* it was she'd said she was going? (Surely that was not to risk another cramp, or sneeze . . . ?) But he had to check his stall, then stop by the Crescent Alley to see if Pheron's workshop were tightly secured. Carnival time always created more than enough mischief.

On his way back he would stop by Pheron's room, see how he was, if he needed anything, talk with him a bit if he was up for it. (Pheron had had one of his looms brought to his room. Sitting with him, watching him thrust the shuttle through quivering strings from shadow into sunlight, Zadyuk had thought: it's as if his thinned arms and narrow back have become, for me, work itself. What has been pared away by the illness is all that's in excess of labor. Why do I have this feeling so much less when I watch Nari lug wet cloth to lob it over the cart rail, or when I see my own stall porter drag in hide bales by the twisted yellow vines? Why does it vanish when I put knife or needle to leather?) He would leave Pheron the dried fruit.

But he was *not* going to tell him about the Calling of the . . . whatever-it-was.

8.5 ". . . you do not read Nabokov as a document of the times," writes Dillard on page 31 of *Living by Fiction.* I just wonder how she read the first third of *Lolita, Pnin,* or the "Introduction" in *Pale Fire.* The Nevèrÿon series is, from first tale to last, a document of our times, thank you very much. And a carefully prepared one, too.

So.

Some documentation on Joey:

8.51 Last summer while we stood together talking, leaning against the wall of McHale's, next to the Fiesta, a heavy black woman came past in a black coat with sequins. She held the hand of a six- or seven-year-old girl in a pink dress, her rough hair pigtailed and beribboned all over her head. They looked like a mother and daughter going to church in Harlem thirty years before. (I wondered if they had anything to do with any of the Broadway theaters down the block.) The little girl pointed at Joey and looked at her mother: "Momma, that's Jesus Christ . . . ?"

The woman smiled, embarrassed. They passed on.

Joey turned to me and gave me a big, disgusted grin. "Man, that happens to me a *lot*! What is it, they all think Jesus Christ looked like some toothless junky?"

Once Joey volunteered to help put a roof on a church nearby that aided local indigents; in Joey's case, they paid him with food and let him sleep on a cot in the basement. For much of that summer, every time I'd see him, he would complain about the money he'd have made if he'd done the work at standard carpenter's wages. "That was a two-thousand-dollar roofing job. Two thousand dollars I could've got. But not me, man! Not fuckin' Jesus Christ!"

8.52 Another time he told me: "This guy takes me home with him—he's forty-one. After we make it together, he takes me in the bathroom with him and tells me to look in the mirror with him. 'Look at yourself,' he says. 'You're thirty, and you look older than I do. You look sixty.' I don't look like no fuckin' sixty, do I?''

Joey was thirty in July of '83. (*I* was forty-one that April!) Whether he looks older than I do has never really struck me before. But there is certainly an ageless quality to his bony face that doesn't fix itself easily to any year.

8.53 This happened, as far as I can figure, about thirteen hundred cases of AIDS ago (when the total was just under three thousand): I was sitting in the Fiesta with Luis.

Joey's white-and-black checked wool hunting shirt lay over the bar beside us. Joey had just ducked out to run after somebody for something and was supposed to be back in a minute.

Luis is twenty-three, thin, hard, and rough looking. He's half Irish and half Puerto Rican, with a story enough like Joey's not to have to repeat it in detail: hustling, drugs, a wife a couple of years older than he is, somewhere in Brooklyn, who kicked him out permanently about a year and a half back, and a kid. Luis is also missing a handful of teeth, but he has a bridge, which, from time to time, he flips loose with his tongue and plays with in his mouth. Over the couple of years I've known him, he's been Joey's 'partner' about half that time. They trade johns, share drugs, hang out with each other. I once asked him: "You two ever make it together?" Luis shrugged: "I wouldn't mind. But Joey don't wanna. He's got rules or something about that." They're still fairly protective of each other. Of course the other half of the time they're on the outs, speaking guardedly to one another, with tales to me and everyone else about how one or the other of them tried to do the other one in. To an outsider these changes, which may start from either one, seem eccentric and unpredictable. While we sat there, waiting for Joey to get back, I asked Luis: "Are you two worried about AIDS? I mean, after all, both of you guys are working men." ('Working men' and 'working women'—interestingly, not 'working girls'— are euphamisms on the strip for hustlers and hookers.) "And I know you been working pretty hard, here, recently, too."

"AIDS," Luis says. "What's that, now . . . ? That's where you get real sick . . . ?"

"You *really* haven't heard of it?" I asked.

"Sure, I've *heard* of it. But I don't know nobody who's got it."

"You should ask Joey about it," I said. Joey and I have talked about it a couple of times in the bar.

Luis ran his tongue under his upper lip, securing his bridge. "Yeah, well . . . you know, Joey's got a lot of other things to worry about, right through here. I don't think he's eatin' too well, you know. Does he look too skinny to you?" He shrugged. "Maybe *he's* got it?" Then he grins at me. "Naw, he just don't eat enough."

"Probably." I nodded.

"Hey, have *you* heard about all the murders . . . ?"

There seems, indeed, to be a whole level of gay activity in New York that goes on as if nothing has happened. (Anecdotal evidence: AIDS is an almost exclusively middle class disease . . . Yeah, sure.) And yet, on this same level, it's certainly thought about. You get odd examples of it here and there. In a pornographic movie house about a block from the bar, there used to be a very active Hispanic midget, who, when he came up for air, would walk down from the back balcony to sit on the steps and chat with the queens who hung out there. We always used to say hello. A few months ago he disappeared, and somehow I got it into my head that he'd probably gotten AIDS. I made up my mind to ask, and finally inquired of a slender black Dominican with whom I'd often seen him talking and whose nickname, as far as I'd been able to make it out from overheard conversations, was Uruguay: "Say, whatever happened to Shorty?" Adjusting a knitted skullcap above a gold-toothed smile, Uruguay had told me in a heavy accent: "He in Peru, now. Shorty get scared of all this AIDS shit, and *take* off, man!"

Luis and I looked up as, in his tank top and shabby jeans, Joey came back into the bar. "Okay, man," Joey said to Luis. "You're on my shit list again . . ."

"Huh?" Luis says. "What do you mean? Aw, come *on*!" He looked at me, shaking his head. "Twenty minutes ago, I'm his best friend! Now I ain't no more." Luis got off the barstool and, still muttering, still shaking, wandered toward the door.

Joey sat down and put his tattooed forearms over white-and-black wool. "You know what I just found out that little bastard done . . . ?" And he began to tell me.

8.54 "I may be a junky, but I ain't no thief," Joey says frequently. "I ain't been arrested for nothin' since I was thirteen!'' This may be the single line I have heard from him more than any other.

He's certainly never stolen or pilfered anything from me—sometimes there may have been loose change lying around on a table or the bar counter: whenever there is, he always says: ''Come on, put that away now. Later, when you can't find it, I don't want you thinkin' I run off with it!'' and once, when my passport fell out of my pocket (the most resalable of commodities on the strip), he came running up to return it to me.

For part of the first winter I knew him, he managed to get down to Florida for a month. I hung out with him the day he did his pretravel laundry and saw him off on the bus; when, a few months later, I ran into him after he got back, he told me that while he was down there he'd been arrested for ''prostitution'': ''I'm in a peep show in Miami, and this guy comes over to me and says, 'I'll give you twenty dollars to suck your dick.' And I say, 'Fuck, yeah!' And his partner, right next to us, arrests me!'' He laughs. ''I wished the fuck he *had* sucked on it. I can't get a hard-on no more anyway, you know? I even come soft—when I come at all. It's the fuckin' dope, man! Anyway, I thought: imagine, this fuckin' cop's gonna suck on a soft dick for twenty bucks? He really should have! Served him right!'' He scratched his head as we walked together up the street. ''I knew he wasn't no cocksucker when he asked me, you know? I *knew* it! He didn't look like no cocksucker. Shit! He looked like a cop is what he *looked* like!'' But, since recounting the happening (over which he spent thirty days in jail), he's gone back to his ''ain't been arrested since I was thirteen'' line.

8.55 How can one make a recognizable pattern that *isn't* a document of its times? Take the limiting case of, say, Kostelanetz's visual fiction *Modulations* (Assembling Press: Brooklyn, 1975): without any words, pictures, or even numbers, a geometrical configuration of black hairlines and circles shifts by an element or two from small yellow page to small yellow page. Even if you don't take from it the strong suggestion of, if not reference to, an urban sensibility as clear as in any Mondrian painting, isn't it a document?

At a certain time a certain artist was interested in a certain pattern. Knowing the certainty, the specificity, the complex meanings associated with any of the three (the time, the artist, the pattern), or the associations between them, is only a matter of reading.

That a moderately sophisticated reader of current experimental work, not specifically familiar with Kostelanetz, would nevertheless recognize *Modulations* as a product of the 'seventies (and would be generally sure it was *not* a dadaist work of the 'twenties, say, when similar aesthetic questions were being asked) only confirms that the pattern is overcoded, recognizable, readable, historical.

If all human production (aesthetic or otherwise) has its documentary aspect (i.e., it can be associated, by a knowledgeable reader, with a time and place), does this endanger its aesthetic aspects *per se*? It is the *richness* of the pattern that is aesthetically at stake. How many art histories does it take to make us understand that reference (a use context) and historicity are not the same?

8.56 To the direct question, ''Do you think of yourself as gay?'' Luis answered:

''I don't know. I like women . . . at least I used to. I ain't been to bed with one in about two years, though. And I'll tell you, I don't miss it. But I like men too. I mean, in the last few years I been to bed with a *whole* lotta you guys, and I sure as hell like what I'm doin'. There's some people I wouldn't want to find out about it, though. I mean even people down here, some of 'em. You out sellin' Valiums and j's and pills and stuff around the corner on Forty-second, and they don't wanna *hear* about no cocksucker down there. But, shit, man, it's *nice* to suck a dick—especially when you're high! I mean, even if you don't get off on it, sometimes it just makes you *feel* better. Know what I mean?'' (I nodded.) ''I *bet* you do!'' Luis chuckled. ''And it's *real* nice to get sucked, huh?'' He nudged me with his arm. I laughed. He snorted and looked forward again, shrugging. ''So, I don't know. Maybe I am. But I don't even think about it, you know . . . ?''

To the same question at another time, Joey answered: ''Sure I'm gay! I been gay since I was fuckin' twelve years ago. I *told* you that, before!''

8.61 I don't even *feel* like writing out the ugly incident from a couple of days ago, the model for the opening of the section below. It began in a movie theater, when some effeminate

Puerto Ricans sat down a few seats away from a (presumably) straight guy, a little man with the muscles of a laborer and glasses (and a down jacket over his lap), who suddenly decided to get abusive—well, since I *don't* feel like it, I'm not; other than to say that when it was over, I felt pretty proud of Our Guys.

8.62 The first morning of Carnival, some dozen tanners were walking together out through the half torn-up Avenue of Refuse Carters for their first six-hour day (rather than the usual ten) at the troughs. One was singing in a high, falsetto voice, making exaggerated mummerly movements to his friends. In an early gesture to the festivities, two—one a barbarian, for there were several tan and sandy southerners among the slim dark men—had tied long colored cords around their heads whose ends, now and again, they tossed back to catch a breeze (and whip at those behind). The women of Able-Ani traditionally wore such cords about their heads in festival times. Two at the back of the group were talking intensely about that—or something else—as they made their way around the heaps of dirt piled at the edges of the excavations that obstacled the avenue.

Ahead, a sudden scuffle: a little man with the muscles of a laborer, a beer belly, thinning hair and weak eyes had brushed by one of the tanners as he came along in the opposite direction. "You!" He stepped away, swinging an angry arm. "Don't touch me, I say! Get away! I don't want your lousy diseases! I don't want one of you gettin' anywhere *near* me. You're sick. You're all sick. I don't want to catch any of your sicknesses. Don't touch me!"

Two of the tanners grunted and barked and mimed his hostile gestures back; and two more stepped up when he stepped forward; so, finally, he went on.

The high voice took up its song again. But the laughter and chatter that had turned around it all along the warm morning avenue was gone.

A dozen steps behind them, on her way to her yard (for everyone in Kolhari it seemed had a double load of linen in preparation for the festivities), Nari watched the little man lope away. She felt the heat of embarrassment momentarily bloom in her cheeks for the young men making their way ahead. As she turned off the avenue down the alley toward the Khora's bank, she remembered something Pheron had told them one afternoon when she and Zadyuk had gone to visit him with cheeses and pickled eggs and spiced meats.

"Now you know," Pheron had said, leaning on the wall at the edge of his roof, where sometimes he wove in the evening and where today they had all brought their lunch, "how certain professions have more than—how shall I put it—their share of high voices and happy hands? Mummers, tanners, and those big, hearty wagon drivers that roll into the markets from the country at dawn—"

"Now that's not true!" Zadyuk had said, turning from the cider jar, where he'd been deviling the cork at knife-point. "You're not going to tell me that all those great, burly men I see each morning rolling and rattling by my stall are—"

But Pheron closed his eyes and fluttered his hands above his ears (making them look their "happiest") dismissing protest. "Anyhow—" He slid his fingers under the sash around his waist, settling his weight on his other foot— "when I was a kid and I first went to work at the tannery, my father took to saying to his friends, to my friends, to me: 'Now don't you think that *every* tanner you see is like that. People shouldn't just go around thinking that because someone works in the troughs, he has to be one of *those*.' And you know I didn't think anything about it at first. That was just my old man; it was the best he could do. After all, he was right. There were, indeed, *two* fellows out there, working with us in all that stench, who I'm perfectly sure had never been to bed with a man in their lives, who were quite mad after the women, and just as nice as they could be to the rest of us. (Frankly, I used to wonder what they were doing there!) Well, after my father and I had our little set-to on the bridge, and it was all out, at some point I heard him say it to someone again: 'Just because some guy's a tanner doesn't mean he *has* to be like that.' So I said—oh, I was a dreadful snot back then; I'm sure he just thought he was protecting me—but I said: 'Look. There *are*, indeed, two guys out there with us who are (probably) not "like that." But why are you always defending *them*? You haven't even met them. What about *me*?'" Pheron raised a hand to slap his chest with wide-spread fingers. "And you know, he *didn't* say it any more." He paused a moment under a sky as blue as any he could weave. "I do miss him. And, yes, I will have some of that, when you get the cork out." He stepped from the wall. "Want some help, Zad?"

Along the alley a heavy young woman raised her hand and grinned, somewhat deferentially, toward Nari: the most recently hired among her barbarian washerwomen—no doubt why she was the first at work this morning. Nari nodded back. Employer and worker made their way together toward the unusual wooden door in the gate of the laundry yard.

8.7 With a shaved head and an ornate turquoise ring, somewhat gaunt Ronald runs a somewhat sprawling, somewhat foundering antique emporium with his rotund partner, Roy. On summer evenings, if the *Closed* sign is out but there're still people inside, you can come in for a vodka martini and find various neighborhood characters sitting around, talking, drinking. "Well, I *had* to do something!" Ronald said to the gathering some time ago: "something" turned out to be going for weekends to do volunteer work at a hospital with an AIDS clinic. Now, sitting beside a bit of Bayreuth kitsch mounted on an easel (a framed color print of Wagner at his piano in an elegant music room, pausing a moment with one hand on the keys, while a grayish cloud emerges from under the raised lid, among whose billows the artist has suggested swans, knights, ravens, gnomes, dragons, armed goddesees in winged helmets, an undraped Venus in the pose of the de Milo, a one-eyed wanderer, and the odd storm-tossed ship), Ronald reared back in his rocker ($290.00 on a white gummed label stuck to the arm): "Now I work with almost seventy-five AIDS patients." (He has not switched to the more cumbersome "people with AIDS.") "And every single *one* of them has mainlined regularly! Now have you ever seen anything like that in print, in either *Time* or the *New York Native*?"

More anecdotal evidence.

8.8 "*You're* not going to the carnival," Larla said, suddenly and accusingly. "You're going to that awful thing they're holding down in the Spur, aren't you? I've heard you mumbling about it all week." She turned to snatch up a mug, a bowl, a cloth, all clutched clumsily in her heavy arms. "You're going to that—that Calling of the . . . oh, I can't even pronounce it!"

The old woman stood in the middle of the kitchen, wrapped in dark brown, while the kitchen girl bustled unhappily about her. She said: "The Amnewor. Yes, I'm going."

"That's just terrible," Larla said, moving here, there,

picking up that, putting down this. "That's horrible. That's no decent sort of religion. Gods don't have names. I've known that since I was a child. And you know it too. What does someone like you know about the Amnewor, anyway?"

"I remember . . ." said the old woman. "A long time ago—a very long time. Something about death. And time. Lots of time. Real death, too. Human beings. You can't appease it with dogs, cats, and chickens, either. It has to be real, violent—"

"Oh, don't go *on*! Please. Not for my benefit. I don't want to hear about such things!" She reached awkwardly out with one hand for a bowl (a knee up to keep held things from falling) to scratch at its inside in case the spot were dirt. "Is that what *they're* talking about . . .?" She looked up at the ceiling. "All those poor, sick men Lord Vanar brought back here to talk? He must have twenty-five of them in there with him! And the two women. Are they really ill with it too? Women aren't supposed to get it. That's what I heard, anyway. That would be just horrible, if *every*body could get it . . ."

"Oh, no," said the old woman. "*They're* not concerned with the Calling. Nor should they be. But they're a few of us who think that, perhaps, if we work very hard, we can concern the Amnewor with *them*." She released a breath and began to walk across the kitchen, while Larla stood very still, hugging the things she'd gathered as if she were afraid; then she blurted: "How did you find out where it was going to be?" Everything clattered to the counter.

The old woman stopped at the door. "When His Lordship sent me to ask around the city for the homes of the other folks ill like himself, I had to talk to lots of people. I learned many things in those afternoons."

Larla looked up again. "Has he carried back every sick person in the city here, then?"

"Oh, no," the old woman repeated. "There're many more of them than that. The ones here now are just a few of those still well enough to travel when a comfortable wagon is sent."

"They *must* be talking about that monster who roams through the city now, corrupting our carnival in honor of the Liberator. Oh, it must come. Otherwise, you *couldn't* call it. The one who's Calling you're going to. Why else would they be here? I've heard it said that a wizard is soon to—"

"Oh, no," said the old woman a third time. "They have their own deaths to deal with. And the lives they've got to live till then. The Calling of the Amnewor is for us." She did not look back at the kitchen girl as she went out the scullery door. "At least I *think* it is..."

8.9 Saw Joey again last night. He says there've been four more hack-jobs on the street-sleepers, and the most recent victim bought it the night before last. "I'm *talkin'* to this guy, two o'clock in the morning, over on Ninth Avenue?" he told me as we sat at the bar of the almost deserted Fiesta, with its orange lights, old jukebox ("I Am What I Am" silent for the first time that evening), and the neon beer sign in its front window making the night beyond the open blinds completely black. "And three hours later, the word comes down he's had his heart cut out in the goddamn park! That's five more in three weeks! Nine all together this summer. Every single one of them hacked up like fuckin' watermelons! And that ain't counting one derelict four Puerto Ricans came by, one night, when he was sleepin' on a park bench, and slit his throat. For the fun of it, you know? They caught *them* right away—for a while they thought maybe it *was* them, or some crazy kids gang that was out to kill us all. But it ain't, I guess. Man, I don't sleep during the night anymore. I sleep in the park in the daytime. I wake up now at five, six o'clock in the evening, and the office girls sittin' around talking to each other after work all applaud when I get up." Joey clapped his wide hands at the end of his tattooed arms. "Yay! Yay! The fucker's up!"

9. The first evening of Carnival, Toplin's mother sat on the side of his bed, supporting Top's forehead with one hand, while he vomited and vomited into a broad crock on the bed's edge: thin, frothy bile strung from his mouth. At the fifteenth or twentieth spasm, nothing much came. Still, every thirty or forty-five seconds, Toplin's stomach clenched hard enough that she felt the shaking in his whole body. She did not say, "I *knew* you shouldn't have gone out to the man's estate today. You weren't well enough. You're very sick. You have to stay in." Actually she *had* said it before, just after the wagon brought him home (though she's forgotten that) and there didn't seem any point to it now. He'd begun to shiver between spasms, and his sight had gone in a welter of

darknesses and little burning spots each time his stomach clutched on the wet emptiness inside it.

The barbarian woman who helped his mother with the house stopped at the door. She'd come up to tell them that, out in the street, the Liberator had reached the city and was momentarily expected to ride by with his entourage. Maybe Toplin would like to go to the window and watch? She would bring in a bench and get a pillow for him . . . Just then, outside, the noise of gathering people broke out in a cheer, usurping her news. So she just stood in the door a few moments, looking at Toplin with the blanket twisted up between his ankles, hunching and hunching as his mother held him over the bile crock. Finally, she took a breath and went back down to the kitchen.

9.1 One afternoon Sarena dropped over, terribly upset. "I just came from seeing Herb in the hospital. He has that AIDS . . . ? He looked just godawful, Chip. Like he's already a corpse, or a ghost, or something. I hadn't seen him in three months. I didn't know it was so bad! You just don't know how shaken I am!" Sarena is from the South and uses words like "shaken" in conversation. "I mean, I'm just not myself." I'd never met Herb, though Sarena had mentioned him to me before. A day later, she phoned in tears.

Herb had died that morning.

The next time Sarena came over, she said in passing: "It's awful. But I'm afraid to hug you, or even shake hands with you! I really am! After Herb, it's just . . . ! Oh, I know it's not supposed to be that contagious. But *suppose* you had it . . ."

And, for the next three weeks, she doesn't—while I read article after article about nurses in hospitals afraid to touch or serve people with AIDS, about perfectly healthy gay men coming to their friends' houses for dinner to be served on paper plates, or reporting to work to find themselves fired (along with Haitians) from their jobs on the possibility that they might be ill, while the governor general of the United States, after pointedly shaking hands with several persons with AIDS on *The Phil Donahue Show*, declares: "From what we know already, AIDS must be one of the *least* communicable diseases we have ever had to deal with. There is no evidence of AIDS being spread by casual contact, food, or water. So far, the only method of infection we can speculate on is repeated sexual contact or an exchange of blood products."

And the conscientious *New York Native* reports that in cases of one of a pair of lovers contracting AIDS, in only 10 percent of the cases has the other lover come down with it.

9.21 You understand, Pryn, I don't believe in any of it: magic, miracles, religion, the calling of the gods, named or unnamed. I make my music; sometimes my music makes people happy—though more often, I suspect, it only makes people remember some moment when music or something else gave them a fine feeling, and they're pleased for the reminder. Oh, when I was a girl much younger than you, sometimes of an afternoon down in Potters' Lane I would see some unglazed amphora, set among other to dry, whose curves and clean flares seemed, in the late sun leaking into the alley, more magnificent than the lean or lounge of any tree; or I would hear some particularly wondrous tale from a teller that revealed in the pattern of its narration a fine and fundamental organization in the real world it mirrored; or I would see some mummer's skit whose songs, dances, and the speeches that came between modeled the entire active and lively flow of living at an intensity, I swear, greater than life's. These moments of vision, prompted by some crafted work, people sometimes speak of as ''supernatural.'' Yet, why should they be less natural than those the nameless gods provide us at a child's laugh, at a sunset seen over great canyons, or at an oceanic storm watched from the shore?

Well, we must get ready, my beliefs notwithstanding. The pudgy barbarian just leaving as you came in—he smiled at you when he went out? Well, *that's* the Wizard who's hired the underground hall in which to hold the Calling. What did he want? Why for us to make music at his subterranean ceremony. It won't be so bad, Pryn. I've known him ever so long, and he's a good sort, really. You have more credence in these things than I, I know. I think it's because you've traveled so much. (In a sense, my provinciality protects me.) But it should be fun to watch him perform his charlatanry from the inside, as it were. Come, gather up our cymbals, drums, harps, and flutes. It's time to go. We should be there to set up, at least a few hours early.

True, I don't believe in it at all. But how could I refuse him? He says my work is magic.

9.22 At the bottom of the steps, Pryn set the bag down on the dusty stone with a most unmusical clanking and looked at the beamed ceiling immensely distant in smoky half-light.

"Ah, my little partridge!" The Wizard who came up to her was something of a partridge himself, with a blond beard and a blue robe with a gold collar. The stems of three or four limp daisies were stuck through his hair. "Where's your mistress?"

"Ah! She'll be along." Pryn glanced back at the wide steps. "She wanted to get some rolls and sausage in the Old Market before she came. She said she thought it would probably be a long rehearsal."

"She knows me, doesn't she?" The Wizard pulled his robes around on the dusty floor. "Well, it's wonderful of you both to participate. It's going to be just wonderful, I know. Come, then. I'll show you where to set up. Isn't this a fabulous space?" He gestured around at the hall. "What in the world do you suppose it was used for?" He started walking as Pryn picked up the sack and hurried along after. "Have you ever been here before?"

"Once." Pryn nodded. "Yes. A long time ago. When I first came to the city . . ."

Raising an eyebrow, the Wizard glanced at her. "Were you, now?"

Water fell from between high pilasters to stream across the floor between stone banks. The Wizard led Pryn across the wooden bridge with the loud waters beneath.

Most of the people were on the far side. Some wheeled by great frames, stretched over with dark skins, dim paintings on them. Others carried poles wrapped around with rolls of cloth. Ropes hung down overhead; two women were hauling up a great sheet of something on which something was pictured, though Pryn was not sure what, as the material flapped and wavered up out of the light.

At the end of the hall, the throne was in shadow. Not far away, a few torches had been set up about the spot where some men were digging, sunk to their shoulders, among piles of dirt.

Perhaps because she was looking at it, the Wizard veered near it, till he and Pryn stood at the pit's lip, watching three naked diggers toiling in the excavation. Pryn was about to ask what they were doing, when one of the men saw something, tossed away his pick, and dropped to his knees to scrape away at the loose dirt wall with his hands.

"What have you got?" the Wizard called down.

The digger was scraping dirt and gravel loose with his fingers, tugging with his other hand.

Pryn ventured: "I wonder what it could—"

It came out in a shower of small stones, leaving a dark niche. Pryn saw them fall across the digger's knee, saw him move a knee on the earth. He stood, beating at it with his hand, and turned to come to the pit's rim holding up his find in the flickering torchlight.

It was a metal cylinder, uncommonly silvery and free of tarnish for its time in the earth. It was somewhat tapered—an arm gauntlet, she realized.

The Wizard took it. Damascened with intricate symbols, there were rings about it that, now, the Wizard tried to turn—and which, astonishingly, did. "That's it!" he called down. "We've got it! That's it!" Turning left and right, he beat about in his robes.

Pryn had been watching the diggers, one of whom was heavily scarred on one side with welts that must have come from a flogging as a criminal or slave. When she looked back at the Wizard, he had already slipped the gauntlet over his rather thin arm—at least under the play of his blue sleeves she *thought* she glimpsed it—and was feeling around in folds and slashes and pockets for . . . something!

What he pulled out was a disk of metal, perhaps the size of his palm. It had been on some leather thong, bits of which hung from it in two uneven lengths. "Here!"

In the torchlight, as another digger reached up for it, Pryn saw the barbaric markings around the edge, the cutouts on the upper layer (for really, it was several disks pinioned together) and the central bolt that held them.

The digger—the scarred one—turned with the astrolabe, crossed the basin, dropped with it to his knees, and thrust it into the niche from which the gauntlet had been taken, packing it with one and another handful of dirt.

"I bet you've never seen one of *those* before," the Wizard said, looking about and not at her as his robes settled.

"Oh, yes, I—"

But the Wizard was calling: "All right, now! Fill it in! Let's get on with it. Fill it in, I say."

The two other diggers had vaulted to the lip and were already shoving piles of dirt back inside with their hands. Scattered clods hit the shoulder of the man inside still packing the wall. He looked up, startled, saw falling earth and dodged away, to leap out and join in the refilling.

Just then a commotion began around them; Pryn saw people looking up, and—just as a shovel and one of the pick axes went into the hole to be half covered by the next dirt load—she looked up herself.

A rumbling sounded from the roof of the underground hall. It was, Pryn realized, horses' hooves, echoing and reechoing overhead through the crypt.

"What . . . ?" she whispered.

"No doubt it's the Liberator's party, passing. If you'd like, you can go upstairs, out through the tavern, and watch at street level." And, indeed, small clusters of people were disappearing off into a shadowed niche that certainly contained some stairwell leading upward.

"Will *he* be coming down here . . . ?"

"Oh, I don't think so!" The Wizard blinked at the ceiling. "I doubt he even knows this place exists. This is one of the most secret and well-preserved centers of Nevèrÿon. No, he's just riding by, in the street—in perfect ignorance, I'm sure, of all we do down here. For we are preparing for the Calling of the Great and Ancient Amnewor. That's not the kind of thing he'd be concerned with, you can be sure."

"And this . . . ?" Pryn looked at the hole, which, in seconds, had been filled by almost a third.

"Ah . . . !" The Wizard bent toward her to speak in a near whisper. "That's the grave where we found the prince! I paid dearly for the information, believe me! We started digging over there, you see," and he gestured off into the darkness. "Oh, only a foot or so down, we were coming upon bones and weapons and bits of ancient leather armor—but before too long, it was perfectly clear that all we'd unearthed was some kind of mass grave. Nothing but ordinary soldiers, or less. Perhaps there'd been a fracas here at some ancient time, and the victims had simply been tossed into a common pit. But that wouldn't do for our purposes, so we chose the second most likely spot, according to the fable—and only a few feet down we found him!" Here, he nodded toward the piles.

Beyond the lowering dirt mounds, Pryn saw the shape beneath the rough cloth.

"Clearly, from his sword, his scant costume, and his meager jewelry, you could tell: he was a real barbarian prince!

The clean parting of his ribs suggests some blade was thrust into his heart to sever the gristle there. He couldn't have been very old, either. Doubtless he was murdered—how many centuries ago, now—not more than a few feet from the foot of that throne . . . and buried where he fell: or not far from it. It's quite a portent, believe me. It bodes extraordinary success for our Calling, tonight. Real death, you know.'' He shook his head and chuckled. ''His corpse will be among our most prestigious spectators this evening. It's grisly, yes. But it's necessary if the kind of thing we're engaged in is to have the proper tone. The Amnewor concerns real death, not some silly substitute.''

There was a muffled cheer, sounding from the overhead street, and more horses' hooves.

But the Wizard was going on: ''The corpse will occupy the throne, of course. I was thinking of sitting you and your mistress on the steps below him. There're some hides to make your seat more comfortable. But everything considered, it might be distracting. So I've decided to put you behind a screen instead—where the sight of your playing won't confuse the congregation. Come along, now. Bring your bag of instruments. I'll show you where you can wait till the rehearsal gets under way. Where was your mistress, again?'' He turned from the lip of the fast-filling grave. ''I hope she gets back soon. We've got pretty much all the preliminary rituals over with, and—if only so all the primary participants can know what to expect—we really *must* get started.''

9.23 Have a bit of sausage, Pryn, and hand me that flute. What? You don't want any? Why, dear girl, you're trembling! Don't tell me all his mumbo jumbo, his bits of carved bone and ancient mummies' fingers—buried for no more than a year, I can assure you—have got you into a state. Honestly, Pryn, it astonishes me. Here you are, a grown woman, who's traveled on her own from Ellamon to the depths of the Garth and back, with adventures under your sash that, when you recount them, cause me to quiver in my sandals: you've flown wild dragons, freed slaves, can read and write and kill, I gather, when you have to—an almost perfectly civilized woman, by my own city-bound account! While here am I, fat, forty, and hardly ever having been outside the city gates, and I'm still more or less comfortable amidst these arcane goings-on. That you came to me, seeking to assist me with my art, well...I take that to be simply another step in your self-education and a confirmation of the success you've had with it to date. But sometimes I think that the range of your experiences allows every little thing about you to take on resonances and vibrations—to become some endlessly shimmering sign, whose clear and concise meaning in the weave and play of meanings is merely terrifying rather than illuminative. I've always felt your sensitivity made you the perfect audience for my playing; has it made you, also, the perfect audience for his? Could it be ignorance that protects me from such terror? Really, Pryn, the magic we do here is harmless, and possibly deeply consoling to those too troubled or too cynical to respond to the political positivism celebrating in the streets. There, dear girl, stay your trembling and hold the drum thus, so that I may rattle on it after I pull an ecstatic glissando from the harp strings. And lay out the flutes for me from high to low as you always have, so that, in this half-light, I may know which one I am picking up to play on, just by feel and habit—those greatest aids to art, which those without them call taste, whether good or bad.

9.3 Ran into Joey a few days ago. Basically the police's response to this maniac has been to start a sweep of their own over the whole area, arresting as many of the street people as possible on drug charges or whatever. (If you put them all in jail, they're less likely to be murdered...?) Some two hundred people have been arrested in the neighborhood in the last week. The kids on the street are really going crazy. Lots of them are pooling their dope money to get rooms, and crashing eight, nine, ten together inside on the floor. Between the maniac at night and the police during the day, they don't know where to shit. Sitting around in the kitchen of one of these ersatz crash-pads one afternoon, while Joey was out "taking care of business," on the permanently out-of-focus black-and-white TV I watched some bizarre rerun of *Ironside*, in which a policeman, who'd been mugged, robbed, and dumped by a road, decides to let himself be treated as an ordinary citizen without identification.

In the midst of all of it, various junkies came running in and out, looking for each other: now a guy with a chain through a hole pierced through one pectoral (a *big* hole too; no tit-ring, this) under his tattoos; now a gaunt couple, he named Mike (thin and sunken chested), she named Karen (with a waist-length hank of black hair), who darted into the bathroom to shoot up, then came out, giving me an enthusiastic disquisition, the two of them, on the size of Mike's equipment and the pornographic modeling session he was to have later that afternoon. (Karen had gotten him the work, and was anxious to be known as someone who could get you that kind of job if you had the Right Stuff.) When Joey came back, he showed me an article cut from the *Times* with a large picture of the cops involved in the sweep—the forty or fifty plainclothesmen and plainclotheswomen—who had been masquerading as street people themselves, pretending to be asleep in doorways at night with portable radios or suitcases nearby to tempt the kids to snatch them; at which point other officers, staked out to observe, would move in and arrest whoever fell victim to the temptation. In the picture, the faces of the disguised policemen were particularly clear, and the street people were passing copies around in hope that they might recognize them when they came across them.

Clear, but not *that* clear. It struck me as kind of quixotic.

There was no mention of the maniac in the paper (there were a few brief page-two and page-three accounts of "nighttime stabbings"), but perhaps the police thought that, in the process of sweeping the area, they'd catch him too . . . ?

So far not.

9.4 They'd set out flares all along the Bridge of Lost Desire, though the sky was still a deepening blue. Some brands burned red. Some burned white. Their light fell on the colorful groups who surged one way laughing, then broke up to run back the other, as still others hurried around them.

Rumors of the approach of the Liberator's entourage— someone had just seen them in the Spur, making their way toward the Old Market—swept new crowds toward the bridge mouth, some of whom jumped up to see over the heads of those crowded in front; other men and women turned to the person next to them: Now, *who* was it exactly supposed to come by?

One man moved distractedly at the crowd's edges. Haft held short in his hand, he carried a stoneworker's hammer. The hair had gone from the top of his head, with the rest in the stubby side-braid of a veteran from the Imperial Army— though his legs were badly bowed. (He could not have put up with those many-day marches.) The muscles on his long arms and bent thighs, however, said he'd worked some years with his mallet. His expression was dazed, drunken, even deranged. He walked by the wall, stopped, turned back a few steps, turned unsteadily again, walked again—bumping more people than most in the boisterous crowd.

As mounted figures rode out into the market square, people cheered. People ran off the bridge to gather at the fountain. The man with the hammer stopped to face the waist-high wall that was the bridge's railing. Taking the handle in both hands, he swung the hammer back over his shoulder, then struck the stone.

He reared back, then struck again.

On the third strike a crack shot through the wall.

At the fourth and fifth, rock splinters fell to the walk.

Some running toward the crowd truly did not see him. A few others saw and sensed in his violence some unmentionable rage and passed on as if they did not see.

The first to take active notice was a sixty-year-old mummer with gold paint still on his eyelids and blue dye darkening his lips. Though a spry old man, he did not look overly strong. He had just finished his skits in the market and was off to join the mummers' wagon, gone by another route to another neighborhood where their performance was wanted to enrich the revelry.

"... excuse me," he said, not terribly loudly. (The white flame set nearest shook at the blow.) Then, perhaps, because he saw something in the unsteadiness between the hammer strikes that, with his years, he recognized and that reassured him, he spoke out in a resonant tone that stopped even some of the passersby. "Come now, you can't do that!" He stepped up and took the man's shoulder.

The man shook the actor's hand away with a convulsion of his whole body—but he stopped hammering; and looked at the old, made-up face.

"What do you think you're doing?" the mummer said. "That's not right, battering like that at public property!"

Blinking, the man looked angry and confused. "I'm tearing it down, breaking it up—this overground sewer! This is where you all come! You can be sure, here is where you give it to one another, like a deadly secret you whisper in the dark from this one to that. Can't you see it? This is where it comes from, the plague!"

The mummer's lips tightened. "Look, friend." He took the

hard shoulder in his hand again. "You—simply—have no right. It's not for you to take it upon yourself to do this."

"No right?" Again the man tried to shrug away the actor's hand; the hammer swung between them. "To protect myself and the other good people of this city from this sickness that kills all who catch it? What rights do I need! What rights must I have? Aren't I doing you fools a favor in the bargain, those too stupid and indifferent to take up a mallet beside me?" He tried to pull away.

"Listen to me." The actor pulled him back. "Rights, you say? *You're* not going to get the plague. You know that as well as I do! Me and my kind, *we're* the ones in danger. And do you think for a minute if I thought there was any right, reason, or efficacy to be gained by tearing down this bridge, I wouldn't have been here days ago with a hammer myself? But that's for us to decide. Not you—" The actor paused, because, from the bandy-legged worker's eyes, two very fat tears, first as glimmerings along his lower lids, then as irregular spills in the torchlight, moved down his dark cheeks toward his beard. "*You* can't take that on yourself," the mummer went on, "to protect *us* from whatever foolishness you think we indulge, no matter how deadly." Seeing the tears, the actor spoke more gently. "Now what is it? You have some happy-handed acquaintance who's ill, dying, or dead of the plague? And now you want to destroy the bridge, to assuage your own fears of a most unlikely contagion?" Behind the mummer the mounted entourage clattered by. People shouted and cheered. More ran about them now. The actor's articulated voice cut through: "Is that what it is? Or perhaps a cousin, a brother. Even a son . . . ?"

More cheers rose at the horses behind them. People stumbling into them pushed the two men closer, the crowd's noise covering the stoneworker's answer. But it was easy enough for the mummer to read his lips. The man blinked; he shook his head; he said: ". . . I have a lover. Not much more than a boy—a student, out at the school. And he's . . . !"

Two or three people trying to see the passing Liberator jarred against one or the other of them, so that they were thrown to hold each other, supporting one another in mutual surprise—till the stoneworker pulled away, flinging his hammer a last time against the wall (that it did not strike someone or fall on someone's foot was a wonder), and reeled away in the crowd.

*   *   *

9.41 Two men had observed the encounter. Indeed, both heard the exchange as we have written it, up until the actor's final question—even as they had missed the stoneworker's final answer.

On his way from the Spur after seeking out Namyuk to ask him if he knew anything about where this Calling of the Amnewor would be held (it was the kind of shady thing his brother would certainly know), crossing the Bridge of Lost Desire, Zadyuk had halted to watch the madman with his hammer banging at the bridge wall and the old queen trying to stop him.

With a single eye, a strip of rag tied around his head to slant across the sunken socket and a metal slave collar around his neck, a short, lank-haired man had been pushed from the crowd and, on recovering his balance, had paused to watch the hammering vandal and the old man in makeup. The one-eyed man had entered Kolhari with the Liberator's party—indeed, had been associated with that great man for some time. But today he'd chosen to walk beside his master's horse rather than to ride. Several times the crowd's pushings and peerings and jumpings about the Liberator's mount had jostled Noyeed away. In the surge of people at the bridge, it had happened again. Once more he had been left behind as the Liberator rode on through the city.

9.42 Not only did Noyeed and Zadyuk both see the incident, they saw each other—were, indeed, left looking at one another when the mummer and the stoneworker had finally moved off from between them in their different directions.

9.43 Zadyuk thought: He's one of those in the collars who roams the bridge looking for violent sex—so, though he's not like my friend, Pheron, he's one of them. No doubt the way he watches me with his good eye, he thinks I'm one too. I wish he didn't. I don't mean there's anything wrong with it . . . after all, I want to help them. Still, I want to be known for who I am. Not mistaken for . . . well, for anything! That, I suppose, is the worst part: to be among them at all means that, to any man or woman who looks at you, you must *be* one. Otherwise, why would you be there at all? It's like some appalling contagion that dwarfs the plague itself. I love Pheron, and would help him in any way I could. Yet, I cannot shake off this sense of contamination. I want to get back soon and tell Nari where we go to find the Calling of this new-named monster.

9.44 Noyeed thought . . . well, it's hard to say what Noyeed thought. To wear the iron collar, even for the Liberator, was to masquerade as a certain kind of monster, a masquerade whose rules Noyeed had chosen to live by long enough so that we would be ill-advised to specify which were merely theater and which were really him, which he had profoundly changed himself to accommodate, and which he only nodded to in their indifferent observance. He looked at Zadyuk. (Zadyuk saw that.) He looked at the hammer fallen among the stone chips by the cracked wall. He looked after the Liberator, riding away by the torches—the fabled figure was almost invisible now for the crowds about.

9.441 Zadyuk started again through the Carnival throng.

9.442 Noyeed, even disliking the torchlight, lingered on the bridge.

9.45 Some of the things Ted told me:
    He met an old trick in a movie house, a tall black guy he'd done some S/M with half a dozen years ago. They were talking vaguely about getting together again, when the black guy mentioned his lover had died about a year or so back.
    "Did he die of AIDS?" Ted had asked. You hear about anybody our age who's gay, dying (Ted said), and it's just the first thing I think of, whatever it turns out to be.
    The guy looked very surprised. "Well, actually, yes. I was—"
    Ted was freaked. "Look, you've *got* to *tell* people that before you set something up with them!" he said. And cut out. He was making it on and off with some concert pianist, who let drop that *his* lover had made it with someone who'd had AIDS and who'd recently appeared on a TV special about the disease—a day before *he'd* died. Ted had seen the special. He cut out once more. And in still another movie house, where he'd been going to cruise regularly, he found written in red paint on the john wall:

AIDS PATIENTS CRUISE HERE!

That one, on top of all the others (he told me), just made me crazy! I kept turning it over in my mind—like one of those three-sided rulers. It could have been someone who knew something and was trying to warn people. It could have been somebody who just wanted to stop the cruising. Or it could have been somebody who didn't get what he wanted there sexually and was just bitching. But any way you read it, I didn't want to be there.

9.46 And so, *Ted explained,* that evening I went walking up somewhere around —th Street, just beyond Ninth Avenue. I was crossing this bridge . . . ? There was some kind of carnival going on, maybe one of the Italian street festivals. Only the costumes people were wearing, I'd never seen anything like them before! And there were a whole lot of people running around, men and women, with not *too* much on at all! They'd set up torches all along the bridge walls. I was looking around and feeling strange, when I noticed this guy cruising me, hard, too. A little guy. Our age. He didn't have a shirt on or anything, and he was wearing this slave collar. When I looked at him directly, I realized he only had one eye! That was really weird. When he finally came over, I just had to ask him: "Aren't you worried about the plague? I mean, this is very serious." (I know you're supposed to call it an epidemic. But I swear, almost every time I ask anybody what they think about AIDS, they look at me and say: "Age? What do you mean, 'age'?" That's happened to me three times now!) He just watched me. "Look," I said. "I mean, I'm horny too, but there're too many people around here, now. We'll never find a place. Why don't you come with me. I'm going to this . . . well, it's like a ceremony. Or a program. For people who're concerned about it. The Calling," I told him. "It's the Calling of the Amnewor. . . ."

Now is that the weirdest thing? I don't even know where the words came from. You tell me I was dreaming, and I won't even argue. But that's what I said. It sounds like something out of one of your stories, Chip. It isn't, is it? (Nope, I said. Not yet.) I couldn't tell you *what* I thought I was talking about when I said it. But I asked him, "You want to go there with me?"

He nodded.

I started across the bridge.

And he followed me. We pushed through the crowd—only, somehow, I must have lost him. Or he changed his mind. Or maybe *he* knew what I was talking about, and I didn't. I remember I got free of the people, crossed the street, and looked back—and, Chip, you know? There wasn't anybody on the bridge at all! No torches. No carnival. It was just one of those walled overpasses that runs across the train tracks, with the tall, bright streetlights at either end. And empty.

Do you know what I mean?

(Yeah, I told him.)

And nobody on it.

I'll tell you, Chip. I'm not doing *any*thing with anybody anymore. This AIDS has got me *really* upset!

9.5 Last February I came down with flu. Two days after I got it, I was in bed with a 102° fever. I stayed in bed for four days, got up—still with a fever—and nearly collapsed when I tried to go to the store. I went back to bed for another week. (I haven't been in bed for two weeks with *anything* since I had pneumonia when I was twenty-one.) At the end of that time, I felt much stronger, but my fever was still between a hundred and a hundred one. I put my clothes on, took it easy, but I felt I had to do *some* work around the house, or make the odd trip out. Slowly, I got back to a more or less normal schedule. But a week later, my temperature was *still* over a hundred. Now and again there would be periods of persistent aching in one or both my armpits, though no apparent swelling. Once, coming home from downtown, I realized my groin was so sore that walking was painful. I went back to bed for two days. Some people get swollen lymph nodes if they go near someone with a cold. Save for the swollen glands under my jaw I've gotten every spring since I was seven, *I* don't. Next morning, I was up—still with a temperature; I decided I was long overdue to see a doctor.

Had I thought about AIDS?

Hour by hour, since I'd first gotten sick.

From a handbook specializing in gay services (*The Gay Yellow Pages*), I got the name of a doctor, himself gay, who specialized in sexually related diseases usually transmitted by homosexual contact. I called. Apparently he was very busy, but I got an appointment for some six days later.

I did *not* have any sexual contacts in the subway on my way to his office—though I could have had, twice.

That office? Neat, well-equipped, efficient, and reassuring. These was a pile of pamphlets concerning AIDS on the white formica-covered table in the waiting room. (I took one, and its very sensible suggestions have been my sexual guidelines since.) In a small examining room, a nurse took my temperature. It was *still* over a hundred—five weeks and three days after the onset of whatever.

A tall, pleasant man in his late thirties, the doctor came in. I detailed my symptoms and history. ("How many sexual contacts would you say you have in a year? I mean with different people, of course." "Till now," I said, "maybe three hundred on the average. That's not counting my steady relationship, which can vary from three times a week to once every two weeks. We're not monogamous." He said: "Mmmm.") My underarms and neck and groin were prodded to the point of pain in a (happily, futile) search for swellings.

After the more usual examination procedure, as well as a set of blood tests, the doctor said, "Well. You don't have either syndromal or prodromal AIDS." (That's the formal way of saying you don't appear to have AIDS or a pre-AIDS condition that should be watched.) "So I wouldn't worry. What it seems like is a *very* tenacious bout of this year's flu. A number of people have been hanging on to this one for a month or more. Now I have a number of patients who do have AIDS; something to remember about AIDS, if you're worried about it, is this: it isn't a disease you *wonder* whether you have. If you get it, you will be *very* sick. Did you take one of our folders there in the waiting room...?"

Three days later my fever went.

9.6 An entertaining man, *the Mummer said*, I've made a few wise men smile, and more than my share of fools howl with laughter. I've fancied that to do it I must know something both of wisdom and foolishness—not that I claim much of either. Really, aside from my mimic talents and my ability to declaim a line or time a fall, I'm a very ordinary man.

Wise men and fools?

Aristocrats and cutpurses?

Well, I've counted all sorts among my friends. I've always seen myself as able to speak to high and low, and to not a few whom others would simply dismiss as mad—like that poor man on the bridge. Certainly Carnival encourages unlikely interchanges. But in my profession, the air of carnival hangs over even the ordinary work-a-day happenings. Certainly among my most interesting and oldest acquaintances is the Master of the academy near the edge of Sallese.

(Odd, that at this particular moment, when, one might think, the general populace joins in the atmosphere I strive to create the year round, my own thoughts wander to such things as they do . . .)

At his school, you know, he promulgates a doctrine of transformation, change, endless impermanence, the evanescence of the visible. Oh, I don't denigrate the precariousness of the intellectual adventure he has undertaken. One must be truly brave to dare such uneasy waters, never stepping in the same stream twice, going with the flow, and all that. Still, he was born into one of the most solid families in the nation— economic rocks, every one!

Fire, flood, earthquake? (With constant reports from my friends of the sickness, I fear to mention plague.) Oh, he's got to worry about those as much as any of us.

But somehow we don't, very much.

I doubt he does either.

I think he got tired of my producing skits about him in the marketplace during which I poked fun at all I took to be his little failings. Oh, he observed my efforts with great good grace, diligently sending his students down to see the enchantments I mounted at his expense, at theirs, indeed at everybody else's. Then, back at the school, he would dutifully draw out the wisdom of it all, even from places I thought they were only clever. (I have never been able to resist a good line. I suspect he has the same failing.) But the truth is, *he* can afford a sense of humor. Mine is won by labor.

About a year back, he began writing a series of dialogues, with ratty old me as the main character! He has his students read the various parts—often playing characters with their own names, when they're not taking turns at being yours truly.

Exercises in argument, he calls them.

Recently he invited me out to a day-long performance. (They *do* go on!) I went. Good manners said I could do nothing else. Some of his students, who have grown fond of my market fare, had with great glee given me *some* warning of what was to come. I expected to see a few well-intentioned gibes, now at my eccentric clothing, now at my manner of speech, perhaps a few cuts at the sexual eccentricities of my youth (or, indeed, of my age), or at the general infirmities time gives to one of my years—the sort I myself mock out on the wagon platform. But what I saw performed in this untitled prince's merchant's imitation of an aristocrat's courtyard (his uncle, I know, still deplores that a lord of Nevèrÿon should gain his living in such a neighborhood) was truly insidious.

With her false beard and scruffy tunic the little girl supposed to be me spouted one and another brilliantly reasoned and beautifully rational diatribes, devastating the callow boys loitering about her and asking one dumb question after the next, egged along in their eager absurdities by her/my eloquence.

But were they *my* arguments?

You must understand, when I was young and the Master younger, we argued, argued, argued! We would wander back and forth across the Old Market often fifty times in a day, one of us always talking.

Yet somehow I never assumed he was arguing *for* anything. (By all the nameless gods, in those days he was too *young* to have opinions!) I assumed he was arguing *against* me for the fun of it—because I was a man and he was a boy—and I gloried in our altercations as a chance to exercise my own rational faculties.

Exercises, yes. That's even what I called them. And from his brightened eyes and quickened breath at their end, I would assume that, as exercises go, they'd been as exhilarating for him as for me.

What I saw his students perform, however, out on his lawn between the smart buildings, was, yes, very much a version of our arguments from twenty years before, but with the imaginative fancy added that he had somehow *won* them all—when I had considered them a draw! It was as if he had come to believe in the interim that, somehow, he had, actually, back then, *convinced* me, so that there I was, in travesty, spouting the exact opposite of what I believed to various interlocutors—and spouting it far more eloquently than *he* had as a youth.

And do you think there was one character in the lot with *his* name? (I've never failed to put actors playing actors—and playing *bad* actors at that—on *my* stage!) Not on your life.

A day of it, and, believe me, the effect was quite disturbing.

But there we were at the end, with all these girls and boys standing about and waiting for my compliments, sure they had all performed quite wonderfully.

And they had! They had!

I hugged them and praised them and clapped like a madman—all the while trying to figure some strategy to counter what, yes, I saw it coming to.

Later, with the clay lamps glimmering on their tripods in the room's four corners as we dined alone in his study—and, yes, no doubt I had been just as equivocal about his production as he can be about mine—I finally chose my tack. (To mime direction by indirection is one of my most successful aesthetic ploys.) I said:

—Now, look. I'm absolutely in accord with what I take, or mistake (for we both know both are possible), to be your basic aim. Still, I see some problems. For one thing, you never bring out that I *am* a theatrical personage. *I* am the one who puts on shows and spectacles for the general public. I think it's a fact that, if it were presented early and clearly, would illuminate your entire effect in a far more subtle light.

—But the point is (we sipped pale cider from old crystal; and he always serves the best), save for the odd note a hired scribe can make, you never write your speeches down. Now my dialogues are transcribed, word for word, in the Ulvayn Island system. By comparison, your performances are spontaneous, free, improvised. They're not fixed forever like some unreadable barbaric script incised on stone. They have the play of interpretation built into them! If, in my texts, I were to give you more authority than I already have, that lifelike quality to your utterances, which *I* can only catch by pinning exact wordings to parchment, would be lost. As it is, I think it comes across.

What could I say?

I said:

—And another thing. Half your students are girls—more than half, actually. Why are all the people you have me talking to, played indiscriminately by maidens and ephebes, *boys*?

—But you *like* boys! he protested, with that wide-eyed surprise that betokens true bemusement. You've never made a secret of it.

—Oh, really! I said. Of *course* I like boys. But three-quarters of my friends are women. Always have been. Always will be. *You* know that. And besides, I don't—as a rule—like the *kind* of boys you have here; and that, in your plays, you have me going on to, endlessly. I haven't made a secret of *that* either. You know as well as I do, my tastes are far more, well . . . trashy.

—You liked *me,* he declared, almost petulantly. Besides, not everybody is an expert in the particular set of nastinesses you indulge in down atn the bridge. *I'm* certainly not!

—All right, I said. Why, for instance, do you have a girl play *me*?

—Your voice, he said, is rather high.

—I am an actor, an artist, I declared. A high voice carries, clear and comprehensible, half again as far across the market as some fuzzy, booming basso. I have *trained* my voice to be thus, through many years of practice. And unlike some who are born with it naturally, mine did not start off that way. Tenors and sopranos will be our heroes for a long, long time, my friend. Get used to it!

And this very wise man gave me a surprised look that declared he'd never considered before this basic fact that has fixed the careers of generals, admirals, and politicians as well as actors and singers since time's dawn—a fact I must explain to three out of five aspiring hopefuls of either sex who come to our wagons for work.

—Oh, come on! he said placatingly. What's to the point isn't that *I'm* not an expert in your wild and marginal ways, but that the young people whose educations have been entrusted to me, and for whom these pieces are written, are not. I dare say some of them will be. No doubt they'll go on to point out all my failings as sharply and as cruelly as you have—no, *not* cruelly. I can say that. You are, and always have been, a very kind man. That's why I love you. But what I'm trying to tell you is . . . these productions of mine are not expressions of the real. They are in dialogue with it. "What if?" That's the game's name! You told me yourself, that's what all speculation is about. What if you *hadn't* abandoned your wife years ago? I'm sure she'd be just as I portrayed her—like the wives of all thinking men: shrill, resentful, obsessively *there,* and awful. I admit it, in those parts I'm talking about why *I'm* not married, not about why or how you once were. (*That* aspect of it had, I confess, struck me as so "off the wall," as the young people say, I had not even retained it in memory to critique!) Suppose you *did* lavish all your wit, wisdom, and affection on the best young men of Nevèrÿon instead of the half-wits, hustlers, and ne'er-do-wells, the silly actresses, simpering market girls, and sly old countesses that you do—

—*You* are not a half-wit, I said. But you even admit it: all you have presented, in *my* name, are *your* fancies.

—The voice, he said (with the naïveté, incomprehension, and sense of total rightness at any and every appropriation that always terrifies me from one of his class and caliber), is, nevertheless and certainly, my own.

I returned to our wagons here in the market the next morning—of course, he wouldn't hear of my walking back that night. I shouldn't worry about all this, you know, but his dialogues *are* written down. He's quite proud of them—justly too. For they *are* beautiful compositions. And he has been having copies made and distributing them to people who can read and write, among both the aristocracy and tradesmen, and even to a few workers I hear, who've mastered the skill—for in practice he's very egalitarian. The details and mannerisms he had taken from me to decorate, as it were, "his" voices are clear enough so that, in a city as diminished in size by writing as Kolhari, I am clearly recognizable. After all, I am something of a public figure, with my minimal dollop of fame.

Yesterday, in the Old Market, during our performance, when I was in the midst of what I've always considered my most innocent depiction of the failings and foibles of our most aged and mindless minister of state, some young man in the audience suddenly shouted:

—Fools! You fools—the lot of you! Every single one of you—duped fools! Don't you know that *he* is the one who has been out with the teachers of Sallese, corrupting our best young men with his disrespect and insidious argumentation—which, here in its vulgar form, you go on to laugh at? Haven't you *read* the accounts of his lectures to the young, taken down by the Master? Do not laugh and applaud. Drive him off the stage, rather! Stone him! Kill him!

It brought the performance to a halt. And it left an old actor *almost* too shaken to go on. The audience itself was discommoded and, finally, reduced by a third. My performance was not at its best for the rest of the day. When the show was over, only an old friend who happened to be there, an unremarkable and even disreputable man in many ways, applauded with any vigor—and, I fancy, some real anger at the interruption. I was grateful to him, but still disheartened. And even he did not come back to see me afterward.

But the fact is, and it takes an old man to say it:

The reign of our empress is violent and vigilant.

It is too easy in our day to see such tendencies getting out of hand, leading, who knows, even to my death—about which, no doubt, my young Master will write a moving and eloquent account, where my screams and protests, my nose thumbings, farts, and insults—and the curses and violences against me they elicit from violent men—will be reduced to, if not replaced by, some cascade of calm and reasoned rhetoric.

Perhaps a Carnival will be in progress outside the prison, where the children and lovers (in all combinations) wandering through the market will be asking: Where is the old mummer who used to make us laugh and cry so? Will the shouts and music in the streets drown out my screams? But you can be sure, that's another thing he will simply omit. (This Calling of the Amnewor? No, I do not intend to go anywhere near it, I tell you. I have seen it all before, and besides: I have more than enough work of my own to do!) No doubt, I *will* have my calm moments during it all.

Still, it is not his style to be as flamboyant, or, indeed, as outrageous, as I. But, then, it is not my style to be as persistently rational as he in the face of unjust madness—a human failing I am now old enough to have seen in all too great amounts.

Oh, there will be bits and pieces of me in his dialogues that I or anyone else would recognize—the details with which he will decorate his text. But there will also be much that only I could give the lie to. And over everything, what his account will not encompass in any way is my real death at their hands.

(His writing has made of me a monster!)

Though he is a prince, and I am an old actor, he will have me die in his dialogues as he would die himself, could he, by any jest of the nameless gods, be calumniated, accused, apprehended, and executed in the same mode and manner as he may so innocently cause me to be. I think on some terribly personal level he sincerely feels his writings have cured me of all my abhorrent opinions, while I fear that, with them, he has put me in as grave a danger as if, instead of cider that evening, he had offered me a goblet of bitter, vegetative poisons.

9.7 Got a flyer from Temple University about a symposium, "Post Barthes/Post Bakhtin." I was familiar with—and great-

ly admired—the work of over half the participants: Michael
Holquist, Carol Emerson, Barbara Johnson, Samuel Weber. I
had a layman's familiarity with Barthes and had read Bahktin's
The Dialogic Imagination in the Holquist and Emerson
translation. Two years before, at the "Innovation/Renovation"
conference at Wingspread, I'd first sketched out a Nevèrÿon
story, "The Tale of Plagues and Carnivals," after a presentation on Bahktin's notion of "the carnivalesque" as an initia-
tor of critical dialogue. I decided to treat myself to a trip
down to Philadelphia, then, and attend.

The conference began at nine on Saturday morning, so at
four, I was up and, by four-thirty, on my way through the
foggy November black, darkness, and the glimmer of not-
quite-rain, struck through by New York's street lights, to the
Port Authority Bus Terminal.

The terminal has a strange kind of life at that hour.

Joey, Jimmy, Johnny, Jamal, and José among the street
people have all mentioned to me using the station to sleep in,
and I was on the lookout for somebody I knew. But I didn't
see anyone.

All the concessions were still closed, but as I walked
through the broad glass doors and across the deserted concourse,
I passed a shutdown news kiosk, beside which stood a boy
about sixteen or seventeen. His jeans were baggy, dirt-blackened,
and torn. One of his sneakers had come off and lay on the
floor about ten inches from a very dirty foot. He had no coat
and just a T-shirt on that was too big, ripped at the neck and
yellow from wear. Head bent forward, with a very dirty hand
he pulled and pulled and pulled at a lock of black, longish
hair.

I went on downstairs to the Greyhound gates. As I came
down the steps, half a dozen black kids, boys about fourteen
or fifteen, were horsing around on the stairs. One leaned
heavily on the banister, running now up, now down. A few
standing at the foot watched him—one smoking—laughing at
his antics.

As I turned to sit on a waiting room chair, I looked back up
the steps. A middle-aged white couple, who must have been
walking only steps behind me, but whom I hadn't seen till
then, came down. The woman carried their bags. The man
looked possibly infirm.

The kid on the steps let go of the banister and turned:
"Hey, white folks!" he called. "Where you goin'?"

The couple ignored him and continued down.

"Don't worry, I ain't gonna hurt you!" The kid continued beside them, squatting on each step. "You don't have to be afraid of me."

The couple looked like they might have been exhausted at that hour. They didn't look very frightened.

"What's a matter? You afraid I'm gonna rob you? I'm gonna mug you?" At the stairs' bottom, he laughed and bounced in a squat, looking at the couple, then at the other boys, some of whom were giggling, some not.

The couple just walked over to the seats as if they hadn't heard.

Leaving my briefcase on the black plastic chair between some passengers, I went into the men's room. There were half a dozen other black kids inside, and a few Puerto Ricans, most of them older or younger than the ones fooling around on the steps.

Just as I came in, a tall black guy with glasses, who may have even been twenty, folded his arms, reared back, and actually said to a boy who couldn't have been more than thirteen: "Hey, what's a kid like you doin' up this late?"

The boy folded his arms indignantly and declared: "I told you before, I ain't no kid!"

"Yeah," declared his even younger companion: "He knows his way around!"

Stifling a laugh, I went to the urinals.

At the far end stood a particularly good looking black guy in a gray Confederate cap; he seemed to be there pretty permanently.

A minute later, I came out to see the kid who'd been horsing around outside look up the steps again, where a tall, rather refined looking white man, with silver hair and an expensive gray suit, his overcoat over one arm and carrying an attaché case, was starting down.

The kid dashed up the steps. "Hey, white man!" he demanded. "Where you goin'? You afraid of me? You afraid I'm gonna follow you where you goin', I'm gonna beat you up, I'm gonna rob you? Now, you don't have to be afraid of that!" As the boy came on down the steps beside him, calling out his taunts, the man paid as little attention to him as had the couple.

At the bottom of the steps, among the other boys, an older

black kid, maybe seventeen, suddenly called up: "Nigger, why you acting like such a fool!"

The boy clowning on the steps didn't even glance back: "Now you don't have to be afraid of me. I ain't gonna hurt you, white man!"

As the first kid reached the bottom the second kid stepped up on the stair: "Hey, nigger! Why—"

The first boy danced back, grinning. "I'm just askin' these white folks where're they—"

Suddenly the second grappled the first boy in a headlock. "—do you talk like such a *fool*!"

"Hey! Let go of me!" The first, his mouth muffled by a forearm, giggled—"Let me go, you . . . crazy nigger!—" while others, who'd been watching and chuckling themselves, turned away as the kid was dragged off.

I was still standing almost inside the men's room door. As I stepped away, a nondescript, middle-class black woman in a brown coat and hat absently wandered in. "Excuse me, ma'am," I said, turning back. "That's the men's room."

"Oh, it is?" she said. "Well, where *is* the lady's room?"

"About three yards down the hall, ma'am," said a Puerto Rican boy from inside, loitering by the basins.

I got my briefcase again and for a while strolled about the Greyhound departure area.

Wearing a ratty thermal vest and looking disheveled and unwashed enough so that it was moot if she were a passenger waiting on a bus or a bum in to keep warm, one teenaged white girl sat by the wall near her knapsack, bound closed with dirty twine. (If she were a derelict, she'd probably taken pains to achieve the ambiguity.) In a cloth coat and a knitted cap, a shopping-bag lady wandered along the far gates with her bundled sacks of paper and cloth, muttering to herself, occasionally spitting, now and again snapping out some curse.

At one point, as the woman passed almost directly in front of her, the girl looked sharply away.

A man perhaps thirty slept on the floor, wedged into the corner by the transparent plastic wall of the north-end waiting area. New black work shoes. Stained and ancient workman's grays. A middling old pea-jacket fallen open over a shirt with some name stitched in yellow thread, soiled and worn to unreadability, across the torn pocket. His black beard was more or less neatly shaven; his hair was fairly short. When the great cleaning machine, pushed by a black attendant, sudsed over the floor, its spinning brush dangerously close to his face, he sat up suddenly, lurched to his feet, and, one hand out before him, staggered into the waiting area and collapsed on a row of black plastic seats without—as far as I could tell—even opening his eyes.

A bunch of tough Puerto Rican girls in very thick makeup and blue down coats, none over sixteen, kept moving in and out of the ladies room, sometimes razzing and sometimes being razzed by the black and Puerto Rican boys lounging about, but more often just in their own, harsh, serious little world.

I hadn't been in a bus station at that hour for over a year. A clear difference from the last time, however, was the increased number of people sleeping on the seats, floor, or benches who looked as if, three weeks or three months ago, they might have been working—a very different population from the eternal indigents (still there of course) who wander about such places year in and year out.

On line behind me for the Philadelphia bus was a bearded college student on his way to visit friends and family at home. His calculated casualness and studied disarray strangely reflected what ambled and stumbled all round us: his beard and long hair worn that way because he liked it, not because he couldn't afford to cut it; the clean, pink shirt left out of his old, white corduroy pants because it felt comfortable that way, not because he'd forgotten it was possible to affect your appearance by the exertion of such small energies; the old sneakers worn because they were comfortable, not because he'd found them in a trash can after spending four days with no shoes at all. His wire-framed glasses were clean. His watch was on time—at one point I asked him what time it was, and the next thing you know we were having an astute enough conversation about economic conditions in the country and how they were reflected in what passed around us.

He sat in the seat ahead of me on the bus, listening to the earphones of his silent Walkman, while we rolled through breaking dawn, down to Philadelphia.

Another journal entry, based on notes made that morning in November and written out more fully a day or so later.

Another (very minor) reason the Nevèrÿon series is a document.

9.81 How did I find out *where* it was? It was rather easy, *the Master explained*. In every group, no matter how carefully you select them, one or two are always more disreputable than the rest. Even in this school, we have ours. So I went to one and told him: "Look, I want to know where they're holding the Calling of the Amnewor." My voice let him know that, while I was serious, I wasn't accusing him of anything. When he told me, of course, I knew I'd had my suspicions all along.

Where else in Kolhari *could* they have held it?

By late afternoon, most of the students had gone off for Carnival. At five o'clock, I went out, pausing on the lawn while a cricket, who'd somehow found her way into town, chirruped in urban isolation and despair. I looked at the infirmary. Another student was laid up, all sad-faced at not being able to attend the merry-making, but—bless her—she'd only sprained an ankle. (Earlier, when I'd visited, she'd made noises about using the time to study.) Walking out toward the Pavē, I turned down the slope between the sycamores, some of which I'd replanted and some of which my neighbors had brought in, after my example.

Well, I asked myself, why are you going to this uncivilized affair? Is it for Toplin? Is it for the ill, the harried, the worried, the ground down? But with only the silent street about me, I could not answer a strict yes. Pure curiosity? But I'm of an age to know that little if nothing in this strange and terrible land is pure.

The problem with these practices—and I've attended enough, both inside the city and out—is that I frequently know more about them than the benighted jungle bunny hopping up and down performing them.

Doughty old servants when I was a child—with the family how many generations and forbidden to talk of such things— oh, they delighted in terrifying spoiled aristocratic brats, whining for an hour before bedtime, with the very tales and terrors aristocratic parents had fled long ago and wherever.

In the south, of course, it's Gauine: a great dragon of jewels and gold, long as the land, with a wingspread wide as the sky. She's supposed to guard some town that doesn't exist any more—though I looked for it long enough when I visited the area.

Up north it's Ropig Crigsbeny: a boar the size of a mountain, who gobbles whole tribes at a mouthful and shits man-high piles of skulls. But there've been enough wars around there—and enough hacked-off heads—to understand why nobody wants to talk about *him* much.

I confess, the Amnewor is new to me. Yes, I've heard the name—as a minor fact in some other god's story. Precisely what it did, though, I can't remember. That, of course, makes it more intriguing. Death. It was associated with endless, mindless, pointless death. But which of them isn't? I recall—

9.811 The problem with the "suspension of disbelief" theory of fiction in general and of F&SF in particular is that it makes art (however willingly) a kind of cheat. People who want to preserve art's privilege of subversion (and of, yes, shock) have said: "Fine, let it *be* a cheat!" e.g., Picasso: "Art is the lie that makes the truth bearable." But certainly *this* is not an enterprise where I want to cheat at all.

As did writers from Flaubert and Baudelaire (who vacillated) to Pater and Wilde, I believe art is wholly a formal enterprise, encompassing almost all the tenets that the nineteenth century spoke of as *l'art pour l'art*, tenets which have made twentieth century's experimentation possible. (What postmodern doesn't?) How, then, to reconcile that belief with all this topicality.

I think the answer lies in that the writer is *always* generating *meanings* (and *not* organizing references), even the most topical meanings. Reference, after all, is only a particularly limited sort (or better, use) of meaning in a particularly limited context: and that is neither the subject-dominated literary text *nor* the object-dominated paraliterary text.

(To refer to reference always requires a frame, and is always therefore an act of meaning . . .)

9.82 Journeying through the city, what I recall (and I always do, whenever I go any place where the street noise lowers enough for me to hear myself think, *the Master said*) is my journey through Nevèrÿon when I was seventeen.

For that was when truly I first learned of monsters.

Nevèrÿon.

Officially, I was crossing it.

What I wanted to do, of course, was flee it—though I couldn't tell my uncle that.

I could hardly tell myself. But that was my secret plan.

My overt object and itinerary as I presented it to my uncle was, however, of the highest moral and intellectual order. I wanted—I told him—to seek out all the works, monuments, and remaining memorials of the barbarian inventor, Belham. There were enough traces of his handiwork here in Kolhari to excite any boy with a like penchant for invention. Born in southern lands, he'd come up to lay out some of our city's finest avenues and estates; then he went north . . .

But his architectural innovations preserve the High Court and make it livable to this day.

Coinpress? Corridor?

He was responsible for both.

And there are a dozen gardens, both in Sallese and Neveryóna, where his fountains still plash among the greenery and flowers. Moving about the city, you think of his as a wholly urban sensibility. But the traditions are clear. He was not born here; he did not die here.

He came from somewhere else.

He left for somewhere else.

And at seventeen, my adolescent obsession, my first mission, my purpose and passion was to reconstruct that journey, that life, from origin to end; for the wonders left in Kolhari alone suggested the most marvelous and misty cross-section among complex endeavors that covered the country.

In preparation for the journey, for almost eight months—a long time for sustained effort from someone seventeen—besides visiting every architectural structure in Kolhari that boasted Belham's hand, I'd met with every relative I could, resident in the city or visiting, to get information about him as well as a list of locations for whatever of his projects might remain in our nation. (Some, of course, had vanished in small time, but an impressive number endured.) In this wise, I'd constructed a map and with it, made notes, from which I seriously considered writing a detailed account of Belham's life and works, like those that various councilors were forever proposing to put together about some of our queens and kings, to have them carved on certain walls at the court—and never getting round to it. You must understand that this was before the writing system from the Ulvayns came to the mainland: that fixes specific words to parchment, stone, or papyrus. But in those days, we had only the various commercial scripts, with their signs for amounts, products, ideas, names, and injunctions, and it was in the two of these languages I'd mastered that I intended to write this work.

The ease with which you could write it today makes my

adolescent ambition seem a grandiose dream verging on the preposterous. Contemplating it in the light of the newer writing, I am only more impressed than ever with that early and ambitious foolishness.

What do you take on a journey if you are a seventeen-year-old prince who expects to be gone a year? Money, of course. And tents. And provisions; and tools to set them up. Of course a chest of sumptuous gifts for the noble houses at which, from time to time, you will be a guest. And another of bright trinkets for commoners who aid you and require recompense. And two closed carriages to carry it all in. And six armed soldiers, skilled with spear, sword, and bow, to protect you from bandits. And three men to rotate as drivers and general grooms (though they, too, should have weapon experience). And a body servant—some soft souls say two, three, or more. And a caravan steward to coordinate it all. My uncle assured me I would need a companion of my own class and interests, as well. I made noises about stopping off to pick up a young cousin of mine from some castle or other in the west—a move, once we started, I had no intention of making. Very few of my class *have* my interests; and among those who do, that cousin was not one.

The night before we left, my uncle held a party for me—to which I arrived late: I'd finally gotten a chance to visit a merchant woman in Sallese whose gardens boasted a set of Belham's finest fountains. The spewing jets played at the four corners of a bridge across the stream at the bottom of the falls foaming behind her house. As I recall, she was quite anxious to show me something else, kept up in a maintenance shack at the top of the garden rise. She said it held Belham's own garden maquette—but I had seen many like it before—as well as something created by another inventor, a contemporary of, or an assistant to, Belham, when he'd worked there for her father.

She wouldn't tell me what it was.

But Belham alone was my Great Man, my Hero, and my only Passion—also I was late.

So I thanked her, declined her invitation, examined her handsome fountains and their ingenious tributary pools on the gardens' upper level; and left for home.

Next morning our caravan pulled out of my uncle's gates, while the gatekeeper, up later than I at the night's revels, planted the end of the crossbeam in the dust to lean on it, yawning, as the sky's deep blue lightened moment by moment toward a gray that threatened rain.

It didn't break, as I recall, till our third day out from the city.

The outlines of Belham's story are widely known: born in the south and distinguishing himself there by his mathematical and architectural ability, he soon came to the attention of local nobles, who encouraged him to work at various holds about the land. Finally he was summoned by Queen Olin to Kolhari, and later worked here for various lords and wealthy merchant families. But he was a drinker, a womanizer, and a commoner to boot, as well as a ranging and restless spirit. After Olin was deposed, he traveled even further north, where he finally died from falling down a cliff, while drunk, one cold and rainy evening, near a village just beyond Ellamon.

The map I'd made indicated forts, temples, bridges, roads, and fountains all over Nevèrÿon that Belham's name was connected with. How did I intend to reconstruct the journey from south to north that was his life? I joined each point on my map by a single line to the point nearest. Certainly that was the most logical path he would have traveled. And one drizzly afternoon, perhaps a week beyond our departure, I sat under a tarpaulin that had been put up for me at our camp. A hickory fire burned near me, from logs that my caravan steward, suspecting rain, had put by in our wagon the day before. I unrolled the map from arm to arm of my lounging chair, now and again sipping a berry drink through a brass straw. The liqueur was local to the town just above which we'd stopped, and my man, Cadmir, born there and boasting of it half the day before, had run down and back to purchase a jar and bring it up for my enjoyment.

Three of my soldiers squatted by a wagon wheel, tossing bones with one of my drivers—for the sprinkle was not so fierce as to distract them from their gambling.

Suddenly they laughed.

The driver had told them, I realized, the perfectly foul joke that, after some deliberation as to whether or not it was meet for one of my station, I'd told to him that morning as we'd sat together on the carriage's rocking bench. ("And make sure you tell it to Terek," I'd suggested, for the dark, lanky soldier had already struck me as the most sullen among my men, though sometimes he could give out with a startling smile.) I glanced up, to see first Terek (of the dark skin and broken nose), then the others, grin in my direction. I grinned back: of course, the driver had told them what I'd said about Terek as well. But none seemed to have taken offense. Feeling supremely well liked, I went on looking at my map. I still recall the pride I felt, that cool afternoon as I moved a forefinger over the vellum. Clearly this was the opening of my Great Work. The logic, the order, the sheer reasonableness of it, in the lines that crossed the geographical signs for mountains and rivers and forests, was as beautiful as—I thought then—truth must always be.

There was Belham's life!

I sat gazing on the totality out of which all Belham's creations had grown.

Had it occurred to me that perhaps one or two of his marvels had missed my notation? Yes, I knew for a fact I had left out at least two, because though I had their descriptions from several people, no one knew exactly *what* towns they were in. Did I suspect that perhaps he had not gone quite so directly, now and again, between proximate locations? From stories I'd already gotten from various noble cousins, I was sure there were three places from which he'd gone on to some far place to build before returning to a nearer town to build again. Had it occurred to me that a few of the works bearing his name had probably not been built by him at all, but were imitations by others in his style? I had down three such for certain, since, despite the name, others remembered the true builder. But these bits of special knowledge were what gave me the expert's sense that spiced my general pleasure.

What did I think, then, of all these mistakes and exceptions? What did they mean for my serpentine pattern winding Nevèrÿon?

I was convinced, as only youth can be, that if new wonders by Belham were reported to me that day, that if new forgeries were at that very moment unmasked, the revisions would surely lie so close to the lines I already had down—that any corrections to be made in such an astute picture as mine must be so minuscule—that, were he looking over my shoulder, Belham himself would praise my method and take it for his own, astonished at how precisely any addition he might make already lay within the general curve and contour of his life as I had sketched it.

Somewhat eccentrically, my quest's first goal was the town, in the Faltha mountains, of Belham's death. I wanted to stand atop the ledge where he had stood, had staggered...and had, drunkenly, slipped down. Indeed, I wanted to climb to that ledge's bottom and stand at—even lie upon—the place where he had lain, with his broken legs, to die. I wanted to see if, in my youth, gazing on the rocks and trees he'd gazed on, I could intuit from them the final thoughts of the aged and injured genius. And I was determined not to stop off at any of the other monuments on my map until I'd had this moment of terminal empathy.

From his dying place I'd planned to move back, then, along the line I'd laid out, to his last accomplishments at Ellamon—the landscaping and fountains of my cousin's gardens at the Vanara Hold. Then, wonder by wonder, I would follow that line (skirting only Kolhari), till, sinking into the south, I reached his place of birth. Thus at each station, I could contemplate the marvels there in terms of all that had lain ahead for him, which I would now know, though it was unknown to him. What more reasonable way, I thought, was there to comprehend the great and sweeping pattern of a great man's sweeping life?

As we drew deeper into the Falthas, of course it rained—rained as though the gods' own cistern had cracked open to spill endlessly over the woody, rocky slopes we rode: it rained for the whole three days we approached Ellamon.

The road grew treacherous.

Soon my balding and heavy-lipped caravan steward climbed into my wagon to confer with me, his robes drenched, his bushy eyebrows water jeweled, and an edge in his voice betraying his impatience with my impractical notion of bypassing the fabled High Hold: *Could* the young master see his way to stopping first at Ellamon proper and importuning some hospitality from his fabled relatives—enough to wait out this bad weather?

I was, of course, as wet and as cold as any of my men, for several times I'd had to leave my wagon when we crossed a particularly narrow stretch. As we rolled, with the steward sitting beside me, I looked through the wagon's forward window, between the driver's legs: our horses went unsteadily on the branch-strewn, runneled path. While we joggled, damp and cold, the wagon slid about.

"Of course," I told him; "we'll stop at Ellamon first,"

and saw my orderly dream, like an overloaded wagon slipping from a muddy mountain path, go smashing over the rocks at the roadway's edge.

At Ellamon an aged cousin—whom I'd never met till then—took us into his great house with much goodwill and solicitousness, putting my servant with his in the scullery and placing my soldiers first in his empty barracks, then bringing them in to dine with us—at *my* egalitarian suggestion. For when I learned they would be served the same food as we, prepared in the same kitchen, there seemed no need for such a lonely meal with only the two of us in that long, echoing chamber.

My cousin was honestly pleased with the suggestion and seemed to enjoy the resultant jokes, laughter, battle tales, and pleasantries, while we ate his parsnips and roast mutton and the windows, flaring with lightning, dripped on the western wall.

The next morning the rain had stopped. Once there, however, I had to stay the day. I'd told my cousin of my interest in Belham. He was a well of information. As he took me out to show me Belham's fountains in his own gardens he gave me instructions on how to get to the town nearest Belham's demise, down to the specific landmarks and the turns I would have to take at them to reach, first, the town, then the ledge outside it, where the Great Man had fallen. (Could we have gotten there without him?) He told me of the inn, long since come down, where Belham had drunk his last mugs of hard cider before wandering off into the evening; he told of a half-witted, fourteen-year-old goatherd, who'd glimpsed the Great Man, still alive, struggling at the cliff's bottom on two consecutive days, but who later confessed she'd been too frightened to help him or tell anyone, since someone had told her that the barbarian stranger was a wizard who could move great rocks at will. And he told me of the quarrymen who, a day later, came upon him and brought him up—barely breathing by the time they found him and dead when they got him back to the inn. In short, he made the whole harrowing and horrid incident live.

After his tale, I said I planned to locate the inn by its foundations and follow Belham's path straight from it to the fatal ledge.

"Well," he said, "that might be difficult, as the whole town has moved over at least two stades to the east, even since my childhood. Also, one must remember, Belham was very drunk.'' My cousin smiled. ''And a drunken man does not necessarily walk the straightest line.''

I think my laughter surprised him. ''Of course!'' I declared. ''And Belham was not only drunk with cider, he was drunk with genius!'' Did he suspect how sure I was that my own cleverness could untangle any and all mysteries about Belham or his life? ''Well,'' he said, ''not only has the town itself moved, it's perhaps half its former size—really, it's just some houses going by the same name. But did you know,'' he went on, ''that there's a peasant woman today, who lives not very far off, on the outskirts of Ellamon itself, with whom Belham lived awhile, here in the High Hold? Why not visit her? She's in her sixties now—possibly even her seventies—and is supposed to be quite a character in her own right. Certainly she'll share her memories of the transient architect and inventor.''

But didn't he stay *here,* at the Vanara Castle, when he was working on the gardens . . . ?

''Well—'' my cousin smiled again—''the story has it that Belham was a rather difficult man. I believe my uncle, for whom the fountains were actually built, then Suzerain of Vanar, put him out at one point!''

I was appalled—at my late uncle!

But my cousin seemed impressed with my commitment to the memory of the Great Man, and wished me luck. The next morning my carriages rolled off for that tiny, mountain hold.

An hour on, again it poured.

Early that evening, drops still hammering the carriage roofs, we rolled in among some hovels of sopping thatch, all brown and hide patched, which were—probably—the village my cousin had told me of. But at least once, when I'd been up with my driver on the bench, I'd inadvertently had him go right when we'd been supposed to go left—and probably, at another point, had gone left instead of right.

In the downpour, no one seemed about; no work-hardened hand pushed back a leather hanging to let creased eyes blink out at us through the rain as we rode past the huts. (One had fallen half in and was obviously abandoned.) As I looked out the carriage's dripping window, we clattered and splashed over what may or may not have been a road between them.

Beside me, Cadmir wanted to know: ''Should we stop to ask if this is—''

"No!" I declared. "No. We have our directions. Drive on!"

Looking out, I tried to imagine among the ancestors of those impoverished dwellings—two stades to the east—one that might have once served as an inn, or even as a drinking establishment where a man such as Belham could have entered, seated himself, and found enough conviviality to reach the necessary drunkenness to bring about his evening's wandering—and death.

It was very hard.

Fifteen minutes or so beyond the enclave, we rolled out onto a long ledge from which—along parts of it—a man might have fallen. I leaned out the window in the rain to look down on the uneven ground at what, scattered among the rocks and leaves, my driver called back to assure me was wild dragon spore. But by then, I was sneezing regularly, and so told myself that the two mistakes (if, indeed, we'd *made* two) surely canceled each other out.

At last I climbed from the carriage, hunching in the downpour, to walk along the precipice in the peppering drops and gaze off at other mountains, wrapped half-round with mists. Going on a little further, staring over into the dripping undergrowth, I realized there would be no climbing down. Indeed, minutes later at a less steep place, clambering over those wet stones, my sandal missed its footing and I slipped and slid some six feet to an outcrop below, landing in leaves and twigs, scraping my thigh and wrenching one arm. Breath knocked out of me, I lay there with my face full of leaf dirt, a speck of something in one eye, gasping and astonished, while a branch jabbed at my leg.

I blinked and grunted in the rain.

My first thought was that, in moments, someone would be running up to help.

But do you know, not one of my servants, soldiers, or drivers saw me go over? They were all inside the carriages to keep dry, no doubt convinced that their young master, off slogging about in the wet, was quite out of his mind.

I climbed back up on my own.

But as I stood once more atop the ledge, sore, scraped, and still sneezing in the torrent, I knew that, in such weather, there was also no possibility of "quiet contemplation" of the last thoughts and hours of the Great Man.

It was raining too hard.

Minutes later, back at the carriage, I did not even mention my fall, though Cadmir asked as I climbed up inside if there were something wrong. No. No, I said. No, I was just wet and leaf-stained. As we jarred and joggled back through the town—if town you could call it—I told myself that, whether or not I'd stood on the ledge from which the drunken genius had fallen, whether or not I'd gazed down at where he'd lain for three days until he died, I'd surely been close enough to it, if not in space, then in kind, so that I should be satisfied. Besides, even if I had fallen upon the spot itself (for couldn't an older man, landing just so, have broken his legs in such a tumble?), in the time since, new trees would have grown up and old ones must have come down, so that the actual site would appear different, anyway, in just those details I'd hoped, till then, to recapture by my presence: I had looked from a ledge on a view near enough to the last Belham must have seen for me to be content. And didn't fable hold that the night of his fall had been cold and wet? Belham had been drunk with cider and genius? I'd been drunk with Belham! He'd fallen. And I . . . ? Well, as I sat sneezing in the carriage with Cadmir now and again pushing more blankets up around me, I decided my experience of the ledge—the severity of the fall excepted—was probably more like Belham's than I had bargained for!

My revised plan had been, of course, to return to my cousin's at Ellamon. But an hour later, Cadmir took his hand away from my forehead with a worried look to state that I felt feverish. The caravan steward was called in from the other wagon (where he rode with the soldiers). And I surprised everyone, including myself, by suddenly ordering that we bypass the High Hold of fabled Ellamon and continue to the next spot on my map.

"But my young master must know that," said the steward, "in his condition and this weather, such action isn't wise . . ."

Cadmir even brought up that my cousin had promised to take me out on my return to see the flying beasts from the corrals above the High Hold that so many people talk of. Certainly Belham had gone out to watch them up on the hillside, as did all tourists who came through fabled Ellamon.

Cadmir, of course, knew me better than the balding, bushy-browed steward. At another time it might have worked.

But I was persistent.

(I was feverish and, in a word, unreasonable.)

I'd not come to *be* a tourist, I declared. I'd come with a purpose and a passion. I'd already seen Belham's fountains in my cousin's garden. Now I'd seen his place of death. Thus my purpose, in these parts, had been fulfilled. Also, I *hadn't* seen them in the order I'd intended. Now I wanted to go on—to repair my injured plan by continuing with it as though nothing had gone amiss. And that did *not* allow for going back!

So that is more or less what we did.

But, bundled in furs lest my indisposition turn into some serious catarrh, as the wagon jounced through the evening along the soaked mountainside, I knew why I did not want to return to my cousin's.

I have never actually told anyone this, though it is simple enough to say.

Cadmir no doubt thought that it was because I did not want my cousin to confirm as fact that we had, indeed, found the wrong turning, the wrong town, and the wrong ledge. Had he dared say that in the jostling carriage, sullenly I would have agreed.

My real reason, however, was the same one that had prevented me from dismounting to ask directions among those poor, crumbling huts to verify the town, make sure of the ledge, or even to help me find the old inn's site.

It was that peasant woman.

A city lad, I had not spoken with many peasants before—and certainly none who didn't at least work for someone related to me. I'd only just managed to quell, through dint of almost forcible companionship on my part, an even then occasionally resurgent, if unmotivated, embarrassment before my own soldiers and drivers. And they, at least, I paid. Certainly I could demand of myself, in those days, no more! The notion of speaking to such a person, an ancient, dense, impoverished, and imperceptive crone, no doubt half-senile in the bargain, seemed by turns preposterous, impossible, and, even more so, terrifying. A peasant woman, I kept repeating. A simple, stupid peasant. A seventy-year-old peasant. And a "character" too, whatever that meant. Certainly I knew Belham was, by birth, a peasant himself. But that he had been ejected from a royal hall to go and live with a stupid, dirty peasant . . .

That I should be expected—for whether or not my cousin expected it of me, I certainly expected it of myself—to

confront this aged wall of belligerent, senile dementia, to sit
in some drafty shack, trying to pry out from that unyielding
common blankness a few pebbles of truth, fact, and firsthand
information, when the earth and air itself already seemed to
conspire around me to yield only approximations of what I
wanted, was simply too frightening for someone so newly
loose in our strange and terrible land.

Later that night we made camp—

But let me skip ten months, or eleven, or possibly even
thirteen, for I have calculated the time differently on several
occasions by several methods. Suffice it to say it was in the
last weeks of my trip.

It was night.

We made camp.

Deep in the southern forests, our fire burned within the
makeshift ring of stones we'd pushed together earlier. Supper
was done. The three of us sat around the flame—

Who—? you ask. *What* three—?

Certainly the tired young man scraping charcoal away from
the burnt end of his empty roasting stick with his thumbnail
was a leaner, browner, and, I would guess, a more levelhead-
ed fellow than I'd been the night we pulled away from the
Ellamon road. My hands were harder, too.

It had begun with that brazen and much sweated over
decision to eat among my own soldiers at my cousin's court.
But between then and now many distinctions of class—at
least, I like to think so—had fallen away.

My fear of peasants?

Well, by now I'd had slept in my share of chill, smelly
peasants huts, and, in several more, had eaten my share of
oddly spiced meals (as well as some spectacularly tasteless
ones). Here and there three or four commoners, come to my
rescue out of simplest kindness and without a suspicion I was
a prince (and most I never told), I'd even called friends. In
that time I'd managed properly to bed my first woman, a
peasant widow, four or five years older than I. She, I confess,
I told about my lineage in what I'd call *exaggerated* detail.
But though I don't know whether, a day later, she believed
me, she seemed fascinated during the account—though possibly only by the complexity of what she may have taken to be
some imaginative merchant's son's preposterous dreaming.
She smelled of cows, I remember, and knew all about country
remedies for ailments I'd never even heard of before, though

I was sure, after a few hours' talk with her, that the country witch could have cured my poor father, without a doubt. And a night later, at a royal relative's great granite home, I snuck through some lightless stone corridor behind a frizzy-haired princess, three years younger, and far more highly born, than I. She was the orphaned ward of another noble cousin and wore a black gown, bronze jewels, and carried a smoky brand high ahead. Finally, on the dirt floor of the castle storage room I showed her some of what I'd learned not a full day back in a common woman's arms . . .

I had no other woman for over a year—though the very range of my encounters was enough to make me think myself at least as much an expert on sex as I was on Belham, if not the final authority on womankind itself.

I'd also managed to learn the lesson easy for rural nobles but hard for the heads of our urban upper classes to absorb: in the right situation, peasant wisdom can outshine all others. In my case, one of our carriages put a wheel over the road edge and, after we'd all gotten out, in our effort to right it the whole wagon suddenly toppled over the side, overturning at the bottom of a five-foot slope with a great crash—just as five dirty, silent, and absolutely unprepossessing bumpkins came wandering along, two women among them, only to gape and giggle at us, I was sure. But I had the good sense to be polite, and after five or six grunts with a minute or two between and many, many, many shakes of their heads, suddenly they went to hauling at limbs and uncoiling ropes, barking brief and incomprehensible instructions, now to one another, now to my wary soldiers, till, with this and that, they managed to lever the carriage up, a bit at a time, propping it now with this rock, now with that log, till it was again on the road with only a snapped trace. And as I stood about in embarrassed gratitude (no, they would take no money, but were happy for the worked-metal jars and plates I gave them as gifts), I found myself thinking that their method must be very near to one Belham himself might have devised to move the incredibly heavy stones from quarry to building site, how many decades ago.

But my material losses in those months must be mentioned along with my intellectual gains, or this is no true account.

Cadmir was the first to go. My fever and sneezing had vanished with a week's cough and a somewhat raspy throat. But soon it was Cadmir himself who was feverish, with a

constant hacking that alternated between painful dryness and
bouts when he would bring up phlegms, green and yellow—
and sometimes even blood.

When we met another caravan, this one commercial, returning
to Kolhari, I paid them to take him back to my uncle's in the
city where he might be better cared for in familiar surroundings.

The soldiers? Well one, for instance, came to me to say we
were within stades of his home hamlet. Could he stop off for
a day's visit? He knew our itinerary and promised he would
catch up to us within the week. Against my steward's advice,
I let the man go—and have not seen him since. But a week
after that, two more soldiers took off, just on their own.

"Comes of being lenient with the first one," some said to
me with sympathy, some with censure.

The two closed carriages were eventually lost:

The first went one hot morning when the other trace
snapped, and *two* of my drivers simply walked away in
disgust. But by then I'd had two more caravan stewards since
the first (whom I'd never really gotten along with) had
abandoned us to take on, I can only assume, a more profitable
and, certainly, more sensible job with yet another commercial
venture heading toward the desert; which he'd heard of, so
Terek later informed me, at our stopover in Varhesh. Since we
were low on soldiers, drivers, and provisions, we decided to
consolidate with the remaining carriage.

Then, wouldn't you know, we were attacked by bandits
somewhere in the western woods. I *say* bandits, but truly I
think they were two mounted guards from a noble house
where only hours before we'd been—oh, politely enough—
refused any hospitality at all and sent on our way:

The master, they said, was not in.

The three soldiers left had been inside the carriage with me
when we stopped outside the castle gate, and I think the
guards who decided to follow us wrongly assumed my single
carriage caravan had no soldiers at all. When they stopped us
on the road with a shout and an arrow through my driver's
arm, before I was even sure what was happening, Terek took
up his spear beside me and thrust it mightily from the
carriage window through the flank of one of the bandit's
horses, felling her on top of her rider—I almost lost a tooth
when the spear's end hit my jaw. Then we were all out of the
carriage, fighting the remaining rider. I really only looked on
as they ran down the second on his horse, cutting at his legs,

at the horses's legs, until both went over all bloody and they killed them. Then they came back and Terek put his sword through the neck of the bandit who'd fallen first. His leg broken and pinned under his horse, the man screamed horribly when, for the fifteen seconds before it, he realized what the tall dark soldier with the broken nose ambling leisurely toward him with his sword out was about to do.

We now had a wounded driver, and there was speculation among the men as to whether we would have avoided the fray if they had been walking along outside, visible, as was usual, where the sight of them might have discouraged attack. Terek commented, sensibly I thought, that if three soldiers and a steward had been outside, the bandits, before pouncing, would simply have picked them off from the cover of the trees with bows and arrows, just as they'd shot the driver—who listened to it all leaning against the wagon, a pained expression on his face and his arm now bandaged in a piece of old cloth and a leather sling. We left him off at the next city— where there was a particularly fine, circular grain-sellers guild building, built by Belham.

While I was out looking at it, two more of my soldiers made up their minds to leave my employ, but they at least had the courtesy to stay long enough to tell me, and even to help me sell off the last carriage and horses to a merchant family there and replace it with a sizable two-mule provision cart with a canopy over its back half that could be taken down if needed; Terek and I could manage it alone.

"You know," Terek told me as we were taking stores out of the carriage and hoisting them up over the cart's edge to pack them under the cart cover, "we'll have less trouble with bandits in this thing than we would with that. A closed carriage on these roads just *looks* like nobility, and if there's not a sizable number of guards in evidence, it cries out to be attacked." That made sense, too.

I became the driver.

Sitting there, reining my mules before me, I was, in just about equal measure, proud of my maturity and of my actual, physical control of our destiny; I was also, yes, frightened lest some arrow strike me from the trees.

The morning after, my last, diminutive, redheaded steward left me—with reasonable warning the night before: "This isn't really a caravan anymore, little master." (I was more than a head taller than he, and, though he was fifteen years my senior, this had been his joke from the beginning.) "I'm a good caravan manager, but there's no one here for me to manage, now. By the same token, I'm not a soldier. Why should you pay me a steward's wages to tag along behind your cart beside your young guard, there?" A little later I called the lanky, still somewhat sullen Terek to me and sat him down on a log across from me for a serious talk.

"The truth is," I told him, "you too should probably quit my company. Certainly you'll be better off making your way alone than weighted down with worry about me. I'll soon find another relative in some great house, whom I intend to implore to get me back to Kolhari—but this has been the most reckless and costly of trips. And I must think of remedying it."

Terek was twenty-three then. Born somewhere off in the country—precisely where, I never did learn—he'd managed to join the army a year or two younger than was permissible. By sixteen or seventeen, he'd seen combat and killed several men; by twenty he'd been the last pupil of the great strategist Master Nabu, and had been made a minor officer in the Imperial Army—where he'd gotten his nose smashed and a scar down his thigh from a young noble-born officer who'd grown jealous of him and, in an argument, had slashed his leg. (He'd slashed back, I'd heard him boast to the other soldiers; then, suddenly, he'd glanced at me, realizing I was listening. I'd just nodded, as approvingly as I could.) After that, he become a private mercenary, hiring out as a caravan guard.

Yes, while I was impressed with his bravery and fighting skills, I was somewhat afraid of this dark, tall man, with the broken nose, the slightly turned-in feet, and the wide hands on which the nails were gnawed down almost to nothing— bitten worse, indeed, than I've seen on *anyone* else in my life.

As I talked to him, telling him he was free to leave me, Terek sat on his log, sword, spear, and bow on the ground between us, clutching his knees and listening as intently as (I imagined) he might to some superior officer explaining a particularly complex battle strategy. "You go too, Terek. It's just not fair. I can manage the wagon alone. There've been no bandits in this part of the forest. And even if I eventually have to abandon the cart, well . . ." He was growing, I could see, more and more uncomfortable, till he blurted:

"Where should I go? You want to get rid of *me*, now? Where do I go, then? What do I do without your damned wagon and your damned mules? And what will *you* do without *me*? You're a boy and a fool! No!" He shook his head, violently. "No, you shouldn't send me off. It's no good! What will happen? To me? To you? I won't go! No!"

My till then controlled fear became simple surprise. But at last, as I had given, somewhat reluctantly, that first soldier permission to leave, I gave this last one permission to stay. My discomfort? It was simply the realization that, from then on, we were *not* Master and man any longer. We were simply a somewhat quiet, though well-trained, twenty-three-year-old soldier and a somewhat precocious, if slightly pigheaded, seventeen-year-old prince. We were traveling together with the same mule wagon; whether I liked it or not, I *had* a companion.

Indeed, it was not long after, nor many villages away, that we crippled Arly, a barbarian outcast in his own village. One leg was gone high at Arly's thigh in a snarl of scarred, hard flesh from some appalling fall as a five-year-old from the front of a runaway stone cart beneath its loud and murderous wheels. Older than I, younger than Terek, and certainly not long on intelligence, he nevertheless had a good imagination, as well as that high humor you sometimes find among the deeply injured; and he was willing to do almost anything in order to come with us—then, indeed, to stay. His arms were thicker than Terek's—though he was shorter than I was. And his remaining leg was strong. He spoke three languages barbarically, where I could converse only in two. (Terek had only one.) Bound round its length with hairy, mint-scented barks, his single crutch was as nimble on rocks and roots as any of the four feet Terek and I had between us; and, on his back, holding it over his shoulder with one hand, he could carry a heavier sack than I could with two. Nothing tied him to his village, where he was usually just tolerated—and sometimes tormented—as a drunkard and an idiot. (He behaved only intermittently like either—and then, usually, with reason.) I suppose the fear and ignorance he shared with his fellow villagers had kept him from running away till now, though he told us he'd thought of little else in the last few years. For his ignorance wasn't so great that he didn't realize his own fear could probably be overcome simply by staying close to someone, like myself, with less than he.

Yes, *please,* he wanted to come!

The reason I took him, however, was that he amused Terek—for all through my good soldier's sullenness, I could still get a grin from him now and then with a dirty story. And to that end I'm afraid I'd used up not only my peasant widow and dark-robed princess, but their sisters and their serving maids, their cousins and their mothers, all in a perfectly shameless manner. Arly's accounts of his one-legged exploits among the village women (as much exaggerated, I'm sure, as my own) gave me at least some respite as we made our way.

With Arly I could become audience to the strings of lascivious tales instead of actor.

Terek's weapon skills were joined with fair hunting ability. Often he speared us rabbits, small pigs, and turkeys. Arly's infirmity seemed to have lent him a mania for physical accomplishment. Already a decent shot with rock and sling, he badgered Terek for spear-throwing lessons, which the young soldier was happy enough to give; and through the' weeks the one-legged barbarian, with his crutch under one shoulder and Terek's spear held over the other, made a committed and purposeful headway that often left me hot-cheeked as I watched, real respect for him contending with real jealousy. Arly had an extraordinary knowledge of edible leaves, roots, pods, nuts, and fungi—passed to him by the same old woman who'd staunched his severed leg and with whom he'd lived till she'd died, when he was fourteen or so and from which time his pariah status in his village dated. Oddly, then, as well as our driver, I became our company cook with what the other two provided. And with only a few culinary disasters (Arly sneezing at some over-peppered stew; Terek frowning at some particularly pasty pudding I'd prepared from Arly's vague recipe, with what I'd thought were only some simple, sensible corrections), it worked fairly well. Since then, I've several times noticed that in such small groups as ours, whoever prepares the food becomes the leader—or stops cooking.

Despite my youth, you see, I still felt in charge of our movements.

And what had happened to my quest for Belham in all this? Well, somehow, aside from these transformations in materials, men, and methods, I'd still managed, before and after, to visit more than half the locations on my map. Whether the true authority lay in me, or in the piece of vellum, now rolled up and stuffed down inside the wagon, I couldn't say. Perhaps I only retained my leadership because from time to time I could take our wagon into the yard of some lowering castle and, after five minutes' conversation with an upper servant, secure an audience with the resident lord, and from there usually gain an offer of hospitality—food, company, and more or less comfortable sleeping accommodations for the three of us—for a day or three's relief from travel.

Another interesting transformation:

On the road, I really felt the three of us were simply friends.

But as soon as we entered one stone gateway or another, Arly would wordlessly become my most attentive, if preposterously clumsy, servant. (His comic confusion in our first such visit, getting lost here and there in the low-ceilinged halls, as he sprinted off to get me water, washing cloths, a bowl of fruit, till I had to go find him, is a tale in itself!) But, do you know, till after he'd taken on the role three times during three such stops, we never discussed it?

At the same time as Arly became my comic man, Terek would transform into my silent, loyal bodyguard.

I don't think they particularly relished being subservient, or even—particularly—felt it. Yet somehow, without question, the pressure of some noble's (or even some noble's servant's) gaze would force the three of us into this hierarchical order, me as well as them—a hierarchy that would vanish minutes after we'd pulled outside the gates. But these visits were rests, as well as social adventures. (Though of a different order for me: in them I learned more than I wanted to about the vulgarities, pretensions, and sheer madness of the provincial rich.) Really, there was no other way for us to negotiate them, and Arly and Terek could not have had them without me. Perhaps, then, that was why, on our days in the forest, mountain, or desert, when I took out my vellum, squinted up at the sun, then pointed now here, now there on the much marked map, unquestioningly we went where I said.

Indeed, without more than the most passing mentions from me, they even began to develop a kind of respect for Belham and my quest—at least after they'd seen a few of his works, or sat in the corner of some sooty-ceilinged hall, while I discussed him with this heavy-robed duchess or that potbellied duke, with the same round eyes and broad cheekbones as I.

But despite my own commitment and my companions' growing respect, the map itself had undergone as many changes as I had; and while, my losses notwithstanding, I'd changed (I think) for the better, the map, for practical purposes, was a mess. Oh, I don't mean that the parchment itself was in tatters. *That* was safe enough—only worn a little at the edges where, from time to time, I'd gripped it too tightly. But the stability of the object only fixed the chaos that had come upon it. For though I had visited more than half the locations marked, by no *means* had I visited them in order. The confusion in my initial trip to Ellamon and the tiny town beyond only hinted at the confusion my quest had met with throughout the rest of Nevèrÿon:

Buildings and bridges built by Belham and said to be at one town or city had several times turned out to be at others, two or three days away. The map itself had contained its own errors, with villages supposedly situated on one side of a river turning out to be a day or two's ride from the other. What had been marked as a stream turned out to be a wide river. And a goodly number of wide and rocky streams—known as rivers locally—turned out not to have been marked at all. On several occasions, when two of my carefully noted cities were, indeed, physically close, some unscalable mountain ridge or unclimbable chasm or unfordable river—at least at that spot—lay between them, so that direct travel from one to the other was all but impossible.

At first I made myself the excuse that Belham, unlike me, as a Great Man, would have been undaunted by the unclimbable, the unfordable. But soon I had to admit that, to the extent he had been a great traveler as well, he must have been an efficient one, and in Nevèrÿon's varied and variegated landscape, the shortest distance on the map was not always the most practical one to pass across. There were simply too many places where it was easier to go a greater distance over easier terrain than a shorter one across the impassable.

Of course I'd tried to revise my map in the light of this new geographical information. For hadn't I learned from an elderly woman of Able-Ani, who recalled working as a youngster for an older Belham, hauling water for his workers building the stone temple for which the town today is famous, that there was a bridge in the town, already years old when she was a girl, which Belham had also built across the river that divided it? For a fact, she knew that he had architected the bridge years before when he was in his twenties, and that he'd not been in Able-Ani for twenty years since (he'd told her these things himself), and had now come back, in his early fifties, to construct the temple at the local lord's request. Now Belham's time and work in Kolhari had clearly been done after both: the woman recalled his great excitement at receiving a messenger from the High Court. That, she was sure, was the first time he'd been summoned to the court by the queen, not only from Belham's own words to her as she'd poured out water for him at the temple site, but from everyone else's excitement over the new commission. And she was sure he'd left from Able-Ani to travel direct to the High Court at the queen's command the very week the temple was finished.

All of this seemed proper from what I knew.

But there was no line direct from Able-Ani to Kolhari on *my* map; nor were there two lines to that small, elegant city marking two separate visits, to build two separate monuments (one stone bridge, one rock temple), twenty years apart. Sitting by my camp's burnt-out fireplace one chill morning, before anyone else was up, I'd tried to draw in these revisions along with the dozens of other geographical corrections I'd learned about, only to realize that, as I worked with my brush at my bit of pumice-rubbed goatskin, that where, before, I'd had supreme order, now I had incompleteness and imprecision superimposed on inaccuracy and error.

Another problem: many times by then I'd heard the name that plagues any researcher into the late works of Belham: Venn. (How I'd avoided it till now, I've often wondered since.) Here and there—and almost always in tiny, provincial holds where the inhabitants had forgotten all facts concerning Belham the man, so that I clearly knew more than anyone there about the stretch of road cut through impossible rocks, or the great stones of some archway balanced impressively together—along with Belham's bridge or building, I'd find "Venn's Stair" or "Venn's Rock" or "Venn's Cut." Someone, I don't know who, said he *thought* Venn was a woman Belham had . . .

Lived with, like the old peasant at Ellamon I'd been afraid to see?

Been in love with?

Been furious at?

Both?

Neither?

Logic suggests the aging inventor, infatuated with some young, pretty, scatterbrained thing, had begun to name some of his minor works after her. But was she a superstitious peasant he'd diddled behind a barn when she'd offered the old man a cup of beer, or was she some prattling princess with whom, groping after her in some castle chamber where he'd pursued her in the dark, he'd managed (once more?) to disgrace himself? I did not know then, and I do not know now. Perhaps it was some merchant who'd financed him. Perhaps it was some noble friend he'd chosen to honor. No one I happened to meet seemed to know—though at Narnis I found an obviously manmade promenade, with great rock steps cut down to the river; and at Aldanangx, near Makalata, we were directed out to an immense cave that had clearly been cut artificially into the mountain, huge and echoing, with carved columns along its sides. Both bore only Venn's name—both, truly, greater than any work by Belham I'd seen.

As we stood in the cave's cool hollow, with his crutch end tapping about on the stone floor and his eyes gazing at the distant ceiling, Arly made the most preposterous suggestion yet: perhaps she—if it was a she—was an inventor and architect herself, comparable to, if not greater than, my Belham. In the columned, echoing space, Terek and I howled and threw our arms around our bellies and doubled over at that one. But the truth is, as we walked out onto sunlit sand (teasing each other with japes about the bandits we'd heard occasionally used the place for a stopover), as we reached our wagon beside the scruffy desert bushes, I realized I simply didn't know. And in such a situation, the joking logic of a one-legged barbarian counts no less, certainly, than the considered reason of a Nevèrÿon prince. But I'd begun to learn how suspicious were all products of logic. So that now, whenever I encountered Venn's name, it was not as a bit of revealing information but only a frayed thread pulled loose from the weave and fallen from time's crowded and confused worktable.

We had recently swung down and around into the lush and forested south, till we were not far from the spot on my old and marked-up map where Belham was supposed to have been born. Certainly I'd given up on the pristine order of my

early plan—advice I'm sure, that, had I asked for it, my first
and long-gone caravan steward would have given me directly,
that feverish night in the Falthas.

But as we'd come closer to what my map fixed as Belham's
point of origin, benefactors both high and low, on hearing of
my goal, had told me that, while, yes, Belham was indeed
rumored to have been born in that particular little town, he
also was rumored to have been born in another as well—also
in several others. And each smiling prince or grinning peasant
gave us his (or, in two cases, her) own perfectly logical
reason why, of course, this one, that one, or another was,
indeed, the *most* logical choice.

By the morning we started out for the place itself, I had
five villages down, each with its claim to be the birthplace of
Belham. The five were not, indeed, far apart—or at least after
the traveling we'd been doing, they did not seem so. The
three of us were able to get our wagon from one to the other,
with a few hours to explore at each, within four days. Nor
were we bothered by inclement weather. And by now, trotting
in after them among the chickens and the dogs, I could stop
any wizened old man or woman, any big-eyed, bandy-legged
boy or girl, give them a smile and a nod, and, after the
necessary moment of suspicion, usually get a smile back and
at least a gesture toward further information, if only the name
and whereabouts of someone else in town who might know
more about my question.

Yet what I'd found in my five villages of his birth was in its
way as disconcerting as my experience of his dying place.

For the first of the towns simply and wholly no longer
existed: we found its foundations, yes, some fallen walls—
but not one building still stood. There were signs of fire. We
left our mule wagon to tramp about the wreckage. While I
speculated aloud as to how many years ago this was likely to
have occurred, with his spear Terek turned up a bit of burnt
board from the body of a cat, whose wet loins, as he prodded
it, spilled out a slough of maggots of maggots!

The destruction was only days—no more than weeks—old,
or the carcass would have been all bone . . .

But for all we looked about that afternoon, the three of us
whispering quietly, or searching about stealthily, skittish as to
lurking marauders or even, perhaps, slavers (none of whom
materialized), we could learn no more.

The second barbarian enclave we found was normal enough—

though, for all of us, the destruction we'd seen the day before returned and returned to mind, the way sun, flashing on a stream, repeats and repeats in the eye after you've moved off into the woods. Yes, the yellow-headed, sun-browned inhabitants knew that Belham had been born there. (They pronounced his name just differently enough to leave a suspicion that we were not talking about the same man, but I'd already learned to put such doubts straight out of mind.) Well, then, did anyone know *precisely* where? Did his parents' house, perhaps, still stand? Did relatives still live here who could tell stories that might have come down through the family about what was supposed to be, after all, a most prodigious childhood?

That drew great laughter from the barbarians who'd gathered to gape at Arly's crutch, dropping to the dust in place of his leg, or to poke and point at the spear Terek, in his kilt and stained leather chest-guard, leaned on like a staff, or simply to blink at me (at my dark, noble, northern features, I presumed), or our wagon, or our mules. From their lapping chatter I learned that this forest village, like the mountain town he'd died near, had also moved about a bit over the years.

Well, where had it moved *from*?

Astonished, I watched this one point in that direction, while another contradicted him, explaining that the other was thinking of a much more recent time, while an aged woman on a stick pushed ahead of them all to tell us that, no, most of the houses used to be down *there*, drowning out a gap-toothed boy who had just been saying earnestly, a moment back, how his old grandfather had clearly told him, years before, that over there...

Terek, Arly, and I looked at each other.

None of the barbarians truly knew.

Or, if one did, none of us three could learn from listening— or from any of our further questions through the day—who was right.

The third town we came to, larger and far more settled looking (perhaps it was the odd stone building, or the wooden fence along one side of a small, partially paved, market area), produced just as many barbarians claiming just as surely that Belham had been born here (part of his family had *come* from another town, you see; but that emigrant relative had been enough to make the other village—not among my five—try to appropriate his birth). This time my question as to where,

then, specifically, young Belham's home or hut had been led
us, after much barbaric chatter, to an elderly man with a cloth
wrapped in a kind of turban around his head, who volunteered
to walk with us awhile. He would explain.

He walked.

We walked with him.

Other barbarians kept a respectful distance.

For distressing minutes our man was silent, and I thought
either Arly or Terek would soon grow bored and start some
jest, for though they had developed a certain respect, neither—
when the other was there to clown about with—had developed
much patience.

But finally he spoke.

"You understand," he told us, in a shrill, measured voice,
as we walked among the huts and houses, "none of what you
see, stone cabin or thatched hovel, has been here more than
twenty-five years. Is that your age, boy?" he asked Terek,
who nodded, even though he was less. "Sometimes it's been
slavers who've devastated the land. Other times, it's been
soldiers who've marched through, killing, burning, destroying.
Villages don't survive that sort of thing. When I was a child,
I can remember even earlier slavers, worse than the Imperial
soldiers—indeed, in the early days I used to think they were
one and the same. They came with the same metal swords,
the same leather armor—" He glanced toward tall Terek's
spear and gear—"and dealt out much the same destruction.
The only difference was that one took prisoners and the other
left all as corpses. But I was only six or seven back then.
Belham? I've heard of him. I've heard that he was born here.
But I've heard that he was born in practically every village in
the south—even in some I know for a fact have existed less
years than the youngest of you has been alive." He glanced at
Arly; and I felt proud that I looked so mature. "But we have
little left to boast of here, my noble visitor." He nodded
toward me. "So you mustn't be surprised if our various
villages share the little we have."

Somehow the next two towns we stopped in, looking for
the birth of Belham, seemed to offer even less than the first
three in terms of certainty. But among them all, at the last of
the five, though I did not say it to either Terek or Arly, what I
was most struck by was that, in their limited, brutish, and
impoverished life, just as I had not been able to imagine a
proper inn in the town of his dying, I could not imagine what,

here, some hundred years ago, might have inspired a barbarian boy to the discoveries about numbers, circles, triangles, rock cutting, levers, pulleys, and the motions of water and wind that had been attributed to him by the time he left it at the behest of some local noble not much more advanced, I suspected by now (judging by the few who had recently given us shelter), in anything save their brutish power over these common folk who had been their subjects, than the commoners themselves. Yet somehow between then and now, I'd become humble enough to see this lack of imagination as *my* failure, *my* want of a comparable genius, the uncrossable distance at which *I* stood from the accomplishments of the Great Man.

Despite the failings I'd learned existed in me, however, along with what strengths I'd found as well, I'd learned that Belham's birth, only a little lifetime before his dying, had somehow become even less specific, even more generalized, than the tenuous fact of his death. Yet now I knew also that, while at (or near) his dying spot I'd seen one town and been able to tell myself, wrong or not, it was probably characteristic of the right one, here at these several places of birth and better trained to observe by my travels, I'd taken from these five possibilities—though all were southern, barbaric, and small—only a set of extreme and fascinating differences; differences which overturned all certainty that, how long ago now, some haphazard huts I'd stumbled on in the mountains (or in the desert or the forest for that matter) could be truly "characteristic" of any others. All towns were individual. Each was unique. And Belham's ability to create wonders of abstraction and stone design from what *he'd* seen in them was just not the same as my little ability to re-create what even then I was becoming more and more wary of calling his "life."

It was only days after we had left the last of these villages—

But I have already said:

We made camp.

The three of us sat by the fire, in our shell of leafy dark, my most recent meal (rabbit and small wild tubers) not much in the past, sleep not far in the future. Terek had just declined a game of bones with Arly, who sat now, both hands holding his knee, looking about us for (I suspect) the demons of darkness ceded him, along with her knowledge of edible

plants, by the crone who'd staunched his stump. Suppose
either one of them, I thought, my "servant" or my "soldier,"
were asked to reconstruct even this little hour of our history,
even as the three of us were enmeshed in it, here and now
(there and then). Suppose they were asked to recall what
we'd eaten, to guess at the order of our bedding down? Would
either of their accounts be accurate? Would two tales from
any of three of us be recognizably the same? How then could
I presume to retrieve the true tale of Belham, as my own story
was congruent with his neither in time nor in space?

For in those old commercial scripts I had to work with, one
could write: "I saw..." or "She was..." or "He did..."
But those useful and efficient marks gave us little or no way
to write: "I might have seen something somewhat like..." or
"Maybe somebody had been near someplace more or less
similar to..." or "It's conceivable that perhaps somebody
who was almost the same as..." But as far as Belham's life
was concerned, that was the only tale I had. In general, writing
is precise and speech is imprecise. But what the unknown
genius of the Ulvayns has given us is a tool to render
precisely speech's imprecision. To be a boy in Nevèrÿon
before that genius sent his system abroad to us, however, was
to have no such tool, and thus to experience precision and
imprecision as separated by some uncrossable chasm which
Belham could not bridge from his side nor I, I'd finally come
to admit, from mine. What came to mind, then, with that
firelit realization?

Do you remember my secret plan?

As I sat by the fireplace that night, contemplating all the
ways that time and the land had smeared my vision of order,
the articulation of my wish to move beyond everything about
me that confined me silently returned.

Contemplating what I took to be the wreckage of my quest,
I realized I could not make that wreck clear to my two
friends—which made them now seem less than friends, but
rather some overpowering responsibility I could no longer
carry. For while Terek had once called me a boy and a fool,
he'd nevertheless assumed from the beginning that I was at
least master of the information I'd sought, found, and sifted.
And each bit of contradictory confusion Arly had watched me
arrive at, he'd simply assumed was what I'd been looking
for all along.

Well, I'd found nothing save a bunch of buildings, roads,

and rocks, some of which were where they were supposed to be and some of which weren't.

And because I could not tell them I had found nothing, for fear I would lose the little authority I had, I only wished to be free of them.

As my thoughts came back from the hard peaks, the tangled forests, and the glaring deserts of my own ignorance, this was the fact I returned to. Yet, oddly enough, right here, at this place, on this evening, I felt as if I might also be face to face with something new, something in no way involved with Belham, something not called Nevèrÿon, something wondrous I might see or feel if only I was free, of them, of it. For here was also the possibility of leaving behind all the tangles of humanity and history Nevèrÿon herself seemed to have made hopelessly problematic in these last months:

Our country is not, you understand, mapped to a precise border the way some of our central counties have recently been marked out by Imperial surveyors. Still, we were at the southernmost edge of what is called Nevèrÿon.

I knew it:

We were at the southernmost edge of my map.

And that map *was* Nevèrÿon.

I had come as close to the points of Belham's birth and death as I was able. It was not that I had seen all, or so much, or even enough of the life between to abandon my quest. Rather I knew how that "life" was no longer there to be known, so that my quest was not so much over, or sufficiently completed, or even reasonably begun. Rather, it had been revealed as an impracticality and an impossibility at once.

On the map a rocky river, which we'd been following for a day between the last two villages, ran off the bottom. If I followed its watery murmur, soon and somewhere, I would be beyond Nevèrÿon.

The most logical way to go on was, of course, simply to wait till next morning. Then, once we were all up, I could take out my map and announce we would now travel even further south. But somehow I had begun to have suspicions that the authority did *not* really lie with me, but in the quest itself; and though, with the fiasco of Belham's 'birth,' *I* knew something terribly important in that quest had irreparably fallen to pieces, my companions didn't. I wanted to shake myself free of the whole thing the way, I fancied, any of my soldiers who had so long ago deserted me must have felt when they, for whatever reasons, suspected things were not going well with my long-lost caravan.

Suddenly I stood up, walked away from the fire—at the edge of the bushes I looked to see, sitting back by the provision cart's wide wheel, Terek glanced up at me with only the slightest questioning, then look again at the flame. Certainly he thought I was going off into the woods to relieve myself, or masturbate—as more than once I caught *him* off doing. Arly yawned at the fire and did not even look. I pushed into the darkening underbrush, stepping slowly, feeling beside and ahead of me. After ten steps it was black enough so that I might have been moving through the trees in a blindfold. Now a branch hit my face, my chest. Now I nearly walked into a tree. I felt my way around a rough trunk. Now my shin came up against a fallen log, and I climbed slowly over, reaching for the ground with my foot and wondering if I weren't about to go over some slope as steep as the cliff where Belham—or I—had fallen.

Thirty steps, forty steps, fifty steps on I came out into some bushy clearing.

There was no moon. But the wide and lucid night was salted with stars as thickly as I'd ever seen. The dusty river of the Milky Way slanted through those cold sparks. I looked down to see that I was at the edge of some field-wide clearing, scattered with brush and near the river. To my right, I could make out rocks and the foam breaking round them. The air was hugely still. The water whispered like wind.

Because the nameless gods of craft we nod to in Nevèrÿon are so much like ourselves, no one ever pictures them. It would be redundant. Still, not only servants, but barbarians and even the odd nobleman had, by now, mentioned to me some of the names of those other, older entities—and a few had even taken me out, on the odd evening, to explain how some of their ancestors had pictured this one or that one among those stellar points. That night, standing there, I had a sudden fancy that, so many stars were out, there were now, hanging above me, pictures of all the gods there'd ever been, as well as all the gods there ever would be, named and unnamed, alike and overlapping, all looking down at me, as I made my way across that little meadow, seeking to flee—my gait slow for the night—beyond our odd and undefinable border.

I tried to mark in the river's foam-shot black the current's thrust, to aid my direction when I'd once more entered the woods.

Another thirty steps, and tickling leaves and prodding twigs received me. I would keep the river's sound constant by me, I decided, as I moved, slow step by slow step. I wondered whether exhaustion or sunlight would find me first. I felt at once idiotically foolish and amazingly brave. My body seemed to glitter blackly in the midst of this transgression of a boundary all but inarticulable. But not for a second did I think of turning back.

Now I have told you of the monster I live with, today, here in Kolhari—my "reputation" as a teacher and a wise man. Well, at that time I had little sense of the reality of the process by which such monsters form, at least as one was to form about me. But in my search for Belham, I had already begun to learn something of the process in the abstract: for all men—famous, infamous, or most extraordinarily ordinary— have such monsters. Didn't Arly and I sometimes speak of Terek when he was off hunting? Didn't Terek and I sometimes joke over Arly's antics when he was not there? No doubt the two of them were talking of me now: making monsters! But as soon as any of us dies, there is *only* the monster left. What I had been pursuing was not Belham but the monster *called* Belham. And what my whole journey had taught me was precisely what *sort* of monster it was: it was made, as all such monsters are, of contradiction, supposition, miscalculation, impossibility, and ignorance. Well, for nearly a year—a long time for sustained effort from one of eighteen—like some fabled hero the mummers might mime on their wagon stage, I had not only pursued this "Belham" monster, but I had fought it and hacked at it, and cut it apart, and pulled it to pieces, and, finally, had tossed away its disparate limbs, till, on that very night, it was truly dispersed, vanquished, gone— all, that is, except the ineluctable force that had first held it together. All that was left was what ever had sought and sucked and gathered and contorted all the fragmentary "facts," was whatever had bound them into that monumentally resist- ant coherence I had begun my journey with, that coherence which, indeed, I had begun by seeking to confirm.

That force still traveled with me as I stepped into the darkness that night—a force which, now naked, was doubt- less even more powerful for what had been yanked apart from it, stripped free, and hurled away.

As I inched forward, moving among black trees, I heard it, I think, on my left—high up too—like the smallest change in the river's susurrus. A night bird, perhaps? But almost immediately, I heard it again, not so much as something that had *moved* closer, but as though another part or limb of it had moved, which *was* closer.

I halted.

Save the river's whisper, it was *very* still.

I started walking once more, hoping my own movement through the brush would be more frightening than attractive to whatever it was.

Three steps on, again I heard it—now near the ground.

Had it dropped from the branches?

Then, while I definitely *wasn't* moving, *it* moved. I swallowed and pulled back, hitting my shoulder against a trunk. Part of it was high, and part of it was on the ground. Whatever it was was simply *very* large.

At first I didn't hear it, but above me a handful of stars between two branches went out as something moved in front of them. Then, slowly, it bent down in the dark and . . . touched me!

Reaching for me, it brushed against my arm, wet and crumbling as some rain-soaked mountain slope. At the same time some change in the night breeze came about, so that I *smelled* something rotten as a week-old cat carcass, its immense body no doubt starred with the same white, wriggling grubs.

Whatever it was was immense, moving, and dead as Belham himself!

I didn't scream, but I gasped in a fetid stench, pulled away, and ran. With ten steps my foot caught something, and I fell, rolling in leaves—and heard *its* foot fall on the earth behind me, loud and large as my whole body. Pushing to my knees, I hurled myself on in the dark, while it breathed, hoarsely, wetly, above me.

I ran, stumbling, scraping myself, hitting myself, hurting my ankle on a rock, my hand on a tree; somehow I tore into that starlit meadow. But five running steps among the ghostly brush, I heard a thundering behind me loud as a tree crashing down through leaves and branches. Then, over the length of an indrawn breath, the starlight on the brushes and ground wiped away, as something huge and cold moved above me and under the night—as I crashed into the trees.

I tripped. I fell on some small slope that would never have felled me in daylight. I practically crawled over some large log. Then, again, I ran. My eyes, blinking and tearing open, filled with firelight as I crashed through more leaves—

Terek looked up from the flame, frowned at me—then scrambled to his feet in a crouch, snatching his spear up over his shoulder with one hand, pulling loose his sword with the other. Arly looked around, then levered up on his crutch in a motion, beginning to take small, hopping steps back.

I looked over my shoulder at the branches quivering in firelight. A breeze had come from somewhere. The forest shook, and the campfire burned high within it. Turning around before the fireplace, I backed away from the trees.

My own shadow grew huge on the shaking leaves.

Still crouching, Terek asked: "Is it bandits . . . ?"

Arly whispered: "Some animal . . . ?"

Terek stepped forward now, hefting his spear threateningly. Without looking at me, he said: "Is it slavers out there . . . ?"

I could only gasp for breath and shake my head. But as they glanced over at my scraped and dirty face, my bleeding hands and legs, they too began to realize it was no natural thing I'd come on in the leaf-canopied and star-pricked night. For I had met some monster god who roamed our borders, preventing such defections as I had foolishly hoped for. Nameless? Certainly not. But I suspect from what I've learned in my travels since that I was fortunate not to have previously encountered some local witch or shaman who might have told me the entity's name. For had I called it to me by its proper appellation as it stalked the forest night, hearing me it simply would have devoured me in its immense, rotten mouth.

I wouldn't let Terek put out the fire that night—not that he really wanted to after I blurted my first protest. Soon we were all sitting practically with our buttocks against the hot stones and our shoulders by one another's. Now and again one or the other of us would get up for a new piece of wood, till the wood within sight was pretty much gone. Once Terek proposed arranging an organized watch, but somehow we never got to it. (There would have been no point against that deity.) Later, I suddenly came awake when one or the other of them fell, asleep at last, against me, and I blinked, surprised, with stifled breath and only the coals' glow behind me for light. Then, morning sun was flaking among the branches, falling on my scratched knees, as first Terek, then I, and at last Arly pushed to our feet, stiff, chill, and all of us feeling as though we'd had no sleep at all.

The cart cover was undisturbed over the provisions wagon. Save for a few more fallen leaves, our camp was as it had been before darkness fell.

We had been spared.

And so, as I had done many mornings before, I reached over the cart's side, slipped my hand, despite its scratches, down between the wood and the money sack, till I could finger up the scroll of goatskin. I unrolled it—the edges were truly frayed now—to examine the confusion of lines and marks and corrections.

A lapwing called shrilly through the morning twitter and warble, over the nearby river's hiss and whisper.

"I guess," I said, as Arly turned on his crutch to listen and Terek paused in wiping his sword blade free of speckling dew, "we've seen just about everything we can of Belham. I've visited the place he died. We've been to the place he was born. And I've looked at just about every spot he worked at in between. I have more than enough information for anything I might want to do with it. And I've been traveling a long time now. What's proper at this point would be to return to Kolhari."

So we swung the cart to the north, riding or walking through the morning, till, by mutual consent, we stopped beneath a protective overhang hard by a cliff wall, took out blankets, and slept a few hours to make up for what sleep we'd missed.

After that we fed the mules and ate.

Then we walked on beside the wagon several hours through the rest of the day till, toward sundown, we made camp for the night.

Monsters are real.

9.821 What are the SF (or fantasy) models for this enterprise— which is, after all, not SF but sword-and-sorcery? Sturgeon's *Venus Plus X*, Russ's *Female Man*, Malzberg's *Galaxies*, Disch's "334," Ellison's "Deathbird" . . .

In what sense are their problems the same as mine?

More important, in what specific ways are they different?

And how much, right at this moment, do I believe in the monstrous specificity of my own solutions . . . ?

9.83 The Bridge of Lost Desire is not my favorite city passage, *the Master explained*. Its libidinous atmosphere does not make me comfortable. Several libidinous friends have suggested that what disturbs me about it is its too-great sense of life, its suggestion of control always a breath away from animal abandon.

That's nonsense.

I feel life when man and woman, together or apart, labor and ponder to nurture, console, or entertain a child, a friend, or some aged body. But there's no particular vital excess where a vicious, bored, fifteen-year-old and undernourished barbarian sells herself for a quarter of an hour to some forty-year-old warehouse loader with enough beer in his belly so that he will remember neither her face nor her name when he ambles by on his next day off—the girl having rushed away moments after their over-quick exchange to swab between her legs with volatile, noxious liquids, while fear of conception nags nevertheless over the twenty-eight days between moons.

Still, at Carnival time that feeling of distress, so intense on the bridge (life? Isn't it, rather, high frustration? It's certainly not rampant satisfaction that gives the place its air), is dispersed throughout the several celebrant neighborhoods. At the same time, the bridge becomes more populous with people who never go there normally, so that the air of life, frustration, or whatever (why not call it lust?) is somewhat mitigated, and its crowded flags seem like any other city thoroughfare, for all the high spirits passing across it.

I passed across.

Flares burned along both sides. Now and again, I overheard in this conversation or that: the Liberator and his entourage had ridden over only a bit before I came by.

As I made my way between raucous revelers still thronging the Old Market of the Spur, I thought about that boyhood trip, and I wondered, as I had, many times since (and many times upon the trip itself): suppose, in the same way as I had sought Belham, someone else came along, seeking me—oh, not the whole of my life, certainly, pieced out some impossible hundred years hence. But suppose somebody, today, hearing of my journey with all the inaccuracies entailed—the interview with my parents, and such—decided to reconstruct only that year's wandering, setting out to find only what that journey had meant for me. What traces of it would be left?

Suppose they did not ask me, but—however honestly—only researched the monster?

Suppose they asked my uncle?

He could tell approximately when I left and when I returned—though several times of late I note he's mistaken the year.

What would some of my relatives say at whose great houses we stopped? What of my visit would they remember?

What would some of the peasants who aided us recall of my passing?

What of my big, bald steward?

What of my little redheaded one?

What tale would the soldiers who deserted me tell?

What about Arly and Terek?

What of the princess or the peasant widow?

Ten years ago I got a partial chance to find out.

The school, you see, had finished its first year successfully. At the beginning of the second, I declared a six-week spring recess so that the students could return home awhile. And I took the same time to visit a friend in a town a day's cart-ride west of Kolhari, which had recently made much economic progress; as well, it had begun to support its own barbarian community as some of those southern-born workers grew disgruntled with the big port city and moved on.

I had been at my friend's house three days and, on the first truly hot afternoon of the year, had tried to take a nap as the rest of the family did; but a restlessness came over me, and so I went out to walk in the warm streets and explore a little.

Ambling along a sun-filled alley, I suddenly saw a powerfully built barbarian with one leg, helping himself along with a single crutch.

Such severe and singular infirmities are rare in Nevèrÿon; I thought of Arly immediately. I stopped, but he didn't seem to notice me and went into a daubed building through a crooked door-frame with no hanging. On impulse I hurried after him, stepping into a shadowed storeroom. From chinks and out-right holes in the roof a dozen beams of sunlight lanced through floating dust.

"Excuse me," I said, "but you're not . . . ?"

In one of these beams, the man on the crutch turned, frowning. (Wasn't he both too short and too thick to be my old barbarian friend?) What I first saw were all the differences in that barbaric face from Arly's: the broader cheeks, the slacker lips, the receding hair at the forehead—while the hair

on the chest was far heavier than I remembered, with half of
it grizzled white. Then, suddenly, the frown became a grin.
And the face simply ... *transformed* into Arly's! "You ... !"
he said. "You? No! What are you doing here? Is it my young
nobleman? No ... ! But why have you come? After all these
years! What has happened with you? Why in the world do
you come to see me like this? Here? Now? No! But it's *really*
you!" Arly came forward, grinning, to clap a broad hand to
my shoulder while, with a grin as large, I shook him happily
by both of his, so that he swayed on his bark bound stick; and
I thought, after all, if I'd changed as little as he, the more
than twice-seven years since we'd seen each other had indeed
been generous to us both.

Arly now worked swabbing resin over the insides of barrels,
he told me. His hands were foul with the stuff all the way to
his elbows, and his bare foot was stained with it to the knee.
Oh, he'd been in this town for *years*, he explained. He'd just
stopped off in the storage building here to pick up a sack of
something he had to take to someone else. But come along
with him. Yes, come along! I must visit his home and sit with
him—if I would so honor him—and we would drink and talk
of the old days. That is, if I could spare the time for an old
friend ... ? If I could pass an hour with a cripple such as
he ... ? If I could see my way to talk with a poor, one-legged
barbarian ... ?

He got his sack, hoisted it around over his shoulder—the
bag still twice as heavy, I'm sure, as any I could carry—and I
followed him out into the street. He bent a little more and
went a little slower than I remember, under such burdens.
But three streets away he left his load with an old, taciturn
oil-seller, and we started off through the town in a direction
I'd never been, till we were among some thatched shacks that
brought back to me nothing so much as that clutch of
mountain hovels where Belham (may have) died.

These, at least, were sunlit and dry.

Before one a woman with dark, sweaty hair worked at a
stone washtub, with two near-grown girls helping her and
three or four youngsters crawling naked in the spilled water
that made mud about the trough.

Arly went up to her, calling out: "Hey, you must see who
I've brought!" As he put his arm around her shoulder, the
woman looked up, surprised and shy—she had a harelip,
wouldn't you know. Hopping on his crutch, Arly herded her

toward me while the big children blinked and the little ones
ignored all, and the woman looked down at her dripping arms
and shriveled hands. I smiled, spoke to her, thinking she must
be Arly's woman. Certainly some of the children looked as
though they might have been his. But *she* knew who I was,
Arly prompted. She knew all about me! Hadn't Arly told her
the story of our travels together, years ago? Didn't she
remember? Of *course* she did! *I* was the nobleman who had
given him the money to come here! He'd *told* her that. Yes,
of *course* she knew of me.

Whether she did or not, I don't know. But *I* was struck with
a memory absent for years. When we'd reached Kolhari, I'd
paid Arly a servant's wages for the three or four months he'd
traveled with me—no great amount, but more than the young
barbarian had ever held at one time before. Three days later,
he'd disappeared from the servants' quarters of my uncle's
home. For a few weeks, I recall, I'd wondered if he had come
to harm in the city, for he'd never turned up again. Could he
have caught some market wagon directly here and settled
down, to live all those intervening years?

But now he released her to lead me on further among the
huts. His woman? No, she was only a good friend. A fine
figure in the neighborhood. She'd helped him many times—as
she'd helped many others here; he'd wanted her to meet his
noble visitor. For, he explained, she was as good and fine a
person of her class as I was of mine.

Several huts away, he pointed out his. It was smaller and in
worse repair than most of those around it, and on the very
edge of the enclave, with scattered branches and bits of refuse
lying about: a split-log bench with two legs broken off so no
one could sit on it, the wheel from some sort of wagon, its
rim split.

We didn't even go inside.

I was thankful, for the whole neighborhood had that smell
I've always assumed comes from continually cooking in pots
never thoroughly washed. What that would become within the
shack I didn't want to imagine.

Arly sat me on a firm, overturned basket near his door,
ducked within the ragged hanging, then came out, the handles
of two unglazed clay cups hooked on the stained fingers of
one hand and a jar in the crook of his arm. He lowered
himself by his crutch to a rock to sit before me, then let the
crutch fall to the worn grass. Leaning forward he poured out

a liquid clear as water. Then he sat back, the jar held up at his right shoulder in both hands, waiting for me to taste mine before he poured his own—the way, indeed, I'd instructed him to pour at table so many years before!

As we grinned at each other, I picked the cup up from the ground and sipped: it was not water. It was sharp and went along the throat with all the aspects of fire save heat. At the same time, there was a strong feeling that, had it gone at only a slightly different angle, it would have slid in as coolly as a mountain ice chip. What he'd served me, I realized, was one of the strong Avila rums.

I said once that Arly had the unearned reputation of a drunkard in the tiny barbarian village where we found him. Well, I began to realize, over the years he'd hobbled a few steps along toward earning it.

There are many who claim the drink is poisonous.

But I will say, after he had poured his own, and I had taken several sips more, it lent a warmth of spirit to the already hot day. And I was not about to judge my old traveling companion in what was after all only his hospitality toward me.

As we talked of this and that, his life, mine, then, now, and the time between, I asked him: "Tell me, Arly, what did you think of that whole trip? What's the part you remember best?"

He look at me slyly. "*You* know which part I remember." He jabbed a stained finger at me with a complicitous grin.

"I know which parts *I* remember," I told him. "But you must tell me for yourself."

"That time," he prompted me, "you know. In the castle. Of one of your cousins."

I smiled, nodding, thinking he meant his first visit to a royal house with me, when he'd gotten lost and I'd had to go searching for him. Indeed, I'd told that story with numerous embellishments, many times since. But Arly went on:

"You know. The one where your noble cousin had killed himself."

I frowned, suddenly lost.

"You remember," Arly said. "We took the wagon through all those broad, endless orchards of fruit trees. And finally, when we came up to the stone gate, the woman you told me later was a slave, though she wore her iron collar under a jeweled neck-piece, said to us that the baron was dead—they had found him only that morning in the gardens, where he had eaten many, many of the small, poisonous petals of the white ini flower...?''

I must have still frowned, though a memory was beginning to flicker; because Arly frowned a moment at me, before he went on:

"When we went inside, the whole castle was in confusion. They could only give us a single room to stay in for the night—"

"Of course!" I exclaimed. "The Baron Inige!" I *didn't* remember the orchards. But now I began to picture a servant (slave?) standing at a half-opened gateway between two high, stone newels, telling me that we could not be received within because there had been a great tragedy in the house. The baron was dead, and by his own hand. "But we *didn't* go in," I protested. "Did we?" The whole incident would never have come up in any spontaneous account from me. As it was, I could only recall that moment at the entrance. "Certainly we went on somewhere else, Arly. We wouldn't have gone inside after that."

"Oh, yes!" Arly nodded. "We did! I was very frightened, and I didn't want to. That soldier with us—what was his name?"

"Terek."

"Yes, that soldier stood by me, while we waited behind the wagon. He *knew* I was frightened, too. He nudged me with his arm. I was *so* frightened—and *he* thought it was funny! You were at the gate, talking with the slave. Oh, so gently and persuasively, with such smiles, you went on—you told her just how you and the dead man were related, and how terrible it must be for all in the castle, and that perhaps we could be of some help, and that you understood how upset everyone must be, and, no, you wouldn't *think* of intruding, but we had traveled *so* far, your guard and your servant were *so* tired, and we would not be any trouble, so that perhaps if they could find rooms for us simply for a night and—"

"Arly—" I laughed—"I have *no* memory of any of this!"

"—finally they let us in," he finished. "We brought the wagon right inside, through the gates of the dead man's house. *You* knew I was scared too!" he added, accusingly. "You looked at me when the mules went by the big stone posts and grinned!" Then, smiling down into his cup, he shifted on his rock. His scarred stump moved in a kind of sweeping motion that would have placed the missing limb at no particular position, save possibly kicking into the air. And I thought, how many hundreds of times have I seen it do that? Yet, I'd never thought of it once in all these years. "They told us to take a single little room on the castle's top floor, up some old, steep, stone stairs. And you got very angry afterwards, because it meant all three of us would have to sleep in the same chamber, and you said you didn't want to have to sleep in the same room with a smelly barbarian and a dirty soldier—"

I started to protest. "Surely I'd only meant it wouldn't look proper to the great house's remaining servants..." My picture of myself for that period was (and still is) wholly egalitarian—more, perhaps, than was even wise. But the truth is, once within the baron's gates, *I* had no memory at all. Till that moment, had you asked me if I'd ever been inside the home of my tragic relative, the Baron Inige, I'd have answered, "No," convinced I spoke the truth.

I said: "Terek *could* let himself get rather dirty, couldn't he?"

"I wanted to stay in the room, because I was scared to walk around in the halls and corridors where the dead man had walked. But when it got dark, you and the soldier— Terek? Was that his name?—decided to play a trick on me and took me up on the castle's roof. I didn't want to go. But you *made* me!"

"Now *how* did we get you to go anywhere that you didn't want to?" For I had a few solid memories of Arly's stubbornness—an all too fabled barbarian trait.

"*You* went," Arly said. "*I* wasn't going to stay in there alone!" He drank more rum. "There wasn't any wall around the roof, either. And there were lots of stone things—like stone huts and places where windows stuck up and things. Part of the roof was sloped, too, right down to the edge." Certainly I knew the kind of castle roof he meant. But equally certainly I had no memory of ever being out on one with Arly. "It had been raining, and the roof slates were still wet. And you know this—" he bent to slap his hand against the flattened and frayed end of his crutch—"doesn't hold so well on wet stone as this—" and he swung his soiled hand back against the cracked and blackened sole of his foot. "The clouds were blowing fast, now over the moon, now free of it. One minute it was dark as pitch. The next it was light. The two of you ran away and hid from me, and began to make strange noises, and pretend to be demons and monsters and strange beasts, and chase me around and hide from me again.''

"But you must have known it was only us...?''

"*Ahhh*!'' Arly's voice rose, with his chin, in dismissal of my protest. "I knew it was you. But in such a house, perhaps the demons that haunted the place actually now possessed *you*. That's why you played such pranks. That's why I was so afraid. In such a house, with such a death only that morning, it was a reasonable fear—at least from the way you carried on! Once, when I was running from you, the soldier stuck the end of his spear out from behind some stone abutment and tripped me, so that I fell.''

"Arly—!'' Though even as I spoke, memories returned of moments when Terek's teasing (if not my own) of the one-legged youth had probably gone too far. What came back even more strongly, however, were those chases and games of tag where all of us contended that Arly on his crutch was a fast and agile as either of us—which was, indeed, *almost* true. Some of those chases were at night, even in the moonlight—but surely not on the roof of my dead cousin's house. "Arly, I just don't think we—''

"Then you ran right out into me.'' He put his cup down and clapped his blackened hands together. "And knocked me over. Then you laughed, while I rolled down the slope toward the edge of the roof. Oh, I *knew*, then, that monsters chased me, and that I would now fall to my death!''

I swallowed another mouthful of rum. "But didn't we catch you...?''

"*No!*'' Arly declared, an astonished questioning to it even greater than the exclamation, as if there was no reason in the world to think we might have. He said: "I just didn't roll that far. I hurt my leg real bad, too, when you pushed me down.'' He reached forward to rub his calf, as if memory brought back the pain. "Then the soldier came out and stood there and laughed at me because I was such a frightened fool. But I was afraid to say how much it hurt, because I thought you might start in again and say you would leave me behind to be a slave in that haunted and frightening castle.''

"But—'' As I started to protest again, the faintest memory returned, however: Terek standing with his spear, in light dim enough to have come from a beclouded moon, laughing over a seated, unhappy Arly, who had just slipped or fallen across his crutch, while I looked on. Could that have been atop the castle roof? Could my purposeful push have been the cause of the fall? The memory was no clearer than that of the servant woman at the gate. And even had I recalled the two faint recollections on my own, I never would have remembered that they were from the morning and evening of the same day, or what Arly claimed lay between.

Arly sat, rubbed, smiled. "We had some good times, then, didn't we? I went a lot of places with you, saw a lot of things."

"Yes," I said. I was still trying to think: *Could* I have been a partner in torment of a lame, ignorant youth—and forgotten it? "We did." But the topic itself seemed too complicated to pursue through the warmth of the day and the glow of the rum. "Well, tell me: did you ever learn any more of Belham or Venn, after our trip? I've often wondered how all that struck you."

Arly looked at me and frowned. "Belham?" he said. "And that other name? Were they some peasants we let ride in the wagon once?"

"*No,* Arly!" I was both astonished and amused—happily so, as it drove away some of my discomfort. "*Don't* you remember—?"

But he had reached out for the jar to pour himself another cupful. "Belham, that's a barbarian name. But not the other. 'Venn,' it was? It sounds like a name from far away. Maybe from the islands or someplace . . ."

Somewhere a crutch tapped on the rock floor; barbaric eyes lifted toward the cave ceiling . . .

We talked about many other things that day. Oh, I mustn't suggest that we had *no* memories in common. We talked a lot of Terek, and even though Arly had not remembered his name, we were still soon mustering new opinions about him, as if our friend were only off for a walk in the woods and was expected back in minutes—though neither of us had seen him in more than a decade.

I supposed we helped to elaborate *his* monster.

Although with each cup of rum he drank, Arly would again declare how fine a time we'd had together, in general his memories were not as pleasant as mine. But then, neither had his life been as pleasant, before or since. Also, I thought later, he had the recollections one might expect from a man who, with great bravery, had traveled only once—and that in order to get from the village where he'd been born to the town where, in all probability, he would die. Through the afternoon, somehow I never brought up my own (nor questioned Arly's) reminiscences of the border god who'd terrified us the night I'd tried my futile flight. It just did not seem the proper time to speak much more of monsters.

Yes, I met Terek once, too—a little over a year after my afternoon with Arly. It was high summer in Kolhari; a day off from the school, and I'd gone to visit a merchant friend, a man of some travel himself. I was to meet him not at his home but at one of the caravan yards among the store buildings adjoining the New Market. Indeed, I'd known he'd been awaiting the arrival of a large commercial caravan for some weeks now: it had been gone seven months and was expected any day.

The half-dozen closed carriages and several high-piled wagons must just have pulled into the yard minutes before I strolled up. The drivers and grooms were joking with one another around the horses. The loaders had not been given their instructions yet and lounged by the warehouse wall. And the caravan soldiers sat about the yard in little clusters, playing bones, or stood leaning on their spears and watching.

My first thought was that my merchant friend would probably not be able to go to lunch with me now as we had planned. I did not see him in the yard. No doubt he was within, conferring with Her Majesty's inspectors. But as I made my way toward the lashed-back hanging over the wide door, I saw a soldier standing by the wall, leaning on his spear before him, rubbing his chin on his forearm.

I frowned.

Could it possibly . . . ?

I walked toward him. Tall, dark, lanky, yes, the man had a once-broken nose. As I neared, he let go his spear with one hand to reach up and rub his cheek. The same gnawed pits of broken and scabby horn were sunk on his fingertips, well back from the crowns. I glanced below his leather kilt, for the scar on his leg.

It was there.

"Terek . . . ?" I said.

He didn't turn.

"Terek . . . !" I stepped before him.

His eyes blinked in a gaunt, weathered face that, save the

nose, I must say did not seem overly familiar, now that I was closer.

"Your name's Terek, isn't it?"

The soldier gave the smallest nod—and waited. Clearly, he did not recognize me.

I smiled. "Do you remember me? You were a guard on a caravan of mine, oh—more than ten years ago now!"

Among his sullen features, a smile only threatened his mouth and eyes—but not of recognition; it was the one you give a stranger who's made some well-intentioned mistake. For all his identifying marks, he looked less and less familiar, so that, again, I asked: "Your name *is* Terek . . . ?"

"Yes . . . ?" He waited for some explanation.

"Well, you were a guard. On a caravan of mine. It was a rough one too. It wasn't as big as this. But we lost both our carriages. We traveled most of the last months with just a wagon, and only the three of us—you, me, and a barbarian called Arly. He had only one—"

"You mean—" shifting position, he said suddenly—"when we went through the Menyat? Where the stores ran out and half the guards mutinied? I had to stick my blade in the gut of three of my best friends on that one! Then we were stuck down in the canyon, and all there were was berries and cactus pith, for four months, caught down in those rocks!" (The sudden outburst in the sullen demeanor *was* Terek—the Terek I remembered. It made me smile—and perhaps he thought, from that, I recognized his account.) "We didn't dare come up, because of the bandits . . ."

While I smiled, at first I wondered if this were simply another incident he recalled that I'd forgotten. But no; neither my carriages nor my cart had gone as far west as the Menyat Canyon. "How long ago was that?" I asked.

(What my own memories brought back as I had struggled a moment with his was a young, broken-nosed man on a leafy road thrusting his blade through the neck of a shrieking brigand.)

"Four years." Terek considered. "Maybe five years back. I was out almost two whole years on that one."

"No," I said. "What I was talking about was over ten years ago. And I don't think it was *that* rough."

He reached up to rub his neck again. "More than ten years," he said. "That's a long time ago. Were you the steward?" He sounded doubtful.

"No." Still smiling, I shook my head. "We knew each other. You told me all about how you got that scar. The young officer in the army—" I pointed to his leg. (He glanced down then looked up with a raised eyebrow like someone who'd forgotten a scar was there.) "We were friends, you and I. I was practically a boy. You stayed on when the others left me. In the end, it was just three of us and a wagon: you, me, and a crippled barbarian—he lives off to the west of the city, now. I saw him just last year. It was . . . my caravan." I really felt odd saying that, for I truly treasured the memory of what I'd still thought was a three-way friendship among equals, even with Arly's additions. "You don't remember?"

He gave a shrug I want to think was so small because he might have been embarrassed. "Maybe," he said. He pursed his lips a moment. "I don't think so."

"Well, ten years . . ." I shrugged too. "That *is* a long time. But it was you."

"Maybe," he repeated.

I watched him, remembering the strange transformations of recognition in those moments meeting Arly. This lack of recognition was, in its way, almost as interesting. Terek had not grown particularly bald or fat, nor had he gone through any other great bodily change. Where before he'd been a young soldier, now he was a middle-aged one. He'd guarded caravans before mine; clearly he'd guarded them since. The trip with me had simply not been that memorable. I thought of trying to identify it further for him—tripping Arly on the castle roof? The terror at the border? Perhaps with a drink or two he might have been prompted to recall . . .

But many men simply do not set much store in memory. They are just not interested in what happened more than three months back, and then they only retain the incidents about those who are currently their friends.

I put my hand on his shoulder. "Well, it's good to see you again, Terek. Good luck."

He looked at my hand (rather as though it didn't belong there), looked back at me with narrowed eyes, still wondering, perhaps, if he *had* known me.

I nodded to him, dropped my hand, and left to go look for my merchant friend. Indeed, I had to go in and out of the warehouse several times to find him. Each time, I glanced at the soldier standing by the wall.

He looked at me only once—and I had the sudden notion

that he did not even remember our conversation from minutes before, or, at any rate, was by now quite convinced that I had been mistaken.

I found my merchant friend. Yes, he could slip off for a quick bite at a tavern close by. I remember all through our meal I was on the verge of telling him about my encounter with his caravan guard. And didn't. But now that I think of it, I never mentioned my encounter with Arly to my hosts in that town I was visiting, back the year before, either.

I crossed the Old Market square that carnival night remembering memories of Arly and Terek—my memories, theirs . . . From that play of the recalled and the forgotten (my forgetfulness, theirs), with whatever distortions lie between, monsters are formed, whether they be gods or great men, or even very ordinary boys, sick unto death with a plague that has much of the monstrous about it.

Yes, I learned about monsters on that trip. And I learned about them in these encounters afterward:

First, monsters are real.

Second, they are us.

I turned down one street where only a few people held up torches.

I cut across a yard to skirt a cistern wall as the half-moon edged its light above a roof.

A few more turnings down a few more streets: I crossed some filled with revelers and some near empty. I went with shoulders hunched through a narrow alley, an arch at its end, and breathed deeply along another street, with only the usual rare night-strollers.

Through the shutters of the old inn, I saw the flicker of lamps. I waited a minute across from the door, to see if anyone entered. Certainly I'd found the proper building. I could have been late or early, of course. Waiting seems to be a part of such disreputable activity. From down the street came voices; red torches moved out from the corner. Someone in the group was playing a reedy flute. So I crossed, pushed back the creaking leather, and slipped inside.

Once within the low-ceilinged tavern, I knew I'd found the place. The way people stood or sat was just not the way people ordinarily stood or sat in a tavern at Carnival time. For one thing, no one spoke. There was an air of waiting. In the light of the lamps hanging by chains from the ceiling beams, I recognized a dark-haired woman at a table with a big barbarian—

both looked up at me. It was the woman who handled the school laundry and the shoemaker she lived with, who sometimes used to drive her laundry cart.

I nodded.

They did the same, looking quickly away.

And I felt as much as they that further talk would be out of place, right here, right now.

I wondered should I go purchase a drink, or simply take a seat, as some had done, or—as had some others—go stand by the wall and wait. As I walked among the benches and tables I heard the hide creak again behind me. I glanced back as an old woman with a brown hood pulled forward about a deeply seamed face stepped tentatively in, peered about, obviously nervous and feeling out of place.

Outside, boisterous revelers passed, singing and laughing.

Through a door near the side of the counter, a yellow-haired man with some limp flowers in his hair, a gold collar, and a blue robe suddenly stepped forward, surveyed the room, clapped his hands before his chest and announced: "Well, there're enough of us to start. You're all concerned about the plague, I know. No one is more concerned about it than we are, here, believe me. We're so happy you could come. We'll take contributions only on your way out. I'm your Wizard for the—" Someone coughed, and he turned with a raised eyebrow. "You're here, of course, for the Calling . . . ?"

Someone said: ". . . of the Amnewor."

Some looked at one another as though that had been a dangerous name to speak.

Nobody answered with an audible 'Yes.' But a few nodded. A few others pushed back from their tables, ready to rise.

"Very good. Very good," the man said. "If you'll all just follow me, right through this way. There're steps down. It's narrow and rather steep. So please don't crowd. Just go carefully."

People began to follow him through the door.

Somehow, in a motion that suggested she was afraid she might be left behind, the hooded old woman slipped ahead of me. She glanced back at me. I smiled. She looked embarrassed and turned away. We followed the crowd.

Over the heads of those before me, I could see that the walls beyond the doorway were rough rock. From somewhere below, I heard an ethereal music. The voice of the Amnewor,

I said to myself, and wondered, indeed, what monster the night would bring.

As I went through the low doorway, ahead I saw the yellow hair of the big shoemaker. He paused, looked down, then, from the way his head lowered, he must have begun to descend the steps.

I moved forward, with the others.

9.84 People who did not attend the Calling of the Amnewor: Arly, Gorgik, Joey, Larla, Meise, the old mummer, Norema, Pheron, Radiant Jade, Samuel Delany (Chip), Terek, Toplin, Toplin's mother, Toplin's lover, and, in general, many, many more, of course, than who did.

9.85 "Failure signs our beginning," the Wizard began in the dark, "for where else can we start, save from weakness, fear, and a crushing incapacity before a purity so rich it sometimes seduces us into thinking our own consciousness is at one with it? Failure will sign our end. Our first step into the darkness here is a realization of that failure—if only the failure to remember what must be remembered if civilization is to persist, our failure to forget what must be forgotten if, personally, we are to endure in it. Harps and cymbals tinkle with rising anticipation. Bring the first brand.

"There!

"Gasp, if you will. But seated on the throne, ribs thrust through the chest's tattered leather, long teeth loose in that nude jaw, it leans, lopsided in firelight, a trace of the life now negated in its brown bones and dried gristle, imbued not with life but with meaning by what passes in positive glory over our heads: the Liberator who is subsumed on this day of Carnival by the true seat of power—which is not here.

"Look!

"Was it righter in life than the master it fell before? Not likely, in the larger scheme. But it lived once; and, dead, it lingers beneath our unholy torches.

"How can we start from any place else before this monstrous and murderous dying, dying, dying which plagues us?

"Amnewor!

"Amnewor!

"Amnewor!

"Drums and reeds echo us. But the Calling is not one we make *to* the monster, through the medium of this desiccated corpse. The Calling of the Amnewor is, rather, the call that the barely believable monster herself will make to this symbol of our mortality that we have enthroned for the night—a Calling that animates it, however marginally.

"Do not look behind!

"Her several eyes, from the size of a minnow's to the size of the full moon low on the horizon and clustered only in odd numbers, open, now here, now there, at your back, across her vast flesh slimed with oceanic slough and filth. The heat of her warms your nape, the joints of your knees. Above you, her many mouths erupt in the loose, liquescent skin, some so small you could not push one finger into their tiny, sucking slits, some so huge and slobbering that the tongue within is sliced to bloody strips by broken teeth (more than a hundred, ragged in the several rows of gum, and each as large as your hand), while others are all soft cheek and uvula and lip— spitting, hissing, sucking—some supported by internal bone, however distorted from traditional jaw and beak, others dangling in immense and flaccid flaps, fluttering and flatulent with the fetid airs, rumbling out here, gushing in there.

"Listen!

"Above the tambourine and sistrum, you can hear her, huge as a merchant's three-story house on fire, *breathing* behind you...Do not look, I say! Do not! High in the suppurating and pulsing meat of her brow, a single jewel, blood red, with ninety-seven flat and glimmering surfaces across it and the size of a baby's head, is sunk in a circlet of iron and gold, bolted to the bone beneath. Once you see it, you cannot look away. (I know! I watch it now!) What does an Amnewor eat?

"Human eyes!

"Human tongues!

"And the hot jelly of human brains! She sucks them through the ear, after piercing the drum and small bones within, using her knobby fingers, all narrow as sapling twigs, from which thin claws grow, six and seven inches. Oh, once you look, once you are hypnotized by the red jewel, she will hold you rigid in her muscular tentacles, while, with her tiny hands, she tears you to pieces...

"Why else have we chosen a decayed corpse for a champion? (Little bells tinkle. The flute flutters eerily.) Eyeless, tongueless, earless, it alone can face the Amnewor from vanquishing distance. It alone can answer her call.

"Do you hear it, now? The music has momentarily halted.
Look at the throne!

"Bring another brand!

"And another!

"There, did you see?

"The dead hand moved!

"It slid an inch on the stone beside the skewed boat of
bone. Now, yes, the slack jaw pulls shut, rattling its remaining
teeth, and the knee swings wide as the foot slips dry tarsal
and metatarsal over the hide on the top step.

"See how weakly it tries to stand! What strength it takes to
vanquish the little bit of death that, so long ago, killed it!
Blind, deaf, dumb, yet it hears the call. We must give it a
guide.

"There, rush to it, little girl!

"She takes up her cat-skull staff to run and stand before the
steps. Someone has drawn a mask across her face, though it's
only makeup, and her clear eyes blink above her full, healthy
cheeks. That health, that innocence (that mask) will protect
her from the gaze of the Amnewor waiting in the shadow
behind you, looking over your heads, as terrible as the gods
who, were they there in your place, might be mistaken for
you yourselves.

"Someone has tied a bit of black and orange cloth in a
cunning cape around the girl's shoulders.

"Beneath it the two ends of a leather thong hang on her
chest, their raddled tips telling of some fetish snatched violently
free. What doom or victory might it have guided her to? It's
gone. We'll never know. She has become merely the guide of
our victory, who—stiffly, unsteadily—manages to rise, now,
from the throne.

"Gongs echo through the crypt.

"It stands on the top stair, as the fat little girl, holding her
staff high, steps back.

"The skeletal foot falls to the step below, and the whole
frame shakes and shivers, dropping dried skin and cartilage
crumbs; a rib falls loose, to click on the stone, rocking. One
toe bone is left on the step above. One finger remains behind
on the seat. Will our champion crumble entirely before true
confrontation?

"But the immense, glimmering monster behind you has
already begun to quiver, heave, and show signs that, certainly,
were you to see them, you'd take for anger and fear, as the

mortal remains of our prince skitter and clatter to the step's bottom. For haven't we all suspected, all along, that human beings are sometimes more godlike than the gods; certainly their deaths are more absolute than the death of any god, named or unnamed, we've ever storied. And as certainly, decay, which is what the Amnewor after all is, cannot feed on the already and absolutely dead. Is that small distinction between the dying and the dead where hope for victory lies?

"The Amnewor is, you know, a god of edges, borders, and boundaries. You may even have encountered her, reeking and putrid on some overhung night, as you tried to get from here to there, all at once too intensely aware of what the separation between them meant. But we have called her, to serve us now—though by this displacement to the center she has not so much changed her nature; for no matter how Nevèrÿon expands, even as it reaches out to encompass death and the stars, she'll still prowl and linger along its rim.

" 'She?' I already hear some of you repeat it, with a note of ironic censure, a moment before turning from me in a positive distinction that will lose you all hope with the return of what we call the real. Stay! Again I say: do not avert your eyes, for many of us know of, and some of us here have even visited, a land that is not Nevèrÿon, but where a similar ritual must be held with a male monster, the corpse of a princess, and a little boy for guide. Though the names might be different, the same, or absent, can't we recognize one monster here, common to us all, prowling the border between one and another, or even between us and a land more different still from ours? I assure you, these are as real as the monster that guards what is, after all, the other's boundary as much as it is ours. For she does not care what distinctions she guards, or how we sex her in a homage to the concept of distinction itself. She only cares that distinctions exist.

"Once more the little girl raises her staff.

"Suddenly there's a sound—

"Keep calm!

"No, please, keep calm!

"Whatever happens, don't look away!

"On the canvas sheet that just unrolled at our little guide's sign, flapping and roaring from the darkness above, like a wind from the edge of forever, you can see a mammoth beast so grossly painted it is difficult to tell whether it is a dragon or an eagle; it wavers there, ambiguous as the stone carving over

the gates to the grounds of the High Court itself. What gazes
out through its hollow eyes? Lust? Pride? Avarice? Ignorance?
Want? The guide leads the skeleton past, and though he
quivers, shakes, and seems fit to fall completely to pieces, he
vanquishes all representations of the enemy by that technique
I would urge on you, at least tonight with regards to the
monster behind you: not looking at it.

"There, another canvas falls open, roaring like pain itself,
among whose folds and shadows a raging landscape glimmers.
Wave or mountain, forest or desert, what is important here is
that the lack of a human figure pictured upon it signs the
whole range of human desolations living men and women can
endure, at least a moment, before they die. And he? He
vanquishes those wastes simply by moving, with his clumsy
and awkward step, across it, appearing—just managing to
appear at all—a human form against it, for all his death and
desecration, an irreducibly social trace.

"Somewhere in that part of our city most separated, most
distant, and, indeed, most protected from the general populace,
the Liberator, already beyond the ambiguous gates, approaches
the castle, a gray wall coming toward him, towering over
him, about to fall on him in some infinitely delayed topple...till
a door swallows him, and he moves forward through wide
corridors, cheering behind him, well-wishers on both sides,
as he strolls closer and closer to the seat of power that has
summoned him here...

"But *here*? In this oldest, central section of our city, the
corpse moves on, limping and staggering, shedding flesh and
mold, till, only inches before you, its dead fingers reach to
your left while its skull drops hugely right, its dry hands
stretch to the right while its skull lolls left, as if it would
determine which way it must go to continue toward the power
that has called.

"The music resounds and pounds with military insistence.

"He reels...for *you* are the border he must pass, transgress,
obliterate with some terminal motion to become one with
what animates him.

"Oh, again I tell you: do not look away from the empty
eyes backed with black bone. For if you are seduced into
turning for a moment by the monster that breathes and hisses
at your back, that heats your shoulders to sweat—that, indeed,
guards *you*—he will slip past.

"*You* will be defeated.

"But see: still making your nostrils pinch with the expectation of a putrefaction he's too long dead to reek of, his scentless joints falter, and he falls, slips, at last clatters to the dusty floor as lifeless as—finally—we always knew him to be, vanquished at your feet.

"That he fails (again, and again, and again) to transgress the boundary you represent, between the possible and the probable, the imprecise and the precise, the dying and the dead, the surmised and the certain, that (once more) he does not join with the absolute outside which, you are sure though you have never seen her, controls you unto life and death, means, somehow, at the High Court, the Liberator may, at least in part, succeed; that our champion may not have been thoroughly subsumed by the power that called *him* back from the border.

"It means there is some hope that we need not close forever and absolutely with the power of our own despair, that some informative contradiction remains to be untangled, which may define the distance between our lives and the plague. And both those of us with, and those of us without, the disease can at least believe we understand the same fact, no matter how monstrous further contradiction proves that belief, that boundary between us, actually to have been.

"The little girl with her cat-skull staff? Ah, while our gaze dispersed the apparition as any group disperses the information that falls into it, she slipped by our legs and passed us—to be caught and devoured by the Amnewor? An innocent, awful sacrifice? So fast and absolute we did not hear her scream? Who can tell.

"We certainly can suspect, though.

"That is very likely the reality of the monster, still invisible behind, as well as the meaning of what lies before, crumbled to dust on dirty tile.

"Only we must admit this final contradiction over the absence at our feet: the skeleton has not really moved from its throne at all, in the course of all this glorious music.

"It leans there, silent, accusing us with void sockets of this last self-deception. Harps and drums! Flutes and cymbals! Friends, when you return to the full, confusing, and fallible world above, speak to others of how you saw, at least, a bony finger twitch, a dry foot slide across the cowhide, how certainly you perceived that little motion in death that must be what life means; for only by that response can you affirm that the Amnewor has called.

"Some of you will even say, as truthfully, that you *saw* the skeleton sit up, stand, stagger down the steps, reel across the tile and dirt as far, or farther, than I have described.

"But remember, as you speak, it is the discrepancy, the contradiction, the gap between what you recall and what you can say (even as you strive for accuracy and articulation) that vouches safe our hope, that indicates the possibility of something more, just as, at this end, its total articulation (the complete knowledge that one lies) signs, again, our failure."

9.86 People who attended the Calling of the Amnewor: the barbarian woman who helped Toplin's mother, Madame Keyne, Kentog, the Master, Nari, Namyuk (Zadyuk's younger brother), Noyeed, the old servant woman, Lord Vanar, a once young smuggler, Zadyuk, and many, many others, though less, of course, than attended the celebration at the High Court in honor of the Liberator.

10. "I'm sorry, Leslie, but that's precisely what he *doesn't* do!" Kermit sat with his knees wide and his arms over them, dangling the paperback from one hand. "He doesn't capture—or 'document,' to use his word—the feel of the gay community between eighty-two and eighty-four, when he was apparently writing his story and the AIDS coverage was at its height. And he *certainly* doesn't document the feel of . . . well, of the day-to-day life of the ancient people who once lived here, in *this* city—" He gestured at the chopped up landscape. A few tents stood about among the diggings and, in a few places, a palm—"or in the towns and villages that we'll presumably find around it. He's just playing at their lives, anachronisms all over the place; and his rituals and gods are obviously phony to the core! I mean, even in terms of his own allegory, just look at what he's done. He starts off promising us a story about various and sundry little people, trying to deal with a medical catastrophe, but slowly and inexorably the Discourse of the Master displaces everyone else's, until, finally, it completely takes over. Soon, it's even speaking *for* the little people—at least those the Master himself wants to consider. In this case that's the military, a soldier who moves from

loyalty to forgetfulness (if not total muteness!) in a *very* suspicious way, and a lumpen laborer, whom he just chooses to present, here, as a comic and a cripple! But at the same time, the Master's Discourse is seducing us with its rhetoric, its insight, its professions of honesty, fallibility, and personal doubt, while he ignores whomever he chooses. In this case (as I can't believe you, a mathematician and linguist, as well as a self-professed feminist, didn't notice), that's women and homosexuals—until, Leslie, in a move that dates back to the time the first Mesopotamian warlord financed the first temple in honor of Marduk or whomever, the worldly discourse of the Master is replaced by the transcendental rhetoric of the Priest—our barbarian Wizard with the daisies—saying more or less the same thing the Master said, only in absolute terms, lest we dare question it. But it's precisely what we heard before, a little muffled, from the mouth of the Master himself: in our failure lies our salvation! And there's even a never-never land, where the low shall be made high and the high made low, off in the Western Cravasse. Well, *whose* failure, I'd like to ask. The Master's? Oh, yes. *Do* tell me another one! You can be sure anywhere *he's* failed, he doesn't have an inkling. Failure, failure, wonderful failure...? Just suppose the people who isolated the virus and who're developing the vaccine took that tack? For God's sake, Leslie, he's even published a roster of who did and didn't attend services! No, I'm afraid Delany's Kolhari is *very* smalltown. It's an old, old, *old,* old story. And for all his marginal numbers, his Benjaminesque montage, or his Bakhtinian polylogue, or whatever, there's not a new—much less radical—thing *in* it! And I don't like it one bit. Nor can I see why you do. Only for some reason you've traveled many, many thousands of miles to bring me a copy (with an enthusiasm that, I assure you, is wholly unwarranted) to ask me what I think. Well, there! I've read it—or skimmed it, at any rate. Certainly I've read as much as I need to. And I've *told* you!''

''Kermi—'' Leslie looked around to brush at the dust beside her that they sat on—''six months ago, you had no idea you'd be working here. No one knew for sure that there *was* a here here. In the Culhar', there's mention of a sickness, and there is clearly *something* odd about it. But Delany certainly couldn't have known, when he wrote it, that a real city would turn up with the same name, so to speak—not to mention a similar epidemic—as the one in his stories. He was going by the same things you folks were: a few suggestions in my book on the translation of the Culhar'. And as far as the allegory, well . . . you have to read the textual shape as just the kind of conservative reification you do, but at the same time opposing it with a vigorous deconstruction of—''

"Leslie, I don't understand a word you're saying. What's more I don't believe you do either. And even if the kind of reading you're talking about *did* exist, somewhere or other, I don't think any . . . text—'' Kermit turned up the paperback and squinted at its cover in the late sunlight blazing copper from under a cord of blue-black cloud—''that goes out into the world with an initial printing of—what? A hundred-fifty thousand copies?—can really look forward to it, assuming it *is* possible.''

"Certainly not if you skim, Kermi.'' Leslie sighed. "You know, sometimes when you make pronouncements like that, you sound like *you're* the one who's appropriated the Master's Discourse, and in its most authoritarian and conservative mode too—you know: good, old-fashioned, never-to-be-argued-with common sense! That's the language the Masters speak *most* of the time, you know. That's the most effective one for keeping things as they are. Though I suppose maybe that's the point: that we all close with that masterly discourse, from time to time, in pursuit of our 'liberation,' whether we like it or not.''

"What do you mean, 'we,' white man?''

"Kermit,'' Leslie said, "*you* are the white man. *I* am a black woman—and your friend for a good many years too. Also I'm a thirty-six-year-old, substantially overweight black woman, with an awful overbite. And you piss me off. I mean, Kermi—'' she turned suddenly on the dusty slope—''if the masses *knew* what you were really saying about them when you come out with something like that—''

"—they'd absorb it, disperse it, and live with it as they do every other piece of real information or horrendous abuse our cultural masters, at whatever level, inflict on them. No doubt that's the way they—we, if you prefer—survive. I'm not a liberal, Leslie. And you know it.''

Leslie sighed again.

Kermit sighed louder and threw up his hands—though the book did *not* go flying over the dug up earth. He held it, looking out across it. "Of course, it couldn't have turned out better for *him*. I mean, really—here we discover an ancient

city, which, if it *wasn't* the capital port of a land some
Mycenean Greek called 'Telepote,' it might as well have
been. *And* they had some sort of epidemic that—at least when
we apply your translation techniques to the texts we found
here at the site—*seems* to have been sexually linked. Though
I gather these things have turned up on and off for some time
now. Somewhere in Romans doesn't it talk about one of these
sexually linked diseases?"

"Also between homosexual men. The Moral Majority quotes
it all the time."

"Oh." Kermit shook his head. "Well that's what comes of
spending so much time off the beaten paths. One loses touch
with these things. Still, it's the sexual linkage *I* think is
awful."

"Of course," Leslie said, "I have no way of knowing
whether the epidemic *here* was limited to men *or* to women—
much less if it was limited to homosexual men. We just know
it's associated with a gender particle, but it's fifty-fifty
whether it's the masculine or feminine one."

"*That's* what I think is awful." Kermit looked over where
two or three workers were moving among the excavations.
"But that's the game your Delany seems to think he's
playing. Ten years ago, Leslie, in that initial paper (and no
matter what I've said, I think it was a very *good* paper, too),
you wrote, quite accurately, 'We have not found the names of
any gods in the Culhar' Fragment, nor in any of the texts
related to it by the most ancient of these fragmentary scripts.'
And three pages later, you noted, 'There seems to be a high
concern with craft among these people.' And what does
Delany do with this in his stories? He invents a whole gallery
of *nameless* gods—all craftsmen, to be sure—who've replaced
a deposed set of named ones! Then he puts them all in the
service of a worldview so modern I just assume he's kidding.
Leslie, that's just not responsible historical fiction. I mean,
how can *you,* who did the original work, countenance that
sort of thing? Your translation of the Culhar' Fragment was
quite ingenious, when all was said and done. But your
friend—"

"He's *not* my friend, Kermi." Across the wide, wide sky
the gibbous moon, a mottled ivory disk, had risen, huge at
the horizon, over the ruins opposite the sunset spectacle.
"I've never met him. We've only corresponded a few times. I
just like some of what he writes. But you've got to be the first

person I've *ever* met to think sword-and-sorcery was supposed to be 'responsible historical fiction'! It's just fun—to sort of play with, in your mind."

"Your privilege." Kermit reached up to scratch an ear. "At any rate, your—metaphorically speaking—friend here writes a book ostensibly based on your findings . . . writes three books, actually. Of which this is, I gather—" he closed the raddled pages—"the third. And I've actually spent an afternoon *reading* it. Well, he *can't* capture the feel of the material lives *these* people lead in zitz-thousand B.C. (Really, all his medical details are opportunistic infection symptoms *with* an advanced medical technology busily at work to waylay almost immediate death—the only way you live with AIDS even for six months is because we *do* have advanced medicine!) But I suppose I can forgive him that. I don't know all that much about what people's life here was like either." Kermit looked at the book again, then out at the excavation. "At this point in our research, *nobody* does. But *why* does he insist on calling the place Kolhari? That wasn't even one of your preferred guesses. That was a real outside shot, if I remember—"

"I assume that's because his whole series is an outside shot." Leslie moved one heavy hip then the other back on the sandy slope. "Kermi, you and Wellman have only been digging here six months—thanks to an appendix in *my* book; and you've been lucky enough actually to *find* your city, in about the right place, from about the right time. When Delany wrote that last story I showed you, there was no way he could have known that there *was* a city on this shore, much less that, for a while, it suffered under an epidemic that, at least in some of its aspects, *may* have resembled AIDS. As far as I can figure out from the dates, you were just leaving to come here back when he was nearing the end of his tale. That's what makes the whole thing uncanny. That's why I brought—"

"Leslie, you've come all the way out here to try to win me over to something. And I don't think I want to be won."

"I came because I was less than three hundred miles away and I wanted to say hello and see what you guys were turning up. And since, however inadvertently, you've written an appendix to *two* of his books now, I thought you might find this third one interesting."

"Someone's paying attention to you, Leslie." Kermit lifted the book again. "And that's flattering. Enjoy it. If it was good for you, it's good for me; I'm happy if it makes you happy.

But we've been friends for a long time. And you mustn't ask me for more than that.''

"We *are* friends, Kermi. Angry as you make me. So you may call it what it is: power. Ten years ago, I wrote some papers, which eventually became a book. I worked on them—my translations and the mathematics they were sunk in—*very* hard. And because of it, someone I've never met but some of whose writing I kind of like has written some stories of his own, three whole books of them. Also, because of it, *you* are now third man down on the totem pole of a hundred-fifty-thousand-dollar excavation that's actually finding some interesting correspondences between what's here and what till recently was considered a minor fictive text—not Delany's, of course. The Culhar'. No doubt you and Wellman will get a book or two out of it yourselves. Yes, I enjoy knowing my hard work was initially responsible for all of that, for all of this. Oh, and *please*, don't *you* forget it when you write *your* book. But if I *did* run into Delany, I'd certainly ask him what he thought of your findings here. I assume he'd answer that they're interesting, but that since all his stories were written before your excavations began, 'interesting' is, finally, about all he could say. Well, that's pretty much all I'm asking you. What do you think about *his* work? But I'm just surprised your answer is so different from the one I'd expect from him.''

"Oh, are you?" Kermit put the book down on the ground. "Well, we might both surprise you. You say you want to know what *I* think, but I really wonder if you *do* want to know.''

"But I do!''

"Are you sure?''

"Very.''

"Well, unlike Wellman, who, when you showed the book to him this morning, went on so about the publicity value for the dig these stories would produce (and didn't read a word!), I *am* gay. I've never made any particular secret of it, at least from you. What Delany is talking about strikes very close to home . . . Look, I was *in* New York that summer, at the height of the media coverage of AIDS. I was in my hotel room, waiting to get on a plane to start on my way here, when I watched a *Twenty/Twenty* coverage of AIDS where they interviewed a 'living skeleton,' who, like Delany's 'Herb' the day after 'Sarena's' visit, died one day after the film was finished. Over a few afternoons, I had to make a couple of trips up to Washington Heights to check on some equipment that was due in; so while I was on the subway, I decided just to drop in on a public john at the Seventy-ninth Street subway stop—a rather active New York sexual congregating spot in those days—just to see how all this was affecting things. Mind you, the johns are *not* my usual stomping grounds, you understand. (Three hundred contacts a year? Good Lord, if I've had three in the last five years, I'd consider myself drowned in a surfeit of orgiastic pleasure!) But with all the brouhaha, the scientist in me was curious. Well, would you believe that, between the first and the second day I looked into that shabby hole with its peeling walls and asbestos covered pipes, the blue and ivory paint soiled almost to one hue, the filthy incandescent bulbs in their wire cages from another era, and only metal partitions between the stalls, someone came in and filled both the commodes and the urinals with plaster of paris, which hardened and bulged up over the porcelain rims, making the facilities wholly unusable—except for the industrial-sized sink in the corner, which, a day later, was fouled with urine, feces, and soggy paper by the desperate.

"Irate straights attempting to render inoperable a well-known cruising spot? Social-minded gays trying to put the place out of operation, assuming they were lowering the chances of AIDS contact?

"No, there's no way to be sure. But from the men who still stood around in it, it didn't stop the cruising—nor, from the condition of the floor and the sink, people using it for a toilet.

"But a few days later, the inoperable bathroom was permanently locked. Don't tell me about mass murders. *That's* what New York felt like back then, to me. And that's what I want to see in his 'carnivalesque' portrait. And also—no, don't stop me. You've got me started, now!

"Also: *Why* hasn't he talked about the attempts to close the gay bathhouses and the harassment of gay-owned businesses, not to mention straight-owned gay bars? *How* many clients did this dead therapist or gay accountant have during the six months or six weeks or six days in which he could still work before he died, but after it was known that he had AIDS? Not to mention Pheron's customers. *That's* what I want to know. That's the political question. Certainly that little homily on the Bridge of Lost Desire—what was it? ' . . . I have a lover . . . '—wasn't supposed to cover *that*, now, was it? Well, I'm sorry. *I have a lover*, won't do! I mean, do you *realize* what was involved in the policing of the baths in San Francisco, or the raiding of the Mine Shaft in New York? These were all things in the gay press the same weeks I was there. It was a complex political situation, with feelings running high among thousands on thousands, if not millions, of gay men—not to mention nongays—in both directions, with people writing articles and letters debating both sides passionately, with most of the gay papers—including some writers with lovers with AIDS—vehemently *against* closing the baths, with the official institutions using the confusion once again to step in and tell gay men how we should and shouldn't live. 'Allegoresis,' my ass! If he wanted to allegorize what was actually going on, he should have had a platoon of Imperial storm troopers arrive at the bridge and just start tearing it down because of *course* it was the source of the epidemic. Then watch the reactions of everyone else, from the market vendors and shoppers with no way to get to their precious Old Market, to the people who, yes, indeed wanted to be free to choose whatever sexual style they—''

"Kermi," Leslie said, "maybe he wasn't *trying* to allegorize a political situation. Maybe he was trying to allegorize a feeling, a feeling probably everybody has had about it at one time or another, no matter what side they finally chose—politically, that is."

Kermit shook his head. "And I'm *still* sorry, Leslie. I don't know about this SF or this 'sword-and-sorcery' of yours; but I *do* know a little about art, literature, and history. Flaubert said it: 'All I require from an artist is that he have the proper sensation.' Well, that goes *particularly* for political art. And in this case, the proper sensation means having some intuition for what *needs* to be written about. I don't really care *what* he has to say about it. Or, at any rate, I don't care a *lot*. But if he's going to present this 'tale' of his as some sort of political meditation and he *doesn't* talk about the proper things, then it doesn't cut the mustard!"

Behind them were dark mountains.

"Well, perhaps—" Leslie shrugged—"he doesn't *go* to the baths."

Before them was the sea.

"Well, at least *one* of my most wonderful encounters, for winter—1979, it was—*was* at the baths; in Cincinnati. (Three

hundred? Oh, I hate him! I hate him!) And believe me—''
Kermit sighed— ''I would't give *that* up for anything! But
it's true. *I* don't go to johns. Or movie houses. And there, I
suppose, you have it.''

Between, on the scarred and interrupted land, lay a kind of
partial map of what had once been a city.

11.1 A single lamp burned in the tavern. The celebrants came
quietly from the doorway, a glow on their shoulders as they
stepped into the street. With Zadyuk's arm around her, Nari
pushed aside the hanging. (Where his arm wasn't seemed so
very chill.) Just then, from around the corner, half a dozen
youngsters ran, torches held high among them. As light swept
the tavern wall, Zadyuk looked aside to see the little girl
who'd taken part in the Calling, leaning there, quite like an
adult, talking to an older, broad-hipped woman. The girl still
wore Pheron's black and orange remnant around her shoulders,
although, as he turned to look at the passing children, he also
saw that the mask makeup had been washed from her small,
round face.

Nari glanced up to see Zadyuk looking and looked too. The
torches swept by, dragging the light away and pulling darkness behind it.

11.2 The artist's performance is always more or less aleatory.

This image of Joey:

He wore dark-blue dress slacks, in which he'd slept for a
week in the park. From his bare chest, minutes before, he'd
shrugged a beige T-shirt with ballooning, metallic letters
across it proclaiming, 'How can you be Humble when you're
as Great as I am?' It hung over the back of the kitchen chair
he sat in. Toes reddened from a summer of ill-fitting shoes
given him by another derelict, instep and ankles peppered
with needle marks, his bare feet were a good yard apart on
the linoleum. Earlier that day, waking sick on some park
bench, he'd shit himself, but as the pants were all he owned,
he still wore them, ten hours later. Rolling up one leg to the
thigh, he bent way over. Brass-colored hair fell forward in
matted hanks. I watched him stick what looked like a toy
hypodermic from a Let's-Play-Doctor kit again and again into
his kneecap, his shin, his thigh, trying for a hit, where, at a
functioning vein, the black-red blood would blip into the
already pale-pink solute at the hypodermic's bottom. Blood

drooled his arms and hands from two-odd-dozen failed attempts in the minutes before, now in his forearm, now between his knuckles, now on the inside of his biceps, now on his wrist, three or four obliquely angled stabs at each location, each time joggling the needle to try and break into his body's more and more well-guarded circulatory system. A dribble over his elbow was thick and long as an earthworm; others looked like red yarn down his arms, over his wrists, stringing his infection swollen hand.

Among the bottle caps and folded bits of wax paper on the kitchen table were two blood-blotched paper towels from where he'd twice wiped away the scarlet drool from his impalings.

Drops of blood trickled his leg. He went on prodding a white, inner thigh with his thick thumb, sliding the inch-long needle to its hilt, out, and in again, lifting thin, inch-high tents of flesh . . .

Under his hair, strained from his bent-over position, he muttered: "Damned if I'm gonna blow *this* hit . . . !" (That's missing the vein and injecting under the skin, so that the liquid blows up a dime-sized bubble, absorbed into the body too gradually for the user to feel any effect.) But most of his accessible veins have collapsed.

Later, he stood up, wiping his arms off with another paper towel, his pants' leg still rolled up. "I look like a fuckin' dartboard, don't I?" Forehead sweating with the first rush after his delayed success, he grinned, showing long under teeth and naked upper gum. "I was at the hospital a couple of months ago, and they're trying to do this blood test . . . ? And I tell 'em, please, please! Lemme do it! Please! You gonna be pokin' around in my arm for an hour and you ain't gonna get no blood."

Joey's daughter, from his marriage when he was nineteen, is one month younger than mine. In the occasional comparisons of the dog-eared photo he had of her for a while and the school picture I carry, it isn't just projection: the two girls look uncannily alike. Three times now, I've known him to get it together enough to make a trip up to Boston to see her. "I only spend a couple of hours with her," he explained on his return. "I don't want to be no trouble for my old lady. Besides, I don't want the kid to know her old man is a fuckin' junky, sleepin' on the street and sellin' his ass." It occurs to me that for anyone—even a ten-year-old—to spend more than a few minutes with Joey is probably to suspect that his situation can't be too much else.

The audience's performance is always more or less stochastic.

My accounts of Joey are only somewhat tightened up from my journals for '82 and '83, about a hustler (whose name does not begin with "J" nor was he born in Boston), some murders (complete with the inaccuracies from "Joey's" account), and a police operation. While that may make them *more* historical, it does not make them *less* fictive.

11.3 Earlier tonight, on a cold, rainy Easter Monday, twenty degrees below normal for the time of year (April 23rd, 1984), after two days of hints in the papers and on TV, the six o'clock news announced an AIDS breakthrough. On the same news program were a few more details of Great Britain's cutting off of diplomatic relations with Libya over the embassy murder of a policewoman in London; there was a minute and a half photographic retrospective for the death of eighty-two-year-old landscape photographer, Ansel Adams; judges called for harsher sentences for New York criminals, despite the fact that our jails are holding 116 percent of their capacity; Harlem dance teacher, Mary Bruce, is determined to fight eviction from the second-floor dance studio she has run at 125th Street since the thirties.

And Dr. Robert Gallo of the National Cancer Institute has isolated a virus (HTLV-3—very similar to ordinary HTLV and possibly much like, or even identical to, LAV, the virus the Institute Pasteur has been studying), which, by reasonable assessment, is possibly the causative agent of AIDS. Secretary of Health and Human Services Margaret Heckler at a press conference in Washington, with hair piled high, pale-framed glasses, and a high-collared red dress, announced across a forest of microphones that we are reasonably six months away from a general test for the antibodies for the virus and two years away from a vaccine—which will then be ready for another year of testing, before it can be used.

That is, of course, if this *is* the actual virus.

Shortly, amidst the peeling walls of the office of the Gay Men's Health Crisis, a gaunt, huge-eyed man with AIDS explained calmly to an interviewer that, while it is hopeful news, it doesn't do much good for the two-thousand-odd people still alive with AIDS today, none of whom, in a word, are likely to survive that long. It's only his work and his will, he tells us, that have kept him alive. (And there have been c. 880 new cases reported in the first three months of this year, 1984.) Later, on Channel 2 there was a remarkably responsible report about AIDS in the Navy, Air Force, and Army. Basically the report says that there *must* be more cases than the five the armed forces have admitted to so far; the news commentator suggests that there are probably somewhat over thirty.

But our microbically unagented terror has, after four years now and a toll of more than four thousand—possibly—developed its microbe.

11.4 *Expand this scene to some six/eight pp.:*

While the last of the night's carnival celebration goes on outside in the street, Nari and Zadyuk get home from the Calling of the Amnewor to their dark house, to find Pheron. (*Wording*: Squatting in the dark before the firebox, Zadyuk swung back the metal door. Coals glowed in the ashes. He picked out one of the hardwood sticks and blew on it. Its end glowed above his fingers. With his other hand he reached for the lamp on top, first accidentally pushing it over a little, then getting it: he brought down the warm clay, touched the stick's end to the wick, which, after a moment, flared red. In the doorway, Nari breathed in sharply. Zadyuk looked at her, then at where she looked. A very, very thin man sat at the bench alongside their table, head forward on his arms. Zadyuk stood up; the lamp flame flickered wildly; red wavered and wobbled in the room. And the man at the table moved a long foot, then a thin hand, and finally lifted his head to blink at them with large, dark eyes, whites showing all the way around. Nari whispered: "Pheron . . . ?" *Clean up some. Work on the red light over the—stone? wood? Omit or change:* "accidentally," "alongside," "the way," "over a little, " "after a moment." *Possibly okay. But clean and clarify: how Pheron got in, etc.*) Pheron looked like a skeleton. (*Wording*: The elbows seemed large interruptions along the thinnesses of his arms. *Okay? Maybe.*) He told them that he'd spent the evening with some of the other people with the disease. (*Where? At Lord Vanar's? At his own house?*) The boy who'd first brought him to the group, Toplin, had died earlier that day at his mother's home. Top's lover, a stoneworker who lived out in the district of Successful Artisans near the school, had come in to tell them, and had broken down in the group. Everyone had been

shaken. And Pheron had realized that, besides the support of
the group, he wanted to talk to his friends. So he'd had the
wagon drop him off here—"Look, I don't want to be any
trouble. I don't, but I just needed to—please, you don't
mind...?"

No, of course not. He was their friend; they were his. (Nari
went to sit beside him on the bench. Zadyuk put the lamp on
the table and sat on the other side of the table.) Really, they
were glad he'd come. Clearly, though, they feel discomfort.
"Are you all right?" Zadyuk asked. "I mean, do you want us
to take you back home...?"

"No...No, please. I just wanted to talk. Let me stay,
awhile. I'm so...I'm frightened, Nari. I want somebody to
do something for me! But what can I ask them for?"

Nari started to say that they'd gone to the Calling of the
Amnewor for him; but Zadyuk stopped her with a look.
Confronted with the reality of their friend, that, they both
realized, had been for them.

"I've always tried to do things for other people," Pheron
went on. (*Wording*: His voice was breathy, as though he spoke
behind cloth.) "I've always tried to help them—you, anybody
I thought needed it. Haven't I? Isn't that true? That's not
bragging, is it? And now, I just want somebody to do
something for me—only there's nothing anybody can do, is
there? And that's not fair. And it's so frightening. I can't
work anymore, Zad. I'm too weak; and I hurt too much. And
when I can't work I get frightened. I'm not afraid of dying.
Not now. Not anymore. But I'm terrified of the next five
days, or five weeks, or fifteen months—with their last minutes—I've still got to live through. Help me! Please, help
me. Somebody, Nari, Zad...Please, I'm *so* frightened...!"

They went on talking, for a long while; then, sensing his
exhaustion and his illness as well, they helped him to lie
down on their bed, where, after a little, he fell asleep. Zadyuk
sat for a while on the bed's edge; Nari stretched out beside
Pheron. Finally Zadyuk lay down too, till all of them were in
the uneasy slumber of three exhausted children, cowering in a
forest, waiting for morning or a monster. *No. Can't write it
out. Not now. Partly because it touches too many emotional
things in me. And partly because, seven weeks beyond my
forty-second year, I'm cynical enough to wonder seriously if a
young, heterosexual, working couple would give up, for a
gay friend (even if he were dying), what amounts, after all, to a*

night's sleep on the last day of carnival before returning next morning to a full work schedule: ten, twelve hours for them both. (They probably would have gotten him home, whether he wanted to go or not, and left him there, feeling vaguely put out.) They cannot bear to think about it directly anymore than can the Master. The relation of those two feelings in me is, of course, the bottom-line political question for this particular scene. Is the cynical response to protect myself from the emotions? Or: Does my knowledge of a cynical truth make the emotions as painful as they are? Or: Are the emotions and the cynicism two valid responses to the world as I've known it at painful play within me, in no particularly contingent hierarchy? Certainly this last is what I suspect. Question? If the whole scene above took place not in the red glow of that particular oil, but in a brighter, butter-colored (i.e., more expensive) light, would that suggest the necessary differences in Zadyuk's and Nari's personalities/situation for me to believe the scene as outlined? At any rate, to sketch out what I hope would happen seems fair. To write out fully what I still can't fully believe seems, however, to be cheating in just the way I wrote of in 9.811. Well, for all those reasons, maybe in a while . . .

11.41 By now I'm willing to admit that perhaps narrative fiction, in neither its literary nor its paraliterary mode, can propose the *radically* successful metaphor. At best, what both modes can do is break up, analyze, and dialogize the conservative, the historically sedimented, letting the fragments argue with one another, letting each display its own obsolescence, suggesting (not stating) where still another retains the possibility of vivid, radical development. But responding to those suggestions is, of course, the job of the radical reader. (The "radical metaphor" is, after all, only an interpretation of preextant words.) Creators, whatever their polictics, only provide raw material—documents, if you will. In terms of AIDS itself, there are all sorts of social practicalities one can endorse: better research, better information, support groups for people with AIDS, support groups for those around them. Yes, I feel the urge to fictionalize these last two, more than the first. (Pheron's incompleteness, we now can be sure, is an incompleteness of the text, not of a person.) I also feel, as I don't (yet) have AIDS myself, and have visited no such AIDS groups, I wouldn't know precisely

how to—though my own experience with the Gay Fathers'
support group certainly urges me to it, and even suggests
what to look for: the first hopes that the group will solve *all*
problems, then the disappointment when they don't, finally
the real and solid help such groups give apart from both
expectations *and* disappointments, and, even, perhaps a measured realization that this *particular* group may not be for you
(while, indeed, another may)—having nothing to do with
expectations, disappointments, *or* benefits. (One could make
Pheron far more "whole" by thinking in fictional terms
precisely where he was among all these possibilities that night
with his particular support group, what precisely had happened,
and how. Go on, then, *mon semblable,—nom frère!*)

12.1 When I was kid, my family had a country house. Down
the road from us a second or third cousin of mine used to
come up sometimes to visit his grandfather. He was about my
age, he had a younger brother, a dog, and played the saxophone.
   He'd been blind from birth.
   We were all very fond of him and his family. I was in and
out of his house and he was in and out of ours all the time.
   One afternoon when I was about twelve and upstairs in our
attic, working on the design for some electrical circuit in my
notebook and listening to the radio (the unfinished attic of our
country house was basically my room), some medical program came on talking about eye injuries and blindness.
Thinking of my cousin, I perked up. The thing I've remembered from the program ever since was one small part of the
discussion: ". . . he lost one eye through an injury in a car
accident, and, two years later through sympathetic ophthalmia,
he lost the sight in the other . . ."
   Sympathetic ophthalmia?
   Always a lover of big words, I'd encountered both before,
but this was the first I'd heard them together. And the idea
that, just because you'd lost one eye, through a weakening of
the muscles and a failure of the nerves you risked losing the
sight in the others seemed the grossest biological injustice! In
the thirty years since, without really trying, I've had a couple
of single-eyed friends or acquaintances. I've always thought
of them as people who've managed to beat sympathetic
ophthalmia. I don't believe I've ever mentioned it to any of
them; still, their triumph seemed important to me.

                    *   *   *

12.2 Anecdotal evidence at work *last* week: In 108 cases of AIDS tested, all 108 exhibited a certain intestinal amoeba. (Sarena says that for three years before he came down with AIDS, Herb spent a losing battle trying to shake these same intestinal parasites.) Perhaps the parasite coupled with excessive use of drugs (particularly amyl nitrite) weakens the system so that...

Of course, what happens to the blood products theory?

And for all the hope that the Easter Monday announcement brings, we're still two years away from a vaccine only ready for testing.

12.3 Here's the ending as I got it to that "Jack the Ripper" account. While walking up Eighth Avenue, I ran into Joey. He was wearing a new set of clothes, including a new leather (more probably plastic) jacket, and clearly feeling very chipper. He grinned and greeted me happily. Obviously, at least for a couple of days, things had been going well for him. I asked him if he was staying anywhere.

He shrugged a little shyly: "I was stayin' with this guy for a couple of weeks. But I'm back on the street now. Been in the Port Authority bus station for the last three nights." He examined the sleeves of his jacket. "I don't look in too bad shape, do I?"

"You look pretty good," I said, with the same phatic content as the usual, I'm fine/how are you? "Did they ever catch that guy who was going around killing people?" I asked.

"Oh, yeah. Caught him two weeks ago." In the midst of his good humor, my question seemed to bother him.

"Tell me what happened," I urged. "Who was it?"

"Just some guy. Some crazy guy who was goin' around killing people. They said he killed five people. But they caught him."

"I thought you said he killed nine...?"

"Naw. Somebody else killed the other four."

"Does that mean somebody *else* was running around, doing the others—"

Joey put one hand on my shoulder. "Man, I'm on the *street* again. I'm doin' pretty well, too. For a while, anyway. They caught him. It's over with. He killed five guys; and I just got to the place where I don't have to think about it *all* the time. So let's talk about something pleasant, okay? Like cancer, or

AIDS, or people starvin' in China...? Now wouldn't you think *I'd* be dead of AIDS by now?" He laughed. "Heroin, homosexuals, hemophiliacs, and Haitians. Well, I suppose I *could* be a hemophiliac Haitian too. Naw, if I had any kind of hemophilia, I'd be dead years ago, huh? Hey, when you gonna break down and help me get another room. I get some place to bring people and I can make a lot more money ...?" But he grins to let me know he's not (as) serious.

12.4 Ted's been reading the Nevèrÿon tales practically since they began coming out of my notebook. Once, last spring, when he came in, he told me: "I made it with Gorgik today."

"What?" I asked, as we walked back into the living room. "What do you mean?"

"I was down at that movie on Third Avenue—you know. The one where I first met you? And I *saw* your character, Gorgik. The Liberator. Actually, I've seen him a few times. As far as I can make out, he's one of the Saturday afternoon regulars. It was all I could do not to tell him: 'Did you know you're the *exact* image of a character in some stories a friend of mine's been writing?' Really, Chip, if you want to see one of your own characters come to life, you should go down there! Christ, he was sensational!"

Yes, the temptation was too great. Next Saturday, sitting in the darkened balcony of what is reputedly the second-oldest theater building in New York City, while for the afternoon its screen was shared between a piece of commercial straight pornography and an espionage rerun, I saw a man some rows to my right and in front of me, pretty clearly the man Ted had gone on to describe: large, hulking, blond(!?), most likely Polish. But no, it would never have occurred to *me* to think he resembled my character. As I went down the narrow stairs into the sunlit lobby, to leave the movie house, I thought (and smiled): Well, to each his own Liberator.

12.5 I was feeling rather down. In entry 5.1, I wrote that the most recent time I'd seen Joey he was doing pretty well: off the street, off drugs? I jotted that down in my notebook at five o'clock the morning after I saw him.

Two nights later, crossing Ninth Avenue at Forty-third, on my way to an editorial meeting of the poetry magazine I've been working on since October, I saw a bunch of young men surging toward me, one of whom, as they broke around me, grinned—and for a moment I thought something was terribly wrong with his teeth. They were moving. And not all in the same direction.

Then I remembered his bridge, just as he tongued it back up into place.

"Luis," I said. "How you doing?"

"Okay." He shrugged, still smiling. "You seen your friend, Joey?"

"Yeah," I said. "As a matter of fact, I saw him a couple of nights back. He was looking pretty good."

Luis shook his head. (The guys with him had wandered on.) "He got beat up last night. They caught him, man, and wiped up the *street* with him!" He started forward again.

With a raised eyebrow, I turned to ask for more details. But Luis smiled apologetically, nodded after the others, who were already at the far corner, shrugged, grinned good-bye, and loped on.

Over the next couple of days, in the Fiesta and around it, I asked a couple of people if they'd seen Joey. I was just curious. Something had happened—though no one was sure what. And he'd hitchhiked out of town. Some said he'd fled to Boston. Some said to Washington.

He showed up about a month later. Once I passed him on the street when he didn't see me. The next day I ran into him, angry, sick, and strung out, running after some black guy down Tenth Avenue as I was walking up, trying to get the guy to trust him "...for the other ten bucks, man! Come on! *Please!*"

In an ancient, funereal suit, the black guy tried to move away.

"Come on, Chip! Tell this guy he can trust me on anything! You know that! Tell him!"

"Yeah," I said. "He's a good guy. You can trust him," and walked on, as Joey ran off after his recalcitrant connection. I doubt it did much good.

Still a couple of weeks later, while I was riding the M-104 bus up Eighth Avenue, I glanced out the window to see him sitting on the steps beside the comic-book store, with another friend, the two of them laughing over something as if they were having the time of their lives.

What's hardest, in the end, for me to accept is that none of these emblematic images fixes Joey's life. Rather, it's the movement between them that the text does not capture—or document—a movement that may, at least in part, be as bewildering to him as it is to me.

13. That night I walked home through our unaccountably cold wet spring. (The day of the Breakthrough announcement three weeks ago, the windchill factor was twenty-three degrees.) Now and again the weather had given way for a half a day or so to something warmer, but always with a nip at either end.

Somehow I found myself walking an almost deserted Riverside Drive, on face-sized hexagonal pavings. Beside me over the waist-high wall, Riverside Park was a shadowy darkness, fronting the river. Above me, trees shattered the mercury-vapor lamps under a theatrically black sky.

Muggers? They're too scared to wander in this part of the city after sundown.

Almost a block ahead, beyond the park wall, I could see a fire flickering in among the bushes. I turned between the stone newels and into the park itself, strolled past the brilliantly lit water fountain and moved away from the playground. As I climbed the brush and tree grown slope, the river cleared to my right and a canyon face of apartment lights—many out now—rose with me at my left above the trees.

He'd built his fire up on the rocks, using some old crates, fallen branches, and newspapers. Sitting on the log beside it, he was waiting, I guess, for the police to come and make him put it out. But the cops are almost as scared of this section of the park as the muggers. He had on a thermal vest, torn over the stuffing at one side, and no shirt under. The muscles on his arms and shoulders were hard and defined. The fire burnished his small, sharp face, much browner than I'd thought it would be.

Around his upper arm he wore a studded leather strap, of the sort that, five years ago, you'd have to buy in some specialty leather shop but which, these days, you could find in any record store with a reasonable punk selection; like his vest, it had probably come from a trash basket. There was something dark around his neck. A leather collar? But from what I could see of it under the vest, it was the wrong color, the wrong texture. In the firelight I would have sworn it was blackened iron.

One eye gazed at the flame. Where the other should have been was shadow. He was small enough so that, looking at him, I thought about midgets, and tall enough so that after a moment I forgot them. His hands hung over his knees—one pants' leg was torn from calf to cuff. He had the rough, thickened fingers of someone who'd done mostly physical labor. Looking at them, you kind of suspected maybe, with another life and another diet, he might have been big; but as it was, his hands were all that had reached full growth. The pants were a lot too large and rolled up so they didn't hang all over his shoes. At first, I thought they (somebody's discarded size twelve runners) were too large too, till I saw his toes coming out a rip in the front. No, like his hands, his feet were just big. He'd knotted a belt with no buckle around the bunched material at his waist.

Standing across the fire from him I finally asked, "How you doing?"

He looked up at me and, after a while, nodded a little.

"You been here long?" I asked.

He shook his head, with a gesture just as small. "No . . . No. I just come, see? Not long." (I'd been thinking Puerto Rican, or Caribbean. But the accent recalled something Middle Eastern.) "Couple of days."

I dropped down in a squat.

He blinked at me with his single eye, curious, as fire flickered between us. Raising one hand, he scrubbed the heel on his mouth.

"Why did you . . . leave?" I asked.

"I can't stay there." He shook his head, frowning. "He don't need me now, no more. Why I stay? I go away, I run—far. Very far. Here, you see?" He looked down, considering a moment. Once he moved his head to the side, reached for some rock or pebble and flipped it away. "Naw, he don't need me, now. He big man. He all in there with those big . . . I can't go in there, be like that. With him. There. Now." Hair, black, stringy, hung in greasy cords at the side of his head. It would smell of dogs and wet leaves. "So I stay, see? On the bridge. Have me some fun." He glanced up, with a quick, gappy grin. "You understand?"

I nodded.

"Then, on the bridge, somebody tell me about . . . and I go to that . . ." Lost for the word, he gave a little shudder. "They try to scare me there at . . . ." Frowning again, he took his hand and mimed pushing something down. He said: "Down. Under the ground, see? When they make the . . . the bones. They walk around. And they try to scare me." Suddenly his hand came back against his chest. "I'm a murderer, you know? I'm a bad man! I'm no good! The bones, they move—like he still alive or something! I'm down there in the dark! The bones, they go here, there, you know, comin' at you, and you can't look back or turn, see? I'm gonna piss all over myself in a minute, you know? I'm that scared! Only I think, Shit!" He grinned again, over an assortment of rottings and holes. "But I move, real quiet, to the side. And I see, there, behind this..." He ran his hand, flat, up and down.

"Screen...?" I offered.

"Yeah! Behind this..." He made the gesture again—"I see this woman. This woman, you know? She real big— here." With both hands he made curving gestures out from his hips—"and she playin' this drum, and this harp, and these..." With hands before his face he mimed some fingered wind. "And this other one, younger, she giving them to her, first this one, then that. So I think: she's there, playin' —nothin' *too* bad gonna come." He pursed his lips tightly, then said: "Not to me. Though I still don't look back, you know?"

I nodded again. "Then what happened?"

He bent his head to the side. "I come here. Later. After it finished with, see? I leave the..." He threw his hand out. "I leave, I run away. From the..."

"City?"

"I leave the city. North. The next day. I go north, on a wagon. And I..."

After a few moments, I decided his thoughts had lost themselves among memories. "But how did you get *here*?" I asked. "From there?"

"Here?" Grinning now, he jabbed at me with his forefinger across the fire. "You wanna know? No, you don't believe me. But it's true. I..." The grin dropped away. His little shoulders went back. He looked up. "I fly! Yes. Flying, on a..." The eye came down, the white stained and bloodshot, the rim of the iris not so definite on the ivory. "You believe that? That hard, I know. For you. But I fly."

I waited. The fire flapped.

"I go to the north, and I fly on a..."

This time when he stopped, I said: "Tell me in your own language. Go on. I'll understand."

He bent his head the other way, so that the blank skin, sealed and sunken in the socket, filled with light.

*   *   *

Three moist and silvery days I waited in the mountains for a wild one, he explained over the fire in the softly singsong syllables of that long-ago distant tongue, *but the single beast I saw through overcast summer green had wings as tattered on the spines as all the leaves around, a ground-bound belly bloated with small deer, eyes rheumy as smashed clams; it was a fair decade beyond flight. I climbed to the corral, then, wedged my nose and eye in the finger width between the boards, and—phew! they grow musty when they muster in groups of more than threes, fetid in fives, noxious in nines. There, they were a gaggle to gag on. But one: I saw it spread, rear on its hind haunches. Sweeping away its fellows with a scaly tail and swaying, he hawed like a mule, as beautiful as the sky we both lusted after. Him! I said to myself, or her—for I could see the egg troughs ranged beyond another fence (such little fruits, with shells like wrinkled leather, to hatch them!)—I'll have it! I climbed inside that night. It's rumored in the Makalata holes that some men long for the small-breasted grooms that care for and curry the beasts, dormed now down the slope. Some have broken in. Seldom have they come out. Monsters, say the good and decent men, hearing of such horrors, meaning the men. Or the girls. Believe it, they deserve whatever they get. But my own desires start at the monstrous: I'm a little man and do not lust after what's little. As I haltered that green neck, jaded with the moon, however, as I beat that scaled side into motion with the flat of my hand, as claws scrabbled on the moonlit dust and the dragon craned to see who'd roped it, I felt, I confess, desire tumble among my body's centers. "Move, you winged worm!" I hissed. "Come on, you four-footed serpent!" And smacked it again, as one might urge on the right sort of lover. It was easy enough to lift the locking beam from its hook. I stuck a stick between the boards and lifted—though when it fell loudly to the rock outside, I started, waiting for guards to fall from all around. (They, no doubt, were elsewhere, busy protecting their glorious store of delinquent virginity that could not have interested me less.) Not even in a shed, but merely under a long, thatched awning on wooden rails, the light, leather gear was ranged and racked. I stood some time in the moonlight, my mount beside me, worrying how I might saddle her for the night. But I've had a hand with horses. And after some moments I simply*

*stalked forward, pulled one set of stirrups free, returned with
the saddle and flung it over the sharp, high back, cinched the
creature, pinched its cheeks to get the bit back in its beaky
gums—while it near hauled me off the ground, tossing its
head on a neck alone half as long again as a taller man than
I. A ledge! Where was a ledge to launch from? But it had already started forward, as if, with its gear, it had put on the
whole of its habitual flight pattern. Holding on, I had to run
after it, trying to haul myself up that heaving side, my feet
dragging on the rocks and ruts it made its way along. Yes,
finally I got myself on, my leg over, when, reaching forward for
the reins, I saw the edge of the world ahead. And moonlit
mountains beyond, thrust among clouds. For the whole corral,
you see, was built along a ledge! We moved toward that precipice with a motion as inexorable as that with which time takes
us toward our death. "Halt!" some distant woman cried—a
guard, certainly, strolling between barracks on her midnight,
moonlight watch. "Halt, I say!" Down wherever she was,
there was more confusion. Then something whizzed by, behind
my shoulders. A spear? An arrow? I only know that, inexorable as that lumbering gait had seemed a moment back, it
seemed now just as unchangeably slow, as we made for the
stony rim. I kicked, I clucked, I rattled its reins, and, without
hastening or hesitating, the maddening monster craned her
head around to see what I was up to! I looked aside at the
incensed women running toward us: the corral guards. Another spear hurtled before me. Something hit my dragon's
leg, but at such an angle—fortunately—that the arrow bounced
free of the hide lapped with its little armors. I looked ahead
again—and realized that the rock we moved across was, now,
the last between us and the sky.*

We went over!

*The broad wings gathered and opened beside me, and in a
roar of air we were caught up on the night. The force of it
nearly jarred me loose! I glanced behind, to see the harridans,
dancing and shouting on the brink, hurling spears and shooting arrows, some of which I saw fall under us.*

Below dark Ellamon lay in moonlight.

*But now I turned forward. For with the night roaring at my
ears and rushing up my arms to beat my chest, with the
beast's wings laboring behind my knees, I put my mind to my
journey. How long, I wondered, could I glide here aloft? The
rumor was that the animals could fly only a stade or so, and*

that in an upward draft. But I've never been a man to believe in limits, borders, boundaries. I've lived beyond them all my life, and I swore I'd get us off now, even if I had to throw the reins and beat my arms in air.

The dragon labored.

The night roared.

I hardly dared breathe.

And we rose awhile under the moon.

Was it minutes? Was it hours? The beast's head began to jerk. Fables all over the land tell how such a motion signals the height of the glide. Well, then you know, I truly began to urge us on. "Up, you low-bellied lizard! Up, I say! Fly for the sun and morning! Don't you dare go down on me yet!" I howled out every curse I knew and then some. I kicked my heels against the wing joints, again and again, to keep them flapping. I knuckled the neck and jockeyed us on through cold air. And for a while, at least, we seemed to move ahead. "You fly, I say! And keep on flying!" Did you know a man with one eye can weep tears hot as a woman with two? Did we cross a desert? Did we cross a sea? I wept and cursed and kicked. "Go on! Go on! Keep flying!" And, believe me, we flew! Somewhere below, I know, we crossed a river. And there were many little lights on both its shores: hundreds of lights, thousands of lights, in orderly rows and lines! At first I thought there must be two vast armies camped, with myriad fires each, on the opposing banks. We swooped, and moonlight sheened the wide water. I pulled on the reins to make her head for some dark among those little flames, where I thought there'd be trees and we might hide from that immense, encircling war—for that is all I could think such lights might mean. But I was exhausted, and once I'd fixed our course I could only fall against the neck and hug it. We fell. I heard the upper twigs tear at the wings. I remember it flapped and trumpeted, banking, back-beating like a bird, attempting to break her flight. Then something struck me, struck at me again, and finally knocked me, numb, from her.

When I came to, in leaves and dirt, I had cuts and abrasions all along one side . . .

He sat up to hold back the vest's torn edge, so that fire lit the scratches and scabs on his ridged, brown flank. "The animal...? I not find," he said, again taking up infacile English. "I look. But she gone, now." He shrugged. "It not fly, now, anyway, no more." Shaking his head, he let the vest fall to and leaned again on his knees. "The wings, now, be all..." He made a few tearing motions. "But I... am here now. You see? Flying. All the way here. All the way. I come from a far when..." He paused, lifting one hand to indicate something vast and unexpressible. "A distant once... across never..." Frowning, first he, then I looked toward the Hudson, at Jersey's massed, Imperial lights. "Across the river," he said, then looked back at me. "You believe that?"

I smiled, shrugged, and shifted in my squat.

We stayed a little longer, while the flames lowered among bits of old board. He blinked his eye and joined his hands, waiting for me to suggest we go somewhere, that I buy him something to eat, perhaps, or that we stay, or whatever.

"Tell me," I said at last, "since you've only been here a little while, how do you find our strange and terrible land? Have you heard that we have plagues of our own?"

Curious, he looked at me across the fire, turned to the river, glanced at the city about us, then looked at me again.

And I would have sworn, on that chill spring night, he no longer understood me.

—New York,
May 1984

I beg my readers not to misread fiction as fact. "The Tale of Plagues and Carnivals" is, of course, a work of imagination; and to the extent it is a document, largely what it documents is misinformation, rumor *and* wholly untested guesses *at play through a limited social section of New York City during 1982 and 1983, mostly before the April 23, 1984 announcement of the discovery of a virus (human t-cell lymphotropic virus [HTLV-3] as the overwhelmingly probable cause of AIDS.*

AIDS (Acquired Immune Deficiency Syndrome) is a disease in which the body's immune system ceases to function, and the body becomes prey to many opportunistic infections, including, among the most common, pneumocystis carinii pncumonia, an otherwise rare form of pneumonia, and Kaposi's Sarcoma (KS), an otherwise rare form of skin cancer. In the last five years, over six and a half thousand cases of AIDS have been reported. There have been no recoveries, and forty-five percent of those to contract the syndrome in these five years are now dead as a result.

There is no evidence that AIDS is transmitted by casual contact (that is, it is not spread by air, food, water, skin contact, sneezes, or the handling of exposed clothing, bedding, or objects). The evidence is overwhelming, however, that it can be spread by sexual contact in which bodily fluids or secretions (semen, saliva, urine, feces, or blood) pass from partner to partner—though it has not been determined how these secretions must enter the partner's body for infection to take place (that is, it is not known if lesions, tears, or small

351

cuts must be present in the mouth, body skin, rectum, or vagina for infection to occur). To date, approximately seventy-two percent of those to get the disease have been homosexual men. The great majority of the men to get it live in, or frequently visit, large urban centers, with New York, San Francisco, Los Angeles, and Chicago far in the lead. The next highest risk-group is intravenous drug abusers: unsterilized and infected needles going directly into the bloodstream are apparently an indisputable point of contagion. Approximately four hundred women have gotten AIDS, the vast majority of whom are either I-V drug abusers, or the sexual partners of men who are I-V drug abusers. AIDS symptoms include unexplained loss of weight, unexplained bruises or lesions on the body (particularly on the legs), swollen lymphnodes (particularly in the neck), along with malaise and general weakness. At the onset of any of these symptoms, singly or in combination, especially in someone in one of the high-risk groups, medical attention should be sought immediately. To date, no adults who have contracted the disease have lived with AIDS beyond three years; and death may come as quickly as six weeks after the onset of symptoms, depending on what opportunistic infections settle in and how they are treated.

The above is some of what is known *about AIDS to date (October, 1984), though what is known has been changing month to month for more than a year and will no doubt continue to change until after a vaccine is developed. (All these statistics will be tragically outdated by the time this book is published.) What follows is generally considered reasonable speculation by the informed, or is based on it.*

Various gay men's groups have advised gay men to put a sharp curtailment on their number of sexual contacts outside of monogamous relationships, or to confine them within known circles, closed if possible. Given the situation, total abstinence is a reasonable choice. Whatever adjustment one makes, one must bear in mind that the social path of the disease is difficult to trace, as the incubation period has been generally estimated at seven months; and, in some cases, three years or more may have passed between infection and the outbreak of symptoms. There is no hard-edged evidence as to when—or for what length of time—someone can transmit the disease during incubation. The possibility of carriers with no symptom is, therefore, highly likely.

*Those wishing further facts and guidelines should send
their questions, stated briefly, to:*

> Gay Men's Health Crisis
> P.O. Box 274
> 132 West 24th Street
> New York, NY 10011

AIDS Hotline: (212) 807-6655*

---

*My warmest thanks go to Dr. Marc Rubenstein for helping me with
this final medical note.

Appendix B:
CLOSURES AND OPENINGS

It is easy to see why Pasolini's arguments could have been so easily dismissed. He himself, only half jokingly, asked: "What horrible sins are crouching in my philosophy?" and named the "monstrous" juxtaposition of irrationalism and pragmatism, religion and action, and other "fascist" aspects of our civilization... Let me suggest, however, that an unconventional, less literal or narrow reading of Pasolini's pronouncements (for such they undoubtedly were), one that would accept his provocations and work on the contradictions of his "heretical empiricism," could be helpful in resisting, if not countering, the more subtle seduction of a logico-semiotic humanism.

—Teresa de Lauretis
Alice Doesn't—Feminism, Semiotics, Cinema

1. For readers who've followed the Nevèrÿon tales through their three volumes, a minuscule gift: "Nevèrÿon" is pronounced Ne-VER-y-on, i.e, four syllables with the accent on the second: *Flight from Nevèrÿon* rhymes with "Octogenarian." The old aristocratic section of Kolhari that briefly lent its name to the entire city is pronounced Ne-ver-y-O-na, i.e., five syllables with the primary accent on the penultimate (and a secondary accent on the ante-antepenult). Thus, *Neveryóna* rhymes with "I love Pemona."

2. I have every intention of making "The Tale of Plagues and Carnivals" a farewell to my nearly ten-year sojourn in Nevèrÿon. The form, however, admits to certain speculations, elaborations, exfoliations. Origins, then?

3. From the time that I became aware the Nevèrÿon tales would become a series—from the time I became aware of a certain dissatisfaction with the idea that a sequence of encounters with a set of socially central institutions was constitutive of the "civilized" subject ("The Tale of Gorgik") and turned back to critique that notion with the idea that a sequence of far more subjective encounters with some far more marginal institutions could be equally constitutive ("The Tale of Old Venn")—I more or less thought of these tales as a Child's Garden of Semiotics.

The five stories of volume one (*Tales of Nevèrÿon*) struggle through the classical notion of the sign (Stoically divided into signifier and signified), posited by the pre-Socratic Greeks

357

and persistent up through Saussure and Pierce, and the conservative notion of social relations that this "classical" sign stabilizes. Under such a program, semiotics becomes the study of the way in which signs are *organized*.

The sixth tale, the novel that fills most of the second volume *(Neveryóna)*, struggles toward a somewhat richer view of the sign, shattering it into sign production (semiosis), sign function, and sign vehicle—the schema that distinguishes Umberto Eco's semiotics as he adumbrated it in *Opera Aperta* (Milano: Bompiani, 1962) and the early essays in *The Role of the Reader* (Bloomington: Indiana University Press, 1984), expressed it in *A Theory of Semiotics* (Bloomington: Indiana University Press, 1976), and (subsequently) critiqued it from a historical point of view in *Semiotics and the Philosophy of Language* (Bloomington: Indiana University Press, 1984). This is certainly the most impressive account of semiosis that allows sign systems to evolve, generate new signs, critique themselves, reorganize themselves, and generally to change. In such a view, semiotics becomes the study of the way in which signs are *generated*.

In this third and, I hope, final volume *(Flight from Nevèrÿon)*, the tales move away from semiotics to a more general semiology, as Barthes described it in his "Inaugural Lecture" for the Chair of Literary Semiology at the College de France, January 7, 1977: for Barthes, semiology was "the labor that collects the impurity of language, the wastes of linguistics, the immediate corruption of any message: nothing less than the desires, fears, expressions, intimidations, advances, blandishments, protests, excuses, aggressions, and melodies of which active language is made." This idea of semiology as the excess, the leftover, the supplement of linguistics brings us round to Jacques Derrida's logic of the supplement, without which semiology and, indeed, poststructuralism in general would be hugely impoverished.

Language in its classical model begins as the grunt spilling out alongside gesture, the excess to indication, the supplement of ostension, the verbal signifier denoting reference. But eventually the grunt, the excess, the supplement recomplicates into meaning, a system so rich it reverses the hierarchy at precisely the point the grunt becomes a spillage, an excess, a supplement to emotion, need, desire (i.e., becomes itself a gesture indicating something otherwise unseeable, that is: at the first infant cry). In its recomplication it becomes a system able to create and to control meaning on its own, developing in the process its own spillage, excess, supplement—writing— which begins to recomplicate all over again, again upsetting the power hierarchy, contouring it not to its former value but toward a new one. Through its richnesses, meaning has become power. . . .

4. In the traditional paraliterary story/novel series, each new tale critiques the tale (or tales) before it. Is it belaboring the obvious to point out that, in the Nevèrÿon series, earlier tales (e.g., ''The Tale of Old Venn'' and *Neveryóna*) dramatically critique later ones (e.g., ''The Tale of Plagues and Carnivals'') as well . . . ?

5. The Nevèrÿon series takes place at the edge of the shadow of the late French psychiatrist Jacques Lacan, from the slaves who have vacated the collars in the first pages of the first story (gone to what manumissions, executions, or other collars, the child Gorgik never knows, though the rest of his life can be looked at as an attempt to find out) to the series of vanished authorities, such as Lord Aldamir: the Dead Father, the Absent Father, the Name of the Law.

At the same time, I have tried to keep a sharp vigil against the muddling results of an essentialist sexuality. As Michel Foucault warned us so pointedly in a lecture at Stanford a few years back: ''We must get rid of the Freudian schema . . . the schema of the interiorization of the law through the medium of sex.'' I deeply feel that in our current social system, almost all claims of such an interiorization are, today, signs of a potential terrorism, wherever they are made, even by groups as seemingly diverse as orthodox or radical psychiatry, or the Moral Majority, or feminist critics against pornography.

The material power of the present father is the material power of any coercive aggressive individual, male or female, armed or unarmed. But it is only the power to coerce that is in excess of immediate bodily force—the power of the ''absent father''—that constitutes authority in our patriarchal culture as a day-to-day social reality. And it is our habitual insistence on reading all such absent-but-functioning authority as male (even when, as in the case of the ''absent father,'' gender is, indeed, materially absent) and at work, usually, on a feminine ground of ''the natural,'' that stabilizes the socio-economic realities of patriarchal society. Social power-relations, from the way embarking passengers wait at a subway-car door for the former passengers to leave the train, to the way a prisoner receives a sentence of incarceration or death from a judge, are very much a language. They involve understood meanings, always more or less accepted, always more or less challenged, always in excess of bodily coercions—in excess of striking body and rebounding body, i.e., of classical mechanics—that contour appropriate *or* inappropriate behavior. But as long as power, whether it goes with or against the law, is named male, the law itself will *be* male—even if justice is a woman blinded by men, with both her hands occupied maintaining a passive and impossibly difficult balancing act.

As language comes from all that is in excess of gesture (unto containing gesture), so social power/authority comes from all that is in excess of mechanical coercion (unto containing mechanical coercion).

The unconscious is structured, declared Lacan so famously in *Ecrits*, as a language.

Well, so is social power/authority.

Indeed, the totality of social power/authority as it is interiorized for better or for worse by each individual may just *be* the structure of the unconscious.

Do I believe, then, Michael Ryan's assertion with which I opened this volume, i.e., that the impossibility of individuating meanings at the level of the word, which Derrida has so powerfully demonstrated (or at the level of the sentence, which Quine has demonstrated with equal power, though with less fanfare; or at the level of any operationally rich, axiomatic system, which was Gödel's originary contribution—Derrida took the term "undecidability" from Gödel), is a *material* force?

Frankly, I don't know.

But I think the possibility must be seriously considered by anyone interested in either language or power, not to mention their frighteningly elusive, always allusive, and often illusive relations.

6. Lacan, and at this point Lacan's commentators even more so, have led us back to a careful reconsideration of Freud's texts with a focus on language. (Our focus? Freud's? The texts'? Often it is as intriguingly undecidable as the terminal prepositional phrase's antecedent in the previous sentence.)

These rereadings have been scrupulously clarifying, profoundly exciting.

The objection to Freud, however, remains. I do not, of course, mean the problem of "vulgar Freudianism," where metonymies are interpreted as metaphors for their originary terms and situations. The valid Freudian enterprise is rather to discern the several social and psychological systems (clearly distinguishing which is which) by which metonymies exfoliate. And Freud's discovery of the force of sex as it worked among the psychological systems was a great one. The problem was, however, not that Freud paid too much attention to sex, but that—paradoxically—he paid too little attention to it. The nature of his inattention manifested itself as a series of metaphors that exhausted sex by purely social analogues. In the Oedipus Complex, for example, the infantile sexual drive becomes wholly entailed with the *emotions* of jealousy, aggression, and fear, which, after puberty, the sexual urge can, indeed, sometimes evoke when frustrated—though by no means necessarily so. Since the sexual drive is *not* an emotion, but an appetite, this entailment wreaks untold confusions in a theory that is supposed to be dealing with drives: in short, Freud does not deal with the sexual drive as an autonomous function that may (or may not) have its own working rules apart from the shifting emotional calculus in which it is embedded.

Freud's often quoted statement, "There is only one libido, and it is male," is, in biological terms, as much nonsense as the statements: "There is only one hunger, and it is male"; "There is only one itch, and it is male"; "There is only one urge to sneeze, and it is male."

There is only one libido and it is neither male *nor* female. If, however, as a number of feminist commentaries on Lacan (most available among them Juliet Mitchell's *Psychoanalysis and Feminism*, and, with even more flair, Jane Gallop's *The Daughter's Seduction*) suggest, Freud's statement should be interpreted: There is only one libido, but since the subject in order to exist at all must constitute itself in a profoundly patriarchal culture, it is understandable that sexual desire must insert itself into the symbolic (i.e., social) order by the means that are historically set up to receive the signifier of desire, i.e., the phallus, whether one is male *or* female . . .

Well, if that *is* the argument, I feel at the very least it is open to a range of profound and empirically based questions. And a careful study of it will, I suspect, reveal that this is simply another case of naming power male, and the arguments for that naming are simply more circular rationalizations for what is nothing more (or less) than social habit. Indeed, if this argument is *not* profoundly questioned, it becomes a feminist defeatism of the silliest, if not saddest, sort.

The objection to Lacan—a paradox that mirrors our objection to Freud—is that *he* does not pay enough attention to language. I am not talking of Lacan's famously recomplicated and allusive style. Rather, in the range of his theoretical elaboration there is little to suggest that, for all his brilliant speculation on the way language works [in] the mind, he entertains any grasp of the primary function of language, not only in the function and field of psychoanalysis, but in the general cultural scheme of things.

Language is first and foremost a *stabilizer* of behavior, thought, and feeling, of human responses and reactions—both for groups and for individuals. Its aid in intellectual analysis and communication are (one) secondary and (two) wholly entailed with its function as a stabilizing system. (It is precisely by its ability to stabilize reactions at the level of the signified that language creates—or "introduces the subject into"—the Symbolic.) Language by itself can call up sexual responses in the absence of a sexual object—and, sometimes, repress sexual responses in the presence of one. Given the tasks we humans find, fixate on, and imagine, again and again our responses must achieve a variety, complexity, and accuracy surpassing those of other species by enormous factors. If there were not an extensive stabilizing system, that variety, complexity, and accuracy could never be achieved.

When the world is projected through the hierarchical oppositions available to the sensory and sensual body (e.g., dry/wet, light/dark, soft/hard, hot/cold, pleasurable/painful, familiar/strange, easy/difficult, dangerous/safe, awake/asleep, alive/dead), it produces a spectacularly unstable text, its objects and locations metamorphosing between states hour by hour, day by day, year by year—a text in desperate need of stabilization if we would maneuver through it to find food, comfort, community, and sexual gratification, much less if we would control it at all with the more abstract hierarchies language lets us develop (e.g., good/bad, right/wrong, efficient/inefficient, beautiful/ugly, etc.). To reduce the world still further to the merely vaginal/phallic is, first, to make a highly Symbolic elaboration the moment the concepts come loose from the human (and/or animal) genitalia that answer the call of desire, and, second, to make an already unstable text reach a totally chaotic state, since everything has an inside and an outside (the projection of vaginal/phallic), fruits, caves, honeycombs, and streams. In the text of the world, various insides and outsides are simply more or less available.

Vaginal symbols can always be unpacked from phallic symbols. Phallic symbols can always be unpacked from vaginal symbols. This may be why this particularly riotous textual play is among the first to be stabilized in most cultures, one way or the óther. But the question as to why it tends to be stabilized toward the phallic cannot be answered by an uncritical appeal either to Nature or the Imaginary (Lacan's register of presocial, Symbolically innocent image). To make the complex, multiple, and unequal alignment penis/outside/something(presence)/desire on the one hand and vagina/inside/nothing(absence) on the other, while it may indeed be among the most fundamental conceptual align-ments of patriarchal thought and one of the most common in the range of human cultures, is nonetheless a highly complex and Symbolic operation. Indeed, it is at least as Symbolic as aligning hot and cold with high and low (as we do on the temperature scale), or as aligning familiar and strange respec-tively with safe and dangerous (this last, an absolute necessity to patriarchal culture and society, and even more common than the patriarchal vaginal/phallic conceptual alignment—though by no means universal). The Imaginary register might, indeed, cover the alignment of penis with outside and vagina with inside. But as soon as we get to the conceptual alignment of desire (much less presence and absence), we are clearly on Symbolic grounds. There are too many "natural" vaginal aspects of desire (e.g., wet, open), so that exclusion of this whole vaginal complex of aspects from an alignment with desire *must* be a Symbolic choice. Indeed, when we look at the male genitalia in Symbolic terms, and the entailed move-ment from flaccid (smaller, soft, more protected) to erect (larger, hard, more vulnerable) and back, the real Symbolic organization of patriarchal culture becomes remarkably clear: larger and hard are Symbolically aligned with male and strength in a single conceptual unit by the same Symbolic act with which the vulnerability of the male genitalia during erection is omitted from mention.

And, sadly, along with vulnerability, desire remains outside this particular fundamental, patriarchal Symbolic complex, which should rightly be named "the phallus" in patriarchal, phallocentric culture. And it is the fact that the phallus is the Symbolic unit that conjoins the notions of masculinity, greater relative size, hardness, and power in the same gesture with which it *omits* vulnerability and desire is the real tragedy of the phallus. But when this Symbolic unit is *used* as a "signifier of desire" (i.e., used to stabilize those responses by which the desired may be possessed, controlled, and exchanged) we are talking about social exploitation, and social exploitation largely of women.

The masculinist bias in the language of patriarchal society and culture in general, and in psychoanalytic terminology in particular, from "phallus," "castration," and "There is only one libido, and it is male," to "absent father" and the exemplary "he," is not the producer of the problem. But it most definitely stabilizes responses and patterns of response *to* the problem—responses now of individuals, now of groups.

A European study of the 1970s has shown that Italian mothers who breast-feed their infants wean their girl children 40 percent earlier, on the average, than they wean their sons. An American study of the same decade has shown that the average white-collar American father physically handles his under-a-year-old infant of either sex less than five *seconds* a day. Male children under five receive on the average more than five times the amount of physical contact, both from their parents and from other adults of both sexes, than do female children of the same age. Infants handled primarily by one adult for their first eighteen months tend to be frightened of strangers and less secure as children than infants handled consistently by two or more adults for their first eighteen months. These and a host of like facts may just *be* among the strongest empirical causes for "patriarchal culture." As one collects more and more of them, one begins to read from them a relative brutalization of the female body and the female psyche in infancy and early childhood that manifests itself in any general collection of male and female adults, in terms of adult physicality, attitude, and behavior; and they may directly or indirectly control both the Imaginary and the Symbolic orders well before the infant grows into her or his *stade du miroir*—that is, before the phallus (as opposed to the female genitalia or the male genitalia) is perceived as a signifier or anything else.

Language is a stabilizer among our responses to the world and to our problems in it. When the stabilizing system is so powerful and important as to make our responses as we recognize them, for all practical purposes (whether they are good responses or bad ones), possible, it is tempting to view the stabilizing system itself as causative of the responses if the responses are judged good, and causative of the problems themselves if the responses are judged bad (i.e., if the responses exacerbate the problems or just allow them to continue). But with the concept of stabilization of response, we can accept the overlap in both these cases while still avoiding its seductive confusions.

To make real changes in patriarchal society and culture will require complex, intricate, and accurate behavior. And things *can* be done about the empirical problems if our responses are stabilized by language.

Lacan's commentators in all of this, however, seem to have forgotten the Saussurean ground rule on which the superstructure of their theoretical elaboration is based: "The sign—the signifier—is arbitrary." It is terribly and terrifyingly easy to create signifiers. If one wants a bowl, the letter "V," the cunt, a twin-tined sword, or, indeed, a macramé tea-cozy to be "a signifier of desire" or anything else, one has merely to speak (write, or even gesture): "Let it signify..."

And it is so.

Resistance to the process *always* comes from a signified, initially constituted by social habit, which can finally be overcome by social usefulness—at which point the useful (always adjusted by society away from its initial theoretical formulation, sometimes for the better, sometimes for the worse) becomes a new social habit itself; but it is precisely within social sedimentation that these battles must be fought. And the "anthropological" evidence that there are "more phallic symbols than all other sorts put together" is only to deny the overwhelming preponderance of pottery, baskets, and containers in general among the tools, functional or symbolic, of "man"-kind. Even for me to claim a masculinistly biased reading at this point simply makes blatant how socially malliable the process of reading (i.e., symbol interpretation) is—and to show how much more of what Lacanians take to be

"Imaginary" is, in fact, like so much else, Symbolic. But when a goblet such as the Holy Grail can be renamed "the phallus," clearly there is nothing "Imaginary" going on here. Such a naming is entirely Symbolic.

To fix appropriate signifiers to appropriate powers, functions, and artifacts is, certainly, no *less* a Symbolic alignment than any that patriarchal society has used to stabilize itself. But that mutual appropriateness must be determined by what one wants the conjunction to stabilize in an always changing social field.

Any two parallel lines create a vaginal symbol. Any two intersecting lines create a vaginal symbol. Cups, containers, and circles create vaginal symbols. In short, human cultures are inundated with them. The question is not why there are "more phallic symbols than all other sorts put together." The question is: Why have the plethora of vaginal symbols not been named? And the answer is that the vast majority of cultures are patriarchal, and patriarchy usually entails, among other things, leaving much that is female outside of language.

History does not exist without theory.

Images do not exist without interpretation.

But it is a very old demystification we undertake here. To claim that what was considered Imaginary is, in fact, Symbolic, is simply another case of claiming that what was once considered Nature is, in fact, Culture. And I can only hope some of our more sophisticated psychoanalytic theorists can recognize that claim for what it is, can recall the history of such claims in our past, and can admit what is at risk by cutting short their analysis where they do.

I am not saying that there is no Imaginary register at all. I am simply saying that it is much smaller than Lacanians traditionally perceive it; as well, it is far more entailed in the Symbolic than, in the case of all things libidinal, they traditionally read it. And when we get to the point of calling grails and cunts "phalluses," this is a good sign that we are far away from the Imaginary and are, rather, about as *deeply* enmired within the Symbolic—within the social—as it is possible to be.

Our earliest and originary Judeo-Christian myth tells us that Adam alone had the right to name—that is, he had the triple right, first, to divide up the world into the semantic units most useful for him, second, to organize those units into the fictions that would stabilize what was most useful to him to

have stable, and, third, to exclude from language whatever
was most convenient for him to leave unspoken. If we want a
world where not only freedom of speech, but freedom of
social determination exists for both sexes, women must seize
this triple right to name, seize it violently and hold to it
tenaciously; and they must use it for something more than
simply retelling *his* old tales. For those tales were what
stabilized patriarchal society in the first place. But only if
they seize and use this right will they be able to stabilize
reactions in both men and women at a fine enough precision
to bring about the desired revolution in patriarchal society and
culture. If women commit this seizure, that revolution, however
painful, may still be a comparatively peaceful one.

If they do not, it will be a bloody one. For, once again,
language is *not* the problem—only a tool to help with solutions.

But at this point the historical battle to name the law and to
effect its constitution within an always-to-be-created society
and culture—already a with less patriarchal for sustaining the
conflict even the length of time it takes to name it—has
always-already begun. And certainly nothing I, a man, have
written, write here, or could write possibly represents or
expresses its origin.

7. If, as it turns to examine the interplay between the healthy
and the pathological, psychoanalysis would untangle specific
failures of the stabilizing system, or would examine ways in
which the stabilizing system itself is unstable or, indeed,
would explore response patterns stabilized in undesirable
ways, all well and good. But it must be prepared to find
destabilizing systems, counterstabilizing systems, and reactions and responses simply too great to be stabilized by the
systems available (reactions both social and psychological),
many if not most of them nonlinguistic. But only with its
object so clarified can psychoanalysis proceed on any front
with any lasting efficacy.

8. The excerpt from Ryan's preface that introduces this
volume ends with a footnote commending the reader to a
number of articles by Gayatri Chakravorty Spivak (from
whose introduction to her translation of Derrida's *Of
Grammatology* I took the motto for the first volume of these
tales), among them: *"Il faut en s'en prenant à elles,"* in *Les
fins de l'homme* (Paris, 1981); "Revolutions that as Yet Have

No Model: Derrida's 'Limited Inc.,'" *Diacritics* 10, no. 4 (Winter 1980); "Finding Feminist Readings: Dante and Yeats," *Social Texts* 3 (Fall 1980); "Unmaking and Making in *To the Lighthouse*," in *Women and Language in Literature and Society* (New York, 1980); "Three Feminist Readings: McCullers, Drabble, Habermas," *Union Seminary Quarterly Review* 35, nos. 1 and 2 (Fall-Winter 1979–80); "Explanation and Culture: Marginalia," *Humanities in Society* 2, no. 3 (Summer 1979); "Displacement and the Discourse of Women," in *Displacement: Derrida and After*, edited by Mark Krupnick, Indiana University Press (1983); "Sex and History in *The Prelude* (1805): Books 9–13," in *Texas Studies in Language and Literature;* "Reading the World: Literary Studies in the 80s," in *College English*; and "French Feminism in an International Frame," *Yale French Studies*.

Let me iterate Ryan's commendation.

In a sense, modern philosophy is a series of introductions to introductions to introductions, the movement between them controlled by the pro-te $\frac{c}{x}$ tive play of forces about desire.

9. Early on, it occurred to me that the relationship of the Nevèrÿon series to semiotics/semiology might be, for better or for worse, much like that of Van Vogt's Null-A series to General Semantics.

I have tried to leave the odd sign of this in the text.

10. Davenport plumbs *Pausanias* (Volume II, Penguin edition, pp. 355–364) for souvenirs of Elis and its resident Skeptic; Mabbott (or Julian Symons? That's where I found it) for young Poe's bogus Russian romp; perhaps Maurois for Hugo's visit, from his exile in Jersey, to Guernsey. But that's very different from the historical enterprise of Nevèrÿon; different from the way I comb Braudel or, for that matter, the *Native*'s D'Eramo.

11. But origins are always constructs, always contouring ideological agendas.

What other kinds of origins, then, am I drawn to discuss? What other kinds or origins am I drawn to exclude?

12. Childhood readings of Robert E. Howard, descriptions by various friends over the years of Leiber's Fafhrd and the Gray Mouser, Moore's Jeryl, Moorcock's Elric? Finally, I

suppose, Russ's *Alyx* series and the introduction for its initial volume assemblage: but those are public precursors for any reader to infer.

I can remember others.

The first Nevèrÿon story, for example, was never finished, never titled; its two fragments, as far as I know, were lost.

In London in 1973, while I was completing the first draft of *Triton* and "Shadows," waiting for my daughter to get born, this image struck:

To a sequestered corral, somewhere near the mountain hold of fabled Ellamon, delinquent girls were sent for incarceration from all over the prehistoric land. There they were put to work as grooms and riders for a breed of flying dragon, local to the mountains, which, for some generations now, had been under Imperial protection.

I made two written starts into this imaginary visitation, both of which I thought might become one tale.

One ran to perhaps a dozen typewritten pages:

In a wagon caravan also carrying goods and stores for the mountain hold, a girl of fifteen was being transported from a primitive city, where she'd been convicted of stealing some coins, to the mountain reformatory. Her overseer was a foreign, Amazon-like woman named Raven, who wore a black rag mask across her eyes and who was to work as a guard at the prison once she had delivered her charge.

In the midst the caravan journey through the forested slopes, bandits attacked the wagons, and, with bow and arrow, Raven killed their chief. (She was a crack shot.) During the attack, she gave the girl some orders, but, more hypnotized than frightened by the violence, the girl did not respond. She was so unused to taking orders, especially from another woman, that it didn't even occur to her to obey—even to save her life and the lives of the others around her. Raven was not so much angered or bewildered by the girl's paralysis as amused. She speculated that a time in the reformatory with other young women criminals might do the girl good. The bandits were driven off, but as the caravan resumed its journey, the girl, who'd always thought of herself as an adventurous, dangerous, and independant sort, was both fascinated and repelled by this foreign woman who killed men for rational reasons.

The other, six-page fragment, written perhaps three weeks

earlier, detailed an incident that occurred some weeks later, with the girl now having become an inmate at the dragon corral and Raven having taken up her job among the guards.

The corral had something of a reputation throughout that primitive land, and from time to time men tried to break into it in hope of the sex to be had there from the young criminals. Led by an older inmate, a young woman possibly psychotic, a group of girls (including the newcomer) had captured such an interloper that morning. Binding his hands behind him, they hung him from a wooden rack (was it built for the purpose...?) by one leg.

Over a day and night, the delinquents tortured, maimed, and—finally—killed him.

Was there some question as to whether the man was a willing victim, who'd let himself be captured and bound, under the impression that the delinquent girls, after they had "enjoyed" him, would set him free...?

Raven learned from the other guards that such male invasions happened two or three times a year—and always with the same end. When men penetrated the mountain reformatory, the more experienced women who guarded the youngsters looked the other way and let them do as they would. At first, when Raven (like the young man) thought the girls would "enjoy" him and let him go, she'd even allowed some of the girls to sneak off to take part. Later, when she accidentally came upon the actual torture, however, she was deeply troubled—particularly by the participation of the girl she'd brought to the compound. While Raven could conceive of killing men (or women) for reasons of self-defense, this Dionysiac slaughter was, to her, deranged—though, unsettlingly, on discovering it, she could not bring herself to step in and stop it, almost as if she suffered from the same paralysis as had her young charge earlier.

That evening Raven decided she would not remain there as a guard but would leave the dragon corral the next morning and go elsewhere...

A third, unwritten scene was probably why the fragments never joined in a single tale. For the strongest of my initial visions was that, at the story's end, the newly imprisoned girl would ride gloriously through the air on the back of a flying dragon—

I begin, a sentence lover, an SF writer; which means I am stuck, willy-nilly, with a certain grammar, a certain logic. It

The Hanged Man from the
FitzGerald *Tarot*, drawn over
'67 and '68; Copyright '69

seemed important that my young prisoner not escape (or die!) at the (potential) story's end. ("Escape" was something only Raven, by her decision, was free to do.) But the notion of all these young criminals, grooming and riding their own means to freedom but never actually *using* them, no matter what limitations they'd internalized through whatever social pressures, no matter how terrible the jungle or rock or desert they might have to struggle in when their dragons landed, seemed an oddity that, finally, just meant there *was* no story.

Similarly, Raven's inability to bring herself to stop the slaughter of the young man seemed as unbelievable as the girl's inability to do anything to help when the caravan was attacked.

Both finally lacked what T. S. Eliot's generation called "objective correlatives," and mine, "psychological veracity."

These two moments of feminine paralysis on which everything hinged were "literature" in its most degraded sense. Neither reflected in any interesting way anything I'd known of women or men in any real situation of material pressure, and both reflected all too much the psychological clichés for heroines of fifties' action-adventure movies.

I felt, and still feel, that it is important for fantasy to have a grasp of the *complexity* of fact, if not of factual content.

So the tale was put aside.

In December 1974, just before Christmas, after a stay of almost two years to the day, I returned from London to New York. When various papers were sent after me, the fragments were not among them.

I haven't seen them since.

In some parallel world that tale may have been written, with all its excesses, unbelievabilities, and contradictions— the distortions that would make it "work" committed largely on the personality of the foreign guard, on her young charges

It's not my world.

Nevertheless, it remains in memory as one lost origin of Nevèrÿon: those two fragments, with the unwritten third, were the logical and grammatical violences against the real, torn apart, recast, recontoured, critiqued, reformed, elaborated in all their various atomika, and their atomika rejoined as this set of intricate lies that have tethered me to this odd structure, the Nevèrÿon series (built for what purpose . . . ?), a decade now.

* * *

13. "The history of thought is the history of its models," Fredric Jameson writes in the opening of his preface to *The Prison House of Language*.

14. The problem as some feminists have articulated it (most recently and brilliantly, Teresa de Lauretis, in *Alice Doesn't— Feminism, Semiotics, Cinema,* Indiana University Press, 1984), is the exclusion of woman as "historical subject" from an overwhelmingly male discourse. This exclusion has been effected by yet another logical contradiction of man: historically, woman has been projected again and again as the subject side of man (i.e., as nature, mystery, the unknown, the site of absence of the social constraints on which all society is grounded, the site of uncontrolled desire) and at once the object of man (sign of male social position, a source of cheap or unpaid labor, the desired object, and the unitary exchange commodity that at once binds, coheres, and generates patriarchal society-as-a-collection-of-bodies).

I would suggest that, theoretically, this "exclusion of woman as historical subject" is a false problem (i.e., a misreading); I would further suggest that, within patriarchal society, the notion of "historical subjects" itself stabilizes the contradiction and thus encourages the exclusion. The real problem, as I see it, is not the apparent contradiction between woman as subject and woman as object and the exclusion it seems to achieve. It is rather the obvious complicity between the denial, first, of woman as historical object and the denial, second, of woman as transhistorical subject: these twin denials, which have nothing contradictory about them, are the real mechanism for the exclusion of women from a cultural discourse, which, by that exclusion, stablizes their social, psychological, and sexual exploitation—an exploitation largely carried out in over-whelmingly economic terms. I truly believe that, restated in this wise, the theoretical side of the problem is solved much the way the goose is gotten out of the bottle in the famous Zen koan. What is left for theory in practical terms, after this theoretical revision, is the specific assertion of women as historical object (research, history, speculation on where woman have been and what they have done) and the assertion of the historical constitution of women as transhistorical subject (how has it been brought about). Lacan and Foucault both would seem to agree that this is identical with the constitution of "man" as transhistorical subject. Certainly there must be an overlap: men and women are less than a chromosome apart. But the very existence of a feminist critique, totally aside from any rightness or wrongness of any of its elements, means that identity does not cover the case.

What the pursuit of the false problem has unearthed that is valid nevertheless can be easily represented under the theoretical rubrics of the constitution of woman as transhistorical subject and woman as historical object.

But the truth embodied in the ideological strategy as I have outlined it should be as axiomatic for the poststructuralists as the earlier Saussurian postulate, "The sign is arbitrary," was axiomatic for the structuralist enterprise against which the array of poststructuralist positions arose in dialogue: "The subject *is* transhistorical." For that is only another way of saying that the subject is fallible: it can, and will, make mistakes.

The transhistoricity of the subject is, of course, an illusion; but it is an inescapable illusion, without which there *is* no subject. (It is, indeed, the ego's belief in itself.) To offer perhaps a somewhat strained analogy: cinema is an illusion constituted of successive frames of light projected on a screen. But without the light or a screen, there is no cinema— no illusion. The subject is a similar illusion, constituted of a sequence of historical responses projected within the sentient body. But without either history or the sentient body, there is no subject—no illusion. Needless to say, the relation between "successive" historical responses is far more complex than that between the frames of a film; and at that syntactic level of complexity of relation and at the neurological level of complexity of the body in which these relations register, we have a human system quite complex enough for, and capable of, true freedom. (Determinism or indeterminism? No, *that* is not where the "illusion" lies.) The historical question is, then, what makes women (or men) experience themselves as transhistorical at *one* point in history; what makes them experience themselves as transhistorical at *another* point. And the structure of oppression is as constitutive of that illusion as the organization of strengths. Historically, these things change for women, for men.

To assert that the subject is always transhistorical (and thus an illusion) is in no way one with the assertion that the historical process of the subject's constitution must (therefore) remain totally opaque and beyond all research and theory. It is simply to say that researchers and theoreticians alike must be careful—and on the watch for errors.

Nor do I mean that progress cannot (or has not) been made under the theoretical program of "historical subjects"—which, in this society, are traditionally male—and its inescapable implication of a transhistorical object, always desired (by whom?), always absent (from what?), an eternally missing factor from the male dominated version of history save as the signifier of desire—the phallus, which woman (supposedly) *is*, but by which she is, the moment she threatens to appear in the Imaginary, displaced by and replaced with a male image, which results in her repression from the Symbolic order through a conspiracy of signs suspiciously similar to, if not identical with, the program by which her productions in society (imaginary, symbolic, and—*pace* Lacan—real), as well as all their rewards, are appropriated by, revalued by, and renamed by men, a program both men and women can recognize as exploitative and oppressive. I mean, rather, that such a verbal theoretical expression centering around the retrieval of "historical subjects" does not *stabilize* the progress made under its rubric. The progress is made—but it tends to be forgotten very quickly, because it is already infiltrated by, and therefore soon dispersed by, the subject myths of patriarchal history with which, unless it remains insistently and programmatically critical of the theory that stabilizes them, it is so intimately entailed.

Counterstabilization, at this point, is necessary.

15. "What is the Modular Calculus?" a reader writes.

The modular calculus began as a science fictional notion that turns out to be somewhat related to the famous Finagle Factor (that illusive constant sought by all researchers, by which the wrong answer is adjusted to get the right one).

Quine has talked about "fitting grammars" and "guiding grammars." In more informal terms, there can be perfectly accurate descriptions of systems, of situations, or even of machines, which, while they tell us what these systems, situations, and machines look like, how they move, how they function (that is, tell us how they *might* work) nevertheless do not indicate how they *do* work. Similarly, there are explanations that tell us, accurately and precisely, how something actually does work, so that we can both recognize and (potentially) construct an object that works in the same way—though often those explanations will not let us recognize the initial object from which the grammar was derived (it doesn't necessarily tell us whether it was a green one or a red one, if its being green or red is not part of its workings) should we stumble over it in life. The first is, more or less, a fitting grammar. The second is, more or less, a guiding grammar. (And a description rich in *both* fitting and guiding elements is what anthropologist Clifford Geertz calls a "thick description.")

The modular calculus is an algorithm or set of algorithms (a set of fixed operations) that can be applied to any fitting grammar to adjust it into a guiding grammar.

A limit case, however, strongly suggests such an algorithm is a total fantasy:

"There is a large red box with a button on one end and a light on the other. When you press the button, sometimes the light goes on; sometimes it does not." The description might go on to include a *possible* circuit that would cause the described switch-and-light operations to occur. There is our fitting grammatical description of an object.

The modular calculus, if such a thing existed, would be a fixed set of algorithms one could apply to this description that would then produce a template of the actual circuitry inside the box, i.e., would give the guiding grammar for the situation.

Well, since there are an infinite number of "circuits" that could bring about these results, some involving mechanical means, some involving electrical means, some involving electronic means, and many, many, many involving combinations of two or all three, obviously no algorithm could specify which *particular* circuit was *necessarily* inside the box from only our guiding description.

We can push our limit case a step further: "There is a large red box with a button on one end and a light on the other end. When the botton is pushed, the light does not go on."

The modular calculus would, again, allow us to know from only this much what is in the box.

Since this box may contain nothing, or, indeed, any broken circuit ever envisioned, or any number of working circuits that just do other things, or a donkey, or a set of the *Encyclopaedia Britannica*, the modular calculus seems again reduced to a fantasy at one with a magic that not only lets you see through walls but also assures that you will understand what you see when you do.

If we allow a certain critical margin into the notion of the modular calculus, however, we at least move back to the realm of science fiction:

Clearly descriptions that grow richer in certain directions move closer to accurate functional explanation; certain descriptions as they become enriched in certain ways take on explanatory force. Also, certain descriptions seem to take on explanatory force that they then don't live up to. Others suggest explanations that turn out simply to be wrong.

Might there be an algorithm or set of algorithms that would tell us how close or how far a given description is from explanation, or that would tell us, from a given description, what kind of explanations may eventually be possible from it, or where the description might be further enriched to achieve explanation. For a limited set of situations, such algorithms might be developed and generalized.

In short, the problem of the modular calculus is: How do we know when we have a model of a situation; and how do we tell what kind of model it is?

16. Clearly the Nevèrÿon series is a model of late twentieth-century (mostly urban) America. The question is, of course: What kind of model is it?

This is not the same question as: Is it accurate or is it inaccurate? Rather: What sort of relation does it bear to the thing modeled?

Rich, eristic, and contestatory (as *well* as documentary), I hope.

17. "Master, save thyself," the well-traveled merchant who had been to Asia and Portugal told his younger brother, the London saddler and narrator of Daniel Defoe's *Journal of the Plague Years* (1722), before going off to join his wife and two children whom he had already evacuated to Bedfordshire.

Yet that strangely faceless, bachelor tradesman (Henry Foe, uncle of Daniel, thirty-five when the Great Plague struck London in 1665...? Daniel himself was five in the year of the plague and "invented" his well-researched memoir only

after news of Marseille's plague of 1720 reached London and
he was over sixty) stayed on in the city, despite his older
brother's advice, out of a combination of self-interest, acedia,
and an odd set of religious scruples (that we, certainly, read as
a rationalization, or at any rate a stabilization, of the first two
motives): while absently turning through his Bible, his finger
fell on the Ninety-first Psalm: ''. . . there shall no evil befall
thee; neither shall any plague come nigh thy dwelling.'' I say
odd, because it makes him cleave to a kind of theological
determinism (God has ordained all things) that is one with the
Asian religion he has been decrying in the account of his
brother only a page or so before.

18. All novelistic narrative, at least from the Richardson/Fielding
dialogue on, takes place more or less against the following
grid: Imagine an equal number of male and female characters.
Now divide both into upper class, middle class, and working
class, an equal number of males and females in each. Now,
for each class and sex, divide your characters into children,
adults, and oldsters. For the more modern tale-teller, the grid
can be refined even more. Split each of the resultant groups
into equal numbers of heterosexuals and homosexuals. If
working class, middle class, and upper class is too gross a
division, we can add students, teachers, blue-collar, white-
collar, management, manual, service workers, civil servants,
and artists, at all levels. A major division must be made along
racial lines: for the United States, white, black, Amerindian,
Oriental, and Hispanic, with most certainly intermediate groups
between all of them. If, similarly, youth, maturity, and age
seems too gross a set of divisions, they can be further
shattered into children, adolescents, young adults, middle-
agers, elderly, and aged. But this chart, this grid must
eventually specify every possible racial/social/age/gender/sexual
type, all of which become ideally equal through their ideal
accessibility on this fictive grid.
  Like the novel itself, this chart has nothing to do with the
statistical prevalence of any one group in our society. (The
Victorian novel would lead one to believe that most middle-
class unmarried women worked as governesses, while at the
same time there were almost no prostitutes in London—whereas
in fact there were remarkably few such governesses [probably

under two hundred in any one year] and possibly in excess of eighty thousand prostitutes in the city.) It is an ideal chart of possibilities.

Immediately on this imaginary chart we must be able to locate the sixty-four-year-old upper-class homosexual Hispanic woman comic-book artist as easily as the twenty-eight-year-old heterosexual lower-middle-class white male private detective.

Next, we must consider a set of novelistic relations: Friendship; sexual love; enmity; economic antagonism; religious approval; etc. Another generation of the grid must be set up where any and all the "characters" can relate to any and all of the others (including characters of their own type) by any one of the possible novelistic relations.

This, of course, only gives us beginning points and end points in possible two-character subplots.

Given any two characters, in any relation, that relation must be seen as having the potential to change into any other. Again, the modern storyteller may always want to complicate this grid further by considering also possible relations between three, or even more, characters, that, in the course of the story, change not between two states, but move through three or more...

That we can, however mistily, conceive of this grid (and I was twenty when I first began to contemplate its multiple intricacies), even as we acknowledge the impossibility of ever completing it in the abstract, much less of actually writing the Great Novel that portrays, with insight, accuracy, and invention, examples of all that grid's combinations and developments, that conception nevertheless allows us to make some purely qualitative observations about the wealth of bourgeois fictions that take place against it, whether the individual novel privileges a single aging working-class man fishing alone off Cuba in his boat, who barely relates now and again to a young, working-class boy, as in Hemingway's *Old Man and the Sea*, or a single elderly working-class woman fishing alone through an absolute chaos of social interrelationships in Canada, as in Sheila Watson's *The Double Hook*.

This grid—as various novelists begin to impose on it their various economies, for their various conscious and unconscious reasons, picking out this character for a hero, that relationship for development, condensing some while blithely ignoring these, those, and the others—supplies us with the ideological contours of the individual novel as it is foregrounded against any historical or statistical grouping of texts. ("Why, through the range of post–World War II American fiction, are friendships between women almost entirely absent until the 1960s?") Yet it also allows us to bracket that ideological weight momentarily because we can at least be secure that every novel has one. ("Because the return of the male work force from the army made possible the destruction of female solidarity in an economy in which driving women out of work and replacing them with male veterans could be fairly easily stabilized by continuing and developing only slightly a preexistent narrative/language tradition." This is an ugly, wholly criticizable, but historically accurate answer—at least in terms of a fitting grammar.)

This grid is what allows us to ask of any fiction: Precisely what does it have to say in excess of its ideological reduction? What does it say in excess of the location of its elements on this grid and the subsequent revelation of vast and overdetermined absences? The deconstructionists have led off this set of new readings most energetically by asking of certain texts: "What do they have to say that specifically undermines and subverts their own ideological array?" As energetic as the deconstructionist foray has been, we must remember that there are still going to be many texts for which we can expect the answer: "Not much."

19. Basil Davenport's fictions have given me more pleasure than those of any single writer I've read in the past three years. Initially I respond to them with complete emotional bewilderment as to why anyone could *want* to write the particular tales he does—why anyone would use what of the method as I can divine beneath his web of allusions and reconstructions. (Is it disingenuous of me to say I find tales such as "Apples and Pears" and *"O Gadjo Niglo"* most interesting when they are at their least homoerotic? Probably. What happens when *"Het Erewhonisch Sketsboek"* reaches the 18th Brumaire?) Within what defines for me, then, an arena of almost total dispassion, Davenport brings me again and again to breath-lost awe at the beauties he manages to construct in that lucid, glimmering language field.

"Robot"
"Dawn in Erewhon"
"The Death of Picasso"
These stories (with the greatest "content," and thus the

greatest accessibility for the reader beginning to enter Davenport's worlds) are among the most carefully constructed art works I know. (In "On Some Lines of Virgil" I only wish Jonquille could have been anchored to parents, home, landscape, and material life with the same precise, lush, and vivid calculus of writerly invention he lavishes so effortlessly on his boys; but it is an old complaint, an old exclusion.) In my personal pantheon they rank with "To Here and the Easle," *La Princesse de Cleves,* "The Graveyard Heart," "The Dead," "The Second Inquisition," "The Metamorphosis," *Le Bal du Compte d'Orgel,* "The Asian Shore," or *Nightwood.* Yet, where one goes after that, amidst Davenport's constructions, delineates where the *unique* pleasure of his envisionings will be found.

The effect for me is totally aesthetic and awesomely pleasurable—or, as I have taken to saying somewhat glibly to my friends: Davenport's tales are rich in everything I personally love about fiction, and almost wholly devoid of what in fiction, today, bores me.

Frankly, I cannot imagine anyone having that initial response of emotional bewilderment to the impetus behind *any* of the Nevèrÿon tales, whatever one thinks of their execution. (In at least one very important sense, its rhetorical urgencies make "The Tale of Plagues and Carnivals" the *least* experimental of the series.) Yet I can imagine a hugely changed world, not a hundred years away, but only ten or twenty hence, where that, indeed, would be precisely the response of the common reader to these stories. That world would be, in many ways, the world I conceive of as a Utopia. In short, I suppose, I write yearning for a world in which all these stories might be *merely* "beautiful."

20. "What are 'Some Informal Remarks toward the Modular Calculus'?" another reader writes.

They are a model of a system.

"Some Informal Remarks toward the Modular Calculus" includes, as Part One, the science fiction novel *Triton* and, as Part Two, "Appendix B" of that novel, "Ashima Slade and the Harbin-Y Lectures." From its position in that book, it is undecidable whether "Appendix A: From the Triton Journal" is or is not a part of Part One. The "Informal Remarks" do *not* include the first five tales in the Nevèrÿon series. The "Appendix" to the first five tales, however, forms Part Three

of the "Informal Remarks." The novel *Neveryóna, or the
Tale of Signs and Cities* is Part Four of the "Informal
Remarks." From their position in that book it is undecidable
whether or not "Appendix A: The Culhar' Correspondance"
or "Appendix B: Acknowledgments" is or is not part of Part
Four. The first two tales of this volume are *not* part of the
"Informal Remarks." The first appendix and third tale,
"Appendix A: The Tale of Plagues and Carnivals," constitutes Part Five of the "Informal Remarks." Again, from their
position, it is undecidable whether these concluding notes,
constituting this second appendix ("Appendix B: Openings
and Closures"), are or are not a part.

21. Any series written over a period of years and published
piecemeal must support inconsistencies. The self-critical nature of the serial form practically insures it; and Alexei
Panshin, writer of that most charming of SF series, the
Villiers books, has even argued that this is a good thing and
claims to have inserted inconsistencies on purpose, volume to
volume. Nevertheless, readers like coherence. And occasionally
even the writer herself or himself glances back at an earlier
tale with a revisionary pang.

I certainly would be happy if any of my readers would
revise the last section of the sixth paragraph on page eight of
"The Tale of Gorgik," in *Tales of Nevèrÿon* (the second
printing or later, that is, with the delightful Rowena cover), to
read: "The pit slave's name was Noyeed. He was fourteen.
He had lost an eye three months back: the wound had never
been dressed and had not really healed. He had a fever. He
was shivering. Bleeding gums had left his mouth scabby. Dirt
had made his flesh scaly. He had been at the mines two
months and was not expected to last a third. Seeing this as a
reasonable excuse, seven men two nights ago had abused the
boy cruelly and repeatedly—hence the limp."

The changes there, in the first tale, largely in the lengths of
time connected with this first mention of Noyeed, seem today
to launch him through the subsequent eight at a better trajectory
to join with his final flight in the last.

Similarly, on page 156 and again on page 159 of that first
volume, in "The Tale of Potters and Dragons," if the reader
will lop five years from each of Madame Keyne's mentions of
her age, some occurrences in the subsequent volume, *Neveryóna*,
will make more dramatic sense.

Indeed, in that first volume, the careful reader will find several inconsistencies in the spelling of the river "Khora" and the suburb "Sallese." Also, there, the accent on "Neveryóna" flops from grave to acute with disarming irregularity. That book contains the odd misspelling (*boney* for *bony*, *scaley* for *scaly*, *velum* for *vellum*, *mullet* for *millet*, and *verdigrised* for *verdigris*) and the odd misplaced apostrophe (4/7/4, 94/3/5) or comma (3/1/11, 130/1/3, and 135/2/3). But these I leave to the diligent reader's marginal markings.

There are, however, a number of other writerly inelegances in the first volume that I long to correct. I list those most painful to me here. Both above and below, the numbers separated by virgules indicate page/paragraph/line(s), followed by the line (or lines) as it (or they) should properly read:

2/2/13:
shirts on bony shoulders, loose or tight around

3/1/1&2:
stringy or fleshy necks, and sometimes even hidden
under jeweled pieces of damasked cloth set with

3/1/9:
some two dozen, cross-legged on the gritty floor-

17/6/3&4:
small, low-ceilinged room with a slit window just
behind her own suite. The stones of the floor and

17/6/8&9:
the end of the first month, both the Vizerine and her
steward had all but lost interest in him. But several

17/6/11&12:
at various private suppers of seven to fourteen
guests in the several dining rooms of her suite, all

22/2/7:
grooved into the floors; dozens of small, lightless cells

25/1/14:
Gorgik might have been, had the play of power five

72/1/12:
at the edge of the net houses to peek at them strolling the

107/2/12:
her shoulders thin.

111/1/5:
short kilt of a cloth made all of interlocked metal

111/4/12:
to have more to do with her talents as a fisherwoman

121/3/2&3:
dark, blotched with fading embers), she turned and
walked back to the woods.

130/3/3:
the evening. Light slanted across dust, scaled like

131/1/1:
some reptile, with myriad lapping footprints; a spilled

134/11/6:
on the waterfront; but without guild protection. Got

135/2/3:
She spoke suddenly, in a sharp and shrill voice that

136/2/9:
narrow back, and wound it high on the other

136/8/1:
   He wasn't a good looking boy. His

143/5/8&9:
other.'' Gorgik's fingers on the barbarian's shoulder
tightened.

146/5/2:
dapplings, squatted too, folding her arms on her own

156/2/4:
Let's sit out under one of those awnings in the front

157/1/13:
who, if we sit out under the awnings, will think their

Any reader (or rereader) of the first volume of this series who makes these adjustments will probably have a smoother narrative ride across Nevèrÿon's textual complexities.

The mass-market (i.e., rack-size) edition of *Neveryóna* corrects some two dozen similar infelicities from the initial, trade paperback (i.e., large-size) edition. Still, some mistakes were missed. Thus, in the rack-size *Neveryóna,* at 18/4/10, the word "pediment" should of course be "pedestal." On the same page, above, at the end of 18/10/3, the word "slowly" should simply be omitted. And on the next page, at 19/1/6, the word "way" should be inserted after "her" in the phrase "making her by broken walls." (This omission wasn't in the trade paperback; and in the age of computer typesetting, it can only make you wonder . . .) On the contents page "Appendix A" has lost its "d." For reasons that still confound me, whoever was assigned to take care of corrections also took it upon himself or herself to insert a wholly disfiguring "a" in the word "scientifiction" at 438/2/11 and to drop a hyphen at the end of 427/1/21. On page 32 the first word of the last paragraph should be "Then" and not "The." At 109/6/4 the third word, "voiced," should of course be "voice." And the line at 115/1/5 should begin: "than it does." (The first "for" should be omitted.)

Readers with the previous two volumes are invited to make these adjustments.

The production folk at Bantam are a kind, careful, and conscientious lot. If my readers, in searching out these errors should find that some or (blessedly!) all of them have been corrected in a printing beyond the second, then she or he should smile and simply consider this note a glimpse into the effort necessary, not only on my part but on theirs, to achieve a bit of orthographic and stylistic punctilio in a set of sword-and-sorcery tales set in the long-ago distant never.

It would seem that any rich system tends to function through an interchange between what is inside the system and what is outside the system (with what is outside frequently fueling the system proper): and there are always certain elements, such as this appendix, which are undecidable as to whether they are inside or outside—often, though not always, those parts that encourage definition and revision.

ABOUT THE AUTHOR

Born in 1942, SAMUEL R. DELANY grew up in New York City. His science fiction novels include a trilogy generally known by its collective title *The Fall of the Towers* (1963–'64–'65), *Babel–17* (1966), *The Einstein Intersection* (1967), the last two of which won Nebula Awards as best novels of their respective years, and *Nova* (1968). His other books include the bestselling *Dhalgren* (1975), *Triton* (1976), the sword-and-sorcery series, *Tales of Nevèrÿon* (1978), *Neveryóna* (1983). His essays on SF are collected in two volumes, *The Jewel-Hinged Jaw* (1977) and *Starboard Wine* (1984). He has also written a book-length semiotic study of the SF short story "Angouleme" by Thomas Disch, *The American Shore* (1978). After some years living in Europe and San Francisco and teaching in the Midwest, he again lives in New York. His latest SF novel is *Stars in My Pocket Like Grains of Sand*.